Lady Wood

Sabina

Lady Wood

Sabina

ISBN/EAN: 9783337044503

Printed in Europe, USA, Canada, Australia, Japan

Cover: Foto ©Andreas Hilbeck / pixelio.de

More available books at **www.hansebooks.com**

SABINA.

A Novel.

BY

LADY WOOD,

AUTHOR OF "ROSEWARN."

NEW EDITION.

LONDON:
CHAPMAN AND HALL, 193, PICCADILLY.
1869.

SABINA.

CHAPTER I.

" Neat was their house, each table, chair, and stool,
Stood in its place, or moving—moved by rule."—CRABBE.

EVER was a mansion better ordered than that in which Mabel Snow passed her infancy and childhood.

She was the second daughter of a very wealthy timber merchant who belonged to the Society of Friends.

His wife and himself were of the strictest of the sect, having become *convinced* Quakers, *i.e.*, not born in the society, but entering it on conviction, after they had attained a mature age.

She was a stern, hard-headed woman, who had enjoyed sufficiently the things of this world, and had seen the vanity of them, before she had cropped her soft brown hair, and covered her head with a Quaker's cap.

Indeed one of the children had dislodged from the bottom of a chest on one occasion a miniature set in a gigantic locket, representing " the mother," as she was called in the family, in a black hat and white feather, and a scarlet riding-habit. It was looked at with awe, and concealed again immediately, as giving an indication that "the mother" had at one time been less perfect than they had ever known her.

Rachel Snow's ambition had been formerly to lead the

1

hunting field in her scarlet dress. Now it was to govern, not
only her husband and her family, but to influence by her
talent the sect to which she had allied herself.

She was pleasant to look at—now in her fortieth year—a
faultlessly fair skin and pink cheeks, with bright blue eyes,
almost too bright and piercing, and her rather too plump
bosom was shaded by a white muslin kerchief; and over her
shoulders, to which it was confined by two pins, hung a
drab-coloured shawl. Her dress was of gray silk, and her
whole appendants betokened the most scrupulous care and
neatness.

Precisely at half past eight o'clock in the morning,
without reference to differing seasons, the breakfast bell
rang, and the mother made the tea for her husband, and
allotted to each child his allowance of bread and milk. Tea
was too expensive a luxury at ten shillings per pound for the
younger members of the family, and sugar was not permitted to any, as it was then bought by the tears and groans
of slavery.

At nine o'clock the father started for his counting-house,
and did not return till six in the evening, when he dined
alone with his wife, the children having partaken of their
meal at one o'clock. When the late dinner was concluded,
they all, with the exception of the infant, came trooping in
to romp with their father, from whom came all the indul-
gences they received, and none of the strict laws under
which they lived.

Poor Mr. Snow had given up his creed, at the endless
solicitations of his wife. He had kept his allegiance to his
Church, so long as he had strength to resist, but her power
increased as his dwindled; and at length his coat lost its
rolling collar and became of the orthodox cut and colour,
and he was carried, an unresisting victim, in a large covered
spring cart, to the meeting of Friends every first day; a
carriage and pair would have been too great a pomp and
vanity for these strict Quakers.

The small ornaments about his room—the framed engravings in which his heart had delighted—disappeared one
by one. The woodman, with his background of snow,
whose long face had for years looked wistfully out of the
picture into the warmly curtained and carpeted room,

and the " Domestic Peace," representing a handsome young man in profile, sitting negligently outside a cottage shadowed by gigantic hollyhocks and gazing lovingly on a sweet-looking woman and her child, doing nothing in particular :— Mr. Snow saw these depart, and groaned in spirit. One treasure remained, a circular mirror, which had belonged to his mother, and had so often represented the family circle of his youth, diminished into fairy sizes.

He had enjoyed to see his own dining table, and his wife's comely form, and the prettiness of his children, made prettier and more delicate in the reflection ; but the harmless glass was doomed, and a deeper red in the circle on the crimson flock paper where it had occupied a place, seemed to blush for its absence.

Women so love power that they enjoy its exercise on the minutest subjects ; and as land, on which the sea has begun to encroach, is nibbled inch by inch into the swallow of the voracious ocean, the man's, if a softer character, is absorbed by constant action of the stronger on its surface.

Mrs. Snow abstained totally from all fermented fluids ; her husband, on the contrary, enjoyed his half-bottle of port every day after a dinner, which he expected to find well cooked and of good material. Like poor Louis of France, he was fond of pastry.

" Will the mother order any mince-meat to be made this season, dost thou know ? " he said timidly, one evening to his eldest girl, who had come in with the rest for her evening's enjoyment.

The query was made at his wife, but addressed to her favourite child. The daughter looked at her mother inquiringly.

" Thou art a great deal too fond of pampering thine appetite, Friend Snow. It is not fitting that mince-meat should be made to minister to thy carnal desires."

Friend Snow succumbed. How could he do otherwise when his wife's blue eyes gleamed menacingly at him, and her hand was raised in admonition ? The port wine was the next object to be attacked. She knew that to deprive her husband suddenly and entirely of the amount of stimulant to which he had been accustomed since boyhood would probably injure his health, so her first step was to change the pint-and-a-half decanters to three which contained half the quantity, for if the truth must be confessed, Friend Snow was sometimes in the habit of taking an extra glass out of the allowance intended for the morrow, when a little more fatigued during the day, or a little increased exhilaration in consequence of a fortunate stroke of business, inclined him to indulgence, and necessitated the opening of a fresh bottle on the following day.

Walter cannot drink more than he ought, if he have it not to drink, was the incontrovertible fact stated to herself by the female Friend, as she ordered the servant to decant half a bottle into a small decanter.

The unhappy man saw it, and made no remark. It was a silent reproof to him for various little excesses of which he was now and then guilty. He felt the reproach and bore it manfully, fearing that a storm might come if he remonstrated, so he drank the reduced quantity, and went his way, lest a worse thing should befall him, and the wine disappear altogether.

One evening, when the party were gathered round the evening fire, one rebellious boy mounted on the back of his father's chair with his legs round Friend Snow's neck, and a beautiful child of five years was danced upon his knee, a female servant knocked at the door and said that a woman in distress wished to speak to him immediately.

The Friend rose slowly—he did not like being disturbed when his day's work was over, and he had begun to enjoy himself. He expected a claim either on his comfort or his purse, or both; but with human imperfections both the husband and wife were thoroughly good, conscientious people. So he repeated to himself—"Whoso hath this world's good, and seeth his brother have need, and shutteth up his compassion from him, how dwelleth the love of God in him?" So he followed the servant to the back door, where he found a woman, whom he recognised as being the sole attendant of a poor widow, who inhabited a ruinous house, about a quarter of a mile from his own substantial mansion.

"Oh, Sir! please will you come to missus. She is a dying, and only the child there, and I dare not go for a doctor, 'tis so far."

"I will come, friend. Go back. I will follow thee." And he returned to the dining-room to say whither he was going.

Mrs. Snow arose and procured from her spirit-stand brandy, and from her medicine-chest sal volatile. She had ever at hand everything which might be required on an emergency. "Thou mayest find these useful, perchance, or, as I should more correctly say, as it may be ordered, seeing that chance is not recognised by a Christian people. If I can aid thee in thy ministration to the widow, and it may be to the orphan, I will join thee at the bed-side, if thou wilt send for me. Sarah had better accompany thee, as thou mayest need a messenger."

Mrs. Snow allowed her children to romp till they were tired, and then astronomical and geographical games for the elder children, and dissecting maps for the younger ones, finished the evening, and the mother went to bed and slept sweetly, though she knew her husband had not returned.

CHAPTER II.

"She was a wayward, elfish child,
    With hair unkempt and gleaming eyes,
Whose steps unwatched had wandered wild
    Beneath bright suns, or sullen skies."

THE next morning Mr. Snow walked into the breakfast-room just as his wife had made the tea.

"I have brought thee a small charge for the present, Rachel," said he, referring to a little child, who seemed about eight or nine years old, in a shabby black frock, whom he led by the hand.

"Thou hast been up all night," said the quick-eyed woman, glancing at the soiled face, dishevelled hair, and tumbled frock of the stranger. "Poor child! I will take thee to Betsy."

The stranger griped the hand of the kind man who had brought her, the only one not quite a stranger in a room full of unfamiliar faces, but had to yield to the determination of the mistress of the house, who hurried her off to be attired in a suit belonging to one of her children, whose size most resembled that of the orphan. The stranger submitted cheerfully to the necessary ablution and brushing; but on the attempt to attire her in a nankeen suit of the Quakeress, she rebelled and insisted on having the old black frock replaced.

"I will wear black for papa and mamma!" and she sobbed so violently that the kind-hearted Betsy, weeping also, brought her a cup of tea and some bread and butter from the kitchen, feeling that she should not like to show a blubbered face in a room full of strangers, were she in sorrow.

Before the ringing of the bell for the servants to attend in the breakfast-room to listen to a portion of the Holy Scriptures, the stranger child had disappeared, and Betsy was scared at being unable to produce her charge. Her absence was observed by Mr. and Mrs. Snow, but not commented on till after the reading of the chapter was concluded.

Mr. Snow always read in terror of the criticisms which he knew his wife to be making on his elocution and manner of delivery, and shrank from the keen flame of the blue eyes, tranquil as the body looked to which they belonged, and quiescent as were the plump arms crossed over the rounded figure.

After the reading, the group remained silent and motionless for a time, during which space they were supposed to be meditating on the holy subjects they had just heard.

This might sometimes be the case with the parents Snow, but if the thoughts of the rest had been proclaimed they might on this occasion have been thus rendered—

Rhoda Snow: The buns for breakfast were stale—I hope we have reached the bottom of the tin.

Mabel Snow: Why did the little girl wear that ugly black frock?

Clara Snow: Reuben is a naughty boy! He broke my doll's nose.

Reuben: If I kick gently I may scrape off a large bit of paint from my chair, and not be found out.

Cook: I don't think Betsy is so well to look at as Richard is always saying.

Betsy: I wonder if cook saw that bit of bacon that went out. I should like to save it for Dick.

The father, having made a rough mental calculation of how much time he should have to spare, gave the signal for dismissal by rising.

"What hast thou done with the little girl, Betsy?" he said, as sternly as he could compel his utterance to be.

"Please, Friend Snow, she slipped away in a moment, I do not know where."

"It was very careless of thee to lose the child," said the female Friend. "I think," turning to her husband, "if thou hast time to call in, thou mightest find her at her own home."

"Thou wilt do well to send Betsy. I shall not have time to return with her, and it is not fitting that the little child should dwell in the house of mourning."

"I will do so, Friend, although I do not hold it to be convenient as a rule that female servants should go forth from the house."

"But thou wilt just this once?"

"Thou hast said it, father," said the wife, who gave way, or rather made a show of doing so, in trifles, that she might govern in essentials, and who frequently addressed him by the name by which he was designated by the household—"the father."

When Friend Snow reached the lonely house, which was large, rambling, and dilapidated, and which, having been left to fall by degrees, had been rented by the widow for a trifle, he found the servant putting aside the remnants of her morning meal, and inquired if the child had returned.

She had not seen her, but owned that she had heard a noise in the death-chamber, but had not had courage to seek from what cause it had arisen.

Friend Snow, who was not troubled by terrors of objects either natural or supernatural, proceeded to the chamber of death, and found the orphan stretched by the side of her dead mother, with her arms thrown over the unyielding breast.

"Thou canst not stay here, poor child! What is thy name? Sabina? That is an unusual name, surely!"

"Sabina, thou wilt meet thy mother in heaven if thou art good."

"I don't want her to be in heaven," replied the child. "She is no good to me there—I want her here."

"Hush, Sabina, thou shalt go to my house for the present. Afterwards thou shalt see thy mother once more; but thou art in the way now. I will bring thee hither myself to-morrow," and Betsy having arrived, he directed the maid to take the child to his house with as many of her clothes as she could carry.

The child thus returned to the house of the Quaker, was conducted safely thither by Betsy, men-servants, excepting coachmen and grooms, being considered unfitting attendants on Friends sixty years since. She was led by Betsy into the school-room, where sat the mother surrounded by her daughters in their occupation of needlework. Rhoda was stitching shirt collars and wristbands for her father's shirts with extraordinary precision and neatness; Mabel was drawing the threads from some Irish linen intended for glass cloths, for the purpose of hemming them in an exactly straight line ; the youngest girl was learning to knit, the mother, with exemplary patience, taking the begun garter from her hand every two minutes to recover the dropped stitches.

"Thou hast come back," said Mrs. Snow, quietly to Sabina, and the tranquillity of her tone kept down the storm of sobs and cries which rebelled in Sabina's breast.

"Thou wilt like to sit down and sew whilst my children are engaged at their occupations. I will give thee a tea-cloth to make. Hast thou a thimble?"

Sabina replied with a little gasp that she did not know.

"We will find thee one. Mabel, thou canst lend Friend Sabina thine, as thou canst not use it whilst thou art busy with the threads."

Mabel presented the thimble, gravely, which Sabina immediately placed on the wrong finger.

"Dear, dear !" said Friend Snow, "I fear thou dost not know how to work. How very sad !" and she looked at the child with real pity. "But do not lament on that account. Sit down on this little chair by my side and I will teach thee."

So the Friend turned down the hem of the glass cloth in a straight line, and fastened, or, in female parlance, *tacked* it, that it might not waver under Sabina's unskilled fingers. The child first unthreaded her needle, which Mabel re-threaded silently and instantaneously, and then Sabina awkwardly pricked her fingers, and a crimson drop stained the cloth, into which she had not as yet succeeded in placing a single stitch.

None of the children spoke a word during the three hours devoted to needlework, and presently the mother took up a book, begun seemingly at some previous time, for the mark was in the middle of the volume. It was entitled "The Influences of the Spirit, as exemplified in the guidance of Members of the Society of Friends," and consisted of anecdotes of the circumstances under which certain individuals had been conducted from danger to safety by attention to the inward promptings of the spirit.

"Two young Friends, a brother and sister, were travelling towards London on business, and, as was usual two hundred years since, the journey was performed on horseback.

"The brother was desirous to push on as far as possible before night, and insisted on passing an inn where the female Friend wished to sleep, in spite of her remonstrance; they had therefore little choice when night fell and found them near a wayside house of entertainment, which stood alone in the midst of a moor. The female Friend was reluctant to enter, from an inward warning; but she disregarded the intimation, and as the people of the house were civil and obliging, she forgot that it had been felt.

"She went to bed, and had not slept more than an hour, when a voice seemed to say unto her, 'Arise, and fly, thou and thy brother, for the slayer of life is behind thee.' She had seen the room where he slept, and by the dim light of a partially obscured moon, she felt her way to his bed, and said in a whisper, 'It has been made known to me that thou must rise and fly from this house directly, if thou wouldest preserve thy life.' He obeyed, clothing himself as silently as she desired, and she led him down through the darkness towards the outer door, which opened towards the stables whither they had seen the men lead their horses. As they proceeded, they saw a light at the end of a passage, and they were afraid, and crouched down within a dark room with an open door, till they saw two men, the host and his son, who passed them so near that they could have touched them. The father bore a large knife, and the son a cord. 'I will manage the man—you shall silence the girl,' said he. 'Shall I strangle her with this?' replied the younger man. The Friends saw them ascend the steps leading to the room they had just vacated, and hastened to the stables, from whence they took their tired horses, and urging them to speed, they fled over the moor, towards the friendly shelter they had previously passed, not venturing, with tired animals, to attempt an unknown distance in the darkness, and thus owing their safety to the monitions of the spirit."

Whilst Mrs. Snow read, Sabina's fingers were still, and her eyes were fixed on the lips of the speaker. The others worked on with placid industry, for outward signs of emotion were discouraged in the Snow family, whose feelings were supposed to be in subjection.

"Thou art not working," said the mother to Sabina. "Thou hast put three stitches one upon the other, and thou hast left a large space with one very long stitch, and that is all. Hast thou not been taught to sew?"

Sabina wept and was silent.

"Do not disturb thyself—thou wilt learn in time. The clock is striking, fold thy work neatly, and go out to play with thy companions."

Very noiselessly they put together their working implements, and Mabel, taking Sabina's hand, led her to the playground. As they passed a looking glass in one of the lower rooms, where the children brushed their hair when they returned from play, before they appeared before their parents, the glass reflected the images of both children. Mabel was twelve years old and dazzlingly fair; her features were perfectly proportioned, and very beautiful; they seemed to be meant to convey only the softer emotions and the fruits of the spirit—love, joy, peace, longsuffering, gentleness, goodness, faith, meekness, temperance. Sabina saw her own reflection close to this beautiful image—dark, flashing, bronzed by the sun, wild and attenuated—and drew back mortified and dejected.

"It is the sun that has burnt thy skin," said Mabel, pityingly.

Sabina shook her head. "No frost would make me look like you."

And the children both hurried away. But in after life both remembered the contrast that day exhibited.

CHAPTER III.

" Children, like tender osiers, take the bow,
 And, as they first are fashioned, always grow,
 For what we learn in youth, to that alone
 In age we are by second nature prone."—DRYDEN.

THE play-ground was a large field, round which was a broad gravelled walk, and at the upper end there were rows of small gardens, divided from each other for the little Snows then existing, and an unoccupied space for the requirements of any future Snows.

There was also a well-built room, in which they had their teas and luncheons in summer weather. During play-hours, they were left to their own devices, without the supervision of their elders ; seeing that Rhoda was but fourteen, and Clara five years old, they got on without more than the usual number of mischances. In a drawer in the cottage, as it was called, there was a roll of diachylon plaster and a pair of scissors, with some rag, so that Rhoda might attend to cuts and bruises without waiting to obtain assistance from the house ; and Sabina, whose life had been a series of *make-shifts,* was astonished at the wealth expended in contrivances for the amusement and welfare of her new companions.

Rhoda went off to her garden to tie up the carnations ; Reuben said Clara should be his horse, and harnessed her with two skipping-ropes.

Mabel looked wistfully at Sabina, whose eyes were filling with tears, and whom she knew not either how to comfort or amuse. They sat down on the step of the cottage, and looked at the others at play.

" I have another brother, called Luke," said Mabel, at

length, as Reuben galloped past them; "I love him best of all. Whom dost thou love best?"

Sabina turned her head away, and said, "I love no one; I have no one to love now; no one who cares whether I live or die!" and she swallowed down her tears, with effort.

"Why dost thou wear that black frock?" inquired Mabel, unable to repress her curiosity longer.

The answer was given petulantly, for the strange child was irritated by having her griefs thus dwelt on.

"Because my papa and mamma are dead; and so would you, if you had lost your parents."

"No, I should not. Friends do not wear what is called mourning. They 'rend their hearts and not their garments, and seem not unto men to fast:' but, Sabina, this thing, what dost thou call it? is unsewn," taking up a bit of crape trimming. "That is untidy. Wilt thou not sew it on?"

"I have no needle nor thread," said the child.

Her companion took from her pocket-book a little needle-book, containing scissors, thimble, needles, and cottons of various tints of gray and drab colours, wound round flat pieces of card.

"I fear," said she, "that I cannot supply thee with black cotton. Dost thou think this dark gray will suffice?" She offered the needle-book to Sabina, and saw, by the awkward way in which she handled it, that she had no idea how to avail herself of the loan. "I forgot that thou canst not sew, friend," said the precise little Quakeress. "Let me do it for thee," and, selecting the darkest cotton, she sewed on the pendant piece of crape.

"Did not thy mother teach thee to sew?"

"No; mamma did all the sewing herself, and said my attention must be given to other things, and that sewing could be learnt at any time;" and Sabina spoke as if she rather disdained the useful knowledge by which she had just profited.

"And what things are those?"

"Music, singing, and elocution. My mother meant to have me educated for the stage. Do you know what is a stage?"

"Yes; there are several in the green-house, on which the plants are placed," replied Mabel, with a puzzled air.

"Oh, those are not the stages I mean. Are you fond of singing?"

"I never heard any. Canst thou sing?"

"Yes, and play on the piano."

"What is that?"

"Oh, a box which makes a noise when you touch it."

"Sing now, that I may know what thou meanest."

Sabina said she would sing a song which her father had taught her, and she sang, with infinite expression, Campbell's "Chieftain to the Highlands Bound."

Mabel was entranced both by the voice and the story. She did not understand many of the words, but the tragedy was clearly made out, and she sat silent when it was over, in deep sympathy with the lady and her lover, and with anger against the father "left lamenting."

She looked at Sabina with greater respect than before, and almost forgot her deficiencies in sewing. Still she had been taught to consider sewing neatly as the principal object in a girl's education, so she was resolved to give her new friend a lesson in that useful art; but that should be a duty —the singing was an amusement for play-hours.

"Where didst thou learn those words, Sabina? I learn verses, but not like those."

"I learnt them from hearing papa sing them; but they are in a book which mamma had, where I often read them. Papa was so fond of it, mamma let me keep it. It is amongst my clothes, somewhere."

"Wilt thou show it to me?"

"Yes; but," Sabina added, ruefully, "I do not know where the clothes were placed, when they were brought here."

"After dinner I will show thee the room where thou wilt sleep, and then thou shalt put thy clothes into the drawers, and show me thy book. Till then we will choose a plot of ground for a garden for thee, and the gardener shall dig it roughly, and we will break the clods and rake it. I will give thee some flower-roots, and Rhoda will do likewise; and if I have money enough of my pocket-money, I will buy thee some flower-seeds."

Sabina looked pleased; she liked the idea of a garden very much; so they set to work to mark its boundaries, and were so busily employed that they were sorry when the sound of the dinner-bell interrupted their occupations.

Their ablutions carefully performed, they sat in silence for a few minutes, and then a universal clatter of knives and forks proved that the meditations had all ceased at the same moment. This would have been strange, had any heavenly inspiration been sought or waited for, but it was a wordless form—nothing more.

The children were helped in rotation, beginning with the youngest, for, as Mrs. Snow sagely observed, they had most difficulty in disposing of their food, and would only delay others if they were helped last.

Sabina, whose dinners had frequently consisted in an apple and a piece of bread, had no particular relish for the soup and fish, roast and boiled joints, and supplementary tarts and puddings; she was tired of sitting on the high straight-backed chairs, cruelly made to compel an upright position to weary spines. She was glad when the dinner was over, and when a few minutes given to meditation had marked its close, the children all rose to leave the table, excepting Mabel, who, with a flush on her face, sat still from her waist upwards, but was making secret and painful efforts with her foot to reach her slipper, which she had kicked off under the table, and dared not own it. It seemed that she was an old offender in this, and many other small faults, and had to pay forfeits constantly from her allowance of pocket-money, which generally found its way into the poor's-box before Seventh day came.

After the payment of one halfpenny for this offence, the children went to the school-room for an hour and a half's sewing. Again and again Sabina got into disgrace with her work.

She had dropped her thimble; she knew not where: it had rolled out of her tea-cloth. This belonged to Mabel, who wished to tell her, but dared not, that it was of no consequence, as she did not want to sew. Mrs. Snow, however, produced another, and Sabina began her work. In a few moments she had unthreaded her needle, and tried vainly for several minutes to rethread it: she bit the end of the thread, and the moisture made it limp: she twisted it with her little fingers, which were tremulous from anxiety, and applied it to the eye, which seemed to contract from a spirit of opposition, or, like a human eye, when approached by any opposing substance. At length with a flutter of hope, she detects that some small fibres of thread had been forced through the eye by her efforts, and seizing them, she draws it through. Alas! only half of the thread follows: the rest is pressed against the side of the eye, into innumerable little circles, and Sabina, hot and despairing, has to pull it out again. The next time the needle, which seemed possessed by a kind of vicious vitality, suddenly jumped out of her fingers. She did not like to move from her place to search for it on the carpet, for Friend Snow had returned to her book on the Influences of the Spirit, and was relating how a Friend had been directed in sleep to rise from his bed one night, and to walk along the banks of a canal, and how, soon after he had reached it,—but here Sabina's impatient interest in the story attracted Mrs. Snow's attention, and she discovered the idleness of the stranger child.

"Why dost thou not sew?"

"If you please, Friend Snow, I've lost my needle."

"Thou shouldest call me Madam, or Mistress Snow, for that is the habit of thy people. When thou art as one of us, thou mayest call me Friend Snow. Here is another needle, and I will thread it for thee this time."

"Oh, here is my own!" cried Sabina, gladly, seeing it glitter on the carpet. "Now I shall not require yours, Ma'am."

"But I must give it to thee, because I said I would, and if I did not, I should tell an untruth," said the scrupulous lady.

At length the hours of sewing, marked by weary sighs from the breast of Sabina, came to a close, and the children were dismissed to play till tea-time. Mabel, whose mind was full of "Lord Ullin's Daughter," asked Sabina to come to the sleeping apartment, which she did, and there drew from the meagre contents of her little trunk a well-worn copy of "Campbell's Pleasures of Hope," and a few of the minor poems which graced the earlier editions. Mabel's eyes glistened with delight at the engravings, for she had never seen any such. True, "Keeper in Search of His Master" had had an ill-executed frontispiece, but it had been neatly excised by Mrs. Snow's scissors so soon as it had been perceived.

Mabel cared little for the grave figure leaning his chin on his hand,—" Andes, Giant of the Northern Star."

But what a charming child, looking round a rustic gate at a tattered venerable old man. What wonderful hollyhocks, just like those in the garden !

What a sweet mother, leaning over the cradle that contains her infant boy, who sleeps with his fingers on his lip !

" Read it to me !" cried Mabel, impatiently. " Let us go somewhere out of the way of the others ; under the trees. Read what refers to the pictures."

" I do not think there is much about the pictures ; nothing to care about ; but I will read you about " Glenara," and about " The Poor Wounded Hussar."

" What is an hussar? A soldier? Ah, I ought not to listen to that, for all soldiers are wicked."

" Surely not."

" I don't know. My mother says it is wicked to fight ; and as soldiers fight, I suppose they are wicked."

" Just as you please," said Sabina, rather affronted, as her father had been a fighting-man, and all her sympathies went with warlike deeds. However, they sat under the trees, and Sabina sang and read, and read and sang again, till Mabel was entranced by the melody of her voice and the charm of the poetry. When they were summoned to the cottage to partake of hot milk, served in a great tin can, and currant buns, Rhoda looked with wonder at Mabel's face, softened to an expression of unusual tenderness.

" Where hast thou been ?" asked the careful sister.

" With Sabina."

" What hast thou been doing ? "

" Nothing."

And Rhoda was silenced, but not satisfied.

Rhoda addressed her mother. " Is Friend Sabina likely to remain with thee long, my mother ? "

" Why dost thou ask ? Does it concern thee to mete out thy father's hospitality ? "

" No ; only, mother, Mabel is always with her ; and Sabina is not a Friend, thou knowest."

That night Mrs. Snow asked her husband if any answer

2

had arrived to a letter he had addressed to a distant relative of Sabina, to whom he had written, describing her destitute state.

Yes; only that morning the expected answer had arrived. "There it is," he said, producing it. "The writer is a harsh man, I fear," said the good-natured Friend.

"HAVEN HOUSE, DEEPINDALE,
"September 18—.

"SIR,

"I have received your letter, describing the destitute state of the child Sabina Rock, my great-niece.

"I never asked my nephew to beget the child, and I consider it hard that I should have this burthen thrown on me. However, as she bears my name, 'needs must, when the Devil drives,' so I send money enough to pay for her coach fare, and I will meet her, if you will let your servant put her into the stage which reaches Deepindale at six o'clock on Thursday evening.

"Your obedient servant,
"MICHAEL ROCK."

"Poor child!" said Mrs. Snow, "my heart aches for her future life; but it will be best for her to go at once. It may be ordered that her uncle may be more gentle when he sees her; not that she is well-favoured; so dark, beside Rhoda and Mabel."

"'Dark, but comely,'" said the father.

"Thou mightest quote better parts of Scripture than Solomon's Song, Friend Snow."

CHAPTER IV

"The balls of his broad eyes rolled in his head,
And glared between yellow and red :
He looked a lion with a gloomy stare,
And o'er his eyebrows hung his matted hair;
Big boned, and large of limb, with sinews strong,
Broad shouldered, and his arms were sound and strong.

DRYDEN.

A FEW days after Sabina was separated from her kind protectors, and sent, with the housemaid as escort, to Deepindale by the coach.

She could scarcely repress her sobs as she felt Mabel's kisses on her cheeks and her arms round her neck, and gave expression to her feelings in uncouth gulps.

She looked up into the faces of her host and hostess, and tried to say something about being obliged for their hospitality, which the housemaid had secretly suggested, but the words died inarticulately. Poor child! she was like a climbing plant, which had just curled its tendrils round the shrubs in chance juxtaposition, and now they were sent away, and she was packed up and sent to some distant, and probably inhospitable, soil.

" We shall hear of thee from Betsy, Sabina. Be dutiful to thy great-uncle, and then thou wilt be happy, and probably well doing."

Mabel retired to the garden seat, to think over the poetry she had learnt from Sabina's book, and to regret that the poems and the songstress had departed.

She provided herself with a bow, which she induced the gardener to procure from an osier bed, and fashioned some wood into arrows, and sat sentimentally in a tree in the thickest part of the shrubbery, fancying herself O'Connor's child; or she walked with downcast eyes examining an imaginary battle-field in search of a wounded hussar, her lover. She had an element of romance about her, which her association with Sabina had elicited. The struggle between this natural disposition and the bondage of her sect, was to be the bane of her happiness. Anything so discordant as these imaginings that filled her brain, with the reality of the primly dressed and stiffly modelled little Quakeress, was never before seen in a Friend's family."

"Why dost thou walk about with thy head down? Thou wilt give thyself a poke of thy neck."

"Why dost thou sit in that tree with a bow in thy hand? Whom dost thou mean to shoot? Surely thou wouldest not destroy life," said the sage Rhoda; but Mabel answered nothing, and concealed for the future the outward expression of the occupation of her thoughts, and longed in secret for the forbidden delights of music, poetry, and painting.

When the coach stopped at the door of the hotel, a hoarse voice was heard, saying to the coachman, "Three minutes late!" and a hand appeared holding up a chronometer in proof of the assertion. Seemingly the coachman was disinclined to dispute it, for he only touched his hat, and said that the little girl and the young woman were inside.

Lieutenant Rock showed himself at the window, lifting his hat, almost reverentially to the beautiful Quakeress servant on whom his eyes first fell. She, all unconscious of the looks of admiration which glanced from under those dark bushy eyebrows, said, "My master has sent thee thy young relative, if thy name be Rock. They charge thee to be tender to the child, who is fatherless and motherless."

The lieutenant's ire was aroused; he was not going to be taught his duty by a lubberly landsman,—a hulking Quaker, who would not fight for his country; but as he was about to answer in wrath, he was arrested by the delicate hectic which asserted itself on the cheek of the girl, and he changed his vituperation intended for the master and mistress into a civil invitation to come to his house and take some refreshment till the coach returned. The maid declined, saying her master had given her money to defray her expenses at the hotel; and taking the child's hand, she bade her " Farewell," and placed the reluctant little palm in the bronzed fingers of the lieutenant, who did not look as if he particularly admired his great-niece.

It must be owned that she did not look to advantage by the side of the beautiful housemaid, who was dazzling fair, and, though fragile looking, was rounded in figure. The child was lean and sallow, with enormous eyes which seemed to occupy the chief part of her face. These were wild, restless and dark, and looked larger from their black lashes, and the purple tint which coloured their large orbits.

Lieutenant Rock looked on her *with distaste. She bore his name and shared his blood, and he saw in her face some likeness to his own; but he had but his half-pay, ninety pounds a year, and that died with him.

She would be a fearful incumbrance during the remainder of his life; and at his death—what could become of her? He could not bear to think that a Rock should be reduced to apply for parish relief. " Well, if I can live till she grows up she must go out as a governess, or a housemaid, and earn her bread."

He declined the offer of the porter to take charge of the child's portmanteau, and, flinging it across his shoulders, he desired Sabina to follow him.

He stopped at a small, new, neat house, which stood alone, opposite the river, with the intervention of a grove which consisted of a number of attenuated trees, which having been too thickly planted and never thinned, had run up, in the desire to obtain more air and sun, by overtopping each other.

The grove was a square with broad gravelled walks round it, which the inhabitants of Deepindale called the Parade, and where young ladies walked, and sighed that the war had taken all the young men, excepting the clergyman and the apothecary; and the school children disported themselves on half holidays.

The lieutenant had painted and yellow-washed his house himself. It was a kind of ship to him. Ah ! how often he had longed for a ship of his own to command; but this blessing had been kept for those better born, and with more influence and less merit than himself.

Some things he had made his own in his naval career—truth, honour, integrity; but he was severe on the infringement of rules he had ever practised, and his virtues seemed to those less virtuous, harsh and repulsive.

Never could such a child as Sabina have fallen to the charge of a protector less suited to the habits of her previous life.

It was a melancholy day for her when she arrived at the small house; shadowed by the spindle-like trees. Some pea-soup and a very tiny bit of salt pork made the frugal dinner. Sabina ate so little that her uncle began to hope that her appetite might prove a small one.

He offered her an apple from the dessert, which was duly placed every day on the table in a broken dish, with plates and dessert knives, and insisted on peeling it for her and cutting it up in small pieces, when she had preferred the primitive mode in which she ate hers. This destroyed Sabina's enjoyment of it. She would have liked to read a book and bite her apple simultaneously.

Her dress was cut low with short sleeves, after the custom of dressing children sixty years since, for it was thought, not unreasonably, that any deviation from correctness in growth could thus be better detected and sooner remedied. However, there were disadvantages in these habiliments—the under garments appeared, pushing up their edges above their proper boundaries. The shoulder-straps would peep out, to say nothing of the top of a pair of stiff stays—a pair of Mabel's—which would show themselves unpleasantly, pressed up by Sabina's position as she sat opposite her uncle, the lower part of them resting on her chair.

Mr. Rock seemed unable to take his eyes off these intrusive articles.

In vain poor Sabina tried to dislodge them. Her efforts to press them down were fruitless.

After dinner he rang for the old servant, and, pointing to the child's frock, said,

"Take a reef up there before to-morrow morning."

"Sir!"

"Take a reef up—a running stay round the top."

The next morning he called the child towards him, and untying her frock-string, he drew it so tightly together, that her shoulders were drawn up to her ears, and looking at her with an air of satisfaction, declared that "it was all 'taut,' and as it should be," while Sabina swelled her chest, and expanded her thin shoulder, to try to escape from the unusual pressure.

She dared not, in her uncle's presence, cut the string ; but should it break, all the better for her.

She tried repeatedly, and at length the material that held the tape tore, and the lifesome form asserted itself once more with wild grace, for she had discarded Mabel's stays, which were articles of dress she had never worn till her brief visit to the Quaker's family.

The lieutenant was not thus to be beaten. He called old Susan to bring needles and thread, and sent Sabina to bed, whilst the top of the frock was plaited in tight folds to produce the effect he had admired when the tape had been used.

With more knowledge or more pity, Susan, though she seemed to obey orders, made the plaits smaller and fewer, that Sabina might feel less cramped ; but that spirited young lady, so soon as the frock was put on, stole into her uncle's room, and borrowing his razor without leave, freed herself from the slightest suspicion of restraint. As Sabina had discarded the stays, they were no longer a cause of offence ; and if her great-uncle perceived that she had beaten him, he bore it with a lofty look of not finding it out.

In an old bureau which had travelled round the world in his cabin, the worthy man kept his accounts.

Each day his expenses were rigidly calculated, and balanced at its close. No indulgence was permitted to himself by this self-denying old man ; but he had a glass of grog for a friend in the evening. After breakfast he walked for an hour up and down the parade trying to fancy it the quarter-deck of a ship. Then he obtained for a penny the loan of a daily paper for three hours. This brought luncheon ; some bread and cheese and a glass of water. Dinner was served at six o'clock, followed by a cup of coffee for himself and Sabina, and at night he partook of a basin of thin gruel with salt, whilst his friend, Lieutenant Orellan, regaled himself with hot whisky and water. "The unknown quantity" of expense introduced in the person of Sabina was a terrible perplexity to her uncle. He looked at his list of expenditure to see, where the difficulty of rendering justice to all was so great, what he could curtail or do without.

How often!—how hopelessly he went over the items. "I have but ninety pounds a-year. Had I but fifty it would be equally my duty to live within my income. This child's food, clothing, and washing, will deduct at least twenty pounds from the fifty. How is this to be met?" He thought of the paper—the penny a-day for the news so dearly prized—for the only link which united the old man to the living, moving, busy world, in which he had once been an actor. This must be given up; but it would only be one pound six shillings towards the twenty pounds.

He had been accustomed to buy three new coats in two years. He was proud of being well-dressed—of looking what he was by birth and feeling, a gentleman. One of the coats must be given up, and every other article of his wardrobe in like proportion. The glass of grog to his friend in the evening; this was the most painful perplexity of all. How could he give up that dearly prized rite of hospitality? He knew that the comfort of those glasses of grog were inestimable to his friend, who had, on *his* ninety pounds a-year, to support a paralytic wife, whom he nursed as tenderly as does a mother her sickly, fractious child.

He thought, with some feeling of relief, that he had just purchased four gallons of whisky at prime cost, and discount off for ready money, and that this store would last his friend for some time. When it was exhausted it would be time enough to meet the difficulty of replacing it.

Sunday came in the midst of these cogitations; Sunday, which was marked by a very small piece of roast beef, which did duty till the following Thursday.

He never missed going twice to church on these days, but twice he considered sufficient; and when the innovation of an evening service was introduced, he sat at home on Sunday afternoons, and joined the evening service.

Now he was to have a companion in these acts of duty, and Sabina, with her face scrubbed, her hair combed, and the strings of her bonnet ironed out, and her frock brushed and sponged, was led by her uncle to church. To pay a guinea a year for a sitting he could not afford ; to leave her at home on Sunday morning might endanger her eternal happiness ; to send her to sit among the servants, with Susan, was a degradation he could not put up with ; to take her into the strangers' pew, which, as few ever visited the remote town of Deepindale, was appropriated to the half-pay officers who congregated there for cheapness—to take a petticoat into that bachelor pew, though that petticoat covered the person of a child only ten years of age, seemed an atrocity only to be equalled by the intrusion of the lady on Saint Senanus.

It was the least of the evils, however, which suggested itself to his imagination. He generally was the first to enter the pew, and take his place at the upper end, which was bounded by a pillar. The church was obscure even at midday, the pew dark oak, the child dressed in black. She will not be much observed, he thought, if she will but be quiet, and not stand up on the hassock and stare about her.

He was shocked to discover that the girl did not know where to find the places in her prayer-book.

"She has been brought up as a little heathen," said the lieutenant to himself. "I must try to make her a Christian."

His notion of succeeding in this task was to dose her with prayers and sermons, which might make up for the deficiency of her early career.

Very tired was Sabina with this morning service, the first she had ever attended. Her uncle had put his large hand on her shoulder, and forced her into a kneeling position on the boards, which were covered only by a bit of worn-out matting. Sabina grew faint and sick during the length of the Litany, and when at length her uncle's strong arm pulled her up, her thin knees were scored all over with the impression of woven flags.

When Sabina began to look about her—not an easy performance, seeing that she was a small child for her age, without stepping on the tempting hassock—her eyes fell on a cluster of fair curls standing before her, surmounted by a delicate gauze bonnet. The girl to whom the curls and the bonnet belonged was standing with her back towards Sabina, and seemed to be about thirteen or fourteen years of age. At the first responses, which were chanted, Sabina heard a feeble little voice chanting very correctly with the choristers, and surmised by the movement of her head in connection with the sound emitted, that the voice and the fair curls belonged to the same person. Sabina envied the lovely hair—her own was black,—she envied the fair skin—the back of the neck, so like marble in whiteness and smoothness; she envied the pretty gauze bonnet, with blue pipings and a pink rose-bud; but she heard the feeble, painstaking voice, and felt comforted. The Psalms were long, and the young lady had chanted them perseveringly and meritoriously, but she was losing power with every fresh verse. By-and-bye a resting-time came, but then the hymn. For this Sabina had reserved herself. When the voice burst forth in the invocation

"Lord of heaven and earth and ocean, hear us from thy blest abode!"

Sabina, who knew every note of the music, and every word of the hymn, sang with such wonderful power, sweetness, and correctness, that involuntarily everyone turned to see whence the magnificent stream of melody flowed—a long resounding voice, oft breaking clear in solemn pauses from the swelling bass. Of the power everyone could judge. Poor Mr. Rock! A boy once went to school with an alarum in his pocket in which he had invested all his pocket-money—the savings of weeks. He could not keep his hands off his darling, and in fingering his new purchase as it reposed in his trowsers' pocket, he set it off in the middle of his class lesson. Whiz went the alarum. The unhappy boy grasped his pocket in the hopes of stopping the accursed thing. It was useless. Like a railing woman, it was determined to have its say out, and the ire of the master, the laughter of the boys, and the shame of its unfortunate possessor, disturbed not the even tenor of its way.

Thus with Sabina's singing. Mr. Rock, but for very shame, would have stopped her mouth with his hand; but neither his manifest vexation at the revelation made of herself by this human alarum, nor the astonishment and curiosity evinced by the stealthily turned heads towards the strangers' pew, in any way discomposed Sabina; she sang

during all the remainder of the service, to the tearful mortification of the possessor of the fair curls and gauze bonnet,
whose voice, already nearly exhausted before Sabina began,
had now become entirely inaudible.

When at length the sermon had begun, Sabina had
managed to relieve the tedium of the service by taking part
in it, and had got through the twenty-five minutes' preaching
by trying to trace distorted faces in the knotted wood of the
old oak pew, and in speculating whether angels in heaven
had gilded wings, yellow hair, and blue petticoats, like those
two which stood over the altar with brazen trumpets in their
hands, and a golden ball each under one leg, which served
as a kind of footstool, and by its position disclosed the knee,
above which the blue petticoat was looped and fastened by
a brooch.

" I can beat her in some ways," said Sabina to herself, as
her uncle, doubtful whether to be most proud or most
ashamed of his new relation, led her up the aisle to return
home, for as she passed the pew she saw Fair-curls still on
her knees—and, as far as her governess knew, devoutly
praying—turn her head, and gaze on her with eyes wet with
angry tears. She had been surpassed in the accomplishment
on which she and her governess particularly prided themselves—her voice and its culture.

> " In thoughts so bold can little minds engage,
> And in soft bosoms dwell such mighty rage ? "

The child with fair curls would gladly have consigned the
girl with black curls to bread and water with solitary confinement for a week.

When the congregation left the church, many inquiring
glances were directed toward the little girl, who had to run
every dozen steps to keep up with the stride of her uncle.

" What a wonderful voice ! " said Mr. Temple, the
German organist, to his wife.

" Humph ! loud enough ! " was the uncomplimentary
reply of the lady.

" My dear, 'tis out of voices such as these that the best
performers are produced. You may direct power and
cultivate it, but 'tis hopeless to try to do anything with a
penny whistle of a voice." The lady and her daughters

were a collection of penny whistles, and she hated Sabina for the admiration expressed by her husband for the stranger child.

After the small joint of beef, baked on potatoes in an earthenware brown dish with yellow stripes, had been partaken of by the lieutenant and his niece and Susan, he thought he would dissipate the inclination for sleep, which *would* come on his unoccupied Sunday afternoons, by taking Sabina for a walk in the country.

Sunday was a day of suppressed yawns with Lieutenant Rock. He dared not give himself the pleasure of yawning a loud hearty oscitation. He would have thought it showed a lack of reverence for the day.

He opened no letter that arrived on Sunday. He would not unlock his desk, lest worldly thoughts should slip out of its recesses, and indispose him to serious reflections.

Yet having thus rendered his mind a blank, with what could he inscribe it, worthy the sacredness of the day?

The poor lieutenant suffered an hebdomadal martyrdom in his efforts to spend this awful division of time as it ought to be spent.

It would never do to let Sabina see his head nodding on his breast in his arm-chair, so he desired Susan to dress her in her bonnet and cloak, and took her out for a walk.

Both the uncle and niece were in good temper when they started, for the autumn sun was shining cheerfully, and making the yellow foliage warmer with its glow.

The child rejoiced in movement, and fluttered along like a young bird who forgets for a moment that a string attached to its leg will in a moment drag it back to its owner.

The uncle could not help watching for coveys of partridges in the stubble; he had been a keen sportsman in his youth, before the heavy sum exacted by government for a license had placed shooting beyond his reach.

No persuasion could ever induce him to fire at a bird without that magical permission in his pocket.

"Take the keeper's gun," said a friend, whom Mr. Rock accompanied one day on the first of September. "There are lots of birds, and I know you are a first-rate shot."

The lieutenant looked longingly at the excellent double-barrel which the keeper offered.

" I have no license," he replied, sadly.

" My good fellow ! No one here will dare to inquire. We shall not go off my own estate."

" I should not consider it quite honourable, you know. Defrauding the king, is it not ? " he replied, gently, for he felt that in thus stating his opinion he was conveying a reproof to his host.

" Just as you like, old fellow ! " said his friend, laughing. " The revenue would be better supplied if all had your scruples."

Whilst the old man was peering into a field over a gap in the hedge, Sabina had found herself a plentiful source of enjoyment in some blackberry-laden brambles, and by the time Mr. Rock, with the quick eye of a sailor, had taken cognizance of the little brown specks in the distant stubbles, and counted their number, Sabina had besmeared her mouth, and torn her frock in five different places—five distinct tears, making two sides of a triangle, and showing a white petticoat underneath, caught her uncle's eyes as he turned from the contemplation of the partridges.

He saw also Sabina's hands full of the ripe fruit, which she was cramming into her purpled mouth, and his ire was aroused. He rushed towards her with his stick uplifted, with no very distinct idea of striking her, but foaming with anger at her greediness, and careless disregard of the destruction of her clothes, so difficult to replace.

Sabina meditated flight, but as she trod on a stubborn branch near its base, the upper portion of it bent toward her, and the sturdy thorns with which it was armed caught the top of her bonnet, which was of white chip, tied with black ribbon so carefully under her chin by Susan, that the brambles had no effect on the sarcenet strings, but the fragile chip gave way at the crown, which came off like a saucer, showing a head covered with black hair underneath. The top was not entirely detached, but swung and danced in the air by a long attenuated piece of the braided chip.

This momentary detention gave Mr. Rock an advantage, and he came so near to his niece as to catch her flying petticoats. She was now too determined on flight to heed remonstrance, and dashed away, leaving her frock unripped from the gathers in his hand.

Just then the wretched uncle heard the sound of wheels, and was aware that a carriage was approaching. There was no time for flight, no place for concealment, and he was revealed in all the light of that sunny Sunday afternoon, with an inflamed countenance and furious eyes, with an uplifted stick, threatening to chastise a child, whose disordered dress bore witness seemingly to his violence.

He let go his hold of Sabina's dress, and tried to stand quietly and bow politely as the carriage passed.

He saw the look of quiet astonishment in the face of the lady, of amusement on the part of her son, the Honourable Wilfred Tresillian,—he saw the smirking grins of the footmen and coachmen, and he burst into a cold perspiration of rage and shame. The young gentleman was a candidate for the representation of the borough of Deepindale, and had called on the lieutenant two days before to ask for his vote.

Mr. Rock had then had the best of the situation. He had been composed—dignified. Had requested time to consider before giving his answer; he had told the candidate that there was a difficulty—that he liked his principles generally, but what were his opinions on flogging in the navy? and did he intend to vote for its abolition? because in that case he must decline to register his vote for the Honourable Mr. Tresillian. The gentleman fenced with the question. He meant to vote for the abolition of flogging, but he did not want to lose Mr. Rock's vote. Thus it had stood, and Mr. Rock felt now, that in the absurd position in which he had been seen, he had lost his vantage ground. The young man would never see him again without feeling moved to laughter and contempt. The carriage rolled on out of sight, and Sabina had long been beyond her uncle's ken or hearing. At first he thought not of her. He was too full of his own mortification to reflect where that provoking imp might have strayed. Then he walked up and down calling for her in vain—he could neither see nor hear her. He went back crestfallen, and depressed—walking slowly, and found the house dark and silent. Susan had been to the afternoon church, and had not returned. No doubt she had stopped to tell some of her acquaintances of the new arrival in her master's house.

He grew impatient and somewhat alarmed at the thought of the child's absence. He wished Susan would return, though he felt ashamed to tell her on what terms he and his niece had parted, and that he was uneasy at her non-appearance. He remembered that she was ignorant of the country, and could not know her way to his house, even if she wished to reach it. With all this, came a feeling of aggravation against her for the shame of the past, and the anxiety of the present time.

Lieutenant Rock was feeble, and had been recommended by his doctor not to exert himself, above all not to agitate himself, yet his heart was thumping now as he stood at the open door very unpleasantly, as he waited in the hope of seeing that little wild black figure, so soon as she came within sight. The house itself was still and dark, but dim lights were gleaming at the lamp-posts, few and far between, along the narrow street which led to Haven House. A soft drizzling rain began to fall.

"She will get wet too, confound her!" muttered the lieutenant.

In the meantime the sound of pattens and a large umbrella, its wet surface shining under a distant lamp, gave token of Susan's approach.

Mr. Rock observed her with some degree of comfort, but could not make up his mind immediately to announce his disquietude.

Susan bustled in; she wanted to take off her bed-chintz gown, and see if the pattens had splashed the skirt. But first she lighted an end of candle for that purpose, and made up the fire and set the tea, before it struck her that she had neither heard nor seen anything of the child.

"Where's Miss, Sir?" she said, going to the door. The uncle was obliged to confess that she had run away from him.

"Away!—by herself!—out in the dark!—all in the rain! Master, she'll die before morning if we can't find her."

"Die! nonsense! A little slut! What should she die for?" said the old man, in a hoarse voice, now thoroughly alarmed.

"Oh, Sir! you're a gentleman that knows nothing about children. Poor lamb; no father nor mother to take care of her! Where did you leave her, Sir? Where can we go to look for her? It's so dark and wet. What if she should fall into the mill pond?"

"Why can't she stand upon her pins? Why should she fall anywhere?" cried the old man, taking down his hat and seizing his stick to go out.

"Oh, master, let me go, you will catch your death of cold going out in the wet," exclaimed Susan. "You sit down and drink a comfortable dish of tea, and I will go out and look for her. I'll get my nevvy to go with me for company; we'll soon find her," she continued cheerily, seeing that her master was really alarmed.

She got ready the tea, and then went up stairs to take off the cherished dress, and put on a common one.

"Damn the dress!" exclaimed Mr. Rock, suspecting why she left the room, and resenting the delay. "Can't you go at once?"

Susan made no reply, but returned in a few moments, bonneted and wrapped in a warm cloak. She took up her lantern, but the candle had burnt out, and she had to find a fresh end to fit and light it, before she left the house, whilst Mr. Rock seemed ready to explode with vexation at the delay.

"You stay here," he exclaimed. "Give *me* the lantern and I will go. You shan't go out into the wet to look for her, a little limb."

"No, master; nevvy and I will go."

"We'll both go then," said Mr. Rock, "we'll go different ways."

"No, Sir, that won't do; if she should come back here and find no one at home, she would be *scart* at the dark and go away again."

The old man still hesitated, but a flutter at his heart made him sit down for an instant, and Susan took advantage of the delay to seize the lantern and hurry off.

"Don't mention it to any but your nephew, Susan," cried Mr. Rock, bitterly ashamed of the whole story.

"Curse her! What a little wretch she is," exclaimed he, apostrophising his absent niece. Drat the child; where can she be now; lying on the wet earth somewhere, the rain beating down upon her? Perhaps she has crawled to some haystack for shelter. Perhaps she may have been met by some ruffian, and, oh Lord!" Unable to bear his own thoughts he rushed to the door, to peer into the darkness, to see if her little figure might be perceived coming along under the lamp-posts, stealing slowly towards her home.

"She don't know where else to go, poor little devil, or she would not come back to me," he thought, full of remorseful pity.

"Afraid of me?—Afraid that I shall beat her? Poor girl; where is she now?—cold and hungry, shivering under some hedge—will be dead probably by to-morrow morning, drenched by the rain, terrified by the darkness and loneliness."

"If she comes back I'll be kind to her. *If* she comes back—Hark! there are Susan's pattens; I'd swear to them in a hundred."

He advanced a few steps from the door into the rain, but his senses had deceived him, it was not Susan, but a woman with a lantern and umbrella, and a little girl by her side.

"It must be *her*," said the lieutenant, regardless of grammar, but the two walked on, talking cheerfully in a tone of perfect accord, which grated on the uncle's mind.

Had he been as kind as that woman, he thought, this terrible anxiety might have been spared.

He walked up and down his sitting-room recklessly, stopping to listen every moment, and hearing only the droppings of the rain-water from the shoot into the puncheon, distinct and loud, at the back of the house. He involuntarily began to count the drops for an occupation, but the rising wind dashed the rain so furiously against the windows in his sitting-room, that he heard single drops no more, in the sheets of water with which the panes of glass seemed deluged.

"What a night for poor Susan, and that child!" he exclaimed.

He looked at his watch; it was near eleven. In his misery he had forgotten the lapse of time. He heard a pair of pattens now — only one pair;—but Sabina had none. He hastened to the door with his candle, but the wind extinguished it immediately.

"Is it you?" he cried, diving his old bald head into the darkness.

"Yes, Sir; 'tis Susan."

"And the child?" he cried, in a voice of hope.

"No, Sir; we can't see or hear anything of her."

Susan came in dripping, and shook the drops from her umbrella.   Mr. Rock sat down and said never a word.

"I went to the lane where you said she was picking the blackberries, Sir; and Billy and I looked about for footsteps.   She must have gone through the gate, or climbed over it, for she lost her little shoe.   Here it is!" producing it, "but we could not see any more of her.   You see 'tis a clover field, and there could not be any marks.   Very likely somebody has found her, and taken her in.   They would not bring her back such a night as this, if they could get shelter anywhere else, or she may have seen a light in a cottage window, and gone to it.   They would take care of her, for she looks to be a gentleman's child, and to-morrow morning they will bring her back."   These were the comforting suggestions of Susan, to which Mr. Rock answered only by a groan.   Susan insisted on making him and herself a basin of gruel, and ordered him to bed.

"'Tis no use.   I can't rest, when she's out in the rain," he exclaimed, his voice going off in a sob.

"Ah! 'twill rest your poor bones, any way," and the lieutenant obeyed for quietness' sake.

When Mr. Rock reached his bed-room, he took off his coat and hung it carefully on the back of the only chair, and kneeling down he wished to change his usual form of prayer for some supplicatory expressions more suited to his pressing anxiety.

The nightly petitions he usually addressed to the Throne of Grace he had devoutly selected from the Evening Church Service.

To pray in any language but that of Scripture, or in forms of prayer sanctioned by the authority of the bishops and clergy, would have seemed to his simple mind to address himself to Heaven in a language which could not be understood, and would have been a useless waste of words, to say nothing of the chance of bringing a judgment down on his own head for his temerity.

So he began.   "Lighten our darkness, we beseech thee, oh Lord! ('tis dark as pitch!)" aside, with a glance at the

windows, "and let not the runagate continue in scarceness"
—this was uttered with a broken voice, thinking of the
supperless child. "Put away the superfluity of her
naughtiness (a cut at her), and make every man swift to
hear, slow to speak—slow to wrath" (a reproof to himself).
" Pardon my offences, gracious Lord, and restore this child
to me ; for greater love has no man than this, that he would
lay down his life for his friend ; and that I would do gladly
to have her back again," was a little natural addendum, for
which he could find no authority in Scripture.

He leaned his head against the side of his bed—that
inartificial and comfortless support consisted of his hammock
slung up—and resting on his sea-chest, he wondered if he had
said enough.

His faltering voice and humid eyes might have pleaded
for him without an uttered word.

CHAPTER V.

HEN Sabina saw the angry countenance and up-
lifted stick of her uncle, her impulse was flight.
She was very miserable in his house. He was to
her an ugly great ogre.

During her mother's life she had enjoyed unlimited indulgence, for that lady's feeble health would have prevented
her correcting Sabina, had she had the desire ; but every act
of that self-willed imp had seemed to her doating mother
"discreetest, best."

"Whither should she go? She cared not. She was not
very hungry—she had eaten plenty of blackberries before
her sin had been found out. She would eat as many as she
pleased, now she was out of the reach of her uncle. Under
cover of his dismay at the sound of the carriage, she had
run down the side of a dry ditch, or rather of one which
seemed to her to be so. When the carriage had driven out
of sight, she thought her uncle would look up and down
the field for her, but she sagely conceived that, if she lay
motionless, she could convey no movement to the bushes
that might betray her, and she believed that the darkness of
her dress might, combined with the rank dock leaves,
entirely conceal her from any search, to the aid of which no
dog was called.

So she lay quite still, and heard her old uncle calling her
in every tone : first of anger, then of anxiety, and lastly of

terror. Now Sabina only became more careful not to move, scarcely daring to breathe, whilst the angry calls pealed in her uncle's deep voice across the meadow. When the tone became plaintive from anxiety, Sabina was half-inclined to crawl out and give herself up, but she argued in her own mind that her uncle's anger would return all the more, from the anxiety he had suffered, so soon as he saw that she was safe ; and as her frock was covered with dirt, she gave no sign.

When his voice was heard no longer, she peered out of the ditch into which she had crawled, to the great detriment of her clothes, and the loss of one of her shoes. It was getting too dark to look for it in the dank ditch. It would have necessitated her crawling back to look for it through the thick weeds and brambles, which she could not push aside—they were too strong and stubborn.

Whither should she go ?

She had often thought of running away during the few hours she had passed at Haven House, and now there seemed nothing to prevent her.

But there were some little treasures in that old portmanteau at Haven House. Three old chains made of that delicate fabric usually procured in Lisbon, a guinea with a hole in it, through which a ribbon had been passed, and worn by her mother, and one or two books belonging to her father. The idea of her uncle's polluting these by his touch, as she would have considered it, made her doubt whether she should not return to possess herself of them, but she remembered the old man's angry face, and hesitated.

She saw in what state her clothes had become: it hurt her to walk without a shoe. The brambles scratched her foot, the stubbles pricked her legs. She sat down on the edge of the ditch, and tried to think. A drizzling rain set in and increased the gloom of the coming night, and Sabina, losing heart and courage, sobbed aloud.

Now it happened that at the houses where Lady Sarah Trelusa and the Honourable Wilfred Tresillian had been paying their visits, that astute young man had picked up certain scraps of electioneering intelligence from which he discovered that his own prospects in the borough were not quite so bright as he had been led to believe.

Not to have to reply to the questions of his lady mother, whose soft, murmuring voice disturbed his meditations, he told her he would indulge in a cigar, and took his seat by the side of the coachman.

His thoughts turned to Mr. Rock—amongst so many doubtful promises his vote would be very important; but then, he might lose more by "going in" for flogging. To him it was a matter of indifference whether every man in his Majesty's navy was flogged daily, from the First Lord of the Admiralty, with whom he was on intimate terms, down to the youngest cabin-boy in the smallest vessel, so long as he was returned member for Deepindale. He must do what would be most likely to lead to that result.

The old man *must* give way. As his thoughts took this direction, the carriage rolled swiftly along the road, for it was now raining thickly and the men did not like to be wet, till they passed the spot where the old man had been seen flourishing his stick over his flying niece. He stopped the carriage. "Shall I open the door, Sir?" said the footman, thinking his young master wished to escape from the rain.

"No, I shall walk home across the fields," was the reply. He laughed and kissed his hand to his mother, as she threw down the glass, and prophesied colds and coughs and in-flammations.

It was really but a short distance, and to the rich, who have abundance of warm clothes at command, getting wet does not mean what it conveys to the poor man whose only suit of clothes is soaked, and who cannot afford a fire to dry them.

Mr. Tresillian's desire for a walk on that wet evening arose from a doubt in his mind, whether a little black heap which seemed to bear some form of humanity, crouched on the wet grass, was in reality a living child, and if so, whether it might be the little girl he had seen in the clutches of Mr. Rock; if so, he might be brought into contact with that gentleman in a manner advantageous to himself as regarded the desired vote, by returning the runaway.

Now, when Sabina saw a man advancing through the dusk with quick steps, she was seized with terror, and rose to her feet to fly, but she slipped about in the wet clay, and found that running away from an old uncle, with a diseased heart, was very different in its results to being pursued by a young man of twenty-five in the plenitude of health and strength.

She heard him coming, and struggled onward, but finding that he was gaining on her, she dived ignominiously into a ditch in the hope of concealment, from whence, with a grasp of his powerful arm, he lifted her by the band round her waist, from which she hung like a lamb in the sign of the golden fleece, with head and arms and legs dependent.

The girl was silent as a trapped wolf, though her heart was beating with fearful violence. Her captor felt it, as he passed his left arm round her waist, thinking the band would give way.

"What are you about here?"

No answer.

"Are you Mr. Rock's little girl?"

No answer.

"I will take you home to him."

She did not speak, but struggled to get away.

"You cannot go till I give you leave—but come, walk on with me to Mr. Rock's house. I suppose you belong to him."

"I belong to nobody, I believe," cried Sabina, with a fresh burst of tears.

"But he takes charge of you?"

"Oh dear!" sobbing. "I wish he didn't."

"Why?"

"Because I hate him."

"Why do you hate him?"

"Because he is so cross, and threatened to beat me, and would have hit me with his great stick, only I ran away."

"Fine, consistent old man! Carries his principles into practice," said Mr. Tresillian, laughing; and then, looking down at the slender child, he could not help pitying her, when he remembered the size and apparent weight of the walking-stick.

"You don't walk very well," said the gentleman, finding it unpleasant to be crawling through a muddy field at a snail's pace, in the dusk, in a pouring rain.

"'Tis because—because," said Sabina, sobbing, "I've lost my shoe."

"What a nuisance," cried the young man. "Well! never mind—we cannot stay here all night; I must carry you," and without further parley he snatched up Sabina like an infant. "Now, put your arms round my neck to steady yourself." She did so, with the shame of knowing that one shoe covered with mud, and one stocking soaked with dirty water, was pressed against his clean trowsers.

The first intention of the young man had been to take Sabina at once to Mr. Rock's house, but though she was not heavy the land was, and clung pertinaciously to the thin soles of Mr. Tresillian's delicate boots, and he found the process of walking under such circumstances rather more fatiguing than he had anticipated. His house was distant but a short quarter of a mile, so he determined to carry her thither, and to send her home to Mr. Rock's, in his dog-cart, so soon as he reached it.

He passed through a small gate leading into the park, and on reaching a summer-house, was glad to rest for a few minutes under the shelter of its roof.

He seated Sabina on the rustic table, and stood thoughtfully by her side a few minutes in silence. The girl could only see the outline of his features, made out dark against the gray sky, but they looked pleasant and sweet tempered.

She nestled closely to her companion, and said, "Where are we going?" and leaning her head against his arm, which she held with both hands, she looked up in his face for an answer.

"I am going to take you to my home first, and then send you in my dog-cart back to Mr. Rock."

Sabina hung her head, and let go her hold.

He did not notice the movement, but took her up again, being rested, to continue his walk. They proceeded in silence till they came near the back entrance of a fine old mansion, and Mr. Tresillian stopped for an instant, embarrassed by Sabina's weight as he attempted to open one of the gates which led to it.

The rain was beating against them, and speaking was not easy, but Sabina, closing her arm more tightly round her companion's neck, whispered in his ear, "Please don't send me home—let me stay with you."

This frank proposition would have provoked Mr. Tresillian's

mirth at any other time, but at present he was too much perplexed to be amused.

The night was so dark, and the child's clothes were so wet,
that he thought, if Mr. Rock had any affection for his little
charge, he would not feel particularly flattered by the way in
which she was returned to him.

Moreover Mr. Tresillian did not like sending his horses
out at night in the wet, and having the risk of their not being
properly dried before they were bedded up for the night; a
circumstance likely to occur, if the servants' hall supper bell
was heard as the groom returned; yet, to produce this child
to Lady Sarah in her present condition was out of the
question; not if the success of the election depended upon
it, would she consent to such a pollution of her drawing-
room. At length he determined on a scheme which presented fewest difficulties.

Mr. Tresillian was a gallant man amongst the fair sex in
every degree, and was on particularly good terms with one of
the head nurses of his brother's children then staying at
Tregear, and taking Sabina still in his arms he entered the
back of the house, and made his way through the lighted
passages to his own dressing-room.

He set her down in the room, dimly lighted by the fire
only, and desired her to remain quiet till his return. In a
few minutes he had explained the matter to his female friend
and told her how important it was that he should propitiate
the uncle by care of his niece, and begged her to arrange
the child so as to make her presentable to Lady Sarah
Trelusa after dinner, and to prepare a bed for her.

Then, rather weary with well doing, he prepared himself
for the important meal of the day by a warm bath, in which
he threw off the stains of mud and clay, which had attached
themselves to his person from his contact with Sabina.

"Dear! dear!" said the nurse, as the light of her candle
fell on Sabina. "Why, wherever have you been, Miss? Did
you fall into the pond, and did Mr. Tresillian fish you out?
Ah! I thought so! Now you must get into a bath, and then
I must look for some clothes for you. Let me see"—looking at her—"Miss Edith's frock would be about your length,
and shoes and socks;—ah! your feet are very small; Miss
Adela's size will do best."

"I fear," said Sabina, "you have no black frock. I don't like not to wear black."

"Who is it for, my dear?"

"Mamma and papa."

"Well, that is right. Only you see, Miss, if they could be asked they would not like you to take cold, and I think they would rather you wore white, or blue, or crimson, than that you should be ill."

Sabina was not sorry to be convinced, and before dinner had concluded, she had been properly washed, combed, and better dressed than she had ever been before in her life.

"How stiff your hair curls," said the nurse, passing the dark rings of hair round her fingers.

"'Tis the rain," replied the child. "Mamma always dipped my hair in water when she wanted it to curl."

"I wish our children's hair would curl with as little trouble," rejoined the servant. "I should not be kept for two hours every evening papering up their heads. There, now, you're dressed, Miss, *a quarter spangles*, as the governess says. Look at yourself in the swing glass."

Sabina felt half ashamed, and did not like to look—besides, a richly-worked flounce which terminated the skirt of her dress occupied all her attention.

She had seen herself often, but such embroidery never. Thus, when she was summoned to the drawing-room she had no clear idea of her appearance.

The footman, opening the door, announced "Miss Rock," and sent her forward into a delicious atmosphere of warmth and perfume, and into a blaze of light.

Dazzled and perplexed, she looked forward and saw another room, as she imagined, in which were seated a strange lady and her new friend. A little girl, in a white frock and blue sash and black shoes, advanced towards her as if to greet Sabina, who, not to be outdone in civility, went up close, and knocked her forehead against a large looking-glass, in which she was reflected, as she tried to kiss the stranger.

Lady Sarah, in great astonishment, turned for an explanation to her son, who, laughing said, "What are you about, Miss Rock? do you want to kiss yourself in the glass?"

The laughter came from behind the child, though she

thought Mr. Tresillian was before her, and she turned, flushing all over at the blunder she had committed.

She had never before seen a glass which nearly covered the end of a room. She looked very handsome with the flush, and her eyes, usually so wild and elfish, were softened into an appealing look at her protector. He arose, and taking her hand, led her to his mother, whom he had prepared for the visit of the strange child.

"Did the nurse give you anything to eat, my dear?" said the lady, kindly; for, replete with the good things of her own table, she felt a generous glow of hospitality towards all persons in general, and towards the little girl in particular, as a possible channel of good towards her favourite son.

"Yes; thank you, Ma'am. I have had tea and toast and —and some chicken," replied the child, her hesitation having arisen from a doubt as to what the white substance was of which she had partaken.

"Perhaps it was turkey," said the lady, meditatively. "We had turkey yesterday. Did you like it, Miss Rock?"

"Yes; thank you, Ma'am."

Lady Sarah had made as great an effort as her son could expect, and with a happy consciousness of having performed her duty, she subsided against the back of the sofa with a sweet smile, and dozed with as much of sleep as to be conscious of enjoying it.

"What is your name?"

"Sabina."

"Do you like looking at prints—picture books?"

"Yes, very much. When they are pretty."

"Then we will turn over these, or rather, I will, for they are too heavy for you."

"I think you have taken too much trouble about me already, Sir. I hope I did not tire you very much?"

She felt she could talk more easily now Lady Sarah was asleep.

The engravings were valuable proofs, and without any lettering to indicate the subjects. Mr. Tresillian gave a little sigh of anticipated weariness when he glanced at the numerous subjects. 'Tis so difficult, as Dr. Johnson says he thought, to talk like little fishes, when required to write a fable about them.

"To talk to this child will be as uncomfortable as walking with a man two feet shorter than yourself, who insists on taking your arm."

So he began. "A man asleep with an ass's head; the fairies took away the man's head, and gave him the ass's."

"Not the fairies, Puck," interrupted Sabina. "'Methought I was enamoured of an ass,'" she continued, roguishly looking up at Mr. Tresillian.

"Meaning me, I suppose," said her friend, laughing. "Well! you make a sweet little Titania," he continued, putting his arm around her waist caressingly.

This disturbed the child, who said, "Show me another, please."

As the engravings were illustrations of Shakespeare, Sabina named the subjects of each, as her companion turned the leaves, and he found, that whilst he only recognised those from the plays which stage representation had made familiar to him, she knew them all, and explained subjects which puzzled him.

"How do you know so much about these plays?"

"Mamma had few books, and so we read them over and over again."

The books were finished, and the girl slid off her chair, and wandered on tiptoe over the luxurious carpet of the drawing-room.

"Oh, what a fine great piano!" touching one of the keys with the tip of her finger.

"Lady Sarah is awake," said her son. "You may touch it if you like. Now, should you not like to play me a tune? I can play the cat's minuet."

As part of this music consists in turning the nail of the first finger on the keys, and drawing it rapidly from one octave to the other, Sabina, forgetting all sense of propriety, put her fingers to her ears with an expression of pain.

Mr. Tresillian pretended to be offended.

"Very well! if you do not like it do better yourself."

"Can you play on the piano?" said the silvery voice of the now thoroughly awakened lady.

"A little, Ma'am. I can play my own accompaniments when they are not very difficult, when I sing."

"Can you sing now?" said her hostess, with some feeble movement of curiosity.

Sabina wriggled herself up on the music stool, and after thinking a few minutes, said, " It is Sunday, so I will sing something sacred."

She began the plaintive movement of Handel's—" ' How beautiful are the feet of those who bring good tidings.' "

That wonderful voice once heard could never be forgotten, even by the most indifferent, and Lady Sarah was exceedingly fond of music.

" You are the little girl who sang in church to-day ? " she said.

" Yes, Ma'am."

" Sing again if you are not too tired."

She went on, and gave with the utmost correctness of the half tones, " ' Behold ! and see if there be any sorrow like unto His sorrow.' "

" Do you prefer sacred music ? "

" No ; only because it is Sunday, you know. I like Italian and English on week days."

She slid down from the music stool, and listened to the striking of the pendule on the chimney-piece.

" Do you wish to go to bed ? " said Mr. Tresillian.

" Oh, no ! I am so very happy," said the child, putting her hands to the back of her head. " I have not been so happy since——"

" But you must be tired," said Mr. Tresillian, who saw tears in her eyes ; " it is getting late ; you had better let me ring for the nurse. Are you not anxious about your uncle ? " said he curiously.

" No ! " replied the girl ; " why should I be ? " and her brow grew sullen.

" Oh ! because he must be unhappy at having lost you."

" No, he would be glad. I am in his way. He hates me —I hate him."

" Hush ! hush ! " cried Mr. Tresillian ; " Lady Sarah will hear you."

" Why not ? " she replied, undauntedly.

" There, I have rung the bell for your ' nurse,' " he was going to say, but changed the word to " maid." He was half afraid of this clever, vixenish child, who might not like to be considered one.

Sabina, seeing that her fate was inevitable, walked up to

Lady Sarah's knee, and said, " I am obliged to you, Ma'am, and I wish you good-night."

She had grown much harder since she could not speak to Mr. and Mrs. Snow without sobbing. She then turned to Mr. Tresillian, and put her small brown hand out.

He drew her towards him, and kissed her, a salute which she returned eagerly, fearing she had displeased him.

" You are so very good to me, and I love you so much," she cried, frankly. Then she followed the nurse to the small bed-room she was to occupy next to the nursery.

" I don't know, Miss," said this woman, " whatever is to be done about your black frock, which is all to ribbons—tore right off your back, I may say ; and black !—no one would ever know it was black, 'tis so smothered in mud. It seems to me, that Mr. Tresillian had better send over to your uncle's house to-morrow, and get another of your frocks, my dear."

" Oh, no ! pray don't ! " said Sabina, with a look of dismay. This had been her best frock ; the other was so shabby. With a sensitive nature which suffered so much from the effects of her own folly, it was a wonder that she did not correct herself of carelessness which entailed such grievous suffering.

" Can't you do anything ? " she cried, despairingly. " Wash it ?—mend it ? "

" Well, really, Miss, I fear 'tis impossible ; but go to bed, and sleep, my dear ; time enough to think of trouble to-morrow ; sufficient for the day is the evil thereof, as I always feel on Sundays, when the clergyman gives us a long sermon."

It seems strange that ladies of rank should care for the tittle-tattle of their servants. To sit and listen to small circumstances regarding their equals picked up by one domestic from another, might, one would imagine, possess not unnatural interest ; but when the information relates to some transactions in the kitchen of some farmer, or the cottage of some labourer, it is difficult to understand the vacuity of mind to which such pabulum can be welcome.

Mrs. March, the nurse who had taken charge of Sabina, talked over the advent of the child with Mrs. Stevens, Lady Sarah's maid. How the poor child's frock was all rags, and

her linen patched and darned all over ; how she seemed
afraid of her life to send for another frock ; and she believed
the old man Rock was a regular old Turk.   The coachman
and William the footman saw him holding a great stick over
the child's head.   She quite pitied the little thing, for her
own part, and would not mind running up a dress, if my
lady would give one of her old ones for the purpose.

This intelligence was conveyed to the good-natured,
placid lady, when her hair was undergoing its nocturnal
brushing and embalming, and melted her to pity.

" Take that black silk, and get some one from the village
to make it."

" Yes, my lady.   Your ladyship may see that the seams
and the hem at the bottom being done, it won't take much
time ; we may get it ready by luncheon time."

" How pleased she will be ! " was the thought of the benevolent lady ; " and how wonderful is her voice ! "

CHAPTER VI.

"The timely dew of sleep,
Now falling with soft slumbrous weight, inclines
The eyelids."—MILTON.

T was some time before Sabina could settle herself
to sleep. Her brain whirled with excitement.
She had had so much suffering and so much
pleasure in a short time—in a succession of a
few hours.

When she shut her eyes the retina retained her uncle's
furious face. She opened them and saw the strange prints
on the wall by the light of the watch-light, and the unusual
aspect of the room. Then her head became dizzy, and she
clasped something very closely, which turned out to be Mr.
Tresillian's neck; but she let it go, and fell with a sudden
start that awakened her.

Then she fancied herself Titania, with a jewelled crown
and a gauze veil, and a beautiful wand in her hand, with
a star at the end of it, and in that happy delusion she at
length slept soundly, and forgot everything.

It was late when she was awakened by children's voices
in the adjoining room, and heard, by the vigorous splashings
going on, that they were in their baths.

" I wonder how I am to get up, and what clothes I can
wear! And oh! my frock!" she cried, sitting on the side
of the bed, with an aspect so woe-begone that even her
uncle might have pitied her.

Presently her kind friend, the nurse, came in. "I will
get your bath directly, Miss Rock, and you will put on one

of my young lady's frocks this morning till you go. My lady says you are to stay and have your dinner at her luncheon time."

This was good news for Sabina, but as she was going with Mrs. March into the day nursery to join the children at their breakfast, the other and rival *bonne* declared that her missus would not like her children to associate with, she didn't know who; children picked up in the hedges and ditches, who might have all kind of infectious complaints about them—scarlet fever, measles, whooping cough and small pox. Mrs. March might take the child to the servants' hall if she liked.

Mrs. March, in dudgeon, took Sabina back to her bedroom, and seeking Mr. Tresillian's valet, confided to him the difficulty, and begged him to ask his master for orders.

Mr. Tresillian sat up in his bed and wrote a short note to his mother, suggesting that it would be a pity now to lose the fruit of all their good deeds as regarded this child, by affronting her at the eleventh hour. Lady Sarah assented, and desired Mrs. March to bring Miss Rock to breakfast with her in her dressing-room.

Mrs. March rejoiced greatly at this tacit snub to Mrs. Cross. The child not considered good enough to associate with *her* charges, was honoured by taking breakfast with her ladyship.

She dressed Sabina neatly, smoothing her beautiful black hair, and led her to the dressing-room, which Lady Sarah had not yet entered. Sabina looked with admiration at the snowy table-cloth, and the old filigree silver service equipage from which the steam was pouring itself in short irregular puffs. She thought herself in fairy land, and when Lady Sarah, enveloped in a soft Cashmere dressing-gown, with her abundant hair falling over her shoulders, entered the room, Sabina thought she saw in her the good fairy from whom all the luxuries around her had proceeded.

The lady desired her maid to pour out the tea and to attend to Miss Rock. She herself, after a cordial nod of good-morning to the girl, amused herself with the last number of the "Lady's Magazine," which was illustrated charmingly by a rising artist named Stodart, and which was light to hold in the hand.

She felt a feeble curiosity about the tales contained in it, though the impressions made by them on her mind were so slight, that her son declared she had read one portion of one of the stories twice over, fancying she was reading the continuation. Sabina soon finished her toast and grated ham, and was anxious to look at some handsomely bound books which came within her reach on the book shelf.

"May I touch them, Madam?" she said, eagerly.

"Yes, certainly. March, take Miss Rock away and wash her hands. Then she may come back."

Lady Sarah was still loitering over her breakfast when Sabina returned, with fingers pink from the friction of the towel, and sat down on the floor to enjoy what was to her a great treat: whilst she read, and looked at the engravings by turns, Lady Sarah had been deep in some love-scene in the magazine.

Part of the description had touched some chord of memory, and she looked off her pamphlet thoughtfully and sadly.

Her ladyship had been a great beauty in her youth, and having married young, had retained a large portion of it, even when grandchildren proclaimed ruthlessly that age had come. There was so much dignity and sweetness in that pensive face, that Sabina left off looking at pictures: and the lady, catching a glimpse of the child's rapt countenance, asked her at what she was looking, and of what thinking.

Sabina's face grew crimson. "I was thinking," she said, "that you were like a beautiful picture I saw in the Louvre of Dido, listening to the adventures of Æneas."

Lady Sarah's face flushed slightly with pleasure. "My dear!" she cried, "you are quite right, I was considered *very* like that picture a few years since." What an intelligent child! was the lady's reflection. Edith would never have thought of the resemblance, nor have said it had she done so. "When were you in Paris?"

"We lived there some time, before mamma was ill. She came over, hoping to find some friends—but "——with a broken voice, "she did not, and then she died."

She prattled on, and Lady Sarah became interested. She was full of pity for the destitution of Sabina's poor wardrobe. She sent a carriage to the best milliner in Deepindale for some chip bonnets, and had a new one trimmed by her maid, under her own directions. She had a slight feeling of malice directed towards all her grandchildren, especially the eldest, Edith. That girl was always calling her "grand-mamma" in the loudest of tones, and the shrillest of voices.

That child, whose inane impertinences were repeated for wit by her absurd parents, was dressed in the finest of linen and fed on the choicest of food ; and here was this neglected child, who promised to be so handsome, and was so gifted by voice and ear, destitute of everything.

She would patronise little Rock, and have her over some day when her daughter-in-law came down, and show her a really beautiful and accomplished girl by the side of that goggle-eyed grandchild of hers, of whom her parents were so proud.

Sabina, unconscious of the thoughts of her patroness, looked at the illustrated books, or at the herds of deer re-posing under the massive elms and oaks in the park.

Presently Lady Sarah observed a curious smile pass over the child's face as she withdrew from the window. "At what are you looking?" said her ladyship.

Sabina blushed slightly. "At a young lady?"

" Yes."

"A young lady with two other young ladies, and an elder one, walking in the park."

"Those are my son's children."

"Yes, Madam. I saw them at church."

" But why did you smile; of what were you thinking?" rejoined the inquisitive lady.

"I was thinking," said Sabina, with a flush of falsehood in her face, "what a pretty gauze bonnet she had on !" She was remembering her triumph in singing.

This reply set Lady Sarah thinking whether it was really a pretty gauze bonnet, and whether pipings of pink satin would not have looked prettier than of blue. Then she remembered the want of contrast which would have resulted from juxtaposition with the pink rosebud in front ; and fancy wandered to a blue convolvulus with pink pipings for her-self; so that Sabina felt she had made "a bold diversion," and got out of the attack cleverly.

But whilst Lady Sarah meditated patronage, she was like

the country maiden, about to overthrow, by an act of her own, all the castles she was amusing herself by building. She went to her cabinet and took out a needle-book, in which she placed something she thought would be useful to Sabina. "It contains needles and cotton and other things, useful to little girls who go out blackberry gathering," she said.

The hour arrived when Sabina had to take leave of her kind friend. She had placed the needle-book in her pocket shyly, when Lady Sarah had first given it to her ; and in the whirl of her emotion at her unusual *entourage*, she scarcely thought of it again.

The child went up reluctantly to Lady Sarah, to say goodbye, after she had partaken of luncheon, brought up into her ladyship's room expressly for her. "I can't bear to go away," said she, "because you look so beautiful and you are so nice to me."

Nothing could have pleased her simple ladyship more. "You shall come and see me again some day," said she, "and mind you keep the needle-book carefully for my sake." The girl will not know the value of what I have put into it, thought she, if I do not impress on her mind that she must be careful.

It was an elegant little Russian leather case, with a coronet and her ladyship's cypher in gold on the outside. She drew the girl towards her and just touched her forehead with her lips ; and then the nurse, taking Sabina to her room, took off the clothes belonging to the children of the house, and dressed her in those which Lady Sarah had ordered to be provided, which though superior in texture, were of the same colour as those which she had previously worn.

Sabina looked about as she was led through the upper corridors, down the grand staircase, across the marble hall, and out at the great entrance, to see if she could perceive Mr. Tresillian. She longed to see him once more, if only to say "good-bye," but that gentleman, conscious that his mother's kindness might be safely trusted, had forgotten all about the child, in his anxiety about the approaching election, and had left home early on business connected with it.

When Mr. Rock had been sent to bed, at the suggestion

of old Susan, he had given way, from a dislike to oppose her, but with no idea of being able to sleep. "How could he sleep?" he said, when the rain came rattling against the window-pane, and the wind made strange noises like cries and moans of a person in extremity. He lay on his right side, and then tossed over on his back. The left side was a forbidden position. The heart could not act so freely when lying in that position. I am afraid he cursed his nephew for having married, also his nephew's wife, who had been *particeps criminis*. "*I* could never afford to marry the girl of my heart," thought the old man. And his memory went back forty years to a small window in a small house, situated just out of Marseilles, which was covered with jessamine, roses, and passion flowers, at which used to be seated a graceful girl called Valerie, whose brunette skin used to flush as she saw him approach.

At a *fête champêtre* given to the officers of "The Seagull," Valerie had been followed there to persecution by one of the junior officers. Timid, and unwilling to draw attention to her dilemma, she only walked faster in the hope of avoiding him, when a sudden turn of the path showed Lieutenant Rock, with his spy-glass in his hand, looking through the trees towards his beloved vessel. A sudden inspiration seized Valerie: she went up to him and passed her arm through his, saying, "I am engaged to dance with this gentleman."

"Is that the case, Mr. Rock?" said the young man, angrily.

"Have you not heard the lady say so? I am astonished, Sir, at your want of courtesy in asking the question after her statement."

The persecutor bowed and withdrew. The girl looked up, the man looked down, and so they fell in love. As the thought, "I never could afford to marry the girl of my heart," flashed across his brain, he seemed to see again the thickly-clustering trees and their cool shadows, the slight girl, with her timid pleading face raised to his, her white dress, looking so pure and bright, half in sun-light, half in shadow, and the straw hat tied under that round young-looking chin with blue ribbon—his favourite colour. Mr. Rock half smiled at the thought how dark and curling *his* hair had then been—himself, how strong, eager and active. That day he had attended Valerie with chivalrous devotion, but he had a widowed mother at home, with little to depend on but what he saved from his pay, or sacrificed at once from his prize-money, and he knew that he could not maintain both a wife and a mother.

A vessel—a French privateer—had been fastened to the French coast by a cable which was inserted in a ring sunk in a steep rock. Mr. Rock and the second lieutenant, his senior, were sent with a boat's crew to cut the cable, and thereby to enable the "Seagull" to carry off the prize. As they landed on the shelving shore the senior in command stumbled and fell, and Rock, springing past him, rushed up the cliff, and hacked at the stout cord with his drawn sword till it was divided, being subject during the whole time to a smart fire from a neighbouring battery which guarded the locality. He was seen from his ship in the execution of his arduous undertaking, and many hearts ached when they saw the gallant young man fall forward, struck with a bullet in the leg. His men hoisted him on their shoulders and carried him back to the ship. The Patriotic Fund decreed him a sword, as a reward for his gallantry, with a suitable inscription; but as the considerate donors knew how poorly filled was Jack's purse, as a rule, they gave him the option of his sword or £90. Young Rock had the aspirations which are so lively in youth. He wished for honours and fame, and he coveted the visible sign of his own gallantry; but he thought of his mother, high mettled and uncomplaining, struggling on in her poverty with his two young sisters, and he gave up the sword, and sent her the £90.

Hard knocks he had had in plenty, but promotion was for those who had friends at the Admiralty, or friends of their friends. And now a sheer hulk, laid up as useless, the only compensation he had reason to hope for, was that he might spend the remainder of his days in peace; of that peace, the imprudent marriage of a nephew he had never cared about, and the orphanage of his little girl, had deprived him.

He tried to sleep. He tried not to care for the driving rain, and the thought that it was drenching her little shivering body. "Oh, God! be merciful to her!" he prayed earnestly. And his old eyelids filled with weak tears, at the image his fancy suggested of Sabina's cowering under some hedge, and shivering in the blast, "and I," he said, "so warmly laid!"

There was a sound along the still street of horse's tread. His heart began to beat fearfully. The child's body had been found, no doubt, and he was wanted to identify it. He sat up in the bed, having pulled off his night-cap to hear better. The sounds stopped at his door—there was an impatient ring at the bell, and a pause. He got out of bed, shaking in every limb, to hear the worst; and, when he had partly dressed and had reached the head of the stairs, he heard a message given to Susan, who stood illuminated by her own candle, which she shielded from the draught, a queer figure in jacket, flannel petticoat, and night-cap.

"Tell Mr. Rock, with my master, Mr. Tresillian's compliments, that his little girl is quite safe, and will be sent home to-morrow."

What a long-drawn sigh of relief heaved the old sailor's breast, as Susan shouted the message from the bottom of the stairs. "Thank God! thank God!" he muttered, "that she is safe and in good hands." And he tottered back to his room, and, extinguishing his candle, got into bed and slept tranquilly.

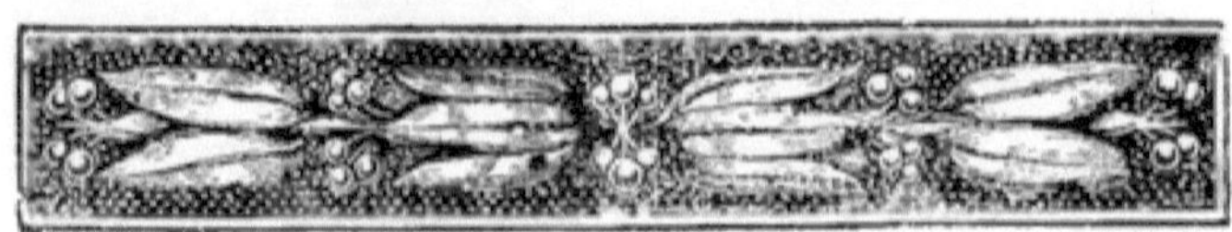

CHAPTER VII.

"An angry care did dwell
In his darker breast, and all gay forms expel."
DRYDEN.

THE old man slept rather later than usual on the following morning. In fact, he had not time to shave before he came down to read the morning paper to Susan. He fidgeted about after completing his post-breakfast toilette ; and could not help giving expression to the thought passing in his mind to Susan, "I wonder when she will be back?"—not that he anticipated any pleasure from her return ; he wanted to know how far appearances had compromised him. He valued the good opinion of his neighbours, he feared he had exhibited himself in a very ludicrous position, if not a tyrannical one, with a huge walking stick lifted over the head of a little girl. What he expected to gather from the child, poor dear old man! was what the great folks had thought of *him*. The columns of the "Times," borrowed from a neighbour that day, had lost their usual attraction, for they seemed incomprehensible. So much had his brain refused to attach meaning to sentences, which he read and re-read, he made up his mind that the writers of the articles were particularly obscure that day.

Susan's thoughts were not of the pleasantest character either. She had her little pride in her master, and the shabby state of Sabina's clothes gave her, in recollection, pangs of which he luckily was quite ignorant. He knew not how repeatedly her stockings had been darned, nor how thin her flannel petticoat had become from long wearing, till the front was almost transparent from the attrition of two little sharp knees. He did not know how the coarse material of her linen had been patched and darned. "And those children up there, dressed so beautiful and so stuck-up, and she with never a bit of night-cap or night-gown to go to bed with."

"Time and the hour runs through the roughest day," and the most dreary also; and about half-past two Susan heard the roll of a carriage coming along the parade, and a sharp rat-tat-tat brought her at once to the door, for she had been waiting breathlessly in the kitchen with her best cap on, and a snowy white apron, which she had that morning washed and ironed for the occasion. Some one would be sure to bring back the child, and she was determined her master should lose no importance by the untidiness of his servant. The footman opened the door for Sabina, and offered his arm to assist her descent; but she jumped out with more liveliness than dignity, and after the footman had received a grim smile and a courtesy from Susan, and had seen the child safely within the house, the carriage drove off.

"Well, indeed, Miss Sabina!" said Susan, seeing her charge, "the same, yet not the same," as to attire. Everything of the same colour, yet of finer material, and with that indescribable look which belongs to well cut out dresses. Sabina took no notice of her. She was full of importance, and swelled in silence. Her great-uncle had many thoughts how to keep up his dignity, though he was longing to go out to meet her. He sat in silent majesty in his little room, and expected a penitent to fall at his feet and ask forgiveness. Sabina considered herself to be the injured person. She did not love her uncle, and had no notion of showing any sorrow which she did not feel. She passed the door of his sitting-room, and walked up stairs with deliberation.

"Well, Miss, was you happy and comfortable at the great house? Was they kind to you?"

"Of course they were," said Sabina, loftily.

"Well," continued Susan, in an injured tone, "a fine job you gave us with your pranks. Just look here," and she turned the child round, and showed a mud-bedrabbled gown and petticoat stretched over a towel-horse. "That's just what happened to me, when I went gandering all over the fields at eleven o'clock last night to find you. And I've got such a hoarseness on my stomach as will last for weeks and weeks, all along of your pranks."

"Uncle should not have threatened to beat me," said Sabina, sullenly.

"Did he?" said Susan. It threw a new light on the affair. "Ah! he was always a hasty gentleman; but then you must forget and forgive, you know."

Sabina did not look of a forgetful or forgiving disposition, but she said nothing.

Mr. Rock wondered that the girl did not come down. He rang the bell for Susan.

"Susan, does she seem sorry?"

Susan's love of truth struggled with her wish to please her master.

"She said nothing, Sir; but I think she looks as if she *might* be sorry."

"Susan!" clearing his throat; "don't you think you ought to tell her to come and kneel down, and say she will never behave so again?"

"Well, Sir, if I was you, I would not drive her too far. She's a wonderful wilful child; but we must make the best of her, and it's no use setting her off again. If I was you, Sir, I'd take no notice."

"Umph!" said Mr. Rock.

He could manage a man-of-war's crew—he knew nothing of the management of little girls; but he felt himself somehow deprived of a due amount of consequence. He succumbed to Susan's better knowledge on this point. He sat down again in his place from which, in his eager speech, he had half-risen, and took up "Anecdotes of Naval History," his favourite reading.

Presently Sabina lounged into the room, with a studied expression of insolent indifference in her face, and walked to the window looking out into the parade, as if she saw something there exceedingly interesting.

Mr. Rock observed her silently over his spectacles, looking down again when any movement in the back of her head indicated an intention of turning round.

Suddenly she left the room again. "I wonder what she is going to do now!" thought the old man.

"Susan!" she exclaimed, "put on your bonnet and come out for a walk with me."

"Well, Miss, as soon as I be finished this saucepan, and put away the bits of cold 'taties for dinner to-morrow, I don't care if I do."

The sight of Sabina's handsome clothes had had a great effect on Susan's mind, and she thought she should like to show her off to her acquaintances, and tell how Miss Sabina had been on a visit to the great folks at Tregear. She thought also that Miss Sabina would tell her more when they were walking—would be "more sociable like." In this she was mistaken. Sabina's wish to go out arose from two reasons—first, that she disliked the old man, and hated to be in the only sitting-room with him; secondly, that she fancied she might have a greater chance of seeing Mr. Tresillian when she was walking, than circumscribed by the four walls of her uncle's house.

Both returned to it, however, disappointed. Sabina chose to tell nothing to Susan of the doings at Tregear, and she was not gratified by even a glimpse of the friend she pined to see again.

"Go in, my dear," said Susan, "go in, and I'll take in tea; and do be sociable with your uncle."

"I don't want to be sociable," retorted the child.

"You had better, Miss—you had, indeed. You can't live with them great folks always. They can't be troubled with such as you."

"Such as I am?" said Sabina, with angry eyes.

"There, there, that will do; now go in, and I'll put away your bonnet."

Sabina sat herself at the tea-table, and her uncle placed a cup of tea before her and a ship biscuit. Sabina took the latter and rolled it round on its edge, to show her contempt for the food provided for her. She liked it really, but disliked her uncle too much to admit it. The old man saw the contemptuous look and gesture, and his wrath began to rise.

"It is not like the fine food you had at Tregear, I suppose," said he.

"No," replied Sabina, shortly, "it is very hard for my teeth."

"I suppose," said her uncle, "that it need not hurt your young teeth, if it does not my old ones."

"I'm not so sure of that," said Sabina, who had caught a glimpse of two suspicious bands of gold in her uncle's mouth. She added nothing to this taunt; no addition was needed. Mr. Rock had false teeth; a fact of which he had flattered himself no one was cognizant but himself and the dentist. Sabina had taken him at a disadvantage. Sabina now began to crumble some of the biscuit into her tea, and to make the best of it.

"Ahem," began her uncle, "where did you have your meals at Tregear?"

"With Lady Sarah," said Sabina, in a conceited tone.

"What !" said the old man, in a stentorian voice.

"With her ladyship," repeated the child, by no means alarmed.

"I am afraid you are telling stories," said Mr. Rock, in a doubtful tone of suppressed delight.

"Don't ask me, then," retorted the girl, "if you don't believe me."

A long silence.

"Who found you ?" he said at last.

"Mr. Tresillian."

"What did he say ?"

"He asked me what I was doing there."

"And what did you say ?"

"That I had run away from you because you were going to beat me."

"Well," said the old man, nervously, "what said he then ?"

"Oh, he said you were a fine, consistent old fellow, who carried your principles of service into private life."

Mr. Rock took it as a compliment. True, he thought the expression "old fellow" was a mark of the want of refinement of the present day, when young men were notorious for their absence of respect towards their seniors; but on the whole he was well satisfied.

"Did Lady Sarah say anything about—— me" was on his lips, but he changed it to "it," encouraged by his previous success.

"Not a word," said Sabina; "she only asked me if I was the little girl that sang so well at church."

"Hum," said Mr. Rock, disappointed. He thought the

circumstance might have excited more interest in her lady-ship's mind.

The arrival of Lieutenant Orellan, and the clearing away of tea-cups, and the arrangement of the chessmen on the board, now allowed Sabina to follow her own devices. She knew the moves, and though unable to pursue the intricate sequences of those made by two good players, she was interested in guessing what plans of attack would be made, and what defences set up. She watched them thus till the whisky-and-water was placed on the table, and Lieutenant Orellan told the little reports of the town—how the dentist, who ought to have known better, found a £20 note on his chimney-piece after Mr. Tresillian's agent had called to ask for his vote, and laughed and meant to keep it. "It is terrible," said one old sailor to the other; and they agreed that pure integrity, honour, and gentlemanlike feeling could spring up and bloom only in the congenial atmosphere of a man-of-war.

"Twenty pounds is a great temptation to a poor man, Rock," said Orellan, meditatively, thinking of his paralytic wife at home, and how many small comforts it would purchase for her. "Then, Mr. Scott may increase his practice in tooth-drawing and tooth-manufacturing, and we, poor devils! are not allowed to do anything but 'stand and wait,' till we are half inclined to cry 'stand and deliver,' because we are gentlemen."

"Yes—but we, being gentlemen, *could* not take a bribe without feeling that we had lost the distinction which we have clung to since we were small boys—we should feel ourselves to be 'dirty dogs and no sailors,' as Jack says."

"Yes, I know 'tis impossible," rejoined Orellan; "but how these £10 and £20 notes do go flying about."

In the meantime, Sabina went to bed, tired and sleepy, and slept in peace. Susan occupied herself in folding up Sabina's clothes, and observing with great satisfaction their delicate texture and fashionable make.

"Something in this pocket," she said, feeling the weight, and diving inside she took it out. "Lawks! this is bootiful! What's this? A little crown all in gold, and a S and a T twisted together! Why, 'tis my lady's own. What's inside ?　O-o-h-h-h ! a £10 note—Bank of England—two !!! £20 !!!!!"

Susan shut them up in the book, and sat down, white and trembling.

"Oh, Lord ! oh, Lord !" she cried ; " the child's a thief ! She's been and stole them !　'Tis like the wicked man in the werses master read me, who was treated so hospitable, and stole a gold mug—goblet they called it.　A little hussey ! That was the reason she was so quiet—wouldn't say a word about how she got on at Tregear.　'Twas on her mind all day.　Oh, dear; 'twill break master's heart that his flesh and blood should turn to thieving—so young, too,—a little baggage—what's to be done?　'Twill be found out as sure as fate, and we shall have the constable coming here to take her up.　'Twill be known all over the town that Mr. Rock— him who has always kept so respectable—Mr. Rock's niece has been took up for stealing."

Susan sat sobbing, and looking impatiently at the quiet sleep of the supposed culprit, till she heard the front door slam after the departing footsteps of Mr. Orellan.　Then she descended, and entering the sitting-room, sat down by the doorway, her white apron thrown over her head, sobbing and wailing in a manner piteous to see and sad to hear.

"What the devil, woman, do you mean by all this non-sense?" said her master, seizing her by the shoulder and shaking her violently.

"Oh, Sir," gasping, "oh, master ! that little hussey—I was always against your taking her home—that vile girl ! She've been and stole a pocket-book what belongs to Lady Sarah up in the great house.　The constables 'll be here the first of the morning to take her up, and our character's gone for ever."

"My own flesh and blood !" said the old man, in a tone of heart-aching agony that wrung the woman's breast with an intensity of sympathy.

"But," said Mr. Rock, "how do you know it is true? How dare you say so of anyone of my family.　Prove it— prove it !" he shouted in her ear, having got his face close to the white apron.

"Ah, good lack ! 'tis true enough, for here it is, with my lady's name upon it, and £20 inside."

" £20 inside ! ! ! "

He had almost repeated the remembered words of his friend Orellan—"£20 notes do fly about the town so !"

Mr. Rock became of the colour of a yellow washed-out silk handkerchief, at seeing what he, as well as Susan, considered as proof positive of Sabina's guilt.

" Fetch her down ! " in a voice of thunder.

" She's asleep, Sir," replied Susan, with a voice of pity for the culprit.

" Fetch her down directly," reiterated her uncle.

Thus coerced, Susan went up, and shaking Sabina by the shoulder, told her that she must get up and come down to speak to her uncle.

Susan put on her shoes and wrapped a shawl round her, and half-led, half-lifted her down the stairs to the sitting-room, where Mr. Rock sat with open mouth, starting eyes, and pale yellow visage, to execute vengeance on the offender. Sabina, half asleep, was too stupid at first to understand why she was awakened and brought down into the presence of her uncle so suddenly.

" What do you mean by it ? " said her uncle, in a hoarse and terrible voice.

" What ? " said Sabina, puzzled.

" Stealing, Miss—*stealing*," and he held up the pocket-book.

" How *dare* you touch that ? " screamed Sabina. " How dare you meddle with what is not your own ? 'Tis *you* are a thief, you ugly, hard old man. I *hate* you. Give me my property."

Mr. Rock could not control his passion ; he hit Sabina a slap on the face with his open hand, which left the crimson print of every giant finger on her delicate face ; the blood sprang from her mouth, which was cut by her teeth—

> " Hard was the hand that dealt the blow,
> Soft were the lips that bled."

For a moment she was stupified ; but the blood tingled back to her face, and made it crimson, and springing on Mr. Rock, she fastened her teeth on the back of his hand, clinging to her hold like a bulldog, crooking up her feet to make the weight greater, till the old man howled with the un-looked-for pain. Agitated and angry before, the pain aroused him to fury, and he shook her off so violently that she swung round and fell, her head coming against the corner of the table, so that she lay senseless on the ground. There are few men who would not have acted with the like impatience ; yet, when Mr. Rock saw the girl lying on the floor, with a serious contused wound on her temple, his agony of remorse was terrible.

"Well, you have done it now, with a vengeance, master," said Susan, "she won't trouble you no more, poor mother-less lamb !"

He did not answer ; he was occupied in raising Sabina tenderly in his arms, and putting back the hair from the wound.

"Up to her bed, Sir," suggested Susan, penitent, when she saw her master's terror and dismay, "she's only stunned —she'll come to herself in a bit or so."

Mr. Rock obeyed, and laid her carefully in her bed, whilst Susan ran to obtain a hot bottle to place at her feet. Mr. Rock sat watching the heavy breathing, and trying with his fingers the constricted pulse at her wrist. His own hand was swollen and aching, but he was unconscious of it. Sabina's supposed theft, and her violence and imperti-nence to himself had faded from his mind. He saw only his great-niece, seemingly nigh unto death from his own violence.

"Susan ! Susan ! stay with her. I must go and get a doctor," he said at last, as his increasing terror battled with his dread of publicity.

"Nonsense, Sir ; don't go on so, bringing shame indeed on a respectable house like this. Doctors go gabbing all over the neighbourhood. She'll do well enough before long —you don't know nothing about children."

Thus advised, Mr. Rock wiped his eyes and his spectacles, and sat by the bedside, whilst Susan bathed the wound with tepid water. Sabina only aroused herself to feel sick, and then slept or dozed again in a way that was alarming to Mr. Rock, who, though he knew nothing of children, had seen men suffering from pressure of the brain. Susan, on the contrary, thought it was a comfort she lay still anyway.

"What a curse this child is !" the old man muttered.

" This is the second night I have been agitated and disturbed. If God don't send us children, truly the devil sends nephews and nieces."

They sat up all night, Susan indulging herself and Mr. Rock in the extravagance of a cup of tea diluted with scalt milk, but without sugar, which Cornish people gave up at the time of the Wilberforce agitation of the slave trade. When morning dawned, Sabina slept more naturally, and the old man was glad to have the occupation of shaving and dressing before he set out to take counsel of his friend Mr. Orellan. This required a great effort ; for though Mr. Orellan was older than Mr. Rock, he was junior in the service, a fact never forgotten by either in their intercourse. Thus, it was with a sense of wounded dignity Mr. Rock put on his hat and walked down by the banks of the river to the small cottage that contained his friend.

" He who calleth on his friend in the morning with a loud voice, it shall be counted unto him for a curse," says Solomon, and some vague remembrance of this proverb flitted across Mr. Rock's brain when he knocked at Mr. Orellan's door, and asked the girl, aged about twelve, if he could see her master. The smutty-faced child who had been disturbed at her task of black-leading the kitchen-grate, wrapped her dirty apron round her still dirtier hand, previous to turning the handle of the door of the small sitting-room, where Mr. Orellan was seated with a very red face, bending over a handful of fire, at which he was striving to make a piece of toast. He was put out at the unseasonable visit, but he rose and placed a chair for his old messmate, and then returned to his occupation, observing that Betsy was waiting for her breakfast, and was rather impatient. A small earthenware teapot with a broken spout, containing weak black tea, a piece of salt butter—(fresh butter was 2s. per pound in those days)—and a very stale half loaf, was all Mr. Orellan had to offer his guest, who declined, saying he had already breakfasted. Then Mr. Orellan poured out some tea, and carried the buttered toast he had made up stairs to his wife, and coming down again, asked his friend whether he could be of any use to him.

" Well ! Orellan "—now that his required adviser was seated opposite, he hesitated—" 'tis a very sad affair "—and then he stopped, feeling rather ashamed of the beginning of the story.

> "The end and the beginning vex;
> His reason; many things perplex;
> With motions, checks and counterchecks."

He had not told Orellan about the visit to Tregear, so he sat looking awkward and saying nothing.

"Hark!" said Mr. Orellan, as a heavy thumping was heard overhead, on the ceiling; and, setting the door open, a feeble, wailing voice was heard from above—"Stephen, I want you."

"My dear Sir," said the poor husband humbly, "I am so grieved, so flattered, that you wish for my advice—so vexed I cannot attend to you now. You see the girl cannot move Betsy, and I have to wash and dress her, and lift her out, to have her bed made. I'm sure you'll excuse me, and I'll call on you about half-past eleven o'clock, when I've made her comfortable."

Mr. Rock took the hint, and retired. Some thoughts of Valerie passed through his mind. Valerie, that sylph of the Marseilles' woods, might have grown unwieldy, fat, and paralytic; might have been the burthen to him that "Betsy" was to his friend. "But then we should have passed through life together, and every act of sacrifice on my part would have been hallowed by love, and now, with this infernal child, I have the burthen, but none of the love."

"She's asleep still, Sir," said Susan as Mr. Rock returned. "I'm sure my heart is up in my mouth at everything that goes by, for I think the constables are coming after that poor wicked young thing; and if I was you, Sir, I'd take the needle-book and the notes, and go to her ladyship, and beg her to take them back quietly, and say nothing about it."

"How am I to get there, woman? Have I got a carriage and horses, to go to Tregear? Can I walk three miles there and three back? You talk stuff; I've no money to hire a carriage and horses. If they send after the purse, there it is for them; I'm too old to go after the great folks. I suppose I must have sinned, for Heaven to have so disgraced my good name as a punishment."

Sabina awoke, and got up slowly and tremblingly, but

was obliged to sit down on the side of her bed several times, before she had completed her toilet. Her head ached—her neck was stiff—she felt miserably ill. Her pretty book had been taken from her whilst she slept, that the beautiful lady had told her to take care of; she had asked Susan for it, but Susan replied that her uncle had it.

Then Sabina remembered the accusation and the blow, whilst she thought but little, if at all, of her retaliation; and she leaned her aching head on her small hand, and brooded in sullen resentment against Susan and her uncle. Mr. Rock did not come up to her room when he knew her to be better. He walked up and down his small sitting-room, and knocked his legs against the furniture. He was waiting for Orellan, and that made a little point of time to which to look forward.

At length Mr. Orellan came, and with many groans and much hesitation, his old shipmate told him all the circumstances. Mr. Orellan was not often elevated into the dignity of an adviser. He made the most of it.

"Hum-m-m!" said he, stroking his newly shaved chin.

"Well! but what's to be done?" said Mr. Rock impatiently. He had got over the misery of confession, and was waiting much too long for his absolution, he considered.

"I cannot decide without much thought," said Mr. Orellan, "on the curious circumstances you have related to me, but I feel disposed to doubt the child's having stolen the purse."

"Damn it! How the devil should she have got it, then?" said Mr. Rock, angrily.

"Might it not have been given to her, Sir?" replied his friend, meekly.

"You talk nonsense, Orellan. Give a child £20!"

At this juncture a carriage was heard rolling past the parade.

"Have you threatened your niece with a visit to Tregear, to return the suspected purse?" said he; "because if she be innocent, she will assent joyfully; if guilty, she would show her distress in her countenance."

"Oh Lord! Oh Lord!" said Susan, bursting into the room. "There's my lady's carriage a-coming, sure as fate, to ask about the purse."

The carriage did not stop at Haven House ; it rolled onward to the principal shop in Deepindale. As they all stood listening to the tramp of the departing hoofs of the horses, they heard the front door shut softly.

"She's gone out," said Susan, with a gasp.

They all proceeded to the door, to see Sabina, without bonnet or cloak, flying after the carriage. They could see, by leaving the locality of the house and advancing a few yards, that it had stopped at Mr. Clemmow's shop. Sabina was running with stumbling uncertain steps towards it. No one, in or on the carriage, saw her. The Tregear folks had only given an order and driven on ; and poor Sabina, breathless, and with a splitting headache, leaned against the low stone pillar that made, united by a chain with others, a barricade against the road.

Mr. Orellan turned back to the house, followed by Mr. Rock. "What do you think now?" inquired he. "She would not go after the carriage as if the devil was after her, if she did not know she had nothing to be ashamed of."

Mr. Rock remembered the bruise on her head, and thought, in that case, he had something to be ashamed of.

"But that £20?" said he doubtfully.

Orellan drew him within his sitting room, and closing the door mysteriously, said, "I told you £20 notes were flying about all over the town. You have a vote, and have not yet promised to give it to Lady Sarah's favourite son, Mr. Tresillian."

"Whew-w-w-w !" said Mr. Rock, with a terrible conviction that he was considered *bribable.* That Orellan should have hit on this by no means preposterous solution of the mystery, mortified his vanity. Why had he not thought of that which now seemed self-evident ?

"How dares he—how dares Mr. Tresillian—how dares Lady Sarah insult me so? And how dare *you*, Sir, to suggest that such is their motive ? "

"Surely, Sir," replied Orellan, meekly, "you had rather that were the case, than that your niece should have committed a theft ? "

"I don't know that, Sir. What the devil is my niece to me? A little limb of Satan. My honour is all that I have —all that I have saved out of the wreck of my life—and you come with this cock-and-a-bull suggestion of yours, to show that those people think *me—me*—an officer in his Majesty's navy, entitled by my profession to appear in his presence—on a par with that fellow who makes false teeth—with the brewer who sells villanous beer—with every pettifogging little scoundrel to whom the word *honour* conveys no meaning. I beg your pardon, Orellan—I am too warm, and I feel," throwing open his waistcoat, "so stifled and bursting *here*," putting his hand on his breast. "Let us go out and walk towards your house ; it is quiet now by the river side, and we will talk of what is to be done in this sad business. If Providence had not sent me that infernal child, none of this would have happened."

Orellan lifted his hat.

" Don't blame Providence, Mr. Rock, nor blaspheme."

They went out together.

Sabina had returned to the house, silent and depressed. She could not run as fast as two fine carriage-horses could trot, she found ; and unreasonable as it was, she could not help feeling as if Lady Sarah and the young ladies in the carriage had known of her pursuit, and had laughed at its failure. Lady Sarah had not been there ; it had contained only the governess and the children, but of that Sabina was ignorant. Her uncle having left the sitting-room clear, Sabina sat down, and leant her aching head on the table. She cried a little, and then became drowsy. She was awakened by hearing Susan's voice, saying,—

" No, Sir ; master is not at home."

"When will he be in ? "

" Oh, in about a quarter of an hour, or twenty minutes," said Susan.

" I will come in, and wait. I want to see him on business," said Mr. Tresillian.

"Oh, lor ! 'tis the *pus* that wicked child stole, no doubt, he's come after ; or, p'rhaps, 'tis election business," thought Susan. She only said—" Please to walk in, and sit down, Sir. Master won't be long."

Sabina started up, and gazed in a startled manner at the person she most wished to see in the world.

Mr. Tresillian, bent on being agreeable, advanced towards her, holding out his hand. " Well, my little friend, what is this?" looking rather shocked at the appearance of one side of her face and head. "Who has used you thus?"

Sabina clasped the hand he gave tightly in both of her own, and tried to speak, but was fearful of bursting into tears; so she stood swallowing in great gulps her inclination to cry, and did not answer at once.

Mr. Tresillian hated scenes, even with children. He thought *his* nieces great nuisances, and it was too bad to be worried by this stupid old fellow's niece. True, he very much preferred that his brother should beget only the frailer sex, giving thereby some future wife of his the chance of perpetuating the family title; but that did not prevent those children being very much in the way when, as now, they came on a visit to Tregear. But he was bent, as I have said before, on being agreeable, and, sitting down, he drew the little girl to his side, and passed his arm round her waist, while, in the tenderest of tones, he questioned her as to the injury to her head.

" My lady—Lady Sarah."

" Yes. What of Lady Sarah?"

" She gave me a purse—no, 'twas a needle-book, with pretty letters outside and a crown, and she told me to take care of it; and—and—when I was asleep Susan took it from my pocket, and Mr. Rock has kept it," and here came a burst of tears and sobs.

" Well! but how came this bruise and cut on your head?"

" Mr. Rock found money in the needle-book, and he was so angry that he knocked me down against the corner of the table there, and that's how it was."

" Well, but surely——" But here Mr. Tresillian flushed, and felt disposed to give utterance to the whew! which had burst from the angry lips of Mr. Rock: but the sound, though the same, was meant to express a different feeling. There was in Mr. Tresillian's mind the consciousness of a blunder committed by his lady mother, in giving the child £20. £20 was the exact sum offered by his agents to doubtful voters at Deepindale. He began to walk up and down the room with a troubled look, which much disturbed Sabina, who preferred the former state of affairs, when his arm had been so kindly placed round her. He was trying to arrange his thoughts so that when Mr. Rock returned, he might be able to say something likely to satisfy the injured honour of the man whose vote was so valuable to him. To do his penetration justice, he never would have offered any bribe so gross as money to a man who, though very poor, was by profession and feeling a gentleman. "Do you know how your uncle means to vote?" said he suddenly to Sabina. "Not for me, I fear, now."

Sabina was mortified. He had appeared so sorry for her trouble, and now he seemed to have quite forgotten it. She answered timidly that she did not know.

He returned to the table and sat down, fixing his eyes on the decaying embers of the small fire, of which he saw nothing.

Sabina came and knelt down at his feet, and threw her arms round both his knees, hiding her face on them, her dark curling hair tumbling over her shoulders in wild confusion.

"Mignon and Wilhelm Meister," said Mr. Tresillian, smiling to himself. "What is it, my dear? Look up—tell me what you wish. Shall I get back your book from Mr. Rock? What is it—the book or the money you regret, or both?"

"Oh!" wailed Sabina, "I want to go away with you. I want to go back to Lady Sarah. I hate him—I hate Mr. Rock. He tries to beat me, and then he knocks me down. He can't bear me. I am miserable here. Oh! I want you to take me quite away!"

"Here's a state of affairs!" said the young man to himself. "Fancy a child taking such a fancy to me. It would be difficult to persuade those children at Tregear that I am so attractive." He raised Sabina, and placed her as she had before stood by his side, and this time he kissed her face tenderly. "Kissing is usual at electioneering times, my child," said he, apologetically, thinking, perhaps, that Sabina might think it improper; but no such thought entered her head; for, passing one of her arms round his head, she kissed his white forehead very innocently and lovingly.

"You are good to me, and I love you so much," said she, "as much as I loved papa, I think."

"Ah!" thought Mr. Tresillian, smiling, "I am not so

flattered after all. 'Tis not a case of Mignon and Wilhelm Meister. I wonder if she thinks me old enough to be her father?"

"You *will* let me go and live with you," Sabina went on to say.

Mr. Tresillian was puzzled how to answer her, without making her cry again. "I will speak to Lady Sarah," he said, temporising.

"Then I shall be quite happy," the child cried, with her face all beaming.

"What a sparkling face it is! She will be wonderfully beautiful as a woman," thought her companion.

A step was heard outside the window, and the flush faded from Sabina's face. She griped the hand of Mr. Tresillian very hard. "Oh! he's coming!" she said; "and I hate him so. I hate the great bald place on the top of his head, and his black beady eyes, and the ugly hairs on the back of his hands."

"Hush! my dear; he's coming in," as Mr. Rock was heard going through his usual exercise, prior to entering. First one foot was drawn over the door-mat thrice; then it was bent down, so as to oppose the outside edge to the friction; then the left or inner side of the boot; then the heel was rubbed, the toe being held in the air; then the toe was pointed, as if he had been about to dance; after which performance the exercise on one foot was considered complete. The same ceremony was gone through with the left foot, during which time Sabina, pricked in conscience, perhaps, at the remembrance of all her vituperations against her uncle, sidled up to the door and stood back as the old man opened it, passing out as he entered, Mr. Rock having been too much occupied by the appearance of his visitor to regard her in any way.

Mr. Tresillian rose, and bowed one of those sharp, short, and decisive bows, introduced by George the Fourth, when Prince of Wales, under the tuition of Madame Micheau; consisting of drawing the foot with a slide to one side, and getting both together, preparatory to a quick bob of the head— the spine being kept erect.

Mr. Rock bent his forward, and bowed both head and body, one leg being sent up behind him in the air, after the fashion of bows from Louis the Fourteenth to the time of George the Third. Then both gentlemen looked at each other. "The foul weather-flag is hoisted," thought the young man. Mr. Rock's face was fixed and gloomy.

" I have called," said Mr. Tresillian, sweetly, "to solicit the favour of your vote, once more ; and I trust this time not in vain."

" Ahem !" said Mr. Rock. He had a remembrance of the ridiculous figure he had cut with his arm raised over his niece's head, and he did not like to begin the old story of flogging again. On other points he approved Mr. Tresillian's principles. He was swelling with anger, too, at the thought of the £20 he had in his pocket. " Before we speak on that subject, Sir," he said, " I must thank you for the hospitality you showed my niece—you and Lady Sarah—to whom I beg you will express my sense of obligation ; and also, I must request that you will return to that lady two notes of £10 each, which her ladyship was probably ignorant were in it at the time when she gave this needle-book to the child." He took out the notes and pushed them towards Mr. Tresillian, who hesitated—a man of the world though he was, he flushed painfully. " I take it for granted," Mr. Rock continued, with a passionate tremor in his voice, " that this—the most favourable aspect in which I can view the affair—is a true one."

" Pardon me," said the young gentleman, smiling, " I think my mother was quite aware of what she was doing, when she gave your little girl the money. Lady Sarah is both wealthy and generous. She was exceedingly delighted with the great talent and magnificent voice possessed by Miss Rock. That is her name, is it not ? And as she would have given Signora Canti a £50 note gladly for an evening's entertainment of a similar kind, I think, as a little token of gratitude for the gratification she had experienced, she placed the notes in the book before she presented it to Miss Rock. So far from any degradation to either party in this transaction, it is not more than ten years since I looked hard at all my relations or friends before I returned to Eton after the holidays, to see what they were about to ' come down ' with, as slang men say." He paused, for he saw he had produced an effect by his statement.

" My niece is not a public singer yet, Sir ; and any gratification she afforded Lady Sarah, she was bound to bestow, in return for the great kindness and hospitality with which she was treated at Tregear. Be so good as to return the notes to her ladyship, and the book. My niece will require nothing to remind her of Lady Sarah's kindness. I shall be happy to register my vote in your favour, Mr. Tresillian."

The young man gathered up the notes and placed them in the case, and, holding out his hand, thanked Mr. Rock very frankly for his promised support. Only a few words more were interchanged. Mr. Tresillian had got all he wanted, and congratulated himself on his tact in getting over the prejudice with which the conversation had begun ; and Mr. Rock was glad to have been soothed into a good temper, and to have sustained his part with due regard to his own honour and dignity.

" That old man has the feelings of a gentleman, though he is somewhat Spartan in his treatment of that child," was Mr. Tresillian's reflection. " Poor little beggar ! how fond she is of me ! I wonder whether I shall get Orellan's vote. Probably. They say he follows suit with Rock."

That evening Mr. Rock intimated to his friend, that though Mr. Tresillian was absurdly crotchety about the abolition of flogging in the navy,—" I should like to see how *he* would work a ship without it "—yet, on the whole, he approved of his principles, and meant to vote for him, and he supposed Orellan would do likewise.

"Yes, certainly," said his obedient shipmate ; and they set themselves sternly to the delightful intricacies of chess. On one point Orellan would never give way. He would as soon have thought of a treacherous surrender of his vessel to the enemy, as of *giving* the game to his antagonist, or not playing his best. Beautiful exercise of the brain ! which needs no foreign stimulus of money to create an interest, nor any charm unborrowed from itself to wrap the players in oblivion as to their proper cares. Mr. Rock and Mr. Orellan forgot they were gentleman-like paupers. Mr. Rock, his tiresome niece ; Mr. Orellan, his paralytic wife. When the game was over, and the hot whisky and water steamed on the little ink-stained mahogany four-legged table, under the weather-beaten nose of one lieutenant, and an innocent basin of gruel, with salt only, comforted the internals of the other, they fought the battle over again, and decided whether Orellan's play of his white bishop had won the game, or Rock's blunder with his rook's pawn had lost it.

The election was over, and Mr. Tresillian had been returned by a small majority, which made him rejoice all the more at his having obtained the votes of his sailor friends. Sabina's heart had been kept in a constant flutter by bands of music, banners and ribbons—by the screams and shouts of the populace, " Tresillian for ever ! Down with the Blues !" &c., &c., &c. At length her hero was chaired. On a platform with four poles, carried by four of the strongest men to be produced in the Borough of Deepindale, or its neighbourhood, an arm-chair was placed, in which the fortunate (or unfortunate, as might be considered) member was placed. On arriving at any building of note, the platform was elevated thrice amidst the deafening cheers of the populace. It must have been difficult for any man to look triumphant under such circumstances, though assured by the inspiring strains of " See the Conquering Hero Comes," notwithstanding which, Mr. Tresillian, standing with his legs apart to steady himself, one hand holding by the arm of the chair, and the other waving his hat, with a quantity of light curling hair, which blew up and down as he was waved in the air, looked as fine a specimen of youth and beauty as ever had dawned on the worthy voters of his native town. His hair was worn in clustering curls—not cut to the length of half an inch as in the present fashion, which gives one unpleasant ideas of hospital and prison discipline. But the pride, pomp, and circumstance of the election was over. Like beggars the candidates disappeared—one having got all he wanted, the other knowing there was nothing to get, and Deepindale sank down into its original stagnation. The carriage from Tregear no longer excited the small shopkeepers to put on their best aprons, as the prancing of its horses was heard in the distance ; Lady Sarah went to Brighton, Mr. Tresillian, like the evil spirit in Job, " up and down the world," and the governess and the young ladies to their paternal home.

Mr. Rock was left with his incumbrance. It was not the old man and Sinbad, but a reverse case. The old man had a monkey-like child compelled to cling to him, though the attachment occasioned as much grief to the child as inconvenience to the old man. But the old lieutenant was softened by the way in which the youthful member had spoken of his niece's performances. " I thought myself she had a wonderful pipe of her own," said he.

As they sat in the twilight by the fire, to save the solitary candle which was all the light Mr. Rock could afford, each was silent, gazing at the fire ; but the compelled inactivity was to " the young heart hot and restless," a weary punishment ; to the old man, who lived in memory over his past life, it was not unpleasurable. He dozed, too, occasionally, with his drooping eyelids shadowing the dark eyeballs, which were fixed on the firelight, and fancied he was again walking on the deck of the vessel outward bound, which had first borne him from his home. The flicker of the fire reminded him how sadly through his boyish tears he had watched the Lizard lights as they disappeared and were seen again, as the vessel tossed and rose or fell in the trough of the sea—all his old yearnings for home returned to his memory ; his mother's form, on whom he doated, and for whose sake he had determined to " do or die," his pretty sisters, who had spent their few hoarded pennies to buy him small remembrances. Then the scene changed—there was the whistling wind, the roar of the waters, the creaking of the masts, the fluttering sails, the strained cordage—they were in the Baltic with the admiral's ship in tow. The vessel in which Rock was, laboured frightfully—if the cable holds, they must perish together—the noble ship in which he was a lieutenant and the unhappy man-of-war they were trying to save—a horror steals through his veins, for a dirk glides down the cable in a stealthy hand, and the ship rides free of her lost burthen—free to return to her native land. Whilst the captain of her more chivalrous consort, who signalled that he should not leave his admiral till he had orders, was soon with his crew sacrificed to their chief, whose frozen body was one of many piled up to defend those still living from the biting wind.

He stirs and shivers, and dreams again. He is full of the fence of action—a man with all of manhood's power and courage—how he climbs up the side of that hostile vessel—

what angry, eager faces are awaiting him to strike him down
as he arrives within their reach—one fires, he is hit, he falls
back—and suiting the action to the thought of his dream,
his feet are extended, and he knocks down the fire-irons, and
awakes to find himself a half-pay lieutenant of sixty-five,
feeble, poor, and with a confirmed heart-disease. No
wonder the noble heart suffered, after the uneasy life its
possessor had led it; always hoping and fearing, never
satisfied with inaction—working incessantly to perform his
own duties, and often those of others, and now he was a
sheer hulk. He did not grumble at the neglect by which
his services had been met—he was quite willing to believe
that the young men who had been promoted over his
head were possessed of good qualities, though he had not
discovered them. The infliction of this child, who did not
seem to have come to him professionally, as it were, was a
grievous irritation;—he had forgotten her in his dream, and
awoke to see her bright, restless eyes fixed on him, whilst
her feet were stretched out to the edge of the fender, and
her fingers twisted themselves into contortions which only
children born in hot climates, as a rule, can produce.

"Can you sing 'The Saucy Arethusa?'" said Mr. Rock
to his niece.

"No! I can't sing anything, because there's no piano."

"Hum! Can you sing the 'Sailor's Grave' when you
have a piano?"

"Yes, and all those kind of songs—'The Heaving of the
Lead,' and 'Sweet Poll of Plymouth,' and 'The Lizard
Lights;' mamma used to sing them all."

This set Mr. Rock thinking of his deficient household arrangements as regarded the education of the child. He had
no piano, and could not afford to buy one. Then his
thoughts wandered to the small house rented by a widowed
lady named Cleverly, and to a miniature little instrument
which stood blocking up the passage, for whose admission
into the sitting-room there was no convenient space. He
would see what could be done; in the meantime, Sabina
could amuse herself by reading anecdotes of "Naval
History"— and here was Orellan.

"Sabina, set out the chessmen."

CHAPTER VIII.

MRS. CLEVERLY was only too happy to lend Mr. Rock the piano for his niece. She feared it was sadly out of order ; but then no doubt Mr. Temple, the organist, would put it right for a trifle. Miss Rock might keep it as long as she pleased, for she, Mrs. Cleverly, " had not the slightest use for it—it was in the way rather than not," thus making what is called a Cornish compliment, with the real delicacy that strives to diminish the sense of obligation.

After Mr. Rock had paid away more shillings than he could well afford in the transportation of the piano, he found it conferred but a mitigated amount of enjoyment to himself —of its effect on the child he could not judge. She played and sung all day, and in the twilight she sang the songs the old man delighted in—" For England when with Favouring Gales," " Fresh and Strong the Breezes Blowing," and " Come all ye Jolly Sailors Bold." This was delightful ; but Mr. Rock's ideas of quarter-deck discipline were stumbling-blocks to Sabina and to himself, as regarded her music. She played mostly by ear, and could arrange a good bass accompaniment ; but by notes she could only perform a few pieces she had been carefully taught by her mother. Mr. Rock had once heard Valerie play the overture to the *Zauberflöte*, and without any regard or knowledge of the difficulty of the piece, he insisted on Sabina's learning it. She tried the first chords successfully, and played about a dozen bars, when she declared it was ugly and stupid, and too difficult, and she would not learn any more of it. In vain Mr. Rock insisted—she took no notice. As a punishment, he closed the instrument and took away the key; she looked in his face and whistled. She knew he enjoyed her singing in the evening, and she did not care to play or sing now that the novelty of regaining a piano was over, so that she felt convinced that the punishment would be greater to him than to herself.

Mr. Rock had hoped that her wonderful voice, if improved by practice, might enable her to obtain a living as a governess, or on the stage. Both plans were repugnant to his feelings, but what could become of her when he died? The thought of her destitution made his old heart ache. Better to bear " the proud man's contumely " than to starve or go to the workhouse for aid.

I fear Mr. Rock is beginning to love this wayward child. He had better try to reach Australia in a cockle-shell of a boat, and thus lose his life, than risk his happiness by fixing his affections on her. Alas! they were already taking root. Since he had stamped out the love of Valerie from his heart, he had had none on whom he might lavish all the mighty devotion of his unselfish feelings. These were now to be given to Sabina.

CHAPTER IX.

MR. ROCK had managed to save £100 out of his income, of which part had been intended to pay his funeral expenses ; £10 to go to old Susan ; and the rest to meet any small sums that might be owing at the time of his decease. "What man, by taking thought, can add one cubit to his stature," or one pound to his banker's account ? There was a charm to him in this round sum ; but the charm was now to be broken in upon. To abstract any more from his household expenses would be, he knew, impossible ; but he thought of Sabina's musical talent, and of his own incapability of cultivating it, and he, with a heavy sigh, determined to sacrifice at least one pound for a quarter's tuition in music. "We shall see if she improves enough to justify me in paying the four pounds for one year," he said, and he walked towards the untidy house inhabited by the German organist, Mr. Temple.

Mr. Temple had £60 yearly as organist of the parish church, and contrived by teaching, and tuning pianos, to add £100 yearly to his income in addition ; but though Mr. Rock had but £90, and kept up the appearance of a gentleman, without owing a single penny at the end of each month, Mr. Temple was indebted to every tradesman in the town of Deepindale, and could with difficulty obtain credit for a loaf of bread, when he required it. Self-indulgence was the habit of the one ; self-denial of the other. Mr. Temple was a good-natured voluptuary, who seemed to consider a tradesman was intended to be the natural prey of the consumer, and considered there was no disgrace, but simply misfortune, in a state of debt.

Clean to scrupulousness in his person, and pure in his ideas of honour and honesty, Mr. Rock would rather have sold his chronometer, his only valuable household god, than have allowed a tradesman to wait twelve months for his money ; yet such was the ungrateful state of the minds of the small shopkeepers in Deepindale, that they preferred Mr. Temple, the jolly companion, who took a cheerful glass with them, and had long unpaid accounts, the items of which he never dared to examine, to Mr. Rock, who looked sharply at their charges, and paid them every week. Probably they each argued thus: "Temple has over £160 a-year ; the money must come to some one, and why not to me? If there be a smash, and we are paid so much in the pound, having overcharged systematically, I cannot be really much a loser."

Mr. Temple was a man of genius ; a first rate musician, both in principle and practice. He was quite pleased at the idea of having a new pupil ; "magnificent voice, only wants a little of *my* training."

He came for his first lesson. Mr. Rock produced a tattered copy of the redoubtable *Zauberflöte.* Mr. Temple smiled at the injunction that Miss Rock was to learn it.

" Certainly, Mr. Rock, we shall be delighted."

When he was gone, Mr. Temple said to Sabina : " You shall learn three bars of this at each lesson ; but it *is* difficult, and requires perfect execution to make it agreeable. To amuse you and exercise the speed of your little fingers, we will also learn, '*Lison dormait dans un boçage,*' with variations." He played the air and the first variation ; but stopped Sabina as she was about to begin it eagerly. " No ; physic first, and sugar-plum afterwards."

Sabina made a wry face ; but obeyed. A shower of rain came on just as the lesson concluded.

" Miss Griggs must wait," said he ; " I can't afford wet boots ;" but he was not bound to teach ; and, sitting down, he modulated on the instrument, and then his fingers stole into the half divine movement of one of Haydn's " Seven Words," " This day shalt thou be with me in paradise."

6

Sabina listened breathlessly and motionless till it was concluded.

"Oh-o-o-h !" she said.   "Again."

Mr. Temple was pleased.   He played it again ; but the second time he introduced a grace of his own.

"Not that ! not that !" exclaimed Sabina.

"Ah ! you have true feeling," cried her master.   "You knew that ornament was not in accord with the genius of the composition."

Master and pupil understood each other ; a new era was begun in Sabina's life.   Tuesdays and Fridays were the two bright spots in her existence ; she forgave her master his dirty hands ; his hair and whiskers, redolent of stale tobacco ; his coat covered with particles of snuff.   I am not sure that she did not tolerate that loathsome powder for the rest of her life, for the remembrance of her lessons.   Mr. Rock's nose was sensitive, and when Mr. Temple had departed, he always set both door and windows open to purify the room.   Sometimes the music-master, whose favourite instrument was the violoncello, would bring it in the evening, and accompany Sabina in the sonatas she had learnt by his tuition.   Poor Mr. Rock was even induced, by the promise of hearing his favourite overture to the *Zauberflöte* performed, to consent to receive two violin players, as dirty and unprincipled as their chief, who executed the piece with Sabina exceedingly well, and took long draughts of hot whisky and water with Orellan afterwards, with a hearty good will, that made Mr. Rock doubt whether they would arrive at their own homes when the party broke up.

Sabina enjoyed her lessons, but felt little love or gratitude to her uncle.   He was often cross and irritable ; he was so particularly, on one occasion, when, at the end of the quarter, he presented his guinea to Temple, and asked for a receipt.

"Two, if you please," said the organist.

"Two !" in a voice of thunder.   "You told me *one* guinea a quarter."

"Certainly, Mr. Rock ; but there is a guinea for entrance."

The lieutenant groaned, and paid it.   It had not been anticipated, and he was cross to Sabina, and reproached her with the expense she had entailed upon him.   She said nothing; but felt the injustice, and was ungrateful for the sacrifice he made in giving her lessons; she had not asked for them.

Children, up to the age when they are compelled to fight their own way in the world, are never grateful for money spent on their education. Even the most clever feel they would rather *not* learn. The old forget that they were ungrateful in their youth, and resent the want of appreciation shown by their juniors for the sacrifices made for their good.

But time made Sabina more and more useful to her uncle, and more beloved by him.

Lieutenant Orellan, for several evenings, could not leave his sick wife, who became more helpless and irritable as her infirmities increased. One evening, when the chessmen were already set out, Mr. Rock looked nervously and repeatedly at his chronometer, finding Orellan was five minutes after his time. "She must be worse, I fear," he said to himself.

"Uncle," cried Sabina, "will you let me begin a game? and I will leave off if Mr. Orellan comes."

"You, you little sprat!" replied the lieutenant; "do you know the moves?"

"That is all," said Sabina, humbly, for her respect for the two chess-players was unbounded.

Of course, she was beaten; but her uncle was pleased. Sabina had had a good lesson in her defeat.

"May I take back that move?" she asked her uncle.

"You may play like a child, if you please," replied Mr. Rock; "but you will never be a good player unless you play the strict game."

Sabina assented, and lost her queen; but she never after repeated the mistake which had so embarrassed her movements in the game.

Poor child! It was well she had resources in Mr. Rock's small home, or her life would have been dreary in the extreme.

Miss Wise kept a seminary for young ladies, who were turned out to play on the parade every day from twelve to one o'clock. When Sabina had first been domesticated with her uncle, Susan had washed her face, combed her hair, pinched her bonnet into proper shape, and sent her out,

6—2

with the injunction,—" Go and play with those pretty young ladies ; 'twill do you good, my dear !"   Now Sabina thought of Mabel Snow, and how nice it had been to play with her, and she bounded eagerly through the trees on the parade to the gravel-walk where the girls were playing " Prisoner's base."

" I'm come to play, too," said Sabina, cheerfully.   " I should like it very much."

They stopped, and whispered amongst themselves.

Sabina felt awkward ; but, as they all moved off in a body to the other side of the parade, she followed, thinking they preferred that side to the one first chosen.

" I'm come to play, too," repeated Sabina ; that time with a little quiver in her voice.

They stopped, and looked at her without speaking, excepting one little girl, who gesticulated eagerly, and made an unintelligible sound.   Sabina tried to understand with ears and eyes.   The oldest girl spoke at length.

" 'Tis useless to address that young lady ; she is deaf and dumb ; and you must go away.   If you don't choose to go we must ; you don't belong to us."

Sabina walked away slowly, and proudly in outward appearance ; but with smothered sobs of mortification and grief.   She walked alone on the deserted side of the parade, and hoped that Susan had not been looking out to see the rebuff she had experienced.   When she returned that old servant hoped she had had a nice game of play with the young ladies.

Sabina said, shortly : " No ; she did not like them."   And Susan thought that she was a queer child, and nothing so pleasant and pretty-mannered as other young ladies.

CHAPTER X.

" Adown her shoulders fell her length of hair,
A riband did her braided tresses bind,
The rest was loose, and wantoned in the wind."

DRYDEN.

FIVE years and a-half passed on ; £10 10s. had been abstracted from the funeral store, for Mr. Rock could not afford her more than two years' tuition ; of this, nine guineas had been paid to Mr. Temple, and one pound for music. With all her energies given to this one study; with no companion of her own age to divert her attention; with a voice so beautiful and powerful that it would have arrested attention even had it been uncultivated, Sabina's proficiency in music excited the envy and hatred and malice of all the mothers with less gifted daughters, who strove in the same race with Mr. Rock's niece.

The beauty which had been prophesied as her future endowment by Mr. Tresillian, had bloomed beyond expectation. She was small and slight, but her limbs had become rounded instead of angular; her complexion was clear, with an occasional flush of delicate pink on her brown skin ; the eyes large, and with a blueish tint in the white, which enhanced the soft brown eyeball, catching velvety lights, like the back of the humble bee ; her hair still fell in curls over her shoulders, and was frequently a cause of offence to her uncle, when the hairs straggled singly on her neck. He had bought a comb, and insisted on its being twisted up ; but the hair was so abundant that it rebelled, and fell down again. At length Sabina, with a carelessness her uncle could never eradicate, left it on the floor where it had fallen, and Mr. Rock, coming into the room suddenly, trod on it, and crushed it into innumerable bits. After that, the curls fell into their usual position, and no further attempt was made to imprison them.

Her uncle doated on her, but with his love came torment; he had the strictest ideas of female propriety. Sabina defied all rules; he thought neatness of dress an almost religious duty; Sabina cared for a rent in her dress as little as the French peasant who danced with Sterne, and sang the Gascoygne roundelay, " *Viva la joia! Fidon la tristessa!* "

" Be

> ' Still, unobtrusive, serious, and meek,
> The first to listen, and the last to speak,' "

said her uncle, but Sabina never could resist a repartee when it rose to her lips. Mr. Rock had obtained permission to occupy, with Miss Rock, a pew which had been vacated by a family gone abroad. He was uneasy if she looked round her in church, and he brought from his stores a French lace veil, in which he had invested when he gave his heart to Valerie. When bought, he had not dared to present it, without an offer of himself also; so he had kept it, with many tender thoughts of how Valerie would have looked through its cobweb texture, till the features of Valerie were seen through a mental mist, and then faded away into indistinctness altogether. Now, it was carefully arranged over Sabina's bonnet when she went out, with an injunction that it was not to be raised on any pretext. Compelled to contemplate the intricacies of the beautiful flowers and leaves, with all their curious entanglements, and wonderful variety of stitches, Sabina's mind stored away all the intricacies of the threads, and on Mondays used to copy them in imitation lace on net. Her uncle had forced the nose of the horse to the water, and fancied that she swallowed; whilst he compelled his niece to the outward appearance of intense devotion and reverence in the house of God, and hoped that she had become religious consequently—Sabina took a malicious pleasure in the occupation she had made for herself, to relieve the monotony of the long church service.

She little knew the envy she excited from the possession

of that old yellow lace veil, in the minds of the young ladies
at Miss Wise's school. Straw plaits were common in Cornwall then, and Sabina had selected her straws, plaited them,
and made them up into a round hat; two yards of ribbon
sufficed for its trimming, and the square lace veil thrown
over it was kept by the brim at a sufficient distance from
Sabina's beautiful face and luxuriant hair to allow them fair
play. The veil was handsome, and gave a look of elegance
to the light-coloured gingham tight dresses which Sabina
generally wore, and which Susan delighted to wash and
iron, so as to do credit to Mr. Rock and to her young lady.
Poor girl! she had not her uncle's strength of mind: she
was naturally fond of dress, and extravagant, nor had she
her uncle's strong perception of pecuniary obligation. Her
dress was very poverty stricken. Miss Wise, who deeply
resented that Miss Rock had never been sent for education
to *her* establishment, could not help revealing her anger
and vexation at having been deprived of a pupil so brilliant
as Sabina.

"What that old man can mean, Mem," she said to her
assistant one day, "I cannot divine. What good he can
ever expect that *gel* to come to, I have no means of judging. But a *gel* brought up from the age of ten to fifteen, by
an old ship lieutenant and a servant maid, cannot be fit for
decent young ladies to associate with. I should not wonder
if she damned and swore dreadful."

"Oh! shocking!" said the assistant. "Did you hear
her, Mem?"

"N—o; I can't say that: but I've good authority for
thinking so."

"Awful!" rejoined the toady.

On several occasions Mr. Temple had asked Sabina to
come and take parts in singing with his other pupils, at the
Town Hall. Sabina was glad of the amusement, for she
gave no labour, but that of love, to her study of music. The
room was long — so long!—built for those interminable
country dances, which delighted our sober ancestors. The
music-stands were placed at the upper end: the door was
at the opposite extremity. The person who entered was
seen, not only in reality, but reflected in a large looking-
glass which ornamented the end of the saloon. Sabina, who

could not always enter the room first, Haven House being
at a much greater distance than the homes of the other
pupils, had the misery of walking up the immense room, a
victim to all the malicious sneers of the girls whom she surpassed in beauty and accomplishments, but to whom she was
immeasurably inferior in dress.

She never could be rendered a tidy girl. If made so by
Susan, she fell to pieces, and relapsed into slovenliness at
the shortest notice. She felt her disgrace painfully ; but forgot it when it was past, or remembered it so slightly that
she never remedied the causes. 'Tis true, her poor little
feet were worn by the often-darned stockings, where little
of the original woof was visible; but it was Susan's imperfect sight which had guided the darning needle, and
the work was *bodged.* Too old, too small, even for her
slight dimensions, were all her clothes ; so when she walked
up the long assembly-room, her frocks were too short,
her darned stockings were visible, and her old shoes rather
down and twisted at her heels, and patched at the toes,
were observed by all the scoffing pupils of Miss Wise's
establishment; the outer covering was a blue pelisse;
navy blue, her uncle had ordered. She had outgrown it ;
the sleeves did not reach the wrists ; it was strained across
her beautifully rounded bosom, because it had fitted her
when she was twelve years old ; and the band of blue
cloth had been pinned and repinned, and strained to
coax it to meet, till the texture would scarcely retain the
pins. Her uncle thought her beautiful, any way. I am
not sure he disliked the look of the strained broad cloth.
He did not wish to think of her as a woman ; she was so
small, so young, so much his own property. He, to whom
poverty had denied all the sweet converse of wedded life, had
had this child forced upon him, and had learnt to pour
out the repressed feelings of his loving heart on her ; the
more violent and intense, as it was the first object on
which they had been lavished. And Sabina loved her
uncle at length. During the five years they had passed
together, Mr. Rock had been seriously ill on two or three
occasions ; then Sabina had been ever tender, anxious,
and watchful of her uncle ; bearing with his impatience,
soothing his irritability, becoming neat-handed in her sick

cookery, to minister to his comfort. These illnesses had been the occasion of an increasing load of vexation to Sabina. On one occasion, Mr. Rock was ordered to eat asparagus; it was too early for any not raised artificially; but Sabina had directed the greengrocer to procure some, not dreaming that what she obtained was fifteen shillings a bundle. I must not give my heroine too much credit. That greengrocer's shop presented temptations which the young lady did not resist, though she might have done so. Ruddy-cheeked apples, with opposite sides of bright yellow, tempted her as one had tempted our general mother. The greengrocer's bill was a heavy one, and Sabina could not pay it. She entreated for time, with a face that flushed and turned pale alternately; and the shopkeeper gave it, and promised not to send the bill in to Mr. Rock, who had been persuaded by Sabina that she had obtained the vegetables through the good nature of the gardener at Tregear. Had her uncle known of this fraud on him, how furious he would have been at the deceit, how broken-hearted at the untruth, how overwhelmed at the amount of the debt, and at the length of time which it had been allowed to run !

About this time he had a recurrence of his attack. Luckily asparagus was comparatively cheap, and for the fresh supply Sabina contrived to pay. He would take no nourishment which he did not believe to be obtained on terms so reasonable that the bills could be paid weekly.

"A man is not bound to remain in the world at the expense of his neighbours," he would say. "He may send round his hat, and beg for charity to support him, if he thinks life so purchased to be worth possession. I do not. But such a course would be much less dishonest than dying insolvent."

Now Sabina had begun to love her uncle so soon as she had begun to pity him; true, her attachment to him was weak compared to that which he felt for her. But where is the young person who ever returns in equal degree the love of his guardian or parent? It seems providential that love should descend rather than ascend, that the young should be cared for rather than those "whose feet stumble in the dark uncertainty of age."

CHAPTER XI.

"Begin ! e'en age itself is cheer'd by music :
   It wakes a glad remembrance of our youth,
   Calls back past joys and warms us into transport."
                      Rowe's " *Fair Penitent.*"

IT was not easy for Sabina to find amusement for her patient, when she had finished reading the paper to her uncle, and the boy had carried it away. Chess was not to be thought of till the evening, or those hours would have been without zest, and Mr. Rock's amusement of dragging a heavy garden-roller up and down the gravel walk of the parade just opposite his house, for the purpose of obliterating the marks made by women's pattens and men's heavy tread, could not be attempted in the face of the doctor's prohibition. Had the exercise been possible at the back of his house, he would have risked it, in the conviction that he should not be seen by his doctor; but he did not care to receive the consequent "jaw," as he termed it in his sailor phraseology. So, after sitting silently for some time, and seeing Sabina quietly working by his side, he reiterated the frequent question,—

"Well, have you nothing to tell me ?"

This query always made Sabina silent, it seemed so impossible to answer. She had been told to amuse her uncle, but not to agitate or interest him too much. She did not care for the small events of Deepindale, and knew not how a sick person, incapable of self-amusement, takes interest in circumstances the most trivial, and which would in health excite no notice.

Mr. Rock, sitting over his fire, made a great circumstance of every shovel of coals he put on, and every accumulation of cinders he threw over them. Before Sabina found this out, she had rudely driven the poker into the dark heap, and upset both the fire and her uncle's temper.

Now she tried to think of something to amuse him.

"Uncle, do you know the townsfolk here are going to get up a concert?"

"A concert?"

"Yes, of amateurs, for the benefit of the Cornwall Infirmary."

"How do you know? You never tell me anything."

"I did not know you would care. I only heard it last evening. Mr. Temple whispered it to me as I was putting by the music-books in the organ loft, and he asked me if I were going to take a part. I said I had not been asked, and he wondered how they could manage without me."

Mr. Rock flushed, and Sabina repented of her repeated observation.

"Who are the performers?" he asked, in a constrained tone.

"Oh, I believe Mr. Temple will perform a sonata on the violoncello, with the accompaniment of two violins played by those musicians who used to accompany me. Mr. Dent, the doctor, will play an air and variations on the flute."

"Puppy! How can he attend to his patients when he is practising such nonsense?"

"Then they are to sing songs in different parts," Sabina went on, without regarding the query which she could not answer.

"Who is to take the female voice—the treble?"

"I suppose Miss Cressy; she has the best ear, and a very good voice."

"Nothing to compare to yours. Why have *you* not been asked, pray?"

"I do not know, uncle."

"I *do* know. They are jealous of you."

Sabina laughed gaily, and just touched her uncle's white brow with her lips. She had learned to love that venerable head, and to admire those black beady eyes—alas! no longer so deep in colour as in the days when he had threatened her with his cane.

"Never mind them, dear. I don't want to sing at their concert." And the uncle was consoled to think that his darling had not set her heart upon it.

But Sabina had occasion for all her philosophy, for rumours of a dissolution of Parliament disturbed the even tenor of Deepindale life; rumours followed by the fact. The family returned to the banishment of Tregear, as Lady Sarah called it, and took credit to herself for the sacrifice of personal comfort she made in coming to the end of the world for the benefit of her favourite son. Committee rooms were taken for the rival candidates at the Whig and Tory hotels, or rather public houses, dignified for the time with a grander title, and all the tradesmen and professions were on the *qui vive* with excitement.

"Would the usual £20 rise to £30 this time?" was the momentous question that made their hearts beat faster at the thought.

Mr. Dent, the apothecary, had a tolerable voice, and had been getting up "The Curfew" and "Blow, Breezes, Blow," with Mr. Grinde, the attorney, and Miss Cressy, the fruiterer's daughter. True, she was not considered "quite genteel," by the female relatives of the professional gentleman, but in voice no one could equal her, except Sabina, who was shut out of the whole affair, for she had never been one of Miss Wise's young ladies, and those fair creatures had spiteful and exclusive feelings, grown with their growth, and strengthened with their strength, and they expended on Sabina more than her full share. Whenever now in the evenings pedestrians passed the closed window-shutters of Mr. Dent's house, they heard, "Look, look, again!" or "Hark! a signal!" whilst little girls in ragged shawls knocked in vain at the surgery door for "grandmother's pills" or "baby's powders." Miss Cressy did not mind stepping in on these occasions, and sang like a syren—all the more as Mr. Grinde, the attorney, who sang bass, was a widower, and likely to marry again, and Mrs. Dent was a fat, good-natured lady, who did not dislike the glass of hot brandy-and-water with which the social evenings concluded. Not having any children, and having been herself the daughter of a cheesemonger, she saw no particular want of gentility in Miss Cressy, and felt rather strongly the feminine desire to make up a match.

Lady Sarah and Mr. Tresillian, and the rest of the party at Tregear, had been asked to patronise the concert, and had graciously engaged two front rows of reserved seats. Saturday arrived; the concert was fixed for the following Thursday. The evening practising grew faster and hotter. It seemed likely that the singers would sing themselves hoarse before the appointed night arrived. They had each studied their parts for six weeks with the most anxious industry. The musical infection spread from house to house. Maid ser vants trundled their mops to " The bells have been rung," and butcher-boys sang scraps of " O'er the dewy green." But, alas ! on Saturday evening, when Miss Cressy should have entered the hospitable house of Mr. Dent, she appeared not, but sent a messenger instead, to say she had a headache, and feared she could not attend the rehearsal.

" Dear me, Mr. Dent, what can be amiss? That girl never has headaches; she's as healthy as a dairy-maid," said Mrs. Dent, who thought herself not entitled to her hot drink, unless she had company.

" I fear, my love," replied her husband, " that I can hardly step over to inquire—not etiquette, you see."

" Etiquette ! fiddle !" cried the lady, and carried her point in making her husband call on the invalid.

He obtained no satisfaction. Mrs. Cressy said her daughter was gone to bed with a 'eadache; had eaten too much boiled pork and cabbage. Mrs. Cressy was of opinion that she would be all right to-morrow. Next day, anxious eyes were turned to the pew in which Miss Cressy ought to have been, but in which was only the cozy figure of her mother. The musical aspirants bustled out after her with their inquiries.

"'Melia has a bad cold, that's all; she'll be all right to-morrow." But on Sunday evening 'Melia's papa called himself on Mr. Dent, and should be obliged if he would look in on 'Melia.

'Melia was found by Mr. Dent to be in a high fever, which would have given him a pleasant hope of a job at any other time, but which now filled him with frightful apprehensions about the fate of his trio.

" That's the dickens," said this elegant gentleman, " of

not standing on one's own bottom. There are three legs to
a trio as it were, and now one leg is taken away, down go
the other two—smash ! Perhaps she may be well enough,
but if she be——, I'll paint my Galen's head into a likeness
of Grimaldi." Then he turned about in his mind whether
another leg might not be found to support the tottering trio.
There was no one but Miss Rock capable of taking those
parts in the trio and quartettes so carefully studied ; and she
had not been asked to take any part in the exhibition of
native talent, and might probably refuse to assist them at the
eleventh hour. " It don't matter for Temple, and those
fellows with their concerted pieces, and as for ' The Soldier
Tired,' *that* might be cut out altogether ; but to deprive us
of our trios, and of the ' Red Cross Knight,' and who the
devil but Miss Cressy or Miss Rock could hold those high
F's and G's !''

He went to Mr. Grinde and found that gentleman just as
indignant with Miss Cressy for her ill-timed indisposition, as
he was himself. In fact rather more so, for inasmuch as
Mr. Dent might draw consolation from the probable length
of his bill, no such happiness could be in store for the
lawyer.

" A greedy creature ! with her boiled pork and cabbage !''
said the unsentimental admirer.

" I'm not *sure* it was the pork and cabbage," rejoined the
apothecary, meditating. " Had it been so, there are means
—but I need not enter into details to an unprofessional
gent.''

" I tell you what you must do; you are attending old
Rock occasionally——"

" Old fellow very close ; *will* have particulars entered in
my accounts. There is really *nothing* to be made of people
who do that. It don't pay me to lose my time in dancing
attendance on a veteran with a heart disease and no money
to spare.''

" No doubt; but you *must* call now, and gammon him
into telling Miss Rock to sing with us. He's a stingy one.
'Tis my belief that he has made his will out of a printed
form, and never came to me as any other gentleman would.''

Mr. Dent, though anxious for Miss Rock's services, did
not like the commission. All the women hated Miss Rock.

What a hornet's nest he should bring around him for asking her.

" I'll just see to-morrow morning how 'Melia Cressy is," he determined, before he concluded his conversation with his friend. " The concert will be as dull as ditchwater without our trios and quartette," mused he.

He called at an early hour next morning, so early that Mrs. Cressy was provoked that 'Melia's room had not been tidied, nor her face washed and hair arranged under a clean night-cap. He came, he saw, and turned pale. There were unmistakable signs in the flushed face, of mischief under the skin, and he knew she would throw out the irruption of scarlet fever before many hours were over. He communicated this intelligence to her parents as he left the sick room.

They were much disturbed, but the instinct of maternal vanity rose over her feeling of alarm. "Of course, Mr. Dent, you and the other gentlemen, as are going to perform, will put off the concert till 'Melia is better."

This was uttered as the door was about to close on the retreating apothecary, and overwhelmed him with confusion. Luckily he was not compelled to answer, as Mrs. Cressy seemingly thought the matter settled. "What *can* I do?" thought the poor man. "To be sure, the family are a good ten pounds a year to me, and they may send for Thomson if I offend them. But then, this concert may bring me into notice with the Tregear family, and be one hundred pounds a year good money to me, when they stay for two or three months here. Children, servants, and all. Why, there's twenty-six servants alone! a colony!" Mr. Dent did not consider that the arrival of the family depended on the number of contested elections; but the crow in the fable points a moral in vain to most people, and there was as much ambition as love of money in his meditations. He called again on his friend Grinde, and the result was that they went together to the house of Mr. Rock, whom they found at home, and by a little skilful flattery they obtained his consent that Sabina should take Miss Cressy's part in the forthcoming concert. "Bless you!" said her uncle, proudly, " *she* can sing 'The Soldier Tired' if you desire it, and all the other parts at sight; you need only alter the name in the bills from Cressy to Rock." Sabina came in before the visitors left, and though pleased, she was somewhat overwhelmed by the consent her uncle had given.

He grew angry at seeing her blushes and hesitation. " Do you mean to say you can't sing the songs they require?" he said, angrily, whilst the musicians, who had no doubt of her powers, felt astonishment at her seeming reluctance.

" Yes, uncle,—oh !—certainly,—I can sing them."

" Very well, then, what the devil do you hesitate about? sing your best !" The flush on her face deepened painfully, but she said nothing.

" Very well, gentlemen,—you may depend on my niece for Thursday evening." And they withdrew.

" What do you mean, Miss Rock, by this behaviour? Why should you be so reluctant to please me? I, who have brought you up for more than five years, have some right to your services, I suppose."

" It is not that," said Sabina, with tears of mortification. " But I—I—'ve no evening dress."

" Go in a morning one, then," said her uncle, who could not enter into the vexation of the young girl. Yet, had Lieutenant Rock ever succeeded to the command of a vessel which lacked the proper amount of paint and gilding, he would have been a miserable man could he not have procured the means of paying for them.

Sabina was silent; visions of a clear white muslin dress floated before her—only 1s. or 1s. 2d. a yard at the most. Mr. Milford, the draper, would give her credit. Her uncle was so particular in his payments that the tradespeople would have given the girl any amount of reasonable time to liquidate her debts. "There is Mr. Cressy's bill," thought Sabina. "I dare say he has forgotten it. It can't matter if I have another with Mr. Milford. I might have my white muslin, and make it up myself in my room, or whilst uncle dozes by the fire. He never attends to women's work, and when I go to the concert, I shall be covered over with a large cloak, so that he will not find it out."

The thought of finding Lady Sarah again was an unmixed pleasure. About Mr. Tresillian Sabina was not so sure. With her present shy sensations of nascent womanhood, she felt ashamed of having clung round his neck, and begged him to take her to live with him. She felt as if her cheeks would tingle with shame when she saw him again. In vain she repeated to herself, "I was but a child, I was but ten years old then." She could not lose her identity, and felt very guilty of forwardness as she lived over her past acts.

Sabina made her dress—the first low dress she had ever had. The mantua maker kindly cut out the pattern of the body, and that had been Sabina's only difficulty. She tried it on one evening before the glass—that tiny glass, in which Susan for years had arranged the bow on the top of her cap, which was denuded in several places of quicksilver, and had lost one side of its frame; but with all these drawbacks she thought herself very beautiful, and she had good reason for her conviction. That evening she went to partake of the tea and toast with which Mrs. Dent provided her, instead of the absent Miss Cressy, and made her hearers thrill by the power of her voice and the brilliancy of her execution in "The Soldier Tired." In the meantime, whilst her voice rang even through the quiet street, nothwithstanding the closed shutters, passengers crowded round to listen, and the fame thereof reached the shop of the greengrocer and fruiterer, Mr. Cressy; in fact, his errand boy, having taken half-a-dozen oranges to a sick lady in the evening, came in open-mouthed at the wonderful singing outside Mr. Dent's windows — a young lady was singing "But should the Trumpets," just like Miss 'Melia used, only a good bit louder.

Mr. and Mrs. Cressy heard and swelled with anger. "That's what they're up to—taking the songs out of my child's mouth, as it were. Sam, if you're a man, you won't stand it."

"Why? What can I do?"

"You're a fool to be bamboozled by that girl, and she owing you seven pounds ten shillings and ninepence-half-penny."

"I'm not bamboozled. She asked me, quite pretty like, to let it stand a bit, and so I did."

"Pretty, indeed! Handsome is that handsome does, say I. That account have stood over this two year."

"Well!" meekly—"what would you have me do?"

7

"Go to her to-morrow, and tell her that if she choose to put our 'Melia's nose out of joint by singing her songs, she must pay her bill, or else you will send the account in to her uncle. That will frighten the young lady, I warrant me, for he's an old Turk, and will lead her a pretty life. Young ladies who can't pay for fruit should not eat it, I say."

"'Twas most for *sparagrass* when her uncle was ill," suggested her husband, apologetically.

"A pack of nonsense! I suppose the apples were for her uncle, too, and he never a tooth to bite them with except false ones."

The result of the matrimonial conversation was that Mr. Cressy, all the more roughly because he did not like his occupation, came up to Mr. Rock's house, and, luckily for Sabina, encountered her at the door before he knocked. In a few hurried and insolent words—more insolent because he had had to force them—he informed her that if she wanted to take 'Melia's part at the concert, she must first pay his old account.

"Very well," she said, taking the "bill delivered," and walking on to get out of his way—"I will let you know."

She walked on without looking back, conscious that he was watching her, as if he could guess from her gait the effect of his threat. Her face seemed in a flame. What could she do? Confess all to her uncle—ah! Those accursed apples! How could she eat so many? She knew that she had told untruths about the asparagus, and her uncle's memory was unpleasantly tenacious; moreover, she knew her uncle could not pay the money without leaving himself penniless. She wished Lady Sarah would give her another twenty pounds without Mr. Rock's finding it out; but 'twas useless to wish. She walked on faster and faster as if to get away from her thoughts; she came to where the plantations of Tregear fringed each side of the road, and the idea of repose and coolness came with the recollection of those solemn giant trees. Further in there was a small gate leading into one side of the estate, and Sabina climbed over it by the help of some overhanging branches, and sprang down on the soft mossy bed beneath her. They would not miss her for a couple of hours. She might remain there, and be miserable at her leisure for some time to come. She would get farther into the covert, she thought, away from any people who might catch a glimpse of her light lilac gingham dress through the trees. On and on she went, stumbling through fern and wild flowers, and startling troops of timid deer with her reckless steps. At length she sank down at the foot of a beech tree, and leaned her head against its trunk, her dark hair conspicuous from its opposition with the silver gray of the bark.

CHAPTER XII.

"Ordinary expense ought to be limited by a man's estate, and ordered to the best, that the bills may be less than the estimation abroad."—BACON.

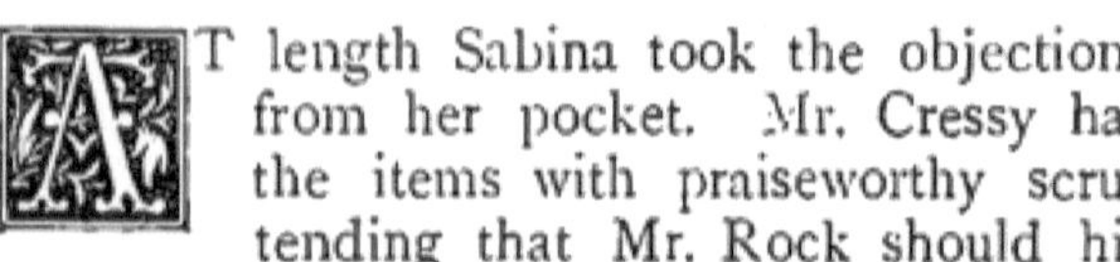

T length Sabina took the objectionable enclosure from her pocket. Mr. Cressy had repeated all the items with praiseworthy scrupulousness, intending that Mr. Rock should himself judge of the extent of the greengrocer's wrongs, should no money be forthcoming. The impression on his mind was that Sabina would make some excuse for not singing, and the concert be put off in consequence. That no doubt of the intention should remain in Sabina's mind, Mrs. Cressy had accompanied the bill with a note, slipped into the cover unknown to her husband, putting the matter, as she thought, in a fair light, as she doubted whether her husband would speak plainly to one so "pretty-spoken" as Miss Rock. Mr. Cressy had no rancour against Mr. Rock, and would not willingly have pressed him for the money; but 'Melia's interests were paramount to everything else. Sabina was a stupid accountant. Her uncle had tried to teach her; but as he began by the rule of three, somewhat as he had insisted on her learning the Zauberflöte, and utterly ignored the first three rules of arithmetic, which he believed she knew, and her ignorance of which she was ashamed to confess, the lesson always ended by tears on one side and ill-temper on the other. Sabina wondered at her own stupidity. Why should she have been *made* so stupid? "It was dreadful," her uncle said, and she quite believed him, and ran to the piano and practised the brilliant passages in "Jubal's Lyre,"

or " Let the bright seraphim." There was no doubt of her success in music. Now she leaned her head on her hand, and tried to pick out all the charges for apples sprinkled through the greengrocer's bill—4*d.*, 2*d.*, 8*d.*, repeatedly, such small sums, yet so large in the aggregate. She puzzled over the division of the articles, and could only try to obtain information by counting on her fingers. She grew more and more perplexed and disheartened, and began to weep bitterly. She had so wanted to go to the concert, to exhibit herself in her new muslin dress, to be recognised by Lady Sarah, and to show her how much her voice had improved ; and now —her uncle, too—he was determined that she should sing, —should she take to her bed and say she had a cold? That horrid Mr. Dent would insist on seeing her, and declare that nothing was the matter. It was most perplexing every way.

At some considerable distance from where Sabina was seated there was a garden-house, which Mr. Tresillian had had built when he was a boy, in imitation of Robinson Crusoe's hut. It was " bosomed high 'midst tufted trees," and approached by a ladder, which Mr. Tresillian drew up when he feared the approach of anyone whom he did not wish to see. By a good opera glass he could command the road which led to Tregear, and if anyone approached whom it was his interest to see, he went up to the mansion to receive them ; if not, he was " out," and it was not known when he would return. Strict orders were always given that he should never be disturbed by any messenger in this retreat.

He was, on this warm September afternoon, smoking his cigar, and looking listlessly through the window of his castle, and thinking of Cowper's lines dinned into his juvenile ears by his governess :—

> " 'Tis pleasant through the loopholes of retreat
> To gaze on such a world."

" Not at all unpleasant after all the *fadeur* of a London season, particularly if one has a good cigar from Beynon and Stockens. 'Tis a comfort to get out of the way of all those girls ! The demireps trying to possess one's purse, the model ones trying to secure both purse and name !

"Who is this coming along? Skimming along, I may say. Something small and bright. Ah! she stops at the little gate. No go, my dear! Locked! Well done! I declare 'tis well the turf is soft there, or you would jar those small feet and ankles of yours."

He watched her hurried scramble through the plantation, and saw her seat herself under one of the beech trees.

"What will she do now? I wish I could see her face. Oh! there goes her hat thrown off, and her hair tossed back. She seems to be very beautiful. I wonder where I have ever seen anyone like her! What's this? Oh! a letter! Yes, a love letter! Of course from some rustic in the neighbourhood, containing the regular poesy,—

> 'When this you see remember me,
> Though many miles I distant be.'

How she studies it! Can't make it out, seemingly! Bless me! there comes her pocket-handkerchief—crying! Poor little head! What's it all about, I wonder — a faithless lover? Yet she is *very* young-looking for a love affair; but of course girls never cry except from what they call outraged feelings. Poor devils! I suppose they do suffer sometimes;" and an unpleasant recollection or two intruded itself on his usually complacent mind. "She's going to get up. There she is! upright, very beautiful,—wonderfully so for so small a creature. Yes, she ties on her hat, and departs. My eyes are beginning to ache. There! she has dropped her letter; she does not perceive it, and is making her way back to the gate. Ha! ha! my pretty dear; you won't find it so easy to get out as to get in—*facilis descensus —sed revocare gradum*—I'll go down, pick up the letter, and introduce myself with that bit of civility."

Poor Sabina walked along with her head depressed, and with slow footsteps. She was in no hurry to get home with such black care awaiting her on the threshold. When, a year and a half before, she had received this dreadful bill, she had tried to sell her mother's small number of ornaments—a brooch or two, and three small Lisbon chains, one of which she had worn round her neck, and the other two as bracelets.

With the exaggerated idea of value, which generally

grows year by year upon the conviction of those possessed of such trifles, she had believed that, could she make up her mind to the sacrifice, she should get at least twenty pounds for her little treasure; but, alas! when offered to the best jeweller in Bodmin, to whom Sabina sent them with a little note, fifteen shillings was the utmost offered for them. She could not give up her mother's trinkets for a sum so inadequate, and they still remained in her little box. Should she take them to Mr. Cressy and beg him to purchase them for his daughter? She thought of that disagreeable girl decked in her mother's property, and cried with vexation; besides, the Cressys might refuse to purchase, and scoff at her for the proposition.

In the meantime she thought she would look at the letter again. She might not find it so insolent on a second reading.

She felt in her pocket but 'twas not there. She must have left it under the tree where she had been seated; but the whole plantation was of giant beech trees, and they were puzzlingly alike. It was easy enough for Mr. Tresillian, who knew every undulation of the woodland, to mark the one under which he had seen Sabina, and to detect the spot of white made by the folded letter; but as the broad trunk interposed between the girl and her lost property, she had nothing but her footprints to guide her back, and the pressure of those were soon filled up by the spongy moss.

In the meantime Mr. Tresillian reached and possessed himself of the letter.

"Miss Rock! Rock!" he exclaimed, meditating. "That's the name of one of my voters. I have it. The old half-pay lieutenant, and Miss Rock must be that child, sprung up into a beautiful girl; she promised to be pretty. By Jove! and she has a lover already. How old can she be—fifteen? sixteen?—not even that, I should think; she wasn't more than nine or ten at the last election."

He held the letter, and looked at the address. Some fellow of a clerk, by the handwriting. He paused a moment with a pang of reluctant honour, and then opened and read the letter and the bill.

"Poor little devil! This is what she was crying about, then. Let us see again what this elegant epistle means.

"'To Miss Rock, Haven House.

"'Madam—We are honest tradesfolks, and don't set up for ladies and gents, as some folks do as hasn't two sixpences to rub one against the other ; but folks must live, and can't noways afford to throw away their money in bad debts. So, Miss, I hope you will not find it *ill* convenient to pay our small account as has been a running now this two year.

"' I consider you've behaved very shabby in putting my 'Melia out of the concert and she so ill, poor lamb ! that she can't speak for herself. I may say that if you did not put yourself so forread, and the concert was give up for want of a fine voice, like my daughter's, Mr. Cressy might be worked upon not to press Mr. Rock for his money, always wishing you to understand, Miss, that if folks want dainties they should go without if they haven't the money to pay for them ; and I am your humble servant to command,

"' WINNIFRED CRESSY.'"

"Asparagus ! fifteen shillings a bundle !" said Mr. Tresillian. "What an extravagance ! I thought Mr. Rock was so economical. Apples ! Ah ! ah ! my little girl ! You are fond of forbidden fruit seemingly—we shall see," and he walked swiftly to the place where Sabina was hunting for the letter.

She heard the rustling of the dried fern, and saw a gentleman coming towards her. She knew her dress was poor-looking, and her eyes were suffused with tears. She began to walk as fast as she could towards the little gate at the termination of the plantation, and then in her anxiety the walk became a run. Mr. Tresillian did not hurry himself; he was tranquilly triumphant with the conviction that Sabina must bring herself up at the gate, which was not easy to climb from the road, but nearly impossible from the side of the plantation.

Reader ! have you never seen an unfortunate cat pursued by a large dog make its way to a sheltering window generally left open, but having her retreat cut off by finding it closed, she turns despairingly to begin the unequal battle that can have but one termination ? Thus Sabina, after shaking the gate with a last vain effort, did not at-

tempt to scale it, but turned and waited the approach of
the enemy.

Why did she *not* make the effort? Mr. Tresillian thought
that she had a lingering desire to meet him, and had only
fled to be pursued ; but the truth was, that had Sabina
had the conviction that her dress was faultless, her hair in
good order, and her cheeks not stained with tears, she
would not have fled from the encounter ; and as for at-
tempting to scale the gate, she was a good climber, and
might have managed it, but she did not try because she
had holes in her stockings, and shoes down at heel, and
these she was ashamed to reveal in what might have been
a futile attempt to escape. So she stood with a wild,
hunted, anxious look in her eyes, panting for breath, and
looking as if she should make a spring past him, and try
to escape through the plantation ; but she was aware that
she was ignorant of the locality, whilst he knew

> " Each bush and every alley green,
>   Dingle and mossy dell in that wild wood."

" What a beautiful wild animal !" was Mr. Tresillian's
thought.

" What a wretch I must be looking !" was Sabina's.

He lifted his hat respectfully, as if in doubt, and then
said,—

" Is it possible that I have the chance of renewing an old
acquaintance with a very young acquaintance ? Have I the
honour of addressing Miss Rock ? Do not tell me that you
have forgotten me, and that delightful evening when——"

" Oh !" sighed poor Sabina, " I remember it *all* !" and
her face hung out a crimson ensign, which, flushing her clear
brown skin, made her look infinitely lovely and helpless.
She glanced up quickly in his face, intending to speak again,
but saw such a pleased smile of triumph that she faltered in
her request. " Could you—open this gate for me ?"

He answered,—" I was once shut up by remaining too
long in one of the parks, and the doorkeeper, instead of
letting me out, kept on repeating, ' But why did you get in ?'
I feel so inclined to say, not only *why* did you get in, but
how did you get in ?"

"I wanted to be quiet," replied Sabina, with a sigh, remembering all her griefs, "and "—thinking she was about to confess something very indelicate—"and—I climbed over."

"Why don't you climb back again, then? Shall I assist you? You know it would not be the first time."

Sabina was silent.. "He is very ungenerous," she thought. "He is laughing at me; but to me it is no laughing matter."

"When I climb, I like to do it alone, Mr. Tresillian."

"Wherefore? I'm sure your ankles are faultless."

Deeper and deeper was the flush on her face. Had it only been the ankles she would not have minded so much.

"Have you not a key to the gate?"

"I have one at my Robinson Crusoe's Castle," replied he; "if you will walk back with me, I will give it to you."

"Thank you," she said, glad of a compromise.

Oh, false Tresillian! you knew the key of the gate was in your pocket all the time.

As they walked along side by side, Sabina's quick eyes darted their brown rays from side to side.

"Have you lost anything?" said her companion, demurely.

"Yes; I have dropped a letter somewhere. I was sitting under a tree, and I cannot tell which tree it was, and these horrid trees are all alike."

"Horrid trees! What an epithet!"

"Oh, yes! Don't criticise, please. They are very fine trees; but just now I had rather they had some distinguishing mark."

"I agree with you in thinking monotony tiresome." This fresh-looking little girl was very original, compared to the girls of the London season just concluded. "Might I inquire," said he, bending his graceful head towards her, and speaking low, "was it a love letter?"

"No."

"Are you sure? Because, as I live here, and you do not, I think I have more chance of finding it than you; and if I do, I shall take the privilege of reading it, considering myself for the time in the position of your parent or guardian."

"Oh, pray, do not!" said Sabina, anxiously.

" Oh, then, it is a love-letter."

Sabina was silent for a moment, and then said,—

" I never had a love letter in my life, nor any letter, till I had this one; and that did not come properly, like other letters, through the post-office."

" Then it was not a pleasant letter?"

" Very unpleasant."

" I have unpleasant letters sometimes—asking for money."

" Bills?" suggested Sabina.

" No-o-o. I generally pay my bills, like your uncle, who, I am told, always pays ready money."

Sabina winced.

" My unpleasant letters from people asking for money are generally disputed election accounts, or from people wanting a small 'consideration' for votes they have given me."

" Oh!" said Sabina, who knew nothing of and cared nothing for this.

" I am going to call on Mr. Rock to-morrow, to beg for the favour of his vote."

" Oh!" came again, but this time with an expression of terror, painful to witness.

" Well, what is the matter? Does your interest lie with the other candidate? Do you not approve of your uncle voting for me?"

" It is not that," said Sabina, her voice going off in a little sob; " but I wish you would not call. My uncle is sure to vote for you without your asking him."

" I am afraid," said he, gravely, " I cannot omit paying that compliment to your uncle. *You* need not see me, if I am so disagreeable," he went on, pretending to be affronted.

Sabina went on, not venturing to speak, but the tears rolled " down her innocent nose."

" What is it?" Mr. Tresillian said, kindly, passing his arm round her waist, and Sabina turned towards him, and, leaning her head on his arm, sobbed aloud.

" Poor little girl! tell me your trouble. Do you hate your uncle as much as you used?"

" No; I'm very fond of him; but, oh! I've done something so very wrong, and I dare not tell him; and—and I'm afraid that he will find it out if you call on him, because he will be sure to thank you for sending the asparagus."

"Asparagus? Did I send any?"

"No, you did not, but—but I said you did."

A little more cross-examination, and he elicited from his small companion the circumstances of the bill at the greengrocer's.

"Surely Mr. Rock would not have been angry had you told him at once?"

"Yes, he would; for he always says, people are not bound to live, but they are bound not to become chargeable to their neighbours."

"A fine principle, very rarely acted on," said Mr. Tresillian, smiling.

"And you see I told him an untruth, because I knew he would not eat the asparagus if he thought it was purchased, and I told him the gardener at Tregear had let me have it for him. He was very ill at the time, and believed it; and if he sees you, he will be sure to mention it."

"Is the bill only for asparagus?" inquired the gentleman.

"No," reluctantly. "When I went to buy the asparagus I saw apples. I'm very fond of them, and I did not think they were so dear, and I owe for the apples and the asparagus."

"Poor little darling!" he said, and he stooped and looked in her flushed face, intending to kiss her; but a new expression of anger and terror came into her countenance.

She withdrew herself from his circling arm, and walked on in silence.

"You kissed *me* when we met last," said Mr. Tresillian.

"When we met last? I was a child then," she said; "though I confess I ought to have known better then: I do know better now," she added, quietly.

"It shall be as you like, my child," replied Mr. Tresillian, who did not wish to alarm her.

They reached the ladder which led to his Castle, as he called it.

"Will you go up?" he said. "Stop till I ascend and steady the ladder."

"Will you not go up and get the key of the gate by yourself?"

But Mr. Tresillian insisted.

He wanted to accustom her to coming to that secret

retreat, where more took place than was ever dreamt of at the mansion of Tregear.

" Let me go up first," said he, remembering divers pictures which had better have a cloth thrown over them before an innocent girl was introduced into the room.

It took a few minutes to arrange these offensive paintings, which he did by taking them from their nails, and piling them under the sofa ; and then he brought the wild bird into his cage. She looked around her with wonder and curiosity.

CHAPTER XIII.

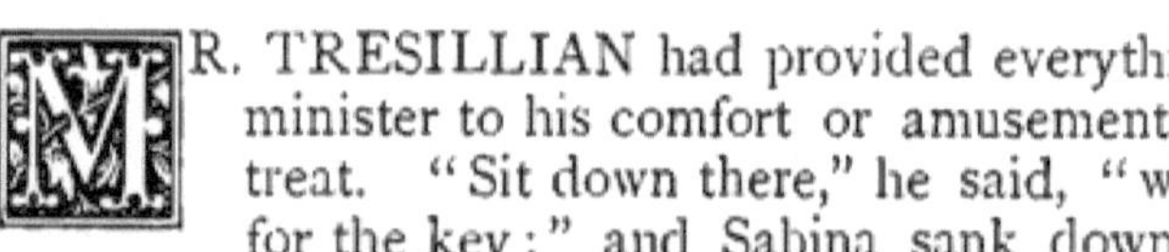

MR. TRESILLIAN had provided everything likely to minister to his comfort or amusement in this retreat. "Sit down there," he said, "whilst I look for the key;" and Sabina sank down into what seemed a bed of down pillows covered with the richest of pink damasks. It was a large old-fashioned sofa, large enough to serve for a bed if necessary; the pillows had been added for modern luxury. "Ah! that is a nice sofa, is it not?" he said, pretending to be looking for the key. "It was too old-fashioned for Lady Sarah, and faded. So I had the down pillows covered to match it as much as possible, not that it *does* match in texture. Our forefathers managed to get better materials than we do."

Lying on part of this couch was a richly-lined fur rug. A glass in one department of the octagon reflected the motley furniture of the room: boxing-gloves, foils, rapiers, fishing-tackle, hunting-whips, a double-barrel gun, and a large case of gunpowder. It was lettered "gunpowder," and Sabina repeated the word with a kind of awe. "Yes!" he observed, smiling, "Lady Sarah will not permit it to be kept at the mansion house, lest we should be all blown to pieces."

"But you?" inquired Sabina, a little too anxiously, and colouring as she became aware of what her tone had conveyed.

"Oh! as for that!" he said, laughing, "when life has become distasteful to me, I can retire here, like Sardanapalus, and set fire to the case, and be blown into air; but where shall I find some slaves or wives? Will you be one of my wives, and consent to be blown up with me?"

"I wish you would find the key, or I shall be blown up without you," said Sabina. "*Please* to find it. I cannot bear to tell my uncle, and sailors are so particular to a minute."

"But tell me what you think of my room?"

"Oh! 'tis a nice room, very," said Sabina, fretfully; "but I would give a great deal to be out of it."

"Very well! here is the key at last; but now I want you to come back again to-morrow morning."

"I don't think——"

"Oh, yes; you will come, I know, if I ask you. Shall I go down on my knees?" and he knelt on one knee, looking up in her face; and Sabina arose from the sofa, blushing painfully.

"I will tell you why you will come. I have something which belongs to you, and if you come, I will give it to you —a little needle-book which Lady Sarah gave you more than five years since. We left Tregear immediately after the election, and as I did not wish to vex my mother, I did not tell her that the book had been returned by your uncle. I locked it up in my desk till I should have an opportunity of giving it to you; and in truth I forgot all about it, till I saw you again."

Sabina's face beamed with pleasure at the chance of getting out of her difficulties so easily: "But," she added timidly, "could you not bring it with you when you call on my uncle?"

"I cannot call on him to-morrow," said Mr. Tresillian, "and from what you told me, I fancied you would be glad of the needle-book at once."

"That is true. I will come. May I come early?"

"Yes, I will meet you here at ten o'clock. Now I will walk with you as far as the gate, and let you out."

As Sabina passed the mirror she saw how common-looking and shabby, her dress was, and how worn the shoes that were half-buried in the thick-piled Turkey carpet; and she was depressed and humbled at the contrast drawn by her fancy between the wealth of Mr. Tresillian's sitting-room, and the poverty of her uncle's home, and of her own habiliments. Mr. Tresillian descended the ladder first, and turning held out his arms to receive Sabina, who sprang into them to conceal her pedal deficiencies. She was small and light, and so beautiful that Mr. Tresillian might have been forgiven the half embrace which he gave her before she regained her feet.

"I wonder if we shall find the letter," she said; "but now I have told you all about it, I shall not care if *you* find it. Ah! there it is!" she exclaimed, bounding to a distant tree, at the foot of which Mr. Tresillian had deposited it, unperceived, when they were walking towards his room. "'Tis very strange—I thought I had looked under all those beech trees."

She had no suspicion of the truth, however, but regarded anxiously the sky, to watch the downward progress of the sun. The thought that her uncle might be watching for her coming step, and disappointed at her non-arrival, made her silent and forgetful even of her companion. So she sped on with swift and unequal steps over the moss and broken ground, till Mr. Tresillian exclaimed,—

"At what a pace you go, Miss Rock! one can hardly keep up with you. It is not much of a compliment to me that you should be so anxious to get rid of me."

"Oh! I never thought of wishing to get rid of you; but I cannot bear to vex my uncle, and here is the gate at last," said she, with a sigh of relief. "Will you tell me what time I have to get home in?"

"It is now just five o'clock," replied Mr. Tresillian, consulting his watch.

"What a beautiful little watch!"

"Should you like to have it?"

"No, thank you," said Sabina, flushing crimson; and fancying her abrupt refusal had given a look of displeasure to Mr. Tresillian's handsome brow, she added,—

"I should like to have it very much, of course, only my uncle says it is not right to take presents from anyone too valuable to be repaid by a gift of equal amount."

"Then," rejoined he, "if you can give me a present of equal or greater value, you will take this in exchange?"

"I may safely promise that," she replied, as Mr. Tresillian unlocked the gate.

"Take the key," he said, "I can get another. I do not like you to climb over like a wicked shepherd or shepherdess into the fold."

She thanked him and passed into the road. Mr. Tresillian watched her till some trees intervening shut her from his sight; but she did not look back as he had hoped.

"She is too beautiful to be walking about on the high road alone," he thought; and he retired to his retreat whence he could watch her onward progress.

Arrived there, he saw a pedestrian following her. She seemed unconscious of it, or at any event she did not quicken her pace. The man came up with and addressed her. Mr. Tresillian saw the start Sabina gave, and that she was hurrying on faster. Presently she was running with surprising swiftness, pursued by the man who had accosted her, and a turn of the road hid them both from his sight. The aristocratic schoolboy, who, "confined to bounds," sees some ragged urchin climbing the tree in which is concealed the nest which he had set his heart on rifling—the sportsman who from a distant field observes on the First of September a trespasser putting up the covey he had marked down as his own—the epicure who sees the coveted slice of venison from "the alderman's walk," carried by a faithless footman to another—may feel aggravation; but not to be compared in amount to that which quickened the pulse and flushed the cheek of Mr. Tresillian, as he imagined the jeopardy of Sabina, that sweet wild rose-bud which he intended should grace his own button-hole, and felt that he could not possibly reach the spot in time to aid her.

He remained watching from the window of his retreat, hoping that he might see some passengers going by, whose presence might be a protection to the young girl. As he gazed a funeral hymn rose on the evening air, and he saw one of those picturesque processions, so common at the period of my story in that remote country, where the dead are carried by the hands of mourners, not on their shoulders, and surrounded by women in their scarlet cloaks, singing their Wesleyan dirges for the departed. Amongst the crowd he marked the man dressed in a velveteen jacket, worn by

8

the pursuer of Sabina, a handsome dissolute fellow, of about thirty-five years, one of the Tregear gamekeepers. "I'll trounce that fellow. What insolence!" was his passing reflection.

When Sabina, hurrying and breathless, reached the corner of the street leading to Haven House, she stopped for a moment to smooth her hair, and retie the strings of her hat, that her uncle might not discover any disorder or confusion in her appearance. When in sight of the windows she saw her uncle's bald forehead pressed against the pane, and knew she was late. He met her at the door, holding up his chronometer. "Three minutes after your time!" he exclaimed. "Miss Rock, if you do this again, I'll make you think that all bags and hammocks are piped up." A threat of driving her to a verge of such distraction as may fill the minds of eight hundred seamen, who suddenly have to answer to their names on deck, each bearing the above-mentioned articles, of which the bags lie in a heap, and cannot be found by their lawful possessors.

Now, had Sabina returned in the depressed state of mind in which she had entered the Tregear plantation, she might have resented the half-playful, half-angry attack made by her uncle; but she had an inward spring of joy which sparkled in her eyes, and expanded her pretty delicate mouth into smiles. The terror inspired by the insolent man who had followed her had passed away from her mind. She only thought that she was relieved from her difficulties, that she should be able to defy the Cressys, and sing at the concert, and be heard and admired by Tresillian and Lady Sarah, and that her pecuniary distress would throw no shadow on her uncle's life. She would have preferred "hanging, whipping, or pressing to death," to the task of confessing her want of truth, and what *he* would have called her want of honesty to her uncle. What deprivation the old man must have submitted to, to make up that seven pounds odd shillings, had he known it! and how deep would have been his sorrow at the cause. Sabina knew a woman who had been beaten to death by her husband, because she had spent four shillings and sixpence he had given her to pay for a lantern. How piteously the poor creature had entreated the tinman to give her a receipt, without being paid for it! How wearily had

she besought the neighbours to club their sixpences to save
her from her husband's vengeance in vain! Sabina would
have had no blows now to suffer from Mr. Rock, but she
thought that she should have died of shame at the confession
had she had it to make.

She kissed his forehead, and made his tea, and as he
drank it she ran to the piano and sang "The Hardy Tar,"
and the uncle's old hoarse voice joined in the refrain—

> "Then oh! reward the hardy tar,
>   Be mindful of his merit;
> And when again you're plunged in war
>   He'll show his daring spirit."

"Now sing what you are to perform at the concert," said
Mr. Rock, proudly.

"There is only one single song, uncle, 'The Soldier
Tired of War's Alarms.'"

"Always soldiers! Sailors are never duly honoured."

"Oh! uncle!"

"Why, child; don't the fools at public dinners always give
'The Army and Navy,' putting us after those rascally land-
lubbers?"

"Perhaps 'tis because A being the first letter of the alpha-
bet, it runs more trippingly off the tongue, than navy and
army; yet in rank you know, uncle, there is no manner of
doubt."

"Well, well, child! I don't know where England would
be without her wooden walls. But surely you ought to
practise your music a little."

"Yes, uncle; when Mr. Orellan comes, I will go and
join the rest of the performers at Mr. Dent's.

The next morning she arose with the lark, though she
could not carry out her intentions till the shops were open.
In Deepindale, as in other remote country towns, shopkeepers are lazy from having few customers to make de-
mands on their time, and so they lie in bed to increase their
resemblance in their own opinion to gentry who are not
obliged to get up sooner than they please. But at length
the reluctant shutters were taken down, and Sabina fitted
herself with a delicate pair of new boots, and some fine hose,
such as had never adorned her pretty feet since the days
when she had been her mother's darling.

8—2

Then, when she had given her uncle his breakfast, having made the tea with the usual accuracy of measurement, and timed the period of its infusion in water, by Mr. Rock's chronometer, she got the newspaper, and having arranged her uncle comfortably in his easy chair, she told him that she was going out for a walk that fine morning, and might not be back till one o'clock. He must promise not to be anxious if she were three minutes late. He assented without reluctance. The little episode of the man who had addressed her she kept secret, lest she might be forbidden to walk out alone. She dressed herself in a clean gingham, tight-fitting morning dress, in which her dainty figure appeared to the greatest advantage, and when she had shook out her glossy black curls, and pressed her light straw hat over them, ornamented as it was with some fresh blue ribbon, and given a glance of pride to the pretty new boots and clean white hose, she was well satisfied with the image reflected in the little three-cornered bit of glass which was an apology for a mirror, and had made, in its more palmy state, part of her uncle's shaving-glass. She was very happy, very young, too young to be so harassed by the load of debt; but this seven pounds odd shillings owed to the fruiterer was a burden as heavy to the poor girl, as the mortgage which has eaten up the best half of the spendthrift's estate.

She trod lightly along the road to Tregear. The autumn sun shone brightly, drawing up from the valleys wreaths of thin mist, the cobwebs glittered in its beams and gemmed the blackberry branches, which had been the first cause of Sabina's introduction to the family of Tregear. "An argument for gluttony and recklessness!" said Sabina, laughing as she tripped along the road. "Had I never picked those purple berries I should not have been threatened by Mr. Rock's stick, nor run away, nor have been picked up in my turn by Mr. Tresillian. How handsome he is!" and she slackened her pace to think of his beauty with more deliberation.

"Breakfast for two in my retreat," said Mr. Tresillian to his valet on the previous evening. "Let it be ready at half-past nine, and call me at half-past eight. You will not be required to wait." The wily servant was accustomed to dual preparations for meals in the woodland, and acted accord-

ingly. As his master, however, had not been communica-
tive as to who might be the second person to be entertained,
he supplied the deficiency by creeping into a hollow beech
tree, after he had made all the necessary preparations for
breakfast, from whence he might watch for the expected
guest. Presently he saw Mr. Tresillian coming through the
woodland. "He've done himself up very handsome, this
morning. He means mischief, he do. 'Taint a man that's
a-coming, *I* know, from the look of his hair. Phew! how
'tis scented!" he exclaimed, as his master passed close to
his retreat.

Mr. Tresillian was a voluptuary. He had youth, intellect,
wealth, and good looks, and proceeded "to make the most,"
not like Doctor Binney, "of both worlds," but of the only
one of which he felt certain.

He schemed to have every sense gratified, in the manner
which promised most enjoyment. He would have the finest
wines of the best vintage, the best French cook, the best
materials for him to work with, and would study with the
judgment of a connoisseur at the theatres the figures of the
unconscious actresses with other thoughts than those
naturally suggested by the characters they represented.—
The creed

> "Which held that women were but dust,
> The soulless toys of tyrants' lust,"

seemed to him very reasonable, as he had great doubts as to
his possessing himself any spark of divinity.

He meant to amuse himself with Sabina, so long as he
remained at Tregear: perhaps even take her to town with
him. But no,—it would not tell well at Deepindale that he
should debauch the niece of an old man so respectable as
Mr. Rock.

"Confound these elections!" he exclaimed. "They are
always in the way of one's comfort." But the idea of the
obloquy, which would fall on him if he pursued his schemes
with regard to Sabina, made him very grave as he walked
towards the gate through which he expected her to pass.

"There she comes! How beautiful she is, face and
figure!" he exclaimed, looking at her critically. "How
smooth and delicate is her skin! how rounded her bust!
Ah! there is no beauty like the beauty of fifteen and six-

teen ! What a nuisance that I must not think of her ! If I were a peer now, I might kick these voters all to the devil !" And his mind wandered to his elder brother, who was drinking away the remains of his liver, in a way which seemed to promise the fulfilment of the younger son's desire to "kick the inhabitants of Deepindale to the devil."

When Sabina met Mr. Tresillian there was trouble on his brow; in other words, he was out of temper. She came on airily enough till she caught the expression of his face, when her look changed to timid wonder and apprehension.

"He cannot find the book for me, I dare say, or perhaps someone has stolen the twenty pounds out of it." Sabina was too poor to realise the fact that the twenty pounds, so important to her, was as twenty farthings, or less than that sum, to Mr. Tresillian.

They met. He looked grave in answer to her timid questioning smile. That she must be forbidden fruit made him feel disposed to sulk with her.

"You are very punctual," he said at length.

"Am I too soon, then?"

"Certainly not. Do you not see I am here to meet you?"

"I think he must have lost the needle-book. Why does he not give it to me?" was the thought in Sabina's mind.

"She is very charming and innocent. I don't see why I should give her up?" was Mr. Tresillian's reflection.

They walked on in silence. Sabina stooped and plucked some purple berries from the nightshade, and began to twist the stem into a wreath.

"For what is that intended?"

"Oh, I scarcely know. I was thinking if I was able to sing at the concert, I should make a wreath of natural flowers for my head."

"Are you going to sing that charming trio which in one line will be so appropriate?—

<blockquote>
"'A wreath around her head she wore,
Carnation, woodbine, lilies, rose.'"
</blockquote>

"No," replied the girl, smiling, "in that case I should not venture to wear a wreath."

"From a consciousness that you resemble the Flora whose beauties are therein celebrated?" continued Mr. Tresillian.

"Why do you try to——?" vex me, Sabina would have said; but, though she shrank from the mocking tone in which he spoke, she did not want to quarrel with him. Was he not the possessor of the much desired needle-book and the twenty pounds?

"Pray, finish your sentence."

"Oh! I don't know. But it seemed that you were mocking me," said Sabina.

The tone of sadness in which she spoke touched Mr. Tresillian.

"If I am a brute, Miss Rock, attribute it to the true cause; I have not breakfasted. All conversations, or rather all fragmentary speeches, before an Englishman has had his morning meal, are cold like the hour, and sharp like the morning air, and generally disagreeable."

"Oh! I thought this morning so beautiful!" said Sabina, happy in the consciousness that she was unusually well dressed, and hoping to get her money. "I have not been so happy for a long time."

Mr. Tresillian put down the happiness all to his own score, and felt self-complacent. They reached the ladder, and he assisted Sabina to ascend into the room, where a luxurious breakfast was prepared for two persons.

The richly chased silver urn bubbled and simmered on the most snowy of fine damask tablecloths. The tea-pot, cream-jug, and sugar-basin were all of the pattern of the tea-urn. The sun gleamed brightly through the leaves of the virginia creeper, red with the tints of autumn, and glittered on the gorgeous tea-equipage. Fish, broiled chicken, marmalade, jams, hot rolls, and a large dish of apples were placed on the table.

Mr. Tresillian looked roguishly at Sabina, and then at the apples. She understood the look and replied to it.

"Ah! these are much finer than those which I ought not to have purchased, but did——"

The speech reminded Mr. Tresillian of the necessity for paying the bill, and he, still smiling, lifted a plate which had been placed in a reversed position on the breakfast-table and revealed to the eager eyes of Sabina the much-wept-for needle-book.

"Oh!" she said; and, for a few minutes, she articulated nothing more.   Then,—

"Oh, dear! how beautiful it is!   I do not think it is in the least faded.   The same paper it had over it when Lady Sarah gave it to me five years ago!"

She wanted to see if the money was safe, but felt ashamed, and stopped, blushing.

Mr. Tresillian understood the feeling and relieved her mind by saying, "The money is all right.   I looked at it this morning, and changed half into gold, which I thought you would find more convenient."

"You are so very good to me," said Sabina, gratefully.

"Do not praise me too soon."

"I do not; you have done what is so thoughtful."

"Let me give you some tea or coffee."

And Sabina was now sufficiently happy to enjoy her breakfast.

She had passed off her shyness, and Mr. Tresillian looked at her with pleasure, and thought her a beautiful addition to his property, which he looked forward to purchasing for his own.

"'Tis very strange," he thought, "that she shows no consciousness of any impropriety of coming thus to a young man's room, and eating her breakfast with him.   By Jove! I believe she considers me an old fogy like her great-uncle! I wonder what relations she has, and whether they would make a fuss."

He spoke, to assure himself on this point: and as a lurcher, knowing the form of a hare, goes around in stealthy circles not to alarm his prey till he is close to her, and seizes her at one gripe, so Mr. Tresillian began at some distance from the point at which he meant ultimately to arrive.

"You are looking forward with anxiety to this concert?"

"Yes—no—not anxiety,—I am too conceited for anxiety, —but with pleasure."

"In what will the pleasure consist?"

Had Sabina told the truth she would have said, "In singing to you, and in your hearing me admired;" but she only answered, "I like to sing, because I do few things well; but singing is one of the few."

" Then your motive is, to be admired ? "

" Yes, and to please Mr. Rock."

" All your relations and friends, doubtless, will rejoice at your success ? "

" *All*," said Sabina, " doubtless. The all consists of two —one relative, Mr. Rock ; one friend, old Susan, his servant. You see I am well provided."

" Has Mr. Rock no friends ? "

" Yes—one old half-pay lieutenant, Mr. Orellan. He seems to have outlived all his other ties, and folks who are poor and old are not sought by new acquaintances."

" Will your uncle go to the concert ? "

" Oh, no, I do not think so. He would hardly like to go out at night."

" His health is very delicate, then ? "

" Yes," said Sabina, " very ; " and a cloud came over her young face.

" She will have no one to interfere with her or for her when this old man dies," thought her companion.

Sabina rose. " It is time for me to go."

" Must you ? " He did not mean to urge her to remain. He would not frighten her away from him entirely by seeming too eager to retain her.

" I will walk part of the way with you."

" Oh, thank you ! but indeed it is unnecessary."

" Not quite. What did that man say to you yesterday afternoon ? You did not seem to like it, for you ran as fast as you could to avoid him."

" How could you know that ? " said Sabina, with her face in a flame.

" Do you not know that I find out all about you ? But who is the man, and what did he want ? "

" I don't know what he said. I was so frightened, that I could not understand him. I think he is mad." And Sabina turned pale in her remembered terror.

Mr. Tresillian was troubled at the recollection as well as his companion.

He would have desired nothing better than to walk to Deepindale with Sabina ; but should anyone meet them— and part of the way was on the high road—how folks would talk ! and how the poor child would be compromised in the

eyes of the townsfolk,—and, worse still, what would not be
said of the young member!

"You must wait a minute or two, Miss Rock," he said;
and going to the door of his retreat, he blew on a shrill
whistle a prolonged note. "There, sit on my sofa and read
a book, like a good child, whilst I go towards Tregear for a
few minutes."

"I shall go if you do not return soon," said Sabina.

"No, you must *not* go till I return," he said, sternly; and
Sabina sat down, quite cowed. In a surprisingly short time
he came back with a smile, and said he was ready to attend
her. He had gone to meet his valet, whom he expected to
see coming from Tregear, but who had taken advantage of
his master's back being turned to crawl out of his hiding-
place, and accordingly presented himself before the astonished eyes of Mr. Tresillian, covered all over with small
fragments of bark.

His master was enlightened; but it did not suit him to
make any observation.

"You will follow us to the gate leading to the high road,
and then keep your eye on Miss Rock without its being
perceived that you are following her, and see that she receives no molestation. When she is within reach of the
town you will return."

He walked by the side of Sabina in silence till they came
to the gate,—

"To-morrow, I think, is the concert?"

"Yes. Are you not coming?"

"I do not know; perhaps I may look in," he said, indifferently.

Sabina felt a choking sensation in her bosom, and the
little of her throat which the dark hair permitted to be seen,
blushed to a pink hue.

"He does not care to hear me sing," she thought; but
she said nothing.

Mr. Tresillian had already begun the cruel sport in which
boys and cats are adepts—the art of tormenting.

"Good-bye," she said, steadying her voice to pronounce
the word with indifference.

He took the little hand which she extended with a light
touch, and dropped it immediately.

"Good-morning, Miss Rock;" and with a smiling bow he opened and then closed the gate after her departing steps. "She begins to love me so soon, that really there will be no effort necessary to win her."

Sabina felt certain, when she had trod that path in the morning, that if she obtained the needle-book with the twenty pounds, and saw her way clearly out of her difficulties, she should be the happiest woman in the world. She had the twenty pounds in her pocket, and she was ready to cry at the fear that Mr. Tresillian would not come to hear her sing, and with the certainty that he did not care whether he came or not.

As, however, she got nearer the town, and saw Mr. Cressy's shop in the distance, and thought how she had always felt it to be "a stumbling-block and rock of offence" whenever she had passed it for the last two years, she forgot some of her vexation, in the prospect of freeing herself from the debt. As she had gone out in the morning she had seen the stout form of Mrs. Cressy behind the counter, wrapping up a pennyworth of bulls'-eyes for a child, and glaring at her through the shop-window simultaneously. She had felt uncomfortable then under her scrutiny; now she was triumphant. Mr. Dent's horse was at the door, and was stamping impatiently under the torment of the flies. They had been troublesome all the morning, and Mr. Dent had wished them all dead, even though they made "the apothecary's ointment to stink," which, as he observed, could not matter much, considering it was the nature of all the contents of his shop. He had found it difficult, owing to the caracoles of his horse, to sing the most difficult little bit in "The Curfew,"—

"Yet where their midnight pranks have been,"

which had haunted him day and night like an unaccomplished duty. To-morrow night must be the scene of his triumph or disgrace as a votary of Apollo,—

"Glorious Apollo! from on high——"

"Oh, here we are," and he pulled up at the private door by the side of the shop.

"Well, Mrs. Cressy, how are we to-day? How is the interesting patient? Getting on nicely?" and Mr. Dent's voice was made up to the most suave of tones to coax Mrs. Cressy into acquiescence with the performance of the concert without the aid of 'Melia's voice.

Mrs. Cressy, who had been swelling with anger at the announcement of the concert for the next night, had a feeling that hers was "the sleeping whirlwind sway" that hushed in grim repose awaited "its evening prey." *They* thought they should sing their trios and quartettes : *she* knew better. She had in her hands the power which governs all things in the civilised world—the power of wealth, and she knew how to apply the screw of poverty to her young debtor. Had Miss Rock had the means of paying, she would have paid at once, she argued. If the concert were not stopped, it should be a dead failure for want of vocal music. They should suffer for thinking her 'Melia could be set aside, as if her absence were unimportant. She thought how well it would have sounded in the county paper, the *Cornwall Gazette*, that the concert for the display of native talent at Deepindale had been put off in consequence of the serious illness of the talented vocalist, Miss Amelia Cressy. As it was going to take place, such a paragraph was impossible, but another might be inserted : "The concert for the benefit of the Cornish Infirmary took place on Thursday, the 16th instant, at Deepindale ; but in consequence of the severe illness of that distinguished vocalist, Miss Cressy (not a word about scarlet fever—that would keep customers away from the shop), a general gloom and disappointment pervaded the assembly, and the company were disappointed of the musical treat, which her well-known talent had led them to expect."

"That will just do," said the mother, satisfied with her imaginary composition, and she could afford to be less sour to Mr. Dent than usual, when, since 'Melia's illness, he averred, not her own sauce apples could equal her tartness. Thank you, Mr. Dent, 'Melia's nicely ; you'll walk up."

"Yes, indeed," said the apothecary, as he descended the stairs—"she is so well that I hope you will favour us to-night with your company at the concert."

" Thankee, no, Mr. Dent; I like the human voice, I do. I don't care for your rosin and scrapings, and violins and violincellers—not I ! Give me a good song, say I."

"Oh, but we shall have——"

"Yes, I know—the peeanner; but that's not much. It don't speak like a human voice, you see."

" I flatter myself," said Mr. Dent, with an air of importance, "that you would not be otherwise than gratified with our vocal strains, Mum."

" Are you and Mr. Grinde a-going to sing duets, then?"

" No, Mum, a trio and a quartette."

" Indeed ! and who is the third, then?"

" Hem ! Miss Rock has kindly——" he blushed, for he knew he was on delicate ground.

" If you mean that Miss Rock is a-going to take 'Melia's place, you're mistaken, that's all. She aint going to do no such thing, or my name's not Mary Cressy."

"You will find yourself mistaken, Mum. Mr. Rock has promised his niece shall lend her aid."

"Then Mr. Rock had better pay his niece's bills and his own. Look here"—putting the large ledger over the counter, and opening it at the letter R. "There, Sir, there ! add up them items, and you will find it comes to 7*l.* 11*s.* 10½*d.* It aint perfessional to tell such things ; but it makes my blood boil, it do—owing this two year ; *she* can't pay it, nor he neither, 'tis my belief; but," continued the furious greengroceress, " if that money aint paid down here before *h*eight o'clock to-morrow morning, I'll know the reason why." She slammed-to the book with a loud smack, and placing her arms akimbo, she asked if Mr. Dent and Mr. Grinde would like to make up the money between them. This proposition was made with a triumphant grin ; she knew how valuable was money to both gentlemen.

Poor Mr. Dent was sadly discomposed at this last blow. He ran over in his mind whether he might possibly lump the money into his attendance on 'Melia ; but no—that healthy young lady was nearly well, and had declined camphor draughts and quinine pills to aid in her restoration ; so he gazed blankly on Mrs. Cressy's infuriated face, and was silent, when a light step was heard behind him, and Sabina tripped into the shop, and in her pretty, childish voice hoped

Miss Cressy was better. She looked pleadingly into the angry face opposed to her; for she knew she had been in fault for what she could not help.

Mr. Dent's kind heart ached for the poor girl. "For certainly she is going to catch it now," said he to himself.

"As to that, Miss Rock, 'Melia will be well in a few days, if folks had but the manners to wait for her."

"The infection, my dear Madam, the infection. The sweet young ladies at Tregear—'twould never do."

"Nobody asked your opinion, Mr. Dent."

"Really, Mrs. Cressy, my professional reputation——"

"Phew! *That* for your reputation!" said the furious woman. "And now, little Miss, are you going to pay up, or not? I don't want no humbug."

"I called for that purpose," said Sabina, taking out the needle-book; and Mr. Dent's face flushed with pleasure, whilst Mrs. Cressy's subsided into paleness. Sabina counted out the money, and waited for the receipt.

Mr. Dent did not leave the shop till he had seen this part of the transaction completed, and then he made a sweeping bow, and went off with a jerk of delight in his gait.

"If I didn't attend them professionally, I'd never buy a two-penny cabbage there again so long as I live; but I can't afford to quarrel with them, though the last potatoes they sent were diseased, and two-pence a peck dearer than Green's at the other end of the town. I don't attend Green's; it's a pity."

When Sabina returned home she had not outstaid her time, though in her newly-born horror of debt she had called on Mr. Milford, and paid the small sum owing for her muslin dress, and had performed the same act of duty at the boot-maker's. She had still ten pounds and some odd silver, and she longed to buy something for her great-uncle and for old Susan. A ribbon to be pinned round old Susan's cap she did buy, not believing she would trouble herself to inquire whether it was paid for, or whence came the money, but she feared her uncle's scrutiny, and felt sure that he would receive nothing of the purchase of which he did not know the history.

CHAPTER XIV

THE morning dawned on which the long-expected concert was to take place. Sabina's muslin dress was laid out on her small bed, with an under-dress of faultless white. She had some ribbons of pale pink, and was wondering from whom she should beg some natural flowers for a wreath.

"There," she said, "it does not matter how I look; he will not be there ;" but there was a little lingering hope that he might come after all.

She was up in her little room in the middle of the day. She heard a knock at the door, and listened. She was sure she distinguished the name of *Miss* Rock, and she called to Susan, after the door had been closed, to come up to her. Sabina had been adding a little lace to her white muslin dress, and having tried it on once more, she was undressed and unable to run down to satisfy her curiosity.

"Coming, Miss," Susan answered ; but she came not.

Presently Sabina heard flap, flap, flap going on in the back yard, and knew that Susan was beating mats against the sill of the back door.

"Horrid old woman ! I hate her !" said the impatient

girl. " I had better have dressed at once and gone down myself."

When she had accomplished this, she met Susan ascending the stairs slowly, with a covered basket in one hand, and a roll of mats in the other.

" You see, Miss, I thought I might as well beat the mats first, just to save two walks up stairs."

" What is it? Where did it come from? What is inside?"

" Lor, Miss, I can't tell. A boy brought it. Says he, 'Do Mr. Rock live here?' 'Yes,' says I. 'Then,' says he, 'this is for Miss Rock;' and he turned away without another word."

Sabina went into her room, and guessed the contents of the basket by the combination of perfumes which it exhaled, even before the cover was removed. It was full of hot-house flowers, exquisite in form, colour, and scent, and cut with the utmost recklessness as to coming buds, which a gardener's hand would have spared for future blossoms. No gardener had collected these fragile beauties. Amongst others there were stems of the passion flower as flexile and far more lovely than the nightshade, which Sabina had half twined into a wreath when she walked through the wood with Mr. Tresillian. She sat down flushed and trembling with her happy consciousness.

It was so very kind of him to remember what she had said. He must like her a little. Then growing pale at the suggestion—" I wonder if these flowers mean anything? Flowers have meanings sometimes." She had some confused notion of having seen a little book called the " Language of Flowers," and of a story—a very old and forgotten one—called the " Indian Cottage," in which a Pariah woos his love by placing in her way a poppy, which was to indicate the following sentiment—" I burn;" the gauzy scarlet leaves being the flame, the heart-shaped seed enclosed by them the heart, and the black stamen representing the ashes into which it was being consumed; but this poppy had been a field flower, and these were all hot-house productions, which, no doubt, accounted for the absence of this expected tell-tale weed.

" I'm glad there is no mignonette; that means, 'Your qualities surpass your charms,'" said Sabina. " Here is a lovely branch of myrtle, with its blossoms like white stars."

"The myrtle bough bids lovers live."

Now, did he mean this? Did he mean anything, or nothing?

Sabina left this question, which has in all time so distracted the minds of her sex, to be solved by futurity. One thing was clear, he had sent her the flowers, and she might arrange a beautiful wreath before night.

She bolted the door of her little room, and sat down to her work. Some flowers were too large, and the stiff stems of others made them unmanageable; but she succeeded at length to her satisfaction, for the three-cornered bit of looking-glass reflected a lovely image.

When this was completed, a terrible thought overwhelmed her. If she wore this wreath of hot-house flowers, how could she account for their possession? She must be reduced, like Faust's Marguerite, to exhibit her ornaments to an old Susan instead of old Martha. If Mr. Orellan should observe on the wreath in the presence of her uncle, into what a labyrinth of lies should she not be plunged to account for her having them.

"Pretty creatures!" said Sabina, placing them carefully in water. "Never mind; they will last longer for not being exposed to the heat of the concert-room."

She took a carnation and a bit of geranium, however, to fasten into the front of her dress, and twisted them carefully together with a piece of netting-silk.

Would it be a fine night? An important question to Sabina's white dress, as she must walk through the town over the streets ungraced by flat pavement.

Both she and her uncle were silent during their evening meal. The old man was revolving a little plan in his own head, which he did not confide to his niece, and she was occupied in nervous anxiety as to the circumstances of the evening. She did not doubt her musical powers; she had the confidence possessed by all endowed with genius, that she should deserve success; but, would *he* be there? What would applause be if he heard it not? She felt a conviction creeping over her that he would not go to the concert, and she was half inclined to sit down and cry.

It was time to go.

She wrapped her cloak over the spotless white dress, and placing its hood over her head, she went into the sitting-room and kissed her uncle's bald head tenderly.

"Wish me success, uncle, and pray do not sit up for me—now mind, you must *not.* Susan, do not let Mr. Rock sit up."

The door closed after her, and she was gone. When she reached the concert-room, which was held at the hotel in the very ball-room in which poor Sabina's mortifications among the pupils had been manifold, she found the performers assembled in the tea-room, in a state of nervous trepidation, which left no space for sympathy with any terrors but their individual ones.

Mr. Temple had damaged one of the strings of his violoncello, and doubted its lasting through the evening. He had sent to the music-shop, but the unfeeling owner of silver wire and cat-gut strings had sent a long-standing account back, with a notice that if Mr. Temple wanted a silver string, he had better pay for what he owed there already. Unless money was forthcoming, the string would not be. Mr. Mudge, of the music-shop, knew that the churchwardens had that morning granted the organist a gratuity of ten pounds in addition to his salary.

Mr. Temple hesitated; perhaps the string might last; but there was a suspicious flaw in the circle of silver wire.

He would risk it. Ten pounds were precious rarities to him, and he could not bear to throw them away on an old account.

Mr. Dent had a "heart bowed down by weight of woe," for he had received a violent letter from Mrs. Cressy, declining his professional services for the future.

"Must call to-morrow, and try to make it up," he said.

Mr. Grinde had made himself nearly sick by eating Mr. Dent's cough lozenges, which Mr. Dent himself was too wise to taste, though both gentlemen had colds.

The pianist could not get the piano and the violins into tune together, and the perspiration stood on his brow in the violence of his efforts.

"Half-past six. They'll be here at seven though it don't begin till half-past. Keep the doors fast for the love of Heaven, till I try once more."

"You are very near it now," said Sabina, kindly; and the pianist was grateful for the first words of encouragement he had heard.

"That is the note which is faulty," she continued. "That A flat is too sharp." He altered the tone a sixteenth, according to her ear, and was satisfied. Now the violin players must do their duty; and the scraping and squeaking was deafening. Sabina forgot her anxieties in the troubles around her, and when the doors were opened and the company thronged in, her heart had ceased to beat so tumultuously.

A green curtain had been placed before the platform on which the performers were raised, as it was thought that thus a better effect would be produced than by their seeing the votaries of Apollo coming in one by one. Before it drew up, Sabina peeped through a friendly aperture, made by a colony of moths, to see who were present.

In the front row sat Lady Sarah, and at the end of the chairs the governess flanked a row of young ladies from Tregear, amongst whom, now grown to womanhood, Sabina recognised her rival of the fair locks; but her heart sank within her, for Mr. Tresillian was not there.

Of what use was now the white muslin so carefully kept from every stain? Of what use the carnation which gave warmth and life to its snowy folds? Of what use the magnificent voice, of the possession of which Sabina was so well aware? In the extremity of her disappointment she cared not for it, nor for anything in life. However, the work must be done, the songs must be sung; but Sabina needed not to appear till they wanted her, and she remained alone in the tea-room.

The overture to *Don Giovanni* was first performed by the piano, violins and violoncello.

It was respectably played, and the audience, not being tired, applauded kindly.

The approbation was not sufficiently continued to demand an encore, however, and "The Curfew" followed, which brought Sabina to the front of the foot-lights.

When she came forward in her simple white dress, her dark clusters of rich hair falling over her shoulders in ringlets, her extreme youth, and the flush on her cheeks, produced by her appearing in the presence of so large an assembly, so impressed the townsfolk of Deepindale that they wondered why they had never before found out Sabina's excessive beauty.

When the three voices began,

> " Hark the curfew's solemn sound,
> Silent darkness spreads around,"

her voice was measured and tremulous; for, several rows back, seated on one of the forms, leaning on that well-remembered stick, was that old bald head, whose dimmed eyes were now fixed on his niece, with a yearning love and anxiety that pierced her very heart.

"How very naughty and imprudent in uncle to come here,—he will be ill,—I must do my best to please him."

These hurried disjointed thoughts passed through Sabina's mind before she arrived at "Solemn Darkness."

By the time that the treble voice rises to and holds the high notes in

> " Heavy it smites on the lover's heart,
> Who leaves with a sigh his tale half told,"

the beauty of the half notes, and Sabina's consciousness of the power and wealth of her voice steadied it, and she gave the passage with a richness and correctness, which affected the company though they knew not wherefore. The beautiful allegro movement, "O'er the Dewy Green," excited the audience, even the least musical, with pleasurable sensations, and the encore was universal.

Sabina withdrew to the tea-room and to solitude, whilst a duet between the flute and piano was executed successfully.

Then followed a fantasia on the piano, which was to be succeeded by "The Soldier Tired."

Sabina had given to this bravura all her care and attention, having heard that it was considered to be the touch-stone of vocal excellence, and that all young vocalists were expected to prove their ability or inability by this test.

The pianist looked round at her to see if she were nervous, but Sabina's hands did not tremble as she placed the open book on the piano for his benefit,—not for her own, for her memory, as well as her voice, was perfect.

As he preluded, she looked at her uncle to judge if he were anxious; another head in the glory of youth and beauty was beside that of Mr. Rock. Mr. Tresillian had come in during the last performance, and the occupier of the seat next to him, seeing the member for the borough looking for a place, had risen politely, and given up his own.

The pleasure of seeing him made Sabina's cheeks flush, and her eyes sparkle into added beauty. She felt triumphant; she knew she should sing well, and poured out such rich and spirit-stirring tones that the audience held their breath to hear, their attention being, it must be confessed, heightened by the evident approbation felt by the Tregear party, headed by Lady Sarah. When her ladyship listened so attentively, and gently beat time with the sticks of her fan on the whitest of kid gloves, the music *must* merit the attention of the townsfolk of Deepindale.

The song ceased, and there was a rapturous call for its repetition. The stick had begun to join in the applause; but struck with a sudden consciousness that the chantress was too nearly allied to him to allow of any expression of opinion without breach of etiquette, Mr. Rock restrained his impatient energies. There was a little pause, and Sabina stooped her pretty head, and whispered something to the performer on the piano, who bowed in reply, and preluding on another key, played the symphony of one of Dibdin's old sea-songs. Sabina felt her power, and determined her auditors should feel the beauty of some of her uncle's favourite melodies.

We give the words, which will sound strange to the ears of the present generation, so wholly are they forgotten, and so completely out of date :—

> " When 'tis night and the mid-watch is come,
>   And chilly mists hang o'er the darkened main,
>   Then sailors think of their far distant home,
>   And of the friends they ne'er may see again.
>   But when the fight's begun,
>   Each serving at his gun,
>   Should any thought of home come o'er their mind,
>   Think only should the day be won,
>   How 'twould cheer
>   Their hearts to hear
>   That their old companion he was one.

> " Or, my lad, if you a mistress kind
> Have left on shore, some pretty girl and true,
> Who many a night doth listen to the wind,
> And sighs to think how it may fare with you ;
> But when the fight's begun,
> Each serving at his gun,
> Should any thought of her come o'er your mind,
> Think only should the day be won,
> How 'twould cheer
> Her heart to hear
> That her own true sailor he was one."

Sabina sang the first four lines quietly, as if relating facts ; but when the movement quickened into,—

> " But when the fight's begun,
> Each serving at his gun,"

her countenance and her enunciation spoke the liveliest enthusiasm.

At the line,—

> " How 'twould cheer,"

her voice rose and held the high note, and giving way to her fancy, she made an *ad libitum* grace, running up the scale and descending in half-notes, till she came to the next line,—

> " Their hearts to hear
> That their own true sailor he had won,"

came with a mixture of triumph and pathos that lived for years after in the memory of her auditors.

In "The Soldier Tired" she had astonished by her brilliancy ; now she touched by her exquisite tenderness. She looked at her uncle, but his head was bowed ; to conceal the tears he was ashamed to call attention to by the use of his handkerchief. At his side the handsome countenance of Mr. Tresillian was beaming with pleasure at her success.

Sabina was very happy.

The concert afterwards flagged in interest till the concluding quartette—"The Redcross Knight," in which Sabina's voice rang out so clearly yet roundly in the high notes, that Mr. Dent, Mr. Grinde, and the pianist, who took the second voice and played the accompaniment, would have felt themselves to have been unheard, had they not each been so self-occupied that nothing but their own voices were present to their ears.

During the execution of this glee, Sabina, free from all anxiety, as the work was so nearly done, had time to look about her. She avoided, shyly, the eyes of Mr. Tresillian, in which the expression was so intense that she dared not encounter it, and looked touchingly on the face of her uncle, who was trying to conceal his triumph and delight under the appearance of well-bred indifference, in which we need scarcely say the open-hearted sailor failed entirely. "The child will have her head turned," he went on repeating to himself, and it seemed not unlikely when at the conclusion of "The Redcross Knight," when the applause had in some degree subsided, Lady Sarah, who was looking younger and handsomer than ever, caught the eye of the young songstress, who had been watching her fair-haired rival of former days, and made a sign to her to come to her. Like the fancied attendants of Malvolio, "twelve men with an obedient start" rushed forward to assist Miss Rock to descend from the platform. At any other time she might have scrambled down as she could ; but now she was favoured by the notice of Lady Sarah, and was the favourite of the evening. During the prformance Lady Sarah had been struck by a brilliant idea. She remembered that crowned heads and great folks often rewarded public performers by some token of their admiration, and of their appreciation of their services in contributing to the amusement of the public, and she thought how grand a stroke of policy it would be, and how graceful an act, were she to sacrifice one of her trinkets in aid of her son's popularity. She looked at her fingers, and saw on one a diamond, which always made her feel melancholy, she said. She had given it in token of girlish friendship, and at the death of the recipient it had been, at that friend's request, returned to her. It was handsome and valuable, but she felt she could part with it with satisfaction in such a cause. When Sabina was led up to her ladyship with great state by Mr. Temple, Mr. Dent and Mr. Grinde following to enjoy the triumph, and perhaps to receive a few personal compliments—at any event, a little notice from the great lady—this majestic beauty made a little speech, which she had arranged in her memory after she had determined on sacrificing her ring to her son's and her own popularity.

"Permit me to offer to your acceptance," said she, "a small token of remembrance of the great gratification your musical talent has this evening afforded me ;" and she placed the ring on the small hand Sabina presented, timidly.

"Oh, my lady, you were always too good to me," replied Sabina, her eyes humid with emotion, expressing all the gratitude which her tongue refused to utter.

The lady was quite satisfied with the giver and with the recipient of the gift, and arose with a stately gesture, drawing the folds of her cashmere shawl around her, whilst Sabina stood by to let her pass. Her son pressed forward to offer his arm to Lady Sarah, and conducted her to the tea-room, from whence he returned immediately, and addressing Sabina, said, " My mother has begged you to accept the use of her carriage to take you home ; she is going to take some tea, and will not require it till it returns." This was uttered in an audible voice ; then, in a low tone, " No wreath ? "

"I dared not," said Sabina, blushing ; "but the carriage— oh, if I might——"

"Might ! of course. Lady Sarah wishes it. It rains, too."

"It is not that," said Sabina, more and more confused ; "but if you would take Mr. Rock ? I don't mind wet in the least—that is —not much," she added, looking down on her dress.

"Hang it !" exclaimed Mr. Tresillian to himself. "I wanted 'sweet Ann Page,' and I have not even 'a lubberly boy,' but an infirm old man thrown into the bargain !" But he only said he should be delighted to place Lady Sarah's carriage at Mr. Rock's disposal, and changed his intention of accompanying Sabina home alone in the carriage, the idea of which had set his heart into tumults, into handing her to the door of it, and then fetching her uncle and de- positing him safely by her side, the old sailor protesting vigorously that he did not desire so unworthily to occupy the vehicle, destined to a fairer freight.

Mr. Tresillian held out his hand to the veteran that he might imprison the soft fingers of Sabina for an instant, who was so disturbed by the pressure of his, that she was scarcely conscious of anything else till the carriage-door was shut, and he was gone.

CHAPTER XV

" Not undelightful is the thoughtful game,
Where martial queens the mimic fray command,
When puzzled ladies blush for very shame,
With furrowed forehead and suspended hand."

H. Maldon, Esq.

MR. ROCK was not insensible of notice from those placed in a higher position than himself: wealth and its possessors, when they are gracious, are so irresistible to those less happily circumstanced. The old sailor sat upright on the spring cushions of Lady Sarah's carriage, with a smile of gratified vanity on his face. One thought was in his breast: " What will that fellow Orellan say to this ? "

" That fellow ! " Yes ; I must confess that the course of true friendship, like that of love, is sometimes ruffled in its progress. Since Sabina had lived with her uncle, Mr. Orellan had been inspired with a frightful jealousy of Mr. Rock's attachment to his niece. " Rock has no one to care for but myself," he used to say on every occasion. " Rock can do nothing without my advice." And when it was suggested that he might live more cheaply in another locality, he had given it as a reason for remaining where he was, that " Rock could not live without him." So long as Mr. Rock found Sabina an intolerable nuisance, and expressed the same in no measured language to his friend, Lieutenant Orellan rather inclined to defend the neglected and contemned orphan ; but so soon as he saw what he designated as " Rock's infatuation about that girl," he became her bitter enemy, and was ever enumerating old offences and ostending new ones, which irritated alike both uncle and niece.

It seemed strange that a man of sixty-five should be jealous of a child, but such was the fact.   His intimacy with Mr. Rock gave him a privilege to be unpleasant; or, as he himself termed it, "friendly in his observations."

"I saw that girl of yours in High Street to-day.   Would you believe it?   There were holes in her gloves, at the tip of each finger!"

"When Sabina called with your message at my house to-day her hat had lost a string, and her hair was blowing about her face in a most untidy way."

The uncle, who was growing very fond of Sabina, could not help boasting of her chess-playing powers.

"Can she beat *you?*"

"No."

Mr. Rock's truth compelled the negative.   Sabina had been too wise to allow herself the luxury of winning a game from her uncle.

Mr. Orellan allowed a slight sneer to curl his long upper lip.   Mr. Rock felt nettled.

"I don't mean to say she will beat *you;* but she plays better than you think."

"We will try, then."

And in the evening, when the game was concluded between the old sailors, by the triumph of Lieutenant Orellan, the victor had challenged Sabina, somewhat mockingly:

"Well, Miss Rock, if you know the moves, I should like to play with you."

Sabina hated him, and did not want to play.   She was afraid of being beaten.

"Perhaps you cannot play?"

"I never pretended to be able to play well."

But, like an unfortunate hunted animal brought to bay, she made a virtue of necessity, and sat down, with a heart so palpitating that she removed her side from the small table, lest the pulsations should become audible to her antagonist.   Nothing, however, could conceal the trepidation evinced by her hand when she was compelled to move her king's pawn in answer to his first move, which he threw for and won.

"Frightened out of her wits, of course!—knows she can't play!   Rock is quite a fool about her!"

Sabina not having had the advantage of the move was

obliged to act on the defensive, a kind of play which did not suit the dashing style which she preferred. She must be careful and watch her opportunity. Mr. Orellan held his childish antagonist in contempt. He ran down his queen to attack her castled king, and so supported her by bishop's knight, that Sabina was within two moves of checkmate.

" A miss is as good as a mile," she said to herself. And advancing her king's rook's pawn, supported by his knight's pawn, she avoided the danger, and so hemmed in her adversary's queen that she could not escape. When she fell a victim to her ignoble assailant, Mr. Orellan could hardly repress a groan. Mr. Rock arose to look over the board.

" For Heaven's sake, Rock, don't watch the game; I hate that."

Mr. Rock gave a soft whistle of "The Saucy Arethusa," and sat down very gently; in doing this, however, he accidentally kicked the fender, and down with a crash came all the fireirons, on which Lieutenant Orellan started up and declared that to play was impossible in such an infernal row, and thereupon he upset the chess-board.

Sabina smiled, a little wicked smile, and picked up the scattered men, replacing them on the board with a tenacity of memory that was quite distracting to the lieutenant.

" It is late; I shall not finish the game," he exclaimed, hurriedly. "Good-night, Rock; good-night, Miss."

" Stop for your whisky-and-water, my good fellow," said his old friend.

" No—no; 'tis too late."

And he was gone.

Now the want of sympathy evinced by Stephen Orellan with Michael Rock's love for his niece had weakened the friendship between them. Nothing could ever re-establish it, but the confession from the latter that his niece was utterly worthless; and, even had he believed the truth of this, he never was likely to confess it. It was this feeling of growing irritation which made him, as the carriage-door closed on him, think, " I wonder what *that fellow*, Orellan, would say to this?"

I have watched two dogs living together on sufficiently friendly terms of intimacy. When one has been caressed by his master's hand, whilst bridling his head, and striking the floor with his tail in token of his pride and joy, he has

turned his eye stealthily to where his friend and rival sat
afar off, to observe if he were conscious of the honour his
companion was receiving.

Mr. Rock's pleasure was enhanced by the idea that
Stephen Orellan would now see that if he, Michael Rock,
were infatuated about Sabina, she had exercised her en-
chantment on others also.

He wondered if he had been present. It did not matter;
if he had kept away from his dislike "to hear that girl
squalling," as he had stated to be his intention, Mr. Rock
would have the pleasure of pouring all the details into his
unwilling ears to-morrow evening.

Sabina, whose fingers had now ceased to tingle from the
pressure of Mr. Tresillian's hand, looked at the open
window next to her uncle, and pulled up the glass. In
doing this the light glanced on the diamond on her finger,
and her delighted relative saw it for the first time.

"Where did it come from? How did you get it? Who
gave it to you?" were the exclamations precipitated one
over the other by Mr. Rock, who had watched the interview from a distance between his niece and Lady Sarah,
and, mindful of the richly-freighted needle-book of former
days, divined the generous donor of the diamond ring. He
did not feel wounded by her receiving a gift from one who
was considered as a queen of Deepindale.

How pleased he was! How he pretended not to hear
what Sabina said, that he might have the delight of having
every word of Lady Sarah's little speech repeated till he had
learnt it by heart, for his own pleasure, and for Orellan's
pain.

"That fellow shall do her justice," he determined.

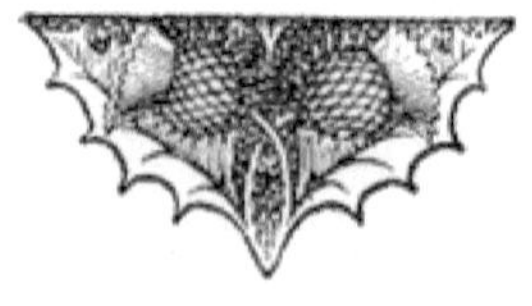

CHAPTER XVI.

"THERE goes the carriage back to Tregear," said Mrs. Cressy, raising herself on her arm in bed, addressing the observation to her sleepy husband.

"Very likely," he murmured.

She laid down her head, but the sound of the carriage pursued her as it passed through the silent town. Folks walked to and from their gaieties in Deepindale, and the carriage from Tregear was the only one in motion.

Presently it stopped. What could that mean? Mrs. Cressy untied her night-cap, and turned back one flap of it, giving herself the look of a half lop-eared rabbit.

It had certainly stopped. There! the door was opened, now shut again; surely it wasn't coming back?

Mrs. Cressy jumped out of the bed, which seemed to spring up when released from her twelve-stone weight, and showed a broad circumference of shoulder and back, arrayed in a short jacket tied round her waist over her under garment worn by day. Mr. Cressy was rheumatic, and when Mrs. Cressy threw up the window, he exclaimed, "My dear!!!" What was rheumatism against curiosity? Mrs. Cressy leaned out till she endangered her falling, in order to satisfy herself that it was really the Tregear carriage which had stopped at Mr. Rock's door; so she pretended not to hear the remonstrance of her quieter half.

At length the return of the carriage, with the drab and scarlet livery, left no doubt on the mind of the indignant cabbage-seller, and she pulled down the sash with a bang, and got into bed again.

"Do lie still, Mrs. C., you bring in such a draught of cold air with your banging about so, window-opening and all, such a sharp night."

"Sharp be blowed!" said the angry woman, turning round indignantly. "You've got no feeling for your own flesh and blood."

"But I have for my bones and muscles, Mrs. Cressy," was the retort; and Mrs. Cressy, finding herself getting the worst of it, pretended to go to sleep.

'Melia was well enough to get up if she had liked it, but she preferred taking her breakfast in bed; and her mother was standing by its side, with a cup of tea and a plate of hot buttered toast in her hand, when the trampling of a horse was heard; and looking over the blind, the green-groceress perceived Mr. Dent, who reined up his steed just at Mr. Cressy's private door.

"He never will have the face to call after the letter I wrote him," said Mrs. Cressy.

"Lor, ma!" said 'Melia, "let him come up; we shan't hear nothing about nobody if he don't come to tell us. 'Tis wuth the five shilluns he charge to hear the news, and pa no need to scringe."

"You've no dignity, 'Melia. You're too kind-hearted." And Mr. Dent, receiving no rebuff from the servant girl, came up into 'Melia's bed-room.

Now Mrs. Cressy would have been glad to have received Mr. Dent in a dignified manner, seated with her hands before her, and to have got up and dropped a stiff courtesy, but the doctor had her at a disadvantage, standing with 'Melia's breakfast in her hands. It obviated the necessity however of shaking hands with him, an omission for which he cared little, as he walked to the bedside and encircled 'Melia's coarse wrist with his fingers.

"Quite nicely this morning, Miss Cressy, I perceive."

"I presume, Mr. Dent, you didn't git my note to you last night, or you was too busy to 'tend to it," said Mrs. Cressy.

"Never too busy to attend to any commands of yours, Mum, and I called just to see if I could not set matters straight between us. You see I'm just back from Tregear, sent for, post haste, this morning, by Lady Sarah—could not do without my services."

"Dear me! what was wrong? Not Lady Sarah, I thought? Good gracious! Surely she's a widdee?"

"Widows, dear Madam, sometimes require medical attendance; but it was not her ladyship, though the summons came in her name—one of the ladies of the household."

"Oh!" said both mother and daughter, much impressed. "What was it?"

"Excuse me, ladies; professional delicacy forbids disclosing medical secrets."

The fact having been that the kitchen-maid had upset a kettle of boiling water over her foot, and as Mr. Dent always attended her mother, a Deepindale woman, the kitchen-maid had sent for him on her own account; and the messenger, to quicken the movements of the surgeon, had used Lady Sarah's name.

"Well, lor! do tell about the concert," said 'Melia; "I'm a-busting to know."

"You were much missed, my dear young lady, and I cannot but say that Miss Rock's performances were very inferior in grace and delicacy to what we might have expected from your gifts. Still the pieces went off smoothly. I don't wish to say anything of my own share in them, but,"— with a simper,—"I think they were noticed by the people from Tregear. Indeed, Lady Sarah expressed her admiration very decidedly, in a pretty compliment to the vocal performers."

"*In*-deed!" said Mrs. Cressy.

Mr. Dent saw the storm rising, and hastened to pour oil on the waters.

"So much so, and so successful was the whole performance in this respect" (slapping his pockets), "and the proceeds are so great, that there are thoughts of having a repetition of the concert when Miss 'Melia shall be sufficiently recovered to take her proper place amongst us."

Both mother and daughter coloured crimson with pleasure at the idea, which had only entered Mr. Dent's head an instant before he spoke it.

"But what was that about the Tregear carriage? What did that mean, its stopping at Mr. Rock's door?" said Mrs. Cressy.

"Oh, Mr. Rock is a very infirm old gentleman, you know, and Lady Sarah is very kind-hearted, so I dare say she sent him home first, as she took a dish of tea at the hotel before she went back."

"Well! I never heard anything like *that*," said the mother, black with envy. "An old man, who hasn't more than ninety pounds a year, to be called a gentleman—hardly enough to keep himself alive; and here's my William, why, he've more money in the funds than you'd think for, and fine houses and cottages, that bring him in—let's see—two hundred and twenty-five pounds a year, and a nice little farm for the wegitables, and he not to be thought such a gentleman as *that !*"

"Really, Mem," said Mr. Dent, "you must distinguish, Mem; there are different grades in society, Mem. First, there is the Church, and then the Navy and Army ; and you see, Mr. Rock is a gentleman by profession, and has as much right to go to court as any lord in the land ; and Miss Rock is the daughter of an officer, and though they're poor, yet she is a lady."

"Never tell me about your ladies and gentlemen as hasn't got a coat to their backs," said the irate greengroceress ; "and them sailors and soldiers, with their uniforms, aint no better than livery servants—that's what I call 'um."

"Never mind 'um, ma, they don't hurt me ; and, Mr. Dent, if you should hear any more about the concert, my voice is come out better than ever, now the rash is gone in."

" I won't fail to let you know when anything is determined on, Miss 'Melia ; and I will say, for a sweet-tempered young lady, I don't know your equal, and so says Grinde to me only yesterday morning."

This last observation softened away any bitterness which might have remained in the breasts of either of the female Cressys, and Mr. Dent took his leave triumphantly, having re-established his footing in the family, to whom he had purposely been silent as to the episode of the diamond ring.

"Let's hope they won't hear of it," said he.

CHAPTER XVII.

> " As she leans—the soft smile, half shut up in her eyes,
>   Beams the sleepy, long, silk soft lashes beneath ;
>   Through her crimson lips, stirred by her faint replies,
>   Breaks one gleam of her pearl-white teeth."
>
> OWEN MEREDITH.

 DIFFERENT scene was passing in the dressing-room of Lady Sarah, at Tregear. She sat before the glass, whilst her maid let down the rich braids of her still abundant and glossy light hair, and enjoyed the repeated passes made by the brush over its smooth surface.

"I wonder, Stephens," said her ladyship to her maid, "whether horses like to be currycombed. I have fancied sometimes it would be very nice, if I were a horse."

" Well really, Mum, I can't say; but the poor beasts kick and snort about for nothing if they do like it; and then them grooms do pull their manes so, it makes my head ache to see it. Nasty rough brutes !"

Here there was a knock at the door, and a message from Mr. Tresillian, brought by his valet, to say that if Lady Sarah were awake he should be glad to be admitted.

" You may go, and leave the hair till by-and-bye, Stephens," and the lady's maid slipped out of the room, gladly, to over-take the valet on the staircase.

" You look quite blooming, my lady mother, this morning. I came to thank you for the sacrifice you made for my popu-larity last night. Never was a son blessed by a mother so thoughtful of his interests as I."

" Ah ! my dear Wilfred, I confess it did give me a pang to part with that last remembrance of my poor dear Adelaide ; but what would I not do for my boy ?" and she shed two graceful tears, without reddening her eyelids or the tip of her nose. Now Lady Sarah did not mean to deceive her son ; she was simply self deceived.

"I do not mean that you should be a loser as to jewelry, though, of course, as far as sentiment goes, I am helpless to supply your loss. I have written to Rundall and Bridge for the emerald ring you admired so much. I hope it will be down by the end of the week, unless the thieves know of its coming, and rob the mail."

"Dear Wilfred ! how *very* shocking ! How can you anticipate so dreadful a loss ! It was very generous in you to think of my little longing for that emerald."

"On *fair* fingers, such as yours, no colour is so becoming," observed the gallant son. "But how did you like the concert ? "

"Oh ! that girl's singing surpasses anything I ever heard, for beauty of tone and finished execution. I doat on music, and her voice, it is a treat to hear. The rest of the performance of course was painfully stupid. How much longer must we stay here, my dear Wilfred? Really, the evenings are dreary to a degree, though you do sacrifice to me at the eternal game of piquet. I think we must hire that girl to sing to us."

"The very thing ! what a brilliant idea, my dear lady ! Now I never should have thought of it ; but as to the question of hiring, the diamond ring will give you a claim on her services so long as I keep you in this dull neighbourhood."

"How then can it be done ? " inquired the lady, languidly. "She is very beautiful," she continued in a meditative tone.

"Oh ! as to beauty," continued her son, "I can see no loveliness in dark hair, when there is such opulence of light tresses before me,"—taking up the rich folds of hair in his hand. "I feel quite proud of my mother's charms."

"But as to this girl, Miss Rock. Catch this singing-bird for me, Wilfred. We will keep her so long as we stay here, and let her go when we return to town."

"You will have to write a note to her or to Mr. Rock, and I will be the bearer of it," said Mr. Tresillian ; and thus it was decided.

When Sabina awoke on the morning after the concert, she saw first the brilliant colours of the hothouse flowers, and all the scene and circumstances of her past triumph rushed upon her mind. Then she remembered the diamond ring, which she had locked up in a little wooden box, much scratched and faded, along with the Lisbon chains and golden cross; but what she thought of most was the pressure of Mr. Tresillian's hand on hers as he had said good-night. She blushed, and thrilled at the recollection.

She dressed herself with more than usual care. Poor little girl, her preparations were of necessity so simple. But she could put on her clean pink gingham dress, and a white collar. She hardly admitted to herself her expectation that Mr. Tresillian might call on her uncle that day; but if he should, he would find her prepared for his reception. She brushed her dark curls carefully, and twisted them round her finger, and went down to make her uncle's breakfast, at eight o'clock. Nothing could be more poverty-stricken than all the circumstances by which she was surrounded; yet her youth and beauty seemed to shed a glory round the room. There was the old sailor, scrupulously clean, and untainted in hair or clothes, by the loathsome smell of stale tobacco, which he held in utter abomination, and feeling a conviction that no smoker could ever be a gentleman. There was the pennyworth of milk for the dilution of the weak tea, for which no sugar was allowed, and the dry toast for Mr. Rock, whilst Sabina ate dry bread,—butter, being two shillings per pound, was beyond their means, and Susan declaring "'Twas quite enough to toast for master, without toasting for Miss. On Mrs. Cleverly's small piano there was abundance of manuscript music. Sabina borrowed the printed music from Mr. Temple, and copied long, intricate pieces, which that spirited organist ordered and did not trouble himself to pay for. The copies were crowded into the smallest possible space, to save the sheets of penny music-paper. The stuff window-curtains, originally green, had faded into a dull yellow; the bureau at which Mr. Rock wrote his letters and small accounts was stained with ink, though bearing the highest polish, the result of Susan's attention; his old arm-chair had sunk into a miserable hollow in its seat, and the faded leather had worn into holes; the others were of the commonest stained wood; the carpet, never of a rich or lasting material, had been darned and redarned till the original pattern was a mystery, so many penny balls of worsted had been used by Susan, and paid for by her out of her four pounds a-year wages.

On this morning, Sabina had purchased an egg for her uncle, and on his reproaching her with her extravagance, she gaily declared that she would sell her diamond ring to pay for it, if he said much more on the subject.

It was a very happy breakfast. Mr. Rock enjoyed his egg, and the remembrance of the last night's success. His delight was unbounded when, in the middle of the day, Lieutenant Orellan called, and asked his old messmate to take a turn on the quarter-deck, as they called the smoothest part of the parade ;—Mr. Orellan full of curiosity to learn some particulars of the previous evening, Mr. Rock all eagerness to pour out praises of his grand-niece.

Some time after, there was a ring at the door. Sabina's heart beat fast ; she felt sure it must be Mr. Tresillian, because he was the person she most wished to see.

How long Susan was in answering the door ! Sabina heard her go to the drawer of the kitchen table, and knew she was going to put on a clean apron. On looking at her hands Susan decided that they were *grimey*, and went to the wash-house to clean them. In the meantime Mr. Tresillian rang again impatiently, and interrupted Susan just as she was half way up to her bed-room in search of the bonnet-box which held her new cap. "Drat the man ; he'll pull the bell down next," and abandoning the idea of the new cap, she descended and opened the door in her dirty one.

Sabina breathlessly heard her say at once, " Mr. Rock is not at home, Sir."

"Oh, Susan ! I could strangle you for that," said Sabina, but a well-known voice replied,

" *Miss* Rock is at home, and I wish to see *her* I have a note from Lady Sarah to deliver to her."

"Walk in, Sir," and Mr. Tresillian found himself in Sabina's presence. He looked very handsome — flushed with exercise—for he had ridden from Tregear very fast, and had put up his horse at the hotel, knowing that Mr. Rock had no one to hold it, and had then watched the walk of the two veterans, and waited till their backs were turned before he rang the bell—the second ring, and the impatient one, arose from the dread he felt lest they should see him on their turning. Luckily for him, they were too deep in conversation to look up, and Mr. Tresillian entered the house unnoticed.

"How beautiful she is!" was his thought, as Sabina stood flushing and palpitating before him.

"How handsome he is without his hat," was Sabina's, as he pushed the light curls from his forehead; those matchless rings of hair, which were so much like floss silk in everything but their superior elasticity; these curled wilfully about the head of this young Adonis.

> "His amber-coloured locks in ringlets run
> With graceful negligence and shine against the sun."
>
> DRYDEN.

"You charmed our ears and stole our hearts by your singing last night. My mother pines to hear you again."

"Lady Sarah is very kind. She pained me by the magnicence of her gift. There is so little I can do, I feel I shall never repay her."

Somehow, both young people felt awkward. Sabina missed the pressure of Mr. Tresillian's fingers. He had not offered his hand on coming in.

"My mother has sent you a note. May I sit down? You have not offered me a chair."

"Pray be seated."

"Well—whilst you read your note."

"Pray, are you looking at the various holes in the leather of my uncle's chair?"

"No," said Mr. Tresillian, looking up wickedly. "I was only thinking of the last time I sat there."

"Yes?" said Sabina, looking uncomfortable.

"Shall I remind you?" said Wilfred.

"No, pray do not," returned the girl, with her face in a flame. "I was a shameless, ill-conducted little wretch, and deserved to be kept on bread and water."

Sabina might have added that such was not an unusual diet for her, though she did not partake of it as a punishment.

"I often wish to recall past moments," said the gentleman.

"Spent with naughty children?" rejoined Sabina.

"Yes; but now, instead of your kneeling at my feet and embracing my knees, I should prefer reversing the positions.

Just read that note, and I will kneel to entreat a favourable answer."

Sabina read, and her face lighted up more brilliantly from pleasure.

Suddenly it clouded. "What is it?" said Mr. Tresillian, answering the look.

"Oh! I should like to go so much, but I don't think I can. You see uncle——"

"Will not Mr. Rock permit you to accept my mother's invitation?"

"Oh, yes! I am not thinking of his permission, but of his loneliness. You see, I am always here to make his breakfast."

"Folks never feel that which they have always, to be a pleasure."

"Probably not; yet they miss it when it is gone."

"Depend upon it, Miss Rock, if you leave your uncle, he will feel like Doctor Johnson's widower, 'afflicted, but relieved.' Remember that you hate his black, beady eyes, and the ugly hairs on the back of his hands."

"I don't hate him at all, now. I think you are very unkind, Mr. Tresillian, to remind me of it."

"How can you wonder at this, Miss Rock? Remember that you entreated me to take you away to live with me; and now, at the end of five years, having duly deliberated over the request, I assent to it, and you, like a capricious young lady, tell me that you cannot fulfil your part of the proposition."

"Very true, Mr. Tresillian; but you see I also have had five years to deliberate, and I have thought better of it. I still want five years of the period of discretion, but I have enough to make me decline."

"Do you not like my mother?"

"Of course I do. She is very beautiful, and very gracious, and high bred; besides being most kind in her manner to me."

"Then I am driven on the horns of a dilemma; either you dislike me, or you like me too much to trust yourself in the same house with me."

"You should not say such things to me, Mr. Tresillian." Sabina thought about "breaking a butterfly upon the wheel," but could not quite remember the quotation.

"You are always right," he said, changing his bantering manner to one at once tender and respectful.

"But do turn it over in your mind ; see if you can give pleasure to Lady Sarah without too much sacrifice of Mr. Rock's comfort. And here he is to answer for himself," he continued, as he heard the preparatory scrapings which announced the advent of the old sailor, who was as anxious to free his shoes from any stray bit of gravel in dry weather, as from mud during the wet days.

Sabina was glad that Mr. Orellan did not accompany her uncle into the house. The room was too small for four persons. The old man came forward to greet his visitor with naval frankness, not unmixed with dignity. He knew that he was a gentleman, though but a half-pay lieutenant, and as Mr. Dent had observed, with as good a right to go to Court as his wealthy acquaintance, the member for Deepindale.

Mr. Tresillian stated why he had done himself the honour of calling on Mr. Rock. Lady Sarah had sent by him a note requesting Miss Rock to favour her for a few days with her company at Tregear. Miss Rock, however, had seemed indisposed to comply with this request, fearing she might deprive Mr. Rock of the comfort of her presence.

"A conceited little minx !" said Mr. Rock, divided between his delight at the honour of the invitation, and his loss of dignity by the supposition that he was dependent on Miss Rock for the comfort of his life. "I contrived to exist for sixty years before I saw that little chitty face of hers. It would be strange, if I could not spend a few days without seeing it. Allow me, then, to decide for my greatniece by accepting very gratefully her ladyship's kind offer."

"In that case," said Mr. Tresillian, "my mother will send her carriage to fetch Miss Rock at any time you may think most convenient this afternoon."

"Oh ! not to-day—not till to-morrow," said Sabina, with dismal forebodings as to her wardrobe.

"Very well," replied the young gentleman, with a shrewd suspicion of the truth ; "to-morrow at three o'clock let it be ;" and not having any great desire to get into a political discussion with his constituent, Mr. Tresillian shook hands with Mr. Rock, and left the house, making only a sweeping bow to Sabina.

CHAPTER XVIII.

MR. ROCK was sorry Mr. Tresillian went so soon. He wanted to ask him a favour, not for himself, but for Lieutenant Orellan. That gentleman had listened with exemplary patience to all the praises lavished by her uncle on Sabina, on the account of her successes on the previous night; and had, in fact, been such a convert to the extent of her perfections, that Mr. Rock had been in the best of tempers, and being wrought up to this point, the crafty lieutenant preferred his petition that Mr. Rock would mention to Mr. Tresillian, or Miss Rock to Lady Sarah, his great desire to obtain a command in the Coastguard. His friend Rock knew what his services had been. His certificates were all forthcoming. Would he not say a word for his old friend?

Mr. Rock said he would do so on the first opportunity, not expecting that talking of his Satanic majesty would evoke his presence so immediately.

Had Mr. Tresillian remained a little longer Mr. Rock would have preferred his petition to the member, or would have tried to discover if he had any interest in the Admiralty; but, when Mr. Tresillian had departed, the old man felt the difficulty greater than he had anticipated, of asking a favour even for a worthy object. He had never asked a favour for himself. In this dilemma he thought of Lady Sarah, and whether Sabina, poor child, could be made to understand the subject sufficiently to explain what was required to that lady.

"Of what are you thinking, uncle?"

"I wish Mr. Tresillian had not been in such a hurry, my dear."

"I wasn't sorry that he went," said Sabina, whose thoughts wandered to Mr. Milford's shop, and to the materials for another evening dress. "All that's bright must fade," thought the girl, and that seems particularly applicable to the purity of white muslin dresses.

"Did you want him to stay for anything in particular?" continued Sabina.

"Why, yes, my dear. Orellan has been speaking to me about—asking me, in fact, to see if Mr. Tresillian has any interest which he might make available for Orellan's benefit at the Admiralty. Orellan wants a command on the Coast-guard station."

"There is no coast here, nothing but a river, and a very small one too."

"You goose, 'tis not here that he wants it. He would leave Deepindale."

"Go away from Deepindale! Why, uncle! who would play chess with you in the evenings?"

Mr. Rock was rather taken aback by this view of the case. He had not thought how dreary would be those hours in the future which had, for years, been spent with his old companion. He cleared his throat. "I should be a selfish old brute not to help Orellan to a good turn, because by so doing I should lose his society."

"Disagreeable old man! I hate him!" said Sabina.

"My dear!" exclaimed Mr. Rock, much disturbed by his niece's vehemence, when he wished her to do the lieutenant a good turn, "I assure you though he may have been unpleasant in his observations on you formerly, he has a great regard for you, and a high opinion of your musical talents."

Sabina laughed a little scornful laugh. "How long has that opinion existed, uncle? Ever since he hoped to please you, and obtain through your influence a Coast-guard appointment," she continued. "But don't be vexed, dear old man!" kissing his bald head. "Do you wish me to ask Mr. Tresillian the question you failed to ask him yourself?"

This was coming to the root of the matter at once.

Mr. Rock did wish it—and did not.   He wanted the question to be asked, but asked of Lady Sarah.

"Yes, I might ask her ladyship," said Sabina slowly, "but I fear she would not understand much about it—it would be really asking Mr. Tresillian."

"Then perhaps you had better leave it alone," said her uncle.

Mr. Rock did not like to ask the member to call on him; he thought of hiring a carriage to go to Tregear, but then, the expense! Sabina saw his trouble, and determined to take her own way in the business, so she said no more. She had enough to occupy her in the preparation of another muslin dress, with pale pink satin ribbons this time: and Susan had some of the gingham frocks washed. Those washing dresses are so delightfully clean. Every article of her habiliments, excepting her shoes, admitted of incessant ablutions, and needed them, for she was always having some misfortune with her clothes, arising from excessive carelessness.

When Mr. Orellan came that evening he heard of the projected visit to Tregear, and tried to manufacture some awkward compliments for Sabina's edification, which that young lady could not listen to without impatience. Luckily, he did not know that Mr. Tresillian had called that morning on Mr. Rock, yet he looked wistfully at his old friend, as if he would have said, "Rock! have you turned over in your own mind the best way of attacking the great man?" Now, Rock was troubled by his own thoughts on the subject —as much troubled as was his old messmate; so both men played so indifferently that Sabina exploded in a peal of laughter, as she looked over the game, on which both players rose angrily, and reproached her for her bad manners, though they mentally admitted that they neither had played with their usual skill.

"An infernal little chit!" was the thought of Mr. Orellan. "But I must hold my tongue, as she is a favourite at Tregear."

They could not settle themselves to the game after Sabina's ill-bred laughter; and both were glad to push aside the board for the whisky and gruel which concluded the evening. Each, as they stirred their beverage, was silent, intent on the Coastguard service; whilst Sabina's pulse quivered and danced at the thought of seeing Mr. Tresillian again on the following day.

"Oh, Susan! what can I do for a box?" said that young lady, breaking into Susan's room when that sleepy old woman had just deposited her cap on her looking-glass—a glass which was the best in the house. Susan had possessed beauty in her youth, and could not forget the lost treasure. Even at fifty-two she used to stretch her large white arms before that little glass, and rejoice in their round whiteness, interspersed with delicate blue veins. It is true that the whiteness existed only from the elbow to the shoulder; for in those forgotten days a servant in long sleeves could not have been found in the United Kingdom. "About a box to hold my clothes to take to Tregear?"

"There's your uncle's great chest, and the old portmanteau, Miss, and——" And she looked at her own deal box, containing all her worldly goods. "I could empty 'em on to the floor, and put a cloth over them."

"Thank you, Susan," said Sabina, in a depressed tone; "I fear it would not do. There will be the muslin dresses, you know."

"There's your uncle's sea-chest——"

Sabina knew it well. It might have contained herself. It was covered with old leather, from which the hair had been rubbed off in patches, and bound with iron, now eaten out with rust. Sabina thought of the footman's efforts to lift it on the carriage, and of the impossibility of its being placed there. Her father's old portmanteau was in pieces. She gave it up in despair. She must go out in the morning, and buy something. How she blessed Lady Sarah for that memorable twenty pounds, which bridged over her difficulties so pleasantly!

When the midday had passed, the carriage drove up, and Sabina, kissing her uncle tenderly, who had come to the door to see her off, proud and pleased at the honour done his niece, sprang into it, and was whirled away amidst the wonder and envy of the inhabitants of Deepindale, and the rage of the grown-up young ladies at Miss Wise's establishment, who had not thought Sabina of sufficient rank to be entitled to play with them in their childhood.

"When will you come back?" her uncle had said to his niece.

"Whenever you like, uncle."

"They said a few days. You had better stay so long as they ask you. Perhaps you might find out when Mr. Tresillian is likely to come into the town."

"I will let you know, my uncle."

When the carriage drove up to the portico of the great house, one of the liveried servants informed Sabina that my lady was walking in the grounds; would Miss Rock wait in the drawing-room, or follow Lady Sarah? Sabina preferred the latter; and after asking the way, and hearing that her ladyship had walked in the direction of the lake, which was seen glimmering through the trees in the glory of the autumn sun, the girl went off gaily over the soft turf to look for her.

She soon found, however, that she was deceived as to the facility with which she had hoped to find her. The lake was large and irregular, and when Sabina thought she had come to its confines, and might go round it, it branched off again into a large space, fringed with rushes and flags. Worse than this, she had got on low ground, and could not see the house. She was lost amongst the bulrushes. She looked anxiously for her feet, which were buried in the tall, rank grass. "Oh, my new boots! if they get wet!" said Sabina. And fancy painted the new treasures soaked with moisture, and placed so close to the laundry fire as to be "shrivelled like a parched scroll."

"I am like the little fairy who was lost in an asparagus-bed," thought the girl. "I wish I were safely out of this. But the water comes so unexpectedly wherever I put my feet. I wonder whether anyone will think of my being lost in the park!—whether Lady Sarah or Mr. Tresillian will inquire if I have arrived, and send out after me? I'll scream for help!" And she screamed, "Help! Help!" But her voice sounded so like the cry of one of the water-fowl, that she would have laughed had she not been more disposed to cry. Presently, she heard the discharge of a gun, and one bird fell near her, in the midst of the covey, which whirred away over her head. She stooped, and picked up the partridge, thankful that it had ceased to struggle.

"In, Dash!" cried Mr. Tresillian to his retriever; and the dog bounded to the spot where Sabina stood, and snuffed about the ground where the bird had fallen. Curious to see why he did not return, Mr. Tresillian strode over the flags, and came down to the spot where Sabina stood, with the bird in her hand, looking rather foolish.

" Upon my word, Miss Rock ! " said he, " I did not kill my bird that you might poach it.   I have lost one before. Do you particularly desire to have a brace for your especial eating ?—perhaps to be served up with asparagus.   I really suspect you have the companion bird in your pocket."

" How can you, Mr. Tresillian ? Oh, dear ! I am like Christian in the Slough of Despond : I cannot move without sinking into this horrid soft turf, which is not turf, but water covered with weeds."

" Remain where you are," said Mr. Tresillian.   " It does not matter whether my shooting-boots are wet, or not." And he strode over to her, and lifted her in his arms like a child. " The second time, I think," said he, " that I have had to do you this good turn," looking up confidently in her face, which was necessarily so near his own.   " The last time, however, you seemed more grateful than you appear disposed to be at present."

" Oh ! " said Sabina, blushing at the recollection how, on a former occasion, she had clung round his neck, and kissed him—" it was so dark then, and I was so frightened."

" Then if it were dark, and you were frightened now, the same amount of gratitude might be exhibited in the same manner," said Mr. Tresillian.

" It is not quite kind," said the girl, with a little tremor in her voice, " to talk to me like that.   You know I was a naughty little girl then.   Cannot you put me down now ? "

" Certainly, if I put you into the soft mud."

She said no more, though she thought he picked out the worst part of the surface instead of the firmest.   In truth, he was strong, and the slight weight of the girl did not incommode him, and he enjoyed the sensation of holding her in his arms.   At length he set her down on *terra firma*, and without taking the kiss from those ripe, red lips which were so near his own.   The gamekeeper was seen toiling along under his well-replenished bag, and he came up to his master to receive the partridge which he believed him to have hit.

" I shall demand my payment on another occasion," said the gentleman.

" I came out to look for Lady Sarah," observed Sabina,

taking no notice, and pretending not to hear the observation, which made her cheek glow to a deeper red.

"I think Lady Sarah has probably returned to the house," said her son; "but whether or no, I shall not allow you to be wandering about here, sinking into Sloughs of Despond. Were those funny little squeaks I heard, your cries for help? I imagined that I was about to find some *rara avis* on the lake utterly unknown to ornithologists. There! will you take my arm, or get over the ground by yourself?"

"By myself, if you please."

"Quite right. 'Help yourself, and your friends will love you the better;' also, 'Heaven helps those who help themselves.'"

"I think it is very disagreeable and ungenerous in you to be vaunting the praise of independence, when you must know that I feel so humiliated by being pulled out of the mud by you."

"Ah! but the proverbs really only apply to men, not to a beautiful, helpless girl," said her companion, turning on her the glory of his radiant blue eyes. "You may demand aid as often as you please, and I shall only think myself too happy to be able to afford it."

"Now is my time for Mr. Orellan," said Sabina to herself; but the thought of what she was about to ask drove every tint of colour from her cheeks.

He saw this, and fancying she was suddenly taken ill, he approached her with the greatest tenderness.

"What is it? Are you fatigued? Ah! I have some sherry in my flask," cried he, taking it from his pocket.

Sabina stopped him.

"It is nothing. I shall be well in another minute." And she made up her mind to put off the evil moment till later in the evening.

"Go into the drawing-room," said Wilfred, on reaching the house; "and I will look for my mother."

So Sabina, in her gingham dress, straw hat, and French veil, was turned into that luxurious apartment.

"How beautiful is wealth!" said the girl, looking longingly at the grand piano, covered with pieces of loose music, and surrounded with a confusion of music-books. She turned to look around her, and saw her little person reflected in the large looking-glass which had deceived her as to her identity five years before. How rich were the folds of the damask curtains! how moss-like the pile of the luxurious carpet! how cunningly inlaid were the various woods in the polished tables! She thought of her uncle's little sitting-room, of the shabby carpet, the faded curtains, the inky table, and repined, " Why should my poor dear uncle have so little, and these rich folks have so much ? "

But fifteen is not given to moralise long. There were ornamental books on the table—Swiss, and Italian, and Spanish views—and Sabina began to turn them over, as she stood by the centre table; but becoming absorbed, she seated herself in one of the luxurious chairs, and pushing back her hat, gave herself up to the enjoyment of so many novelties.

Sabina's father had accompanied Sir John Moore in the retreat towards Corunna, and she was looking intently at an engraving of the ascent of the pine-clad Nogales, and picturing to herself the toilsome march of the troops over the snow-covered mountain, when Mr. Tresillian returned, and she gave a long sigh and closed the book.

" What has engaged your attention so deeply? I was in the room for a minute or two without your perceiving me."

" I was looking at this Spanish landscape, and thinking of my father."

" Why? Did he serve in Spain ? "

" Yes ; and my mother used to tell me about the events of that disastrous retreat, and how my father took a living infant from the breast of its dead mother, and bore it away in his bosom. Poor papa! my memory of his handsome face and carefully tied hair, which seems to me so indistinct and dreamy, acquires consistency when I see pictures of the scenes through which he passed."

Thus spoke Sabina, who was as proud of her father and her uncle in their valour and unblemished honour, poor as they were, and ever had been, as Mrs. Cressy was of her husband's self-made wealth.

Mr. Tresillian wished to please his mother's little guest, and took her to his own sitting-room, against the wall of which was suspended the engraving from the picture of the death of Sir John Moore.

" How proud," said Sabina, " Doctor Moore must have been of his son ! "

"And of the children of his brain also," added Mr. Tresillian. "Have you read 'Zeluco,' and 'Edward?'"

Sabina had not; and Mr. Tresillian went to the library, to fetch a volume of the first-named novel.

"Come with me," he said, "that you may know your way another time." And following him to the finely-arranged bookshelves, Sabina was wonder-stricken at the number of volumes, and the beauty of their bindings.

"What a beautiful collection of books! They look though as if no one ever read them," cried Sabina, with a keen recollection of the tattered "Anecdotes of Naval History," "Cook's Voyages," and her own much-read volume of "Campbell's Poems."

"Don't be so satirical, Miss Rock. Remember we are not often here, and my mother prefers the contents of the boxes of books, which the mail brings from the London libraries, to these, which are old and dry for the most part."

"Do you think so? May I take down this beauty dressed in green morocco?—'The Lay of the Last Minstrel!' I should so like to read it."

"Take any you like."

"She is intelligent, and easily amused," was his reflection, and he thought she would be very fresh and nice for him to come home to, when he had established her in a small house, or convenient lodgings in London.

"Was there no pity, no relenting ruth," in Mr. Tresillian's mind?

No more than exists in the breast of the farmer, who looks at the lamb on which he intends to regale himself at Easter. Its perfections give him the pleasure of anticipation.

Mr. Tresillian meant to be very careful in not allowing Lady Sarah to suspect his intentions. She was an indolent lady, with no very lively ideas of religion or morality, but a deliberate intention to seduce an innocent young lady, because she was poor, and but slightly protected by an aged uncle, would have made her feel that "dear Wilfred was decidedly wrong," the utmost stretch of which her indignation was capable.

He was, therefore, cautiously polite to the young guest, but nothing more in his mother's presence. Sabina wondered that his manner became so chilly, and thought she might have offended him.

"And I have not asked him about Mr. Orellan yet," she said to herself, meditatively.

The dinner was rather a silent one, for the mother and son had no subjects in common with Sabina, and were too well-bred to start any in which she could not join.

After dinner Lady Sarah settled herself to sleep on the sofa, and thus was found when Mr. Tresillian came from his solitary devotions to the wine and dessert. Sabina in her white muslin concert dress looked very lady-like, and by no means out of place in the superb drawing-room. The dinner had been late, and the evening seemed melting away, and with her mind wandering to her uncle's fireside and to his companion, she felt guilty that she had not spoken about the Coastguard. "I am as bad as Joseph's chief butler," she thought, "and have not remembered my uncle's wishes, in the midst of this magnificence." Then she fancied him with the cup of gruel, made palatable only by a little salt, and Mr. Orellan's glass of steaming whisky. She had often attempted to pour a few drops into the gruel, but it was too great an indulgence, her uncle had said—he could not afford it. And here was Lady Sarah expecting an emerald ring, which was to cost more than Mr. Rock had to meet his year's expenditure.

"Will you play a little on the piano?" said Mr. Tresillian, after he had noiselessly offered her some coffee. He wanted to sit near her, and the piano was behind Lady Sarah's sofa; so that, if she opened her eyes, she could not observe the juxtaposition, should Mr. Tresillian stand a little too near the music-stool. Sabina went at once to the instrument, and seated herself. She could play by ear without any effort, and she was hoping to bring the conversation round to the Coastguard, should Mr. Tresillian talk to her.

He stood by her in silence for some minutes, listening to her delicate touch of the instrument, and observing the exquisite contour of her dimpled shoulders and bosom. Her fingers wandered over the keys in "wanton heed and giddy cunning," with the charm which a true genius for music and that only can inspire. Then she began to sing softly, lest her voice should awake Lady Sarah.

> "My love is lord of lofty halls,
> Which crown the woodland steep;
> In valleys where the streamlet falls,
> I tend my father's sheep.

11

> "The youth forsook the higher land
>   To drink the crystal wave;
> And as he scooped it in his hand
>   The stream my image gave.
>
> "'Oh, maiden, yield to me that flower
>   That's placed thy vest within.'
> 'That lily flower is all my dower,
>   And that thou may'st not win.'
>
> "He turned his stately head aside,
>   Too proud to sue in vain,
> And I in sorrow now abide
>   That he sues not again.'"

When she had finished her song, in which each word was, as usual with her singing, clearly enunciated, Mr. Tresillian laughed a little low laugh, and looked at her with eyes brimming with fun.

"The moral is, never to take no for an answer," said he.

"I do not know. I never thought of a moral. 'Tis a translation from the Spanish which my mother used to sing, but if *you* were asked to do anything you did not much like to do, would you do it, like the wicked judge, for much entreating?" said Sabina, talking very fast, with her tongue beginning to cleave to the roof of her mouth.

Mr. Tresillian was puzzled by the change in her colour and tone.

"I do not know. I fear I am not very yielding to entreaties," he said gravely; "but why do you ask?"

"I'll tell you. I want you to do something—something disagreeable, perhaps; for me—no, for my uncle—no, for Mr. Orellan. He wants a command in the Coastguard."

Mr. Tresillian was silent, and the silence continued so long that Sabina felt her heart throbbing so violently that she fancied she heard it.

"Did your uncle desire you to ask me?"

"No," replied the girl hurriedly; "but I knew he wished to ask you himself, had you stayed longer yesterday morning; and I saw, too, that the idea of asking you vexed him. He has never asked favours in all his life for himself, but Mr. Orellan begged him to mention the subject to you, so I thought I would take the pain on myself."

"Does it give you so much pain to ask a favour of me?" said the gentleman, tenderly stealing his hand over to the shoulder farthest from him, and reaching the girl gently towards him.

She arose, and freed herself from him.

"Yes, it is very painful," she said. She fancied he treated her like a child; "but," she continued, smiling, "it will not be painful if you can get from the Admiralty what my uncle wants; but perhaps you do not know Lord Melville; perhaps you cannot do it?"

"I have no doubt I can do it, provided Mr. Orellan's career will bear investigation," said the gentleman; "and I am sure it can do this, or he would not be your uncle's friend."

Sabina looked so beautiful with her brown eyes full of pleasant tears, that he longed to kiss them away. She was more grateful for this unpremeditated compliment to her uncle from Mr. Tresillian than she had been to Lady Sarah for the diamond ring.

"Oh! Mr. Tresillian," she said, kissing his hand, which was outstretched towards the piano to turn over the leaves of the music, "how good and kind you have always been to me. I love you so much!"

She said this with a childish impulse which was very mortifying to her companion. She might love him, but had she been *in love* she would not have stated the fact so openly; however, he was not going to allow such an opportunity to pass unimproved, and he stooped and kissed her cheek kindly, but not in a way to alarm her. "My child," he said, "I will do what I can for your uncle's friend, and so you may tell him when you see him."

It was time that the interview, confidential as it was, should cease, for the footman entered with sherry and soda water, and with him came bounding in a young poodle, escaped from the caresses of the young ladies and the governess. Lady Sarah sat up, and concealed a quiet yawn at the conclusion of her nap, and caressed the puppy with the indolent kindness she felt to every sentient creature.

Then she called on Sabina to sing, and was delighted to find that she knew and could pour forth a succession of those melodies which had delighted Lady Sarah's youth :—

> "Oh, say not woman's heart is bought
> By vain and empty treasure;"

was sung by Sabina with exquisite tenderness; and the repetition of the line, "She loves and loves for ever," Sabina executed with a delightful cadence which excited the admiration of her auditors. The music recalled her youth to Lady Sarah; for "music is the language of memory," as one of the most charming of composers, Mozart, designated it, and Lady Sarah, who had prudently and placidly wedded her deceased lord for his wealth and title, still had a soft regret for a handsome youth, who had neither to offer at the shrine of beauty; he had hung over her enamoured, when in a delicate girlish voice she had sung that song, and he had hoped she would fulfil the expectations it excited, and remain unmarried for his sake till her hair had become gray and her beauty faded. He had left his body in the trenches of Seringapatam, and his form lived in the memory of his friends, an image of beauty and youth and valour.

> " The hero boy who died in blooming years,
> He lives in man's regret, and woman's tears."

Had he come unscathed from that human hecatomb, he might have broken the spell of memory by becoming middle-aged, stout, and bottled-nosed.

There was a marked similarity of character between Lady Sarah and her son, allowing for the differences of sex: her ladyship was passively selfish—Mr. Tresillian actively so.

> " Narcissa's nature, tolerably mild,
> To make a wash would hardly stew a child."

And her ladyship being sweet tempered, her selfishness was softened by the placidity of her disposition. Mr. Tresillian rushed to his object, regardless of the wounds and bruises he inflicted on others in attaining it. His mother, quite as intent on her own gratification, obtained it with such an amount of apologies to the people she incommoded in her progress, that they made way for her willingly, even to their own hindrance. She liked Sabina for the admiration so genuinely expressed by her of Lady Sarah's beauty during Sabina's visit to Tregear in her childhood. She loved music honestly, and found this girl to minister to the gratification of her taste with no trouble to her ladyship. She had her little plans too, which she did not confide to her son, of taking the girl to town next season, and introducing her as her *protégé* in the musical world. It would reflect such glory on herself, she thought, if she turned out a success ; if she did not, she might be easily dropped again quietly at Deepindale, or recommended as a governess, or a lady's maid.

If her ladyship had seen a little girl come through a crowd of horses and carriages, to offer early flowers, at her carriage-window, she would have taken the flowers, and thought nothing of the risk the child would run of being trodden to death before she could return. Sabina must take care of herself. Lady Sarah stood now by the side of the piano whilst Sabina was singing, and turned the leaves of the music book when the song was concluded. The beautiful glee arrested her attention, "Oh happy fair," and she pointed to it ; on which Sabina began : her ladyship took the second, and Mr. Tresillian the bass voice. Sabina's love of music and delicacy of ear, more than any feeling of subserviency to her companions, made her sink the power of her voice, lest, as she afterwards told Mr. Rock, it should swallow up their notes, as did the lean kine of Pharaoh the fat cattle in his dream ; and the lady and her son liked the girl all the more for having made them pleased with themselves. Whilst they had been occupied by the music, they had been utterly unmindful of the pranks of the poodle, whose movements fell noiselessly on the thick pile of the carpet, and who had rolled himself in the valuable lace shawl, which had fallen from the stately white shoulders of the lady when she stretched out her hand to turn the leaves of the music book. When, at the conclusion of the song, she turned to leave the instrument, she saw to her dismay the poodle on his back, swathed round and round in Brussels lace, from which he was trying to free himself, regardless of the rich fabric which he tore with teeth and claw, and which fluttered in ribbons round his agitated body. "Oh, my veil ! my veil ! Wilfred, look at that wretch !" Wilfred laughed, and he and Sabina stooped at the same moment, the girl seizing the jaws of the animal and Mr. Tresillian the fore paws, on which the hind feet kicked themselves clear of the delicate texture by repeated jerks, much to its detriment.

Mr. Tresillian caught up the offender, and Sabina the veil, now become somewhat like a cullender. Lady Sarah looked exceedingly grieved.

"Never mind, my lady," said her son, "I will give you another."

"Another! my dear Wilfred, how you talk! Men never know anything," said her ladyship, plaintively. "Why, that veil belonged to your father's grandmother, and to his mother, Lady Trelusa. The price given for it, originally, was seven hundred pounds, and I paid eighty-four pounds to have it repaired when it came into my possession. Such a one could not now be purchased. Really, my dear Wilfred, that dog shall be hanged, or given away. That girl has no business to bring dogs to my house." And then she stopped, knowing that the house really belonged to "that girl's" father; and that she was there on sufferance, though with her own establishment of servants and horses.

It was Sabina who spoke next. Mr. Tresillian was sorry that he had vexed his mother by underrating her loss, and by the ignorance shown by his offer of replacing the veil. "I think, Ma'am," she said, timidly, "I could mend the veil, if you will allow me."

"You!" said Lady Sarah. "My dear, you are very good to say so, but I think your offer is as wild as Wilfred's."

"I can do lace-work—imitation, I mean. I have a collar I can show your ladyship." And she left the room. What a comfort, to avoid the necessity of lighting a candle! for, with the enviable privilege of wealth, every portion of the large mansion was brilliantly lighted. So she returned with a pretty lace-collar, on which Sabina's clever fingers had imitated all the stitches in the celebrated lace-veil spoken of before, in tearing which she had, as she thought, revenged herself on her uncle for her enforced attention to the church service.

"This is very wonderful!" said Lady Sarah. "Did you really do this? How very well you work! And they charged me over eighty pounds for such small tearings only where the pins had rent it, or the brooches."

"Probably the menders charge for their time," said Sabina. "It is not so very difficult when one once gets into the way of doing it; only tedious."

"Then, will you mend this?"

" Certainly, Lady Sarah ; when I can get some thread sufficiently fine."

" I will send to London for some."

Sabina said nothing, and soon after the trio separated for the night.

A charming room had been prepared for Sabina on that night. Its furniture bore the unmistakable marks of wealthy generations gone by. An old-fashioned tortoise-shell clock, inlaid with gold, ornamented the white marble chimney-piece, over which was inserted, in the panel, an oil-painting, well executed, of King Cophetua and the beggar maiden.

The artist had disdained the usual artifice of contrast between the countenance of a doating old man and a beautiful young woman. The king he had represented as a model of manly grace, whose vestments of purple and fine gold contrasted with the fluttering rags of the beggar-girl whom he embraced. He might have been Prior's " Solomon Raising Abra from his feet to his arms." The girl was dark as to her eyes and her flowing tresses, and beautiful in " her lovesome mien."

" How happy the king must be ! and how very happy the girl !" thought Sabina, who gazed at the pair, till her brain became dizzy and her heavy eyes closed in sleep, as the firelight leapt up and sank again repeatedly, now revealing the picture and its gilded framework, and now shrouding all in shadow.

CHAPTER XIX.

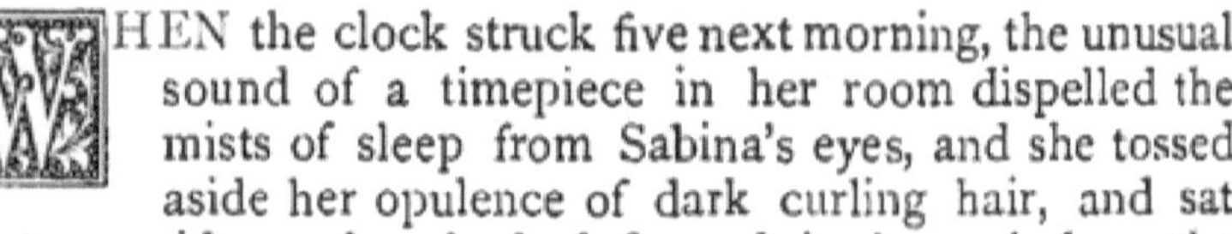

HEN the clock struck five next morning, the unusual sound of a timepiece in her room dispelled the mists of sleep from Sabina's eyes, and she tossed aside her opulence of dark curling hair, and sat up, to consider a plan she had formed in her mind on the previous night.

The realities of luxury with which she was surrounded, did but bring to her mind in stronger contrast the poverty of her uncle's dwelling, and filled her with unspeakable tenderness towards him. She remembered that Susan, whose eyes were not as good as in former days, often brought in his slices of toast with little bits of smut-flakes fluttering at their points, when she had reposed her weary arm, by resting the bread on the bars of the kitchen grate. In this case, her uncle, who was scrupulously clean, used to send away his breakfast in disgust; and Sabina had had the habit of going into the kitchen, and making it herself, under the pretence that she was cold, and that Mr. Rock did not like to see her cowering over the sitting-room fire.

Sabina looked, and meditated, and became impatient of the magnificence by which she was surrounded, and determined to find a door in her gilded cage through which she might take flight to Deepindale for a few hours.

The newly-risen autumn sun was gleaming in long lines of light through the opening of the massive damask curtains, which were drawn to exclude its rays, and Sabina sprang

out of bed, and put them back, and gazed with delight
on the scene before her. "Oh, how grand! how very
beautiful! I don't care for all the rest, but how delicious it
would be to live always in a park!" she cried, as she observed
the massive clumps of trees, of which the foliage was but
tinted with the glow of autumn, and had as yet lost none of
its density. The sun illuminated the solid summits of the
trees with golden light, whilst the park at their base was
bathed in mist. Further out in the distance, the same
landscape was repeated, diversified by hill and valley, and
purpled by distance, whilst spread out like a wavering sheet
of silver, the lake gave up its curling wreaths of white vapour.
Nothing broke the silence save the twitter of a few half-
awakened birds, or, occasionally, the lowing of distant
cattle.

Sabina, having looked long and earnestly on this picture,
now observed what made the framework of it; the carved
tracery of the window, and the rich stained glass which
seemed to nestle in the intricacies of the oak, like birds of
gorgeous plumage in the dark branches of trees. Orange,
purple, crimson, and green, shot bright arrows of light from
each pane, tinted with the colour through which they had
passed, and played fantastic dances on the surface of the
damask curtain.

Sabina arose, and contented herself with the abundant
supply of cold water in her room, as she knew no servants
would be up at that hour to substitute that fluid even in its
tepid state.

"Probably Susie is not up yet," she thought, as she
dressed herself.

With the elastic figure and fresh beauty of youth, her
ablutions over, her toilette was soon made. Cold water was
the only application necessary for that smooth, stainless
skin; and the comb, passed through her curling hair, gave it
all the gloss necessary for its adornment. She *shook* her
clothes over that lithe and delicate figure, and the result was,
that she was dressed without the pressure or padding of
corsets, without the application of *rouge* or pearl-powder.

The boots were not wet, thanks to the care with which
Mr. Tresillian had lifted her on the preceding day. She went
down, but met with an unexpected difficulty at the door.
She could not remove those massive and intricate fastenings.

Were she to descend into the unknown regions of the servants, she should probably be met by the same impediments at the back of the house. She went into one of the drawing-rooms, and managed to find the spring which confined the shutter, and, by a great effort, to lift the heavy sash. That done, she sprang out, alighting on the soft turf, and sped away to Deepindale. "I shall be back again after I have given Mr. Rock his breakfast," she thought, "and long before Lady Sarah leaves her room."

She felt as if she had wings as she flew over the park, scattering the herds of deer which had reposed under the sheltering woods. How fresh and sweet the air seemed! She went through the beech plantation, and saw in the distance Mr. Tresillian's retreat. Ah! how handsome he was! how very nice and kind! She paused for a few moments, and looked at the building, meditating on the perfections of its owner, and wondered whether he was sleeping still, and how he looked with his eyes shut; and the remembrance of his kindness to her uncle led her thoughts to that dear old head which would soon be leaving its pillow, if he had not already dashed above it the large pail of cold water, on the surface of which he had in winter to break the ice before he poured its contents over him, as he stood in a large tub, and gave involuntary jumps and gasps at the chill produced by this inartificial shower-bath.

Mr. Rock had been warned that, in the state of his heart, such shocks might kill him; but he often averred, that in his opinion, if a man could not live clean, he had better die clean; so he continued his customary ablutions.

Everything seemed fragrant to Sabina till she entered the purlieus of Deepindale. The hedges of the high road along which she passed were hung with the feathery seeds of the briony, and were lilac with the bloom of the blackberry. The smell of the moist earth was pleasant to the girl as she passed on. It was different when she reached the town. Congregations of the human species are not agreeable in the odours that surround their habitations in the early morning, unless those habitations have been designed for, and appropriated by, the wealthy. Sabina trod carefully over the noisome gutters, not to soil her boots. Few shutters were taken down; but half-awakened maids, with dirty caps stuck askew on their heads, were lazily beating their mats and bits of carpet, covering themselves with an atmosphere of dust, which made faces and caps still more begrimed. Mr. Cressy's boy was taking the pony from the stable to fetch the vegetables from the farm, and looked curiously at Sabina as she passed. "She had soon been sent back from the great house," he thought. "No carriage this time. She looks quite brisk, though, not a bit down-hearted," gazing after her as she tripped along towards Haven House. She went round by the back door, and sprang into the kitchen, just as Susan, with her back turned to the door, was cutting the slice for Mr. Rock's toast. "*Much* too thick, Susan!" Sabina cried, and Susan dropped both loaf and knife, with "Lor, Miss! how you frighten me! Well! tired of the great folks at Tregear already, I'll warrant you. Glad to come home to your own nice breakfast, poor lamb!"

"Is my uncle down stairs yet?"

But Mr. Rock's deliberate step was now heard as he descended. "He is come to the creaking stair now." How Sabina hated that stair, which always would creak, notwithstanding the many efforts which she had made to avoid the unmusical plank with which it had been invested.

She made the toast before she went to wish him "Good-morning," dreading Susan's ministration, if she were left alone with the cut bread.

"There, Susan! let me cut both pieces. This will do for your breakfast."

"A pretty thing! a fine extravagance for servants to eat toast. You got them notions at Tregear, I suppose."

"You may eat it untoasted if you like. There is no compulsion," said Sabina, as she placed her uncle's two slices in the little old silver rack, and carried it in daintily between her finger and thumb, so that no part of her dress or sleeve came into contact with the simple luxury.

"What! Sabina! Why have you come back so soon?" said her uncle, with a troubled countenance.

"Oh, uncle! I thought you would be so very glad to see me again, and I came in time to make your toast, and to tell you all about everything, and I shall run all the way back, and they will never know it. Lady Sarah will not be out of her room before luncheon."

Mr. Rock's countenance cleared. The same idea had

crossed his mind and that of the greengrocer's boy, that
Sabina had been sent back in disgrace.

How happy were the pair over that niggardly little breakfast-table.   Sabina reproached her uncle with the absence of
the egg she had entreated him to have; but he made the
usual reply, that he could not afford it.

"Oh, uncle!" so sadly, she said.

"If ever I get my share of the 'Eurydice' prize money,
my dear, I will eat an egg every day for the remainder of
my life, if it will give you any pleasure."

"Ah! that prize money!" replied the girl, hopelessly.
"How unjust—how cruel the people are who make these
delays. The eggs you will not eat might keep you alive, uncle!
I wish the officials were wanting eggs to keep them alive!
I wish they were where Eurydice was herself, and had no
Orpheus to bring them back."   Sabina knew the opera, but
Mr. Rock did not, or he would gravely have rebuked the
wish as savouring of profanity.

"In the meantime, child, thanks to Mr. Tresillian, or
Lady Sarah, I shall have a good dinner, for the gamekeeper
left two brace of birds here after you went yesterday, all
young," continued the old man, with a tone of satisfaction.
He had been a sportsman, and had often parcelled out
young and old birds together, or young ones only, when
anxious to please the recipient of the gift.

Sabina's face flushed with pleasure.

"It was Mr. Tresillian, no doubt. Lady Sarah would
not have thought of it."

"I have sent a brace to Orellan. I knew it would be a
treat to Mrs. Orellan."

Sabina did not care for Mr. Orellan, nor for his sick wife,
and had rather her uncle had kept the partridges himself;
but now she told him the good news, and saw his forehead
crimson with pleasure at the intelligence. He was too much
pleased to say much; but Sabina was well repaid. He sat
swelling with the importance of having this to communicate
to Orellan when he should call.

Then Sabina's tongue went glibly. She told her uncle
nearly all that had happened. Not about the quagmire, nor
about the kiss; but she gave a vivid description of the magnificence of the house and furniture, and of the dinner, and
the gorgeously liveried servants, and of the singing. She

omitted how she had escaped from the house, for she imagined justly that her means of egress would shock her uncle's ideas of propriety ; but enough was repeated to give the veteran food for amused thought for the rest of the day.

In the meantime, Mr. Tresillian awoke to the memory of the kiss he had imprinted on Sabina's velvet cheek, and with a great longing to repeat the application. Most people have felt the desire to clasp in reality the phantom which has haunted them in the realms of sleep. In slumber, these creations of our wishes are sweet, loving, yielding, where in life they are probably fenced round by propriety and the tyranny of circumstances. In sleep he had fancied himself to be wandering in some green island, accompanied only by Sabina. All nature seemed like what might be dreamed of Paradise, clustering ivy and the twisted stemmed vine hung over them ; the air was balmy and serene ; she clung to his support, and his lips met hers in one long kiss ; she seemed to be melting away in his arms as he tightened his embrace. He awoke and found it was but a dream, but a dream which he longed to fulfil as soon as possible.

" The little witch is an early riser, I dare say. She will be up before I am dressed," and he rang for his valet, and ordered his bath to be prepared at once.

When Mr. Tresillian was dressed he deferred taking his breakfast, in the hope that Sabina would partake of it.

" Pray, is Miss Rock down stairs yet ? " he said in an indifferent tone.

" Can't say, Sir."

" Find out."

" Miss Rock has not rung her bell yet, Sir, Miss Stephens says," replied the man, after making inquiries.

" Sleeping still ? " he said to himself ; " not accustomed to late hours, I suppose." His heart throbbed violently at the thought which took possession of his brain. " Suppose I go and knock at her room-door, and awake her."

He listened. There is not a sound ! He knocked again. " She's not there ! " He opened the door stealthily, and, deceived by the unwithdrawn curtains at the window, which darkened the room, he moved softly to the bed. " Empty ! " He placed his hand on the pillow. " Cold ! She has not been here for some time ! " Then, after looking suspiciously round the room, and seeing only Sabina's costume of the preceding evening, with the little black satin shoes, and silk hose, retroverted and left on the ground, after the untidy fashion of that careless child, he said—" She's gone down to amuse herself with the pictures," and he went to seek her in the gallery, then in the drawing-room, library, and breakfast-room, growing more angry at every fresh disappointment of his hopes. " If she be not in the house, she may have gone into the grounds," he thought, and, returning to her room, he opened a wardrobe to see if her hat and cloak were in its recesses. No, then she was gone out, and with seeming indifference he strolled out to look for her.

" Stupid girl ! Good Heavens ! If she went to the waterfall, and attempted to cross the small ledge of wood over the torrent—just the thing it would please her to attempt !" He was walking in that direction when he saw small footsteps on the dewy grass, and following their lead, he found she had gone through the beech plantation. He hastened to his retreat in a flutter of hope that he should find her there, but the footsteps branched off to the gate which led to the high road, and then Mr. Tresillian knew she had returned home, and anger swallowed up every other feeling.

CHAPTER XX.

MR. TRESILLIAN went up into his retreat, and looked down the road; for some time fruitlessly; but at length between the waving branches he caught a glimpse of a slight little figure, coming on swiftly between the trees. He determined to remain in silent dignity in his room, till he recollected that, in doing this, he should defer the opportunity of making her unhappy by the exhibition of his indignation, for that she would probably hasten to the house, being ignorant of his vicinity. So he resolved to walk towards her, solving the sacrifice of his own dignity by a determination to make her as miserable as possible by the reproaches he would heap upon her, and by the sarcasms with which he would overwhelm her. He had nearly reached the gate when she unlocked it, and stood before him, her lovely face glowing with exercise, and with the unexpected sight of him whom she most desired to see.

"Oh, Mr. Tresillian !" she said, bounding towards him, but there was no responsive pleasure in his face, when, raising his hat stiffly, he showed the expression of his countenance, which it had previously shadowed.

"What is it ? Is Lady Sarah ill ? Is anything wrong ?"

"Not that I am aware of, Miss Rock."

"Oh, but there is ; there must be. Why are you angry ?

Please don't be vexed with me. What have I done? Is Lady Sarah angry? I hope not," and Sabina passed both hands round Mr. Tresillian's arm, and hid her face and wept. The revulsion of feeling on a morning which had been so fraught with happiness to her was too bitter to bear without tears. They spring so readily to the eyes of the young, the pendulum of whose feelings vibrates so easily between pleasure and suffering. Age, blunted by frequently recurring causes of grief, sheds tears sparingly and seldom.

"When you have finished your weeping, Miss Rock, we will continue our walk towards the house. I am not aware that Lady Sarah has as yet discovered that your impatience of her hospitality was so great, that you took the first opportunity of leaving Tregear."

Sabina drew her handkerchief from her pocket and wiped her eyes, releasing Mr. Tresillian's arm, and walking by his side in silence.

"Now," he said to himself, "if I remain cold and sulky in my manner, and go up into my retreat, she will follow me in the hope of being forgiven."

They had not yet reached that part of the beech wood which led to the ladder, and Sabina, steadying her voice as well as she could, said,

"Please do not be angry with me, Mr. Tresillian ; I owe you so much for your kindness to my uncle, so very much ; and to me you have always been so very good. I only went to see my uncle, you see. I was so glad to be able to tell him. And then his toast—I like to make it myself."

If Mr. Tresillian had spoken his thoughts, he would have said, " What is that stupid old fool of an uncle compared to me?" but he said nothing, and removed, with a slight twist, the arm on which Sabina had timidly placed only the tips of her fingers this time. They were close to the ladder now, and Mr. Tresillian began to ascend it without looking back, or speaking to Sabina. The girl's spirit was aroused, and instead of the reiterated entreaties which the young man expected to hear poured forth, with all the eloquence of love and grief, Sabina compressed her lips, and walked steadily towards the house.

"Checkmated, by Jove !" was Mr. Tresillian's reflection. "Shall I follow her? No. She will now, in her turn, take the privilege of sulking. I must bide my time."

CHAPTER XXI.

LD people have often some cherished hope—some intense love, which exists in a greater force than any experienced by the young. The horizon of youth is diversified by a thousand sparkling beams, caught from the morning sun of their existence. To the aged, how dear must be the lonely light which illuminates the dark midnight by which they are surrounded—

" A single star, when only one
Is shining in the skies."

The attachment of Mr. Rock for Sabina was his absorbing passion. His youthful love had been starved out; his ambition of manhood had sunk into despondency. This child had been thrown on his unwilling support, taken to his protection, because he could not endure that anyone bearing the name of Rock should be reduced to be provided for by the parish, received unwillingly, as a tax on his limited income; but growing by degrees into toleration, then liking, then love so absorbing, that, proud and self-sufficient as the old man flattered himself he was, he could not help owning to himself that he could not be easy in her absence, and had no thoughts of which she was not the centre. He had his little secret from this dear child, and swelled with the importance of it. He had received some information which seemed to promise that the long disputed prize-money of the " Eurydice " would soon be settled; and then !—what would he not do with the money ! How he calculated and re-calculated to a fraction what it would amount to. Then came the anticipated pleasure of spending, and the secret of secrets with which he was to surprise his darling—a new piano ! He was a liberal man in his ideas, poor fellow ! and only kept out of debt by his horror of pecuniary dishonesty. Seven hundred and odd pounds he hoped to receive. What a fortune it seemed ! He would give a hundred of it for a piano for Sabina. He went over in his mind her delight and his. He wrote to Messrs. Broadwood for lists of prices, and for the measurements of their instruments ; for the room was finite, though his desires to please his child were infinite. Where could the instrument stand was a vexed question in his mind. There was the old bureau in the sitting-room, where he sat and wrote, and did his small accounts. If the horizontal grand piano came, that must be dismissed—but whither ? The bed-room he occupied might receive it ; but he was old and his circulation was irregular, and he rather dreaded sitting in a fireless room during the coming winter ; for a fire in his bed-room would have been an unheard-of luxury. True, he might have had an upright piano ; but Mr. Mudge, at the music shop, considered that the silk absorbed the voice, and he wanted Sabina's voice to be heard in perfection. He would leave twenty pounds in his will to Susan, and then there would be six hundred left to invest in the funds for Sabina's benefit when he should die. Six hundred pounds in the funds in those days, meant thirty pounds a-year—a small income for his darling to live on. But she might give lessons, or go out as a governess, and the thirty pounds certain yearly would be a great comfort, he thought. Then, she might marry ; but at this idea his brow clouded. Whom could she marry ? It seemed strange that one so poor should have so profound a contempt for men whose money was supplied by trade ; but it would have grieved Mr. Rock should Sabina have been linked for life with any but a gentleman.

Thinking of his prize-money, and of the pleasure he was about to confer on his friend Orellan, and of the piano with which he was to surprise Sabina, Mr. Rock was quite cheerful, and almost forgot that his evenings would be very dreary without his usual antagonist at chess ; but to act rightly, and bear the result, had been the old sailor's rule of action through life, and he was not going to flinch from it now.

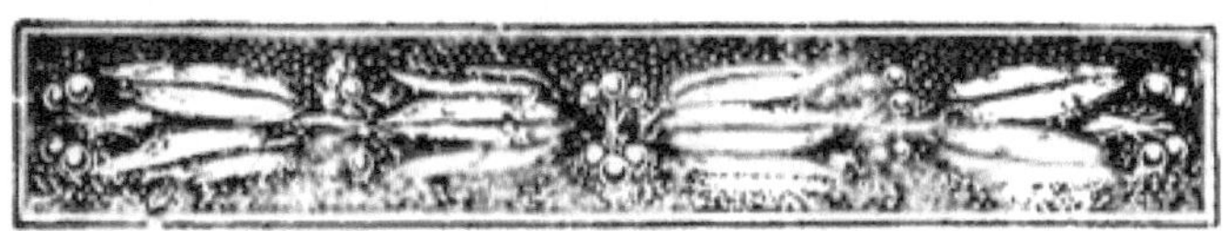

CHAPTER XXII.

Owen Meredith.

E left Sabina hastening to Tregear with a swelling bosom, ready to expand into sobs, and eyes from which she had to wipe the tears, which constantly gathered, and excluded the pathway she must tread.

She hastened to her room, and deposited her hat and shawl, and shortly after Stephens came to inquire of Miss Rock if she would take her breakfast in her own room or in the breakfast saloon. She preferred the latter, for she could not fancy eating or drinking in a bed-room, and determined to despatch the meal as soon as possible, and return to her room to begin the repairs of the veil, some fine thread for which she had taken from her work-box at home, the remains of what she had used for her own work.

The hot rolls, toast and butter, eggs, and fried haddock were rarities to the young girl, who enjoyed them in moderation, and then drank a cup of coffee hastily and escaped to her own apartment, to avoid the angry eyes which she dreaded to encounter, when Mr. Tresillian returned to the house. She hoped he would not withdraw his promise with respect to the Coastguard. What a sad temper he must have, to be so angry for such a trifle ! What could it matter to him that she went home to give her uncle his breakfast ? Was it so very ill-bred as he seemed to think it ? She could not tell; but her face got hot at the idea that she had been guilty of some breach of unknown

etiquette. She wondered when he would forgive her,—
whether he ever would. She rather dreaded seeing Lady
Sarah, lest she, too, should express her displeasure. Perhaps she had not found it out; and Sabina trusted that Mr.
Tresillian would not betray her.

She set to work on the veil, and had mended one large
fracture, before the luncheon-bell rang. Sabina heard it,
but knew not its signification till Stephens came and said
Lady Sarah was inquiring for her. Sabina descended, and
was met by a tranquil salutation and a sweet smile. She, at
any event, was not angry with her; and the girl's spirits rose
at the thought. The butler carved the roasted pheasant,
for Mr. Tresillian did not appear. He did not seem to
have been expected, and the girl knew not whether she was
relieved by, or sorry for his absence. After luncheon, Lady
Sarah proposed to show Sabina her flower garden and
aviary; and they walked together, the one pleased by
Sabina's expressions of admiration, the other thinking such
glorious combinations of flowers had never before been
assembled, for Sabina's memory of Spanish and Portuguese
gardens had become somewhat dreamy.

Whilst the girl was examining some exotics which she had
never before seen, a footman came up and announced the
arrival of visitors, and Lady Sarah gave Sabina the choice of
returning to the house with her, or remaining amongst the
flowers. She chose the latter, for she was very tired with
the length of her walk, and sat down to rest herself before
she proceeded to explore the gardens. At length she recovered sufficiently to go on, and seeing a low door-way in
the high-walled kitchen garden, she opened it and entered.
What a magnificent old place it was! There were long
gravel paths so hard and broad that three carriages might
have passed abreast without encroaching on the venerable
box border, which might have walled in the flower-beds for
the last hundred years—for there was that mixture of flowers,
fruit and vegetables, which makes an old English garden so
attractive. These noble paths or rather roads were planted
at the sides with hollyhocks of majestic height, and of the
largest clusters; every variety of colour was to be seen,
from the pale straw-colour to the richest crimson, interspersed
with white and black blossoms. By their sides, and sometimes supported by them, were those queenly lilies, which

the painters of old made to live on their canvas, as the
type of purity. Each end of the garden road was terminated
by high stone vases, from the summit of which bloomed
scarlet geraniums, mingled with the plumy branches of the
clematis, which hung over the old moss-covered stone, a
contrast in their evanescent beauty to the solid structure,
venerable with its hundreds of years, which supported it.
The gravel which was still glowing, though part of the
garden was shadowed from the sun, was less attractive to
Sabina than a distant portion, which was to be approached
through another low door-way, and seemed full of short
clustering trees. In truth, Sabina's instinct told her that
they must be apple trees, and her old temptation came on
her with fresh force. The peaches and nectarines were
covered by nets, and Sabina had not courage to place a fur-
tive hand within that tantalising defence, through which
their ripe beauties glowed on the heated wall ; but when she
wandered into the orchard all her perceptions enjoyed the
anticipated feast. What a fine old orchard it was ! The
walls were covered with plum trees, some large and round ;
and covered with their purple bloom, seen between the
oblong polished leaves, some magnum bonums oval and
pendant glimmered out unexpectedly from their seclusion.
The gardeners had not thought it worth while to net these
trees ; indeed, from the fantastic manner in which the smaller
branches projected from the wall it would have been a work
of difficulty ; and it struck Sabina that at some past period
of the trees' lives those functionaries must have neglected
that part of the ground in the prolonged absences of the
family,—" Out of sight, out of mind." Probably few persons,
but herself, would have found the orchard so attractive.
Through tall seeding weeds she strode, lifting her feet very
high ineffectually to avoid them, till she got close under a
Pearmain tree—others were more brilliant in the colour of
their bright burthen ; but of the Pearmain, it might be said,
as of the mignonette, " My qualities surpass my charms." A
" sops in wine " seemed to beckon her from the distance,
but Sabina determined to defer her attentions to that till
another day, or, at any event, till she got tired of eating
Pearmains. Unfortunately the best fruit seemed above her
reach—it always is, in some way or other. She stood on
tip-toe, and with elevated arm, and head thrown back,

she just reached the points of some of the leaves, which broke away from her clutch, leaving her hand full only of the torn fragments, and her eyes blinded by the particles of dust and white and yellow mosses which made the trees venerable. The branch laden with luscious fruit swung up indignantly from the effort she had made to secure its offspring; Sabina let go the torn leaves and put her hands to her blinded eyes. The pain was exquisite; she tried to open them, but could not, when a laughing voice cried out—

"Well done, Miss Rock, you always find apples irresistible. 'Feed me with apples, comfort me with pippins,' says the wisest of men. But what is this? no laughing matter, seemingly," continued Mr. Tresillian, who, finding his mother safely occupied by her guests, had determined to improve his opportunity by seeking Sabina. She was in too much pain to express the provocation she felt in being detected in a position so undignified, as that of stealing apples. What could she say? Nothing. She stamped her little foot in the increasing agony of her eye.

"Now you *must* open your eye," said the gentleman, with his cambric handkerchief twisted into a point. "There," continued he, placing her head against the tree, "now do try to open it." Sabina did so, and Mr. Tresillian dexterously inserted the point of the handkerchief and swept off the particle of moss. The pain of the friction of the handkerchief over the ball was very great, and Sabina sank on the ground, and rocked herself to and fro in her agony. "The particle of moss or dust is out,—here it is on the handkerchief. You are only suffering now from the irritation of the eyeball; get up," and as she rose Mr. Tresillian took her up in his arms. "Keep your eyes shut—I'll carry you to the fountain." Arrived there he made her kneel, leaning over the brim, and bathed her eyelids with the cold water; and by-and-bye Sabina's pain abated, and she opened a pair of very red eyes and looked about her.

The fountain stood in a little arched recess, and flung up its glittering waters, which gleamed more brightly from the darkness which half surrounded it. The entrance was shadowed by trees, and ivy clustered round the archway.

"Oh, how beautiful! cried Sabina; I never saw this before;" for she forgot her trouble about her eye, and her shame at her attempted theft, in the loveliness of the scenery.

"No; and permit me to observe, that you would not have been able to see it now, had I not kindly and skilfully taken the mote out of your eye. Oh most shameless of little thieves!"

"You are very good, very kind to me now—and I am very grateful to you; but I thought you very capricious and cross this morning,—but, oh, dear, are my eyes getting any better? I am so afraid I shall not be able to do Lady Sarah's veil."

"Yes, they will soon be well. Never mind the veil. I will admit that I was cross this morning; but then I was frightened, and when people are alarmed they are always cross."

"Who frightened you? How can a great man like you be frightened by anyone?" said the girl, wondering.

"You goose! you frightened me; or to speak more grammatically, I was alarmed on your account. I thought you might have tried to cross the torrent on that little ledge of wood, and fallen over and been drowned; and I went down to look for your body, like a fool that I was; then, when I saw your funny little footsteps on the moist turf in the direction of Deepindale, I was uneasy lest you should be insulted in walking alone, where the road was so unfrequented from the early hour you chose; altogether I had enough to make me cross, and I thought you ought to have come up the ladder and begged my pardon properly."

"I had done so once, and you would not speak to me," replied Sabina.

"Had I not cared for you a great deal, I should not have been so unkind," said the gentleman, looking up at her with eyes full of love; his arm was round her waist, as she stood up by his side, he sitting on the edge of the fountain. Sabina had become familarised with their proximity, and was not startled; on the contrary, she seemed disposed to argue the point quietly.

"It seems to me," she said, "that if one loves a person a great deal one is never cross, but always nice to them; that is my way of loving my uncle." Mr. Tresillian felt inclined to shake her. "It was because I love him more than anyone else in the world that I went home to see that his breakfast was nicely made." Mr. Tresillian removed his arm and taking up a flat pebble made ducks and drakes in the fountain. Sabina, all unconscious that she had inflicted mortification, was rather proud of her triumph in argument, in which she augured her victory from the silence of her companion.

"I declare, Sabina," he said at length, "that I should like to take your head and hold it under that water till you were suffocated."

He spoke as though he would have really enjoyed the performance, and the girl looked into his face, so puzzled and scared, that with a sudden revulsion of feeling he flung his arms round her and kissed her passionately.

"Don't—let me go—I don't like it," said she, struggling —"I don't like it at all"—freeing herself, and standing breathless and angry at a little distance. "No one ever kissed me before—no, that is a story."

"Who did?"

"Poor mamma before she died," replied the girl, almost weeping, "and—yes, one person beside."

"Who?" said Mr. Tresillian,—"Your uncle?"

"Nonsense!" said Sabina. "*He* never kisses anyone."

"Who then?"

"Mabel Snow," rejoined Sabina.

A sudden change came over Mr. Tresillian's countenance, a great gravity and depression, and a deep crimson flush suffused his brow. Sabina looked and wondered, and waited till he spoke again. When he did so, it was in a constrained voice.

"Who, pray, is Mabel Snow?"

Yet he did not seem to be particularly interested in her simple recital, when he had satisfied himself that Sabina had had no communication with the Snows for more than five years.

When Sabina had ceased speaking there was a long silence, which was broken at length by Mr. Tresillian asking her of what she was thinking?

"I was thinking," she replied, "that notwithstanding all my trouble, and the pain in my eyes, I never got any apples after all."

Mr. Tresillian laughed. "What a greedy child you are! Come! I will pick you as many as we can carry; or I will order the gardener."

"Oh, no! that won't be half so nice as picking them ourselves," said Sabina; so they returned to the orchard, and
Mr. Tresillian shook the trees, and Sabina had as many
apples as she desired.

"Are you satisfied?" he said, smiling.

"Quite, I thank you," said the girl, for the vulgar abbrevia-
tion of "Thanks" was then unknown.

"Then," suggested the gentleman, "I want you to promise
me something—not to be running off to Deepindale to-morrow morning."

Sabina's countenance fell.

He saw it, and said,—"If your heart is so set on giving
your uncle his breakfast, I will order my dog-cart for you
at seven o'clock to-morrow, and the servant shall drive you
over, put up the horse for a couple of hours, and then bring
you back."

"Oh, thank you! a thousand times," cried the girl, and
she looked ready to offer to kiss him again; but some recollection of the last embrace withheld her, and she then suggested, that as her eyes were well again, she should like to
return to the house, and go on with the repairs of Lady
Sarah's veil.

CHAPTER XXIII.

OUR history must retrograde for some months, and change its locality for that of the pretty town of Trevedra.

It is the period of the quarterly meeting held in London by the Society of Friends, and Friend Rachel and Friend Walter Snow have gone to attend it, taking with them their eldest girl, whom they consider to be of a marriageable age, and for whom they wish to contract an alliance with a steady man, rather older than the girl might prefer, very stiff and long backed, but with wealth, in abundance, and great capability of accumulating more.

Rhoda Snow was quite aware, without having been told in so many words, that a matrimonial scheme, in which she was to be one of the principal parties, was under consideration, and she had, with increased importance, communicated all she knew, and a good many doubtful suppositions, to her Sister Mabel. They were standing now in their large pleasant bed-room, overlooking the trim but luxuriant garden, rich with flowers and heavy with fruit.

Mabel turned her sweet face from the varieties of crimson, blue, orange, green, scarlet, and purple, which vied with each other in her favourite borders, and looked at the French gray bonnet, of coal-scuttle shape, which Rhoda held in her outstretched hand for Mabel's approbation.

"It is just come from Friend Botlerel, wilt thou look at it? It seems to me that the stitches are not so small as they might be. Thou seest there are fifty-two stitches from the middle to the termination of the first inch, and but forty-nine the next inch. Dost thou perceive that?"

Mabel smiled quietly. "I do not think friends will look at the stitches if they see thy face under the bonnet, sister."

A starched smile struggled on the goodly face of Rhoda. "When I sit next to Friend Stubbes, at the meeting, she always looks at my bonnet, thou seest, and not at my face. She could not see my face, unless I turned my head, which would be unseemly."

"Where will Friend Sturm sit?" said Mabel, wickedly.

"Thou shouldest not say that, Mabel."

"Oh, Rhoda, dear! look at all those bright colours in the garden! Can it be wrong to dress otherwise than in drab, when the Great Father so arrays the lilies of the field? Why hast thou that lovely colour in thy cheek? God gave it to thee. Thou canst not help being comely. If it were wicked to have a colour He would not have given it to thee."

"Friends dress in drab," said Rhoda, "that they may not be tempted to give up too much thought to outward adornment; but cultivate the graces of a quiet spirit."

Mabel was silent; but she thought that Rhoda's excessive care as to the number of stitches in her bonnet, was only a variety of devotion to outward adornment; and she turned the conversation to Joseph Sturm.

"Oh, Rhoda! Canst thou really like him? I mean like him well enough to live with him always."

"*Thou* dost not like him," was Rhoda's evasive reply.

"No, no! he is so ugly, so coarse in his skin, such a long upper lip, and he never says more than 'yea' and nay.'"

"Thou shouldest not call ugly that which God has been pleased to create, and dost thou read what is said—'Let thy communication be yea, yea; nay, nay: for whatsoever is more than these cometh of evil?' Besides, Roscrow is a fine place. Dost not recollect when we used to fill our baskets with specimens of spar and ore which paved the road when Joseph's uncle was alive?"

Mabel was silent. She thought she should not find the same pleasure in collecting specimens of copper, if such a man as Joseph Sturm were the master of Roscrow, so she only sighed.

"Dost thou think thou wilt feel lonely when we are gone

to the quarterly meeting, Mabel? Will it try thee to stay here alone?"

"No, Rhoda. I hope I shall be supported. I wish all the boys were going away too. I can manage the girls."

Many instructions were given to Mabel with regard to domestic watchfulness. Certain portions of needlework were to be performed daily. The butchers' accounts were to be overlooked weekly, and the stockings from the shop were to be run toe and heel before they were polluted by the foot of the wearer.

Mabel was rather proud of being left in the position of mistress of the house, and mother of the younger children in the absence of her parents, and accepted all the instructions with a conscientious determination to carry them out.

Her eyes filled with tears though, as the covered waggon drove off, laden with her father and mother and sister, the last two arrayed in the snowiest of neckerchiefs and the most shining of French gray bonnets, with little, close, neatly crimped caps under them.

Mabel wandered about the house for half-an-hour, listlessly, and then set the younger children their lessons, and attacked the wearisome stockings and socks. As she worked, however, she felt the pleasure of the extreme neatness and regularity of her stitches, and of her mother's anticipated quiet approbation on her return. That would not be, indeed, for six weeks. How very long the time would seem! and how often Mabel thought she should wish those weary weeks abridged. Before one was passed, Mabel would have been glad to have lengthened them to infinity.

Mabel's day passed quietly, for the boys were at school. At night they returned, and had tea, for Mabel gave the eldest youth that beverage, though Reuben was sent to the nursery to take his milk-and-water and stale currant-cake with the younger children.

Very lovely the young Quakeress looked presiding at the tea-table, with a pleasant look of assumption of authority. The youth, who was two years older than Mabel, was plain, and conceited beyond the usual unbounded conceit of foolish boys, who seem self-satisfied in proportion to their small amount of brains. This young gentleman began to disturb the placidity of his sister's temper by finding fault with everything on the table, and then with the Society of

Friends in general, and with his father and mother in particular. All the pent-up insolence of years, all the surging of a rebellious spirit against the strict authority which had repressed it in the persons of his parents, now broke over the slight barrier opposed by his Sister Mabel to the expression of his opinions.

"Thou knowest nothing, Mabel. What can a girl know who sees nothing but what passes between these walls, and is carried in a thing more like a waggon than a carriage, every first day to meeting, as a treat? What a figure thou art in thy brown dress and white neckerchief! Ah! if thou couldest see Caroline Manners, thou wouldest see a girl who knows how to dress!"

Mabel, who had thought her dress very appropriate to a young Friend, winced at this wholesale criticism. "There's not a spot on it, I'm sure," said she meekly.

"A spot! What if there were fifty, so that the gown was well cut!"

Mabel thought she should like to know how Caroline Manners looked; but Luke only said she was the most beautiful creature in the world, and he meant to go to the county ball, to dance with her.

"Ball! Dance!" exclaimed Mabel. "Oh, Luke, what would thy mother say?"

His mother might say what she pleased. *He* didn't care. And he pushed away his tea-cup, and left the room with an air of defiance, which filled the gentle Mabel with grief. She heard him go out of the door leading to the garden, which he slammed in his insolence; and Mabel was disturbed by the fear lest he should not return by ten o'clock, when the quiet household retired to bed.

It is a proverb worthy of all acceptation, that "There is no accounting for tastes;" and certainly no accounting for affection. It is a puzzle to know why the gentle, pure-minded Mabel loved her degraded, hypocritical brother, why she always placed his words and acts in the best light to her parents, and bore blame which might have been more justly his due. Though she was possessed of more sense than fell to his share, she was constantly impressed by his knowledge of facts and people of which and of whom she knew nothing. As, at ten o'clock, she passed the looking-glass in her bed-room, she paused, and examined the reflection of her beautiful person, and wondered what Caroline Manners was like, and how she was dressed. She would get Luke to tell her, when he was not so cross, she thought. Then she looked again, and smiled a little timid smile; for though meek and subdued in her self-estimation, she appreciated the faultless skin and the perfection of her fairness. Her hair was banded over her pure brow, and braided at the back under the transparent cap of white muslin; her throat was rounded and white; and the hair at the back of her neck grew compactly to her head, and did not straggle down on the skin in its growth. She was rather fully formed than slender, which was in her youth an added attraction, but would in middle life degenerate probably into clumsiness.

She went to bed with a troubled mind. What would her mother think if she knew that Luke was not at home? She hoped to hear the door leading from the garden open softly, indicating his return; for though the servants, believing him to have retired to rest, had fastened it so securely, Mabel had gone noiselessly and undone the bolts and locks before she came up to her room. But Mabel dropped off to sleep in the midst of her anxiety, and awoke in an hour or so, thinking that half the night was over, and tormented with anxiety, lest Luke should not have come in. She arose, and dressed herself, being too precise, even in her distress, not to make herself quite neat; and lighting a candle from the rushlight which burnt in her room, she proceeded to that of Luke, in which the bed was empty. He had not come in.

She wondered, helplessly, whether this was the night of the county ball he had talked of attending. She knew nothing, and leant her face against the window-pane, looking into the darkness of the garden, fruitlessly. At length she saw flashes of light amongst the trees on the road leading past the house, and shouts of a multitude of men and boys. That they might have something to do with Luke, and thus be mixed up with the overwhelming anxiety of her heart, she feared, painfully; and her eagerness to know, contending with her natural timidity, induced her to descend into the garden, and open a small door by which the gardeners were used to enter, to save a round by the large gates. She stood outside, partly shadowed by the wall, and the crowd, intent

on their own amusement, did not at first catch sight of her ;
but in her eagerness to see, she advanced a little into the
light of the torches they were carrying, and was greeted with
a shout—"Sweet gal! pretty gal! Give us a kiss!" She
did not listen, but pushed into the midst, where Luke, very
drunk, was staggering along, leaning on the arm of a dissolute woman, oppressed by the amount of stimulants he had
taken, and by the weight of a pole, to which was appended
a large flag, on which was marked, in gilt letters, the Cornish
motto, "One and all." It was at the period of enthusiasm
for war, at the point of the greatest interest during the Pe-
ninsular campaigns ; and Mabel, brought up in the horror,
felt by all true Friends, of arms, saw that Luke, with his
loathsome-looking companion, was heading a procession of
half boys and half young men, who intended to enlist on the
following day, and celebrated their future triumphs by parad-
ing with all the mimic signs of war they could get together.

"Luke, Luke!" said Mabel, catching his arm with an
impetus which nearly pulled him over, flag and flag-staff.
" Luke, come away from that woman. Come home with
me. Throw away that red rag, which savours of blood and
strife. Come home to bed. Art thou mad, Luke?" she
cried, not understanding his glazed eyes and uncertain steps.

The insolent woman, and the crowd of young men and
boys, chiefly from the free school, of which Luke was the
head, bearing their venerated flag (purloined from the town-
hall by one of the boys, who was son of the woman employed to keep the hall), so misused, showered a storm of
abuse on the young girl :

" Quaker! Quaker! thy mother is made of brown paper."

"What do you mean, you young fool, by interfering with
our noble captain ? "

"Brother! Luke!" said Mabel in her agony, for one of
the young men put his arm round her, and insisted on a
kiss.

But Luke, planting his flag-staff as firmly as he could, said
only with a drunken gravity—"One and all !"

"That means we may all kiss her," said the crowd.

" Bravo !" cried the woman, insolently.

Mabel uttered shriek on shriek, as she struggled in the

arms of her captor, when she was suddenly freed by such a blow dealt on the head of her assailant, that she staggered against the wall, whilst her deliverer had enough to do in warding off the attacks which came from a multitude of fists, the proprietors of which seemed to have forgotten "fair play." One young man, however, called the rest to order, and challenged Mr. Tresillian to fight him. The gentleman said he was perfectly willing, if the young lady might first be placed in safety; and taking the hand of the terrified Mabel, he led her to the garden-door, and placed her inside.

"Lock it," he said, impressively.

"I cannot let thee go out to fight for me. I implore thee to stay inside. It is so sinful to fight; and thou mayest be killed. Oh! I pray thee—no, I *beg* thee to stay —'tis sinful to pray." And she clung to his arm eagerly.

Mr. Tresillian looked at her beautiful person with admiration.

"I will return in a few minutes, and assure you of my safety, Madam. These men and boys are all drunk. Oblige me by locking the door; the rest may enter whilst I am engaged with the biggest."

Without saying more, he drew the door close, locked it, and placed the key in his own pocket. Mabel listened and wept, leaning her head against the door-sill. She heard the blows—heard the brutal shouts of the crowd, and believed she heard the inarticulate cries of Luke, urging on the assailant of her protector. She grew quite faint and sick with apprehension. What could she do to help him? Should she return to the house, and obtain the aid of the coachman and groom? It was a good way to go; and then they would know Luke's ill-behaviour. She tried to get out— anything was better than this suspense,—but the bolt of the lock could not be pushed back by her weak fingers. At length there was a louder shout than ever, and then a hushed silence, then murmurs, then trampling feet; and as they died away in the distance, Mabel heard the key applied to the garden-door, and Mr. Tresillian entered.

"Oh! art thou hurt?" the girl cried, tenderly. "Come to the summer-house, and sit down. Dear, dear!" she continued, as he sat down, and put his hand to his head, "thou art hurt. I feel warm blood trickling from thy fore-

head. Lean thy head on my shoulder ; or if thou wilt wait
a minute, I will dip my handkerchief in the water at the
fountain, and wash thy face."

" No," said Mr. Tresillian, clinging to her, for he liked
the proximity sufficiently to wish to retain the situation.
" Let me sit here quietly for a few moments, and the faintness will go off. I really am ashamed, Madam, of thus
intruding."

" I beg thee not to mention it." And there was a silence
—Mabel standing, and Mr. Tresillian leaning his head
against her bosom. All the womanly feelings of her nature
melted into tenderness towards the handsome young man
who was suffering from his devotion to her interest, who
had rescued her from insults, when that craven Luke—her
own Luke—her own brother—had stood by without afford-
ing her any aid. The girl had sprung into womanhood
in the last half-hour. She loved the handsome creature so
strangely placed in juxtaposition with herself. But, for very
shame, she would have bowed her head, and impressed her
lips on his forehead. How fine a young man he had looked
in the torchlight ! how respectfully he had placed her in
safety ! And Luke—but at the thought recurring of her
brother, she began to weep, in grief, anger, and perplexity.

" How could Luke ? " she sobbed at length, thinking of
her woes, and of her companion.

" My dear young lady, which is Luke ? "

"Oh !" said Mabel, with her face flushing with shame,
" Luke was the one with the flag." She did not say, with
the woman.

" Luke cannot be your brother," said Mr. Tresillian, for
he saw no resemblance to the beautiful girl at his side in the
besotted figure of the standard-bearer.

" Yes, he is my brother ; and "—sobbing again—" I wish
he would come home. My parents are gone to the quarterly
meeting, and they have left me to take care of the house
and all the children ; and—and—what shall I do about
Luke !" She did not mean this interrogatively, but merely
as an expression of dismay.

" My dear lady ! "

" I am not a lady !" said Mabel, unconsciously using the
words of Faust's " Margaret," " I am a ' Friend.' "

" My dear friend, then, I will go out and see if I can

13

persuade your brother to return to you. I have small expectation of inducing him to leave his 'rabble rout ;' but I will do my best. The longest orgies must have an end; and his companions will drop off one by one, and he may then listen to reason."

"But thou wilt be hurt—thou art hurt now. Ah! what can I do for thee?"

"My hurt is nothing. I feel well again now ; 'twas but a momentary feeling of faintness. I would advise you to return to the house."

"But how shall I know?"

"Will you show me the window of the room in which you sleep? I suppose you wish to get him in unknown to the servants?"

"Yes, I will show thee," she said ; and she walked, leading him through the darkness towards the house, feeling that he must depend on her guidance. "I have shown thee the window, and now I will lead thee back to the door."

Mr. Tresillian did not object; he felt the charm of the guidance too much. She let him out into the darkness, which was less in the road than under the shelter of the ornamental shrubs of the garden, and returned to the house.

She was less anxious now about Luke; she had rested her cares now on the breast of another and a stronger than herself.

"I fear he must have thought me very untidy," she half uttered, moving to the mirror.

She started at the reflection and saw, for the first time, that the clear muslin neckerchief which covered her bosom, and the shoulder and front of her frock was stained with blood.

"He must be grievously hurt—it was for me,"—this was the tenor of her thoughts. "I must change my dress. What will they say when they see these stains? Oh, Luke! Luke! what trouble thou hast brought on thy sister!"

She tried to wash the marks out with cold water, but she exhausted all that the jugs and pail contained, and the stains seemed indelible. "Oh, mother! what wilt thou say when thou hearest of this?" Then she remembered that her mother must not know it, if Luke's disgrace was to be concealed.

The efforts to cleanse the clothes from the stains of blood passed the time more swiftly, and at length she heard a sound like hail upon the window panes, and going towards it she perceived Mr. Tresillian making signs to her to descend. When she reached him, the moon had shone out from the clouds which had hitherto shrouded it, and Mabel saw that the countenance of her new friend was very grave.

"What is it? Is he hurt?" she cried in a low voice, anxiously.

"I do not think he is hurt; but he is quite insensible," said Mr. Tresillian. "I have got my groom and my valet to carry him, and I came here to know if they can bring him up without awakening your household, or whether they shall take him to the front of the house, and ring the bell."

"Oh, friend, I know not thy name! Who has hurt my poor brother? Why should he be insensible?" cried Mabel, to whom intoxication and its effects was utterly unknown.

"He will be in his usual state to-morrow, my dear young lady."

"Friend," interposed Mabel.

"My dear friend," amended Mr. Tresillian, "we had better get him quietly into his bed and leave him."

Mabel assented, and set all the doors open between Luke's bed-room and the garden gate. Presently she saw three figures coming along the gravel path in the moonlight, bearing a heavy, dark, helpless mass in their arms, one man held it by the shoulders and one by the knees. They moved slowly and noiselessly, sometimes setting down their burthen to rest and recover breath, Mr. Tresillian walking by the side. All expressions of violent sorrow or terror were discountenanced by these Friends, and though Mabel was dreadfully alarmed by seeing her brother in such a position, she swallowed down her tears and concealed her terrors, and lighted the three men up stairs, after they had taken off their boots to move without noise.

Mr. Tresillian whispered to her, "You had better leave us to undress him," and he took the light from her hands, and lighted the candles which stood on the dressing-table, and put her gently out of the room. He had too much respect for this fair young Quakeress to permit her to see more of this degraded youth in his present state, and felt that his groom and his valet had better do what was necessary for his comfort or safety. Mr. Tresillian's faith was great in the youth of this unworthy scion of "Friends," yet his symptoms seemed alarming, for Luke Snow had never before dared to indulge in excessive potations, and the effect on his weak brain, had been greater than it would have been on a habitual drunkard. After he had been undressed and placed in his bed Mr. Tresillian joined Mabel, and said he had done what he could, but he inquired whether he had not better call in the surgeon who attended the family, to see if anything more could be suggested. Mabel listened with a very white face, turned up towards that of her interlocutor so pleadingly, and with an expression of so much trouble, that Mr. Tresillian was touched by it.

"Thou seest that if this disgrace be known to my parents, they will be made unhappy; and if I send for Friend Farley he may tell them. Thou dost not think my brother will die?"

"I do not think it at all likely that he will die, but I think it possible."

Mabel's face became almost livid.

"I will tell you," said Mr. Tresillian, "what I will do, if you wish it. I will sit by his side till morning, or till he recovers consciousness, and send my servants back to the hotel at once. You will not like to be alone under these painful circumstances; but is there none amongst your own servants in whom you could confide?"

"They would tell my mother," was the quiet answer. "But has he been hurt in the head?" she continued, anxiously.

"He has taken too much to drink."

She flushed crimson. "And he went in a procession of mimic soldiers, and carried a flag himself!" she said, in a voice which showed that she knew not which offence would be considered the greatest in the judgment of her parents.

That her dear Brother Luke should be a votary of Moloch, and a man of Belial at the same time, seemed doubly shocking to the simple-minded Quakeress.

"May I see him?" and without awaiting Mr. Tresillian's permission, she opened the door of his room softly, and looked in. The two men-servants drew back from the bed to let her approach it, and Mr. Tresillian stood at the door. Luke Snow had been placed with his head high on the pillows, and had a handkerchief steeped in cold water on his head ; as the candles on the dressing-table illuminated the perfect profile of the young Quakeress in her snowy cap and spotless attire, she seemed to Mr. Tresillian like an angel too pure for sin, yet full of pity for the sinner.

The face of the youth was shadowed by the curtains, but Mr. Tresillian had seen enough of the low, narrow forehead, small eyes, set closely together, long nose, and coarse, animal mouth, to wonder at the blindness of family affection, which could cherish such a creature tenderly.

"If she be wise, not that she seems to be particularly sharp ; if she be prudent, she will write to her people, and make a clean breast of it," thought her companion ; but Mabel was too essentially timid to take such a step, or, indeed, any step. She had never walked without mental leading-strings ; and now, being deprived of them, she leant on the first support she could cling to, without considering whether it might be a broken reed on a spear, on the sharp point of which

"Peace bleeds and hope expires."

Mabel had the tranquil, loving, sensuous nature of her father. In the situation in which she had unfortunately been placed, the qualities of her mother's character would have been more valuable.

Thus Mr. Tresillian took on himself to act at once. He dismissed his groom and valet silently through the garden, telling them he should stay with the young gentleman till he got better, and that they were to be silent on the subject of the night's transaction. Then he returned to Luke Snow's room, and sat down by the bed, wondering whether Mabel would remain or not with the patient. His own head ached unpleasantly, and he was glad to rest it against the back of the chair. He had received a telling blow on the temple, which by cutting the skin had occasioned the effusion of blood, exciting the commiseration of the beautiful Quakeress, and this he had not yet found time to have dressed. Occasionally, he put his cambric handkerchief to his face, and withdrew it still stained by the oozing blood. Mabel perceived it, and left the room quietly, returning with a small basin of warm water and a sponge, and some diachylon plaster. Without speaking, she drew the handsome head towards her, and washed it tenderly, and after drying it with a soft napkin, she applied the warmed plaster. She stood back for a moment to look at her handy-work, and seemed to Mr. Tresillian so indescribably lovely, that he kissed the white hand which had so ministered to his comfort.

She withdrew it with every nerve quivering with an unknown sensation, so pleasurable that it bordered on pain. All mention of love, carnal, sensual love, had been excluded from the mother's thoughts. No books were ever allowed to be read which touched even remotely on the subject. Mabel had been as secluded as the Hero of ancient story, and the seclusion had been as ineffectual. Mabel loved her guest as a woman, young, pure-minded, but passionate, loves—but once. Mr. Tresillian loved her as a licentious man loves every beautiful woman with whom he is thrown into contact. There was something in the *entourage* of this young person particularly piquant to his taste, *blasé* as he was with the women who were the companions of his unbridled hours in town. His last fancy had been an actress, of some talent, and greater artifice; a woman of flashing eyes, violent action, and of exaggerated vocabulary; every pleasure had been pronounced by her ecstatic; every vexation, however slight, overwhelming. She heeded not the recommendation of Doctor Johnson, not to use big words on small occasions. She was a woman made to shine on the stage, her proper locality, and it had been the applause of crowded houses which had been her chief attraction to Wilfred in the first instance. When she was established under his protection, as it was called, her lover had wearied of her society, as he did of most things. He declared that she was as glaring as the stripes of colour in a target, or as one of David's pictures—vivid and shadowless. Their temporary connection had just been severed, when accident brought Mr. Tresillian to the rescue of Mabel Snow, from the insults of her brother's companions, and in the fair Quakeress he found all those soft, neutral tints which his eye and mind seemed to require. There seemed, too, something particularly attractive to his jaded fancy in the innocence of his present companion, and in the seclusion which had surrounded her with such a halo of purity. He remembered

with a hard smile the utter indifference with which Amalie
had kicked aside a young actor, who had also indulged in
strong potations, and was lying at the door of one of the
dressing-rooms at the theatre—not with anger, nor disgust,
but with utter indifference, and it scarcely need be said how
the purity of Mabel rose by comparison.

His imagination was captivated by the young Quakeress,
as well as his passions excited by her beauty. His Lily of
the Valley he called her in his silent vocabulary.

They watched together till the candles burnt low in
their sockets, and Mr. Tresillian, anxious for her reputation,
watched the first yellow tinge of light showing over the distant line of country. Then he rose and made a sign to
Mabel to follow him, taking one of the nearly extinguished
lights with him. He turned into the first open door, which
happened to be Mabel's bed-room. He felt that it was,
though nothing was said, for the clothes were thrown back
from the bed, on the pillow of which there still was marked
the slight pressure made by her head, during that short sleep
from which her anxiety for her brother had disturbed her.

She stood trembling and blushing, with a sense of the
impropriety of his being there, but unwilling to risk the
opening of the door of the sitting-room, which was locked.

"I think," said Mr. Tresillian, taking her hand; "that
your brother is sleeping more naturally, and may be considered to be safe. I must go now, whilst there is enough
of the night left to conceal my departure. May I call to inquire after you to-morrow, or rather to-day?"

Mabel did not answer the question directly, she only said,
"I must walk with thee to the garden door, and lock it after
thee, otherwise the gardener will inquire why it has been unlocked, which may be inconvenient."

So they went together down through the shadowed
garden, and reached the gate;—how well, in after years,
Mr. Tresillian remembered the spot, on one side of which
a tall cypress slowly waved, on the other a tender clematis
hung its graceful and fragrant blossoms, and clustered its
slender branches, with tendrils clinging to the dark fibrous
leaves of its stately neighbour, and quivering with every
breeze that moved his sombre head.

When they had reached the gate, Mr. Tresillian said,
"May I call and see you again? I was only passing

through Trevedra, but to have such a pleasure I would delay my journey, otherwise I shall probably never again meet you."

Mabel held down her head, and was silent.

Mr. Tresillian understood the rebellion in her heart, but desired not to take advantage of it. She was too pure and innocent to be his victim. He was generous enough not to press for the victory he knew was within his grasp.

"You do not wish it—you will not permit it," he continued. "Good-bye, then," and he held out his hand.

"Farewell," she said, placing her own in his, and pressing it tenderly he released it, and went out closing the gate softly.

He listened; she had not locked it—she must be there still. He fancied he heard smothered sobs, and impetuously re-entered the garden. Mabel was leaning, weeping against the door-sill. The sacrifice had been made to propriety and duty, and she was repenting her good deeds, and fearing she should see his face no more. There was no further reserve between them. She knew that he had divined why she wept. She thought he would not have taken leave of her so abruptly.

"May I not return and see you to-morrow—you know it is natural that I should wish to hear how your brother is—when may I come?"

"At eleven," replied Mabel, "at the garden gate."

When she no longer could hear his departing footsteps, she ran along the solitary garden paths to the mansion. She let herself in softly, and visited Luke's room, where he seemed to sleep peacefully. She wound his watch, and placed his clothes in their usual position. He would remember his sin fast enough, without the untidiness of his room acting as a reminder. Then she retired to her own, and sat down to meditate, as is enjoined by the chief amongst Friends, on the events of the past night. Surely, the desire to see after her brother's welfare, which called her from her first sleep, had been an inspiration from heaven. She had been "sent," no doubt. Her mother often felt such impulses, and attributed them to Divine influences. But for her going down, Luke might have been found dead next morning, instead of being warm and cared for in his own bed. Then she thought of the insults offered to her by

his companions, till she felt her cheeks burn with anger ;
then of her deliverer, and of his bruised and wounded temple,
the result of his defence of herself. How fair and comely
he was ! And her face was moved with a beautiful expression
of admiring love. How very different to Joseph Sturm, with
his monosyllabic conversation, coarse skin, and long upper
lip ! She reflected with doubt and shame, on the caresses
she had received. What would her mother have thought !
Should she—ought she—to confess the truth to her ? But
then poor Luke's disgrace must come out ! She was glad
to be relieved of the struggle in her mind by this conviction.
No; she would shield poor Luke. She had a conviction
that Rhoda was not fond of Luke. Rhoda would tell
Joseph Sturm ; for Rhoda would learn the truth from their
mother, who never concealed anything from her favourite
daughter.

Mabel would marry her new acquaintance, she felt sure.
She had an inward conviction that she was to belong to
him. Her father and mother would not consent to receive
him as a son-in-law unless he belonged to the Society of
Friends ; but he would do so, no doubt. She tried to fancy
him in a collarless coat like that of Joseph Sturm ; but by
no freak of that fickle power could she trace any resemblance between the ready, gallant, polished gentleman and
the slow, plain, coarse-looking man of business.

She thought of her new friend's readiness to remain
at the hotel to see *her*, and felt a quiet triumph at the remembrance that Joseph Sturm had left his Rhoda's house,
and town, because, from the unexpected arrival of Friends,
he could no longer have a bed without paying for it at the
hotel. It would be difficult to account for her lover's first
introduction to her. That must be thought of, and provided against. And Mabel fell asleep happily, with the
remembrance of his kisses on her mouth, and a conviction
of future happiness in a life which was to be passed with a
man with whose name even she was unacquainted, and of
whose character and pecuniary resources she was utterly
ignorant.

CHAPTER XXIV.

RETURNED to his hotel, Mr. Tresillian laid his aching head on his pillow, and felt rather disturbed by the conviction that his face would be anything but beautified by the red, yellow, and purple discoloration of the skin which he expected to see by daylight. His admiration for the beautiful Quakeress was but secondary to his sense of personal discomfort. He to her was to be the love of a life ; she to him was but as one of fifty transient inclinations. So, he was glad to go to sleep and forget the uneasiness of his bruises, and she was glad to keep awake and think he had received them in her defence.

When Mabel awoke next morning, she flushed crimson with pleasure and shame at the recollection of the past night. She was early alive to her duties, however, and exactly as the clock struck eight, she was in her place in the breakfast-room, making tea and distributing milk-and-water and buns to the younger children ; after she had folded her plump white hands, and sat in silence for a space, before her, she began her morning meal. The children wriggled themselves up into their stools, small in the seat and straight backed, so as to admit of no repose to the spine from any change of position. Those, whose legs could reach the ground from the height of the seat, found their feet imprisoned in an oblong piece of deal board, which turned out the toes and brought the heels together.

Why a Friend like Mrs. Snow should have desired thus to force the extremities of her children into a position like that of a dancing-master, when she would have considered dancing as a quick movement leading to the infernal regions, I don't know, excepting that few persons are ever thoroughly consistent.

When Mabel had given the children their breakfast, she stole softly to Luke's room, to see if he were awake.

His head was turned towards the wall, and she could not see his face, but she put her hand on his shoulder. "Luke, it is time for thee to get up."

The response was a kick under the bedclothes and a grunt.

"Thou wilt be too late for thy class in school."

"I don't care."

"Oh! but thou dost care. Shall I bring thee thy breakfast?"

This was said in a low voice, overwhelmed at the enormity of the proposition.

"My head aches, and I don't want anything to eat. Bring me some water to drink."

Mabel got some fresh cold water, and when he had drunk, she bathed his head with the remainder.

"That will do. Leave me alone, Mabel. Go away." And Mabel went.

She went through her duties mechanically, a troubled pleasure giving a tinge of colour to her delicate cheeks, and a soft light to her blue eyes.

She had nothing to divert her from dwelling on the image of her lover in meditations, where

> "Hope and memory made a mingled joy."

Her reading had been restricted to a few devotional books; "The Life of Margaret Woods," Moore's "Practical Piety," and "The Influences of the Spirit Exemplified in Passages from the Lives of Friends."

Mabel had read them often, and knew them by heart. She and her sisters had been taught French, but for what purpose it would be difficult to say, unless to read, "Elizabeth, or the Exiles of Siberia," by Madame Cotton, in the original, the only harmless work Friend Snow had found in that language. No intercourse with the Continent was possible in those days of general warfare, so none spoke French unless to some unfortunate *émigré* who had fled to England from the terrors of the revolution in the last century.

Thus Mabel found that running darning-cotton with intense precision into the toes and heels of stockings and socks, did not materially interfere with her thoughts of the visitor she expected at night. She speculated as to the impropriety of the act, but shut her eyes to the suggestion that it might be wrong. She would ask *him* what he thought, and arrange with him for future and open meetings. She must not compromise Luke, of course not.

" The lout fought well," said Mr. Tresillian next morning, as he looked at his disfigured face. " I must remain in my room till I can keep my appointment with my fair Quakeress. She cannot possibly object to discoloration, which is the result of blows received in her behalf."

He meditated on his adventure. The wealth visible in the whole house, though kept in subjection to the eye by the gravity of the colours, was so evident, and the refinement of Mabel's manners and tone so marked, that he did not dare to consider her as an object of legitimate license. She had the simplicity and artlessness of a child, a Juliet who had never read a line of Shakespeare, who never dreamed of any but chaste and honourable love.

He wished to be rid of the adventure without further worry to himself or distress to her ; but here he was laid up by a disfigured face for at least a week, and only presentable at owl's light. And after he had read the " Times " and the " Courier," only three days old on their arrival at the pretty town of Trevedra, he was fain to ask Mr. Prout, the landlord, for the loan of some books, and obtained a " Life of Mrs. Robinson " (" Perdita"), and some account of her treatment by the meanest of royal scoundrels, and the correspondence between the Duke of York and Mrs. Clark, with a portrait of the lady as a frontispiece, so charmingly *piquante*, with its bright eyes, turned up nose, rather full lips, and perfection of figure, that Mr. Tresillian wondered not at the Duke's infatuation.

When he had looked through these records of folly, he found "Chiffney's Defence of the Prince of Wales for Cheating on the Turf," and tossed it away contemptuously. The thought of the pure-minded and beautiful Quakeress was refreshing after such disgraceful records; and he waited impatiently till the hour arrived for meeting her. It would have been better not to go, probably, but he had promised, and should have had a contempt for himself as being deficient in gentleman-like bearing, had he failed in his politeness to a woman, and to a beautiful woman especially.

When the hour appointed came, he flung a cloak over him and proceeded to the garden-gate. He tried it, and it gave way to his pressure; and under the cypress, shivering with nervousness rather than cold, was the slender form of the Quakeress. She looked ghostly in her light-coloured dress, for the brown shawl, in which she had wrapped herself to come out, had fallen in large stiff folds to her feet.

She put forth her hand into that of Mr. Tresillian, and then stooped to repossess herself of the shawl. He placed it on her shoulders without any word but one of murmured endearment, and she drew him on towards a large alcove, where they might be sheltered from the night wind.

Seated there, Mr. Tresillian placed his arm round that of his darling, and would have drawn her closely to his side: but Mabel withdrew herself gently, and said—"I pray thee, Friend, remove thy arm, which is inconvenient for breathing, or, indeed, for the conversation I would hold with thee. Thou hast been very kind to me, and last evening I showed thee that I was sensible thereof. I wish to have thy advice, Friend, and I would learn from thee what is thy name, and where thou dost abide. Thou seest I am, as it were, alone in the house, for my brother, my poor Luke is unable to advise me, and I would that they should know of thy love and tender dealings towards me. Yet I would screen him, if I could, from their censure."

"What an extraordinary girl!" was Mr. Tresillian's thought; but he was silent for a space, and then answered the first part of her questions. "My name is Wilfred Tresillian. I am the second son of the late Lord Trelusa. I live in chambers at the Albany generally, as a bachelor: that is my home, but I stay frequently at my brother's house, Tregear, near Deepindale, where my mother, Lady Sarah Trelusa, is now on a visit. I am a Member of Parliament for Deepindale, as you may have heard."

"I knew it not," said the girl. "I only see thee as thou art—most fair, most manful, most gentle—and so I love thee, and will be thy wife, if that thou seest fit to ask me in marriage of my parents : as Joseph Sturm asked for my Sister Rhoda to wife."

"Who is Joseph Sturm ? "

"He who is about to marry my sister. Dost thou know that my name is Mabel ? "

"Yes, I know that. I learned it to-day from the people at the hotel. It suits us both—you to bear, I to use. *Ma belle !*"

"I suppose it does not matter in French, but Friends do not call anything beautiful," said Mabel.

"For what reason ? " said her lover.

"Probably because 'full of beauty' should not be applied to anything created, but to the Power only which creates all things."

"Pretty creature," he murmured.

"What wilt thou say to my parents—what canst thou say ? How canst thou ask their consent to our marriage when they will not know that we have ever met ? "

"I will think over the subject and let you know, my friend. Do you ever go beyond these grounds ? "

"Yes : on first day we go all together to a Meeting of the Friends at Saltmarsh. The hill at Calcuick is very steep, and we always get out and walk."

"I may say that I met you there ? "

"But thou *must* meet me, or it will not be according to truth."

"Then I will meet you," said her lover, smiling in the darkness, at the self-deception which persuaded her that to conceal the truth was not a falsehood acted, if not spoken, and at the simplicity which could imagine that seeing a young woman once, walking up a hill, was reason enough for asking her to ascend that "hill of difficulty," marriage.

"Mabel," he said, gravely, "you have seen me twice. Suppose you should find qualities in my character, or facts in my past life, which you disapproved. Then you would not like to marry me. Think of this, my child."

"But I love thee! And I am sure that thou art good."

Mr. Tresillian could make no answer to this, but a pressure of his lips on the rosy mouth that had uttered so sweet an affirmation.

He did not half like to be drawn into a marriage at his early age. He was not the head of the family as yet. In the future it might be his duty to ally himself to some titled lady—to some duke's daughter, as his father had done before him. A marriage with the daughter of a merchant, however wealthy, would be considered by his family as a *mésalliance.*

"My Mabel!" he said, tenderly, "I could not at present ask your parents their consent to our marriage. A favour which one is anxious to obtain should always be prayed for face to face. You have not seen my unfortunate face in the daylight. It is so much disfigured by the blows I received last night that I could not show myself in your father's presence without his inquiring how such injuries were received. Let me continue to visit you, either openly in midday at your home, or secretly in this garden at night. You shall decide the manner of our intercourse; but let us associate for the present, and wait for favourable circumstances before I place my present happiness in hazard by asking for more."

Mabel pondered.

"If thou wert to visit me in the day, others might see thy wounded face, and ask wherefore it was injured. Moreover, my younger sisters would be present, to whom I set tasks of needlework, arithmetic and French. Thy coming would be an interruption to them, and their presence would be irksome to thee. Whilst it is fine, thou shalt come to see me every night here. When it rains, I will think of thee in thy absence. I could not have thee run the hazard of taking cold."

She said this so tenderly and yet so modestly, that Mr. Tresillian, hardened *roué* as he was, was touched and charmed into something like real love.

"Thus, then, they met nightly in the garden for a few consecutive evenings, but the climate of England is not so propitious as that of Italy for such assignations, and the time came when there was drizzly rain; and this came on after the lovers had met. Mr. Tresillian complained of cold, and Mabel led him tremblingly up to the house, and raked together the embers in the grate of the deserted drawing-room, and they sat and talked together hand in hand, Mabel's soft profile, with her smooth luxuriant hair, surmounted by the clear white cap, and French gray silk dress, with a snowy neckerchief crossed over her finely-formed bust, was illuminated by the warm light of the fire only. The candles she did not re-light, perhaps from fear of observation.

In this delicious repose conversation was not needed to make the happiness of the pair. The scene and the girl were so unhacknied, so original in Mr. Tresillian's experience, that he desired nothing more for the present, than to sit by the side of the young Quaker girl, and gaze upon her beauty. Her trust in him was so unbounded that he felt it as a point of honour not to abuse it. Her love for him was so honest and truthful, so free from coquetry or thought of evil, that Satan himself might have hesitated before he whispered poisonous words in the ear of such an Eve.

CHAPTER XXV

"What wonder is it that ye know not men?
 For here ye live demure, with downcast eyes,
 And humble, as your discipline requires;
 But when let loose from thence to live at large,
 Your little tincture of devotion dies;
 Then luxury succeeds, and set agog
 With a new sense of yet untasted joys,
 You fall with greedy hunger to the feast."
                                        DRYDEN.

MABEL heard from her mother. Short letters from London in those days cost fourteen-pence. Long ones, or two sheets, twenty-two-pence. So that communication between families was unfrequent, and restricted in its quantity.

"DEAR MABEL,

"We trust that you are well" (Quakers were proud that by the proper use of the pronoun more was implied by the Friends than by the world generally. "You" here applied to the household as well as to Mabel).

"Thou hast, no doubt, been diligent with thy needle, and darned the feet and heels of thy brother's new socks.

"Thy father and I desire to see thee and the dear children mightily; but it hath seemed good to us to see all things done prudently and in order, for thy sister's welfare, when she shall be united in the bonds of marriage with Joseph Sturm.

"Their union will take place shortly before the Friends assemble, and we only wait for the accomplishment of this great happiness for thy dear sister, to return to thee and to the others, our beloved children.

"I often think of thee, especially in the evenings, lest when the little ones sleep thou shouldest feel lonely; but thou hast thy dear Brother Luke as a companion, and it doubtless is pleasant to you both, that he should read some instructive book whilst thy fingers are busy with needlework. For this cause have I sent unto you both by the mail-coach, that thou mayest not find thy evenings wearisome, some passages in the life of one of the ancestors of Joseph Sturm, by name Michael Sturm, showing forth his trials in America when he accompanied the venerated William Penn, and displaying God's providence in supporting him, when the Indians rifled his dwelling and murdered his wife and infants. Yet did he not return railing for railing, but contrariwise blessing.

"By this my dear Luke will see what good things hath He laid up for those that love Him, so that seeming calamities are made crowning mercies when they are received aright. And I would that Luke should lay this to heart, as I have sometimes thought that he allowed his fancy to wander too much to those men of Moloch in red coats whom he has passed in going to the Meeting of the Friends on first day sometimes.

"So I desire that you may be preserved in health and safety, and a pleasant condition of mind, till your father and I may be restored to you. Till then, farewell."

Her sister wrote also—

"Dear Friend and Sister,

"I have been much exercised in spirit at this my first separation from thee, and I fear that thou hast felt lonely in my absence. It will prepare thee, however, for that severance which must occur when I am the wife of Joseph Sturm, though I trust thou wilt take pleasure in coming to stay at Moscrow House with me and my future husband. Also it will be well for thee to conduct the household at Trevedra, which I doubt not thou hast done, keeping all things decently and in order, which will prepare thee for ordering thy parent's house when I am with my husband, or if, perchance, the same good fortune may overtake thee, to be selected as the helpmate to a good man, such as my Joseph.

"I pray thee take care of the bulbs of hyacinths, which

are in our sitting-room. They must be withered now. I have purchased for thee a convenient work-box, which containeth also writing materials.

"One of the young Friends at the Meeting on first day had a cap of leno instead of muslin. For this cause a council of female Friends was convened on second day, and the young Friend was reproved. Also her mother, who had been cognizant of the fact, and had not prevented her daughter's infringement of the rules for Friends' dresses.

"On first day also our dear mother was exercised greatly in spirit, and manifested with mighty strength that which it was given unto her to utter. The subject thereof was the backsliding of a young Friend who had greatly tried her parents by her wilful determination to ally herself to one not of her own persuasion. She was "*out read*" from the Assembly of Friends, and her parents were much overcome by the disgrace.

"I could not but consider myself highly favoured amongst women, that my duty and affection alike direct me to a union with that good man Joseph Sturm, and I trust that thou, dear Mabel, mayest also, one day, find his equal to be thy yoke-fellow—his superior thou canst not find.

"I shall send thee some gold-eyed needles for darning, when your mother sends the book for thee and Luke; and thus I bid thee farewell."

When Mabel read the above, she flushed with different feelings, the predominant one being indignation that Rhoda should exalt the man she was about to marry over the lover of Mabel, of whose existence she was unaware.

Mabel was conscious, too, that Rhoda was exalting herself also, triumphing over her, as it were, on the strength of her coming dignity as a married woman ; and, gentle as she was, she felt a feverish impatience to get the start of her sister in the matrimonial race. She thought how beautiful, how refined, was her Wilfred. How repulsive was the good Joseph. And her heart throbbed at the contrast the brothers-in-law would exhibit. She was scarcely troubled at the subject of her mother's holding forth at the Friends' Meeting. True, Mr. Tresillian was not a Friend, but Friends were right in their views, and when those views were explained to Mr. Tresillian, he would see their justice, and adopt them.

Thus, in the tender delicious dream of love, she overleapt obstacles insurmountable in real life, as in sleep, the dreamer floats through air, scales towers, and fathoms precipices, without the power of exercising judgment as to the impossibility of this achievement.

Grown less apprehensive by habit, Mabel generally brought her lover into the house now ; for it was the month of October, and the nights were frequently wet, and always chilly. Luke Snow had been sullen, self-opinionated, when he did speak, and giving himself those airs of importance which most frequently accompany a weak brain inflated by vanity.

Master Luke had been plucking fruits of the tree of knowledge—of good and evil—and, instead of discovering that he was naked, he believed that he had clothed himself with glorious fruitage of knowledge which all must admire.

It was unlikely that the woman, who had been his companion on the night of Mabel's adventure, should relax her hold on the son of the wealthy merchant, from whom she had received small sums only at that period, the youth having no others in his possession ; but he had told her that, when his father returned home, he was to be received as clerk in the bank, with a small share of the profits, and in the meantime Polly Best thought it would be agreeable to get within the four walls of Trevedra House to see "how the land lay," and whether there might not be some small articles that she might purloin, and use at the pawnbrokers' as deposits.

Whilst Mabel met Mr. Tresillian in the garden, Luke Snow, who went out at the back of the house in the direction of the stables, neither detected his sister in her nocturnal meetings, nor was himself discovered in his irregularities. He had become more wise under the tuition of his female companion, whose object it was to keep things quiet; and instead of defying Mabel and making a quarrel, he simply waited till he believed her and the household to be asleep before he left home, taking care to return before the servants were stirring in the morning.

Had Mabel been less occupied by her love and her lover, she might have detected stealthy sounds in the house occasionally, when she was seated by his side in the dining-room or drawing-room, in whichever the fire burnt brightest; more frequently in the dining-room, which was on one side of the entrance-hall, and which did not necessitate the risk of ascending the stairs and the increased dread of detection.

"Stolen waters are sweet, and bread eaten in secret." I doubt whether Mr. Tresillian might have been satisfied had he met Mabel in her mother's drawing-room daily, and whether he would have found her conversation sufficiently piquant to have tempted him to return again and again to her presence. He delighted in the love she evinced towards him in every look, in every word she uttered—the love of a pure-minded girl, strictly modest, and carefully secluded from the world and its pollutions. He loved her in return, without being in love, as it is called, with her. He delighted to think he had inspired such an affection, but he knew the preponderance was on her side — that for the thousand pounds in pure gold he received, he could give but a hundred in return; still the payment, such as it was, was in specie.

It had been a gloomy evening, succeeded by a night of intense darkness—after more than six weeks had elapsed, spent in nightly meetings between the lovers, and on the night in question the dark, overhanging clouds began to give out a few large drops from their ragged edges—when Mabel led Mr. Tresillian into the dining-room.

She was never weary of asking him to describe his life and its surroundings—his mother, his brother, and his nieces. What they did, what they liked to do—their homes and friends. In return, she showed him all her innocent ignorance of life, and spoke with awe of her mother, and tenderness of her father. He had to soften and subdue in his narrative; for, gently dealt with as his facts might be, they were strong meat to babes. But Mabel had nothing to conceal, and was candid in all her revelations.

They sat together this night, Mr. Tresillian, as usual, holding Mabel's soft, dimpled hand, sometimes spreading it over his knee, sometimes raising it to see the pink fire-light shine through the transparent fingers, when the hand was suddenly raised in a listening position.

"Hark! What is that?" she cried.

Mr. Tresillian listened, but heard nothing.

"Some one is moving in the house. Oh! what can I do with thee? Where shall I hide thee?"

"There is nothing," replied her lover.

"If Luke should have gone out again," murmured the girl.

"Let him go!" impatiently.

"How canst thou?"

"Pardon me, dear Mabel; but you are unreasonably fond of that youth," replied her lover, omitting the adjective which his thought supplied.

"Are we not told to 'love even our enemies, and to forgive our brother, not seven times, but seventy times seven?'"

Mr. Tresillian answered not.

Mabel went on: "I will tell thee what I will do, I will go softly and see if he be in his room; he does not lock his door generally."

She lit a candle, and went up stairs, leaving Mr. Tresillian lighted only by the glow of the embers, and returned presently, with her face working with the effort to repress her sobs.

"He is not there—he has not been in bed," and, with a burst of tears no longer to be repressed, "he has left the lighted candle close to the muslin window curtains."

"Then, depend upon it, he will soon return," said Mr. Tresillian.

"I do not think that follows, for he was always careless about fire—poor Luke!"

"Let me see if the outer doors are fastened; he may be in the house," said her lover.

The back door had been unbolted and opened, and the noise Mabel had heard was its closing again.

"He is gone," said Mabel, leaning her head on Mr. Tresillian's arm, and weeping bitterly. "Thou didst save him once, and this time it may not be in thy power."

Mr. Tresillian felt by no means disposed to try, even for the sake of Mabel.

Luke Snow had not long left the house before the rain came down in torrents, and dashed itself against the dining-room windows, as it was flung in angry jerks by the wind.

"Luke is out in this bitter weather," said Mabel.

"I think I had better go into the bitter weather also," said Mr. Tresillian; "for I do not think he will stay out in it long, and it will not be agreeable for him to find me here."

"Oh! thou canst not go! Stay—I will hide thee, if he returns. Thou canst hide behind these window-curtains."

"Pardon me, sweet Mabel. I cannot conceal myself. If he finds me here he must take the consequences; but for his own disgraceful conduct, I should never have known the happiness of loving you."

They stood together, notwithstanding, in silent perplexity, Mr. Tresillian trying to make up his mind as to what position he should assume should Luke Snow return, Mabel's memory and imagination following her brother all through the darkness and rain down towards the mill, the roaring waters of which had ever filled her childish heart with dread, when she passed the unfenced depth in which the wheel revolved. Then, if he passed that danger safely, there was the broad, deep Leat, with the single plank and no hand-rail, which must be surmounted if he intended to reach the town; and whither else could he intend to go this wild night?

Mabel regarded her lover anxiously. She had a dim and vague conviction that he could follow her brother and bring him back, if he would. He had done so once, wherefore should he not do so again? She knew nothing of the town, excepting of that part which she passed on first day, going to meeting; but with the desire that her lover should leave her to seek Luke, came the dread lest he should be exposed to the storm; and the indecision made her silent and in-active.

Mr. Tresillian did not care whether or no he braved the elements; but he fancied that Mabel would be both help-less and unhappy should her brother stay out all night, or return in a state of intoxication, and be, perhaps, noisy and quarrelsome, or stupid and half insensible. He desired to be free from a very unpleasant predicament, but saw no way of escaping without great personal sacrifices, or without be-having shabbily to a young creature who seemed to be devoted to him.

"I can do nothing for him in this darkness," said Mr. Tresillian, "he has probably attained to some shelter within doors, where I, not knowing his haunts, could never find him."

"But thou didst find him before?"

"My child, I followed the crowd of revellers, and they dropped off one by one and left him lying insensible, and I returned to the hotel and procured the aid of my own servants. I have nothing to guide me now. I am willing to do anything to serve you, Mabel. I will go or I will remain. My advice to you is, to let me go, and to confide your brother's having left the house to the most trustworthy of your father's servants."

"They would tell—they would tell the mother," said the poor girl, wringing her plump fingers. "And Luke, what will become of him ?"

"You are unwise to place yourself in the power of such a brother," said her lover, with some irritation ; "a brother who could stand by and see his sister insulted."

"He was not himself, alas !" cried the girl.

Mr. Tresillian said no more then ; but with all his affection for Mabel he felt he should have liked to shake her.

Mabel, like all weak people, lost the time which pressed for action in indecision. She clung to Mr. Tresillian's arm ; she wished to have his aid and the comfort of his presence, whilst nothing but a chivalrous feeling prevented his leaving her and returning to the hotel.

That which she could not decide, was settled by circumstance.

Polly Best had been urged to obtain money, or money's worth, by the man she really cared for, from the youth who was her gull. Tim Brown was connected with a gang of burglars, and it was their object to get Polly into the merchant's house, and learn if possible the plan of the rooms, the nature of the fastenings, and what plunder might be the reward of their exploit, should they succeed. They did not expect money—nothing of importance ; for Friend Snow was a merchant not likely to keep cash in the house ; but they knew that he had had fine plate before he joined the society of Friends, and expected, not unreasonably, that, as part of the family were still at home, it would not all have been sent to the bank.

Consequently, Polly Best, notwithstanding the threatening of the night, went out to meet Luke Snow, and lay in wait for him in the lane which he must pass after crossing the Leat, before he reached the Hillside Almshouses.

She was shivering with cold, and told him she would walk

back with him as far as his father's house, as her father was at home, and would "kick up the Devil's delight" should she bring her Luke to their cottage.

She said nothing then about being admitted to the house, trusting to chance to befriend her: but she was unusually gentle and tender in her manner to the boy, whom she generally ruled, as bullies are best governed — by harsh measures. They reached the house door.

"Oh, Luke, dear! the cold have got hold of the very marrow of my back. Could you bring me out a drop of brandy, or rum, or gin, to warm my poor body?"

The rain had come down in torrents by this time, and Polly Best had only summer clothing; for though October had come, she had neither money nor credit for the purchase of seasonable habiliments.

"Yes, I dare say you are wet enough ; so am I, for that matter. I don't know about brandy, but I think there is some capital port wine in the dining-room. You stay here, and I will go and fetch it."

He departed to get a candle, and Polly, standing within the shelter of the house, took from her pocket a tinder-box and struck a light, for in those days lucifer matches had not been invented, and examined carefully the locks, bolts, and bars of the outer door, and measured the thickness of the staples in which they were embedded.

She had time to accomplish this ; for though Mabel had the key of the sideboard Luke Snow had another, which he had often found useful for his own comfort when the family were in bed and asleep, and this key he proceeded to his desk to fetch.

He had opened the back door so softly, that neither Mr. Tresillian nor Mabel had heard it, though they were intent on every sound. He did not mean to awake his sister Mabel and let her find out his theft of the wine. He could get at the key of the cellar which was kept in the sideboard, but there was no time for that now, and no necessity. The port wine had remained in the cellaret since the last time a sick neighbour had needed it, and he could replace it from the cellar before Mabel found it out. Softly as he came along the passage, Mr. Tresillian and Mabel heard his footsteps on the floor-cloth and remained motionless, as he opened the door stealthily and came into the room.

Mabel was sitting near the table, partly enveloped by the brown shawl she had worn when she went through the garden to admit Mr. Tresillian. He was leaning on the chimney-piece, nearly obscured by shadows which the dull red light of the decaying fire was insufficient to dissipate. Luke Snow, entering with the lighted candle in his hand, was clearly visible to them, whilst he did not observe the lovers.

The room was large, and his attention was occupied by what he was engaged in.

Mabel looked intently at her brother in astonishment at his possessing her key to the sideboard; for the idea of a duplicate did not suggest itself to her innocent mind, and her hand stole down to her pocket to be sure whether or not she had lost her own. With breathless wonder, which banished every thought of self, she observed him fill a tumbler, which he had brought from his bed-room, with port wine, and drink it off to the last drop; then he refilled it so plenteously that it threatened to run over, and to prevent this, and save the carpet from the tell-tale stain, he stooped his head to the glass, intending to take as much as would enable him to carry it without spilling, to his companion at the door; but Mabel, whose education had taught her that drunkenness was a sin that excluded from heaven, and terrified at the state of insensibility to which she had seen him reduced on a former occasion, forgot everything else in the desire she felt to save him from present and future peril, from impending disgrace and future despair, and walked swiftly across the room, snatching the tumbler from his shaking hand, spilling half its contents on the floor.

"Luke!" she said impressively, "thou shalt not drink this wine; thou hast drunk too much already."

"How! What! Mabel! Leave the wine alone; 'tis mine. I'm master here now *they* are away. What keeps thee up at this hour? Go to bed. How darest thou interfere with me? I'll drink all the wine in the cellar if I choose. Let go my arm, wilt thou?" and he flung her off with such violence that she staggered across the room, and only saved herself from falling by clinging to a chair.

Mabel recovered herself on seeing her brother about to refill the half-emptied tumbler with wine.

"If thou dost that, I will complain to our father of thee, Luke! How canst thou be so sinful?"

"Hold thy tongue, and be d——d," exclaimed the angry youth. "I shall do what I please;" and as she imprudently tried to seize the decanter, the degraded coward hit her a blow on the face. She reeled back with a faint cry, and Mr. Tresillian rushed forward, unable any longer to remain a quiet witness of such a scene, and shook Luke Snow violently by the collar, saying with clenched teeth,—

"You cowardly scoundrel! I'll shake every breath out of your body!"

As he left him free, Luke looked up astonished.

"Eh! what! Who the devil art thou? What dost thou here? Here, with my Sister Mabel!" recovering his breath. "Here in the middle of the night, alone with her!"

Now these were exclamations more easily made than answered, and Mr. Tresillian gave no explanation; indeed, he had no time; for Polly Best having found out all that was necessary on the side of the house through which she had entered, had extinguished her light, and following the murmur of angry voices, had stationed herself at the door, and became acquainted with the fact that there were two couple of lovers in the house by stealth instead of one couple.

She had seen Mr. Tresillian frequently in his ingress and egress from Prout's Hotel, and believed that his designs on Mabel were as illicit as hers on Luke Snow. She had "kept company" with gentlemen before every bit as good as he, she argued; though that was when she was younger. The rain pattered dismally outside the house, her thin and scanty clothing clung to her shivering frame, and the warmth of the glowing embers was tempting. Why should they not all sit round and be comfortable, she thought; and she bobbed a courtesy to the company generally as she stood at the door, and edged herself into the room.

"Begging your pardin, gentlefolks, the rain is hard, and my clothes is wet, and if the young lady allows I should like a warming at this here fire."

Suiting the action to the word, she drew a chair up, and placing her saturated and mud-covered boots on the fender, was soon enveloped in the steam, which rising from her wet clothes, enveloped her in a mist.

"Luke!" gasped Mabel, "who is this friend? Wherefore hast thou brought her here?"

"No harm, Miss Snow. Your brother and I is old acquaintance; and as I was reeking wet, he promised me a glass of something comfortable to drink. You've yot your sweetheart—I've got mine. I don't see a pin to choose between us—not I. I warrant me the old Quakers would open their eyes as much on account of one as t'other." Then, in a whisper to Luke, "Don't thee be put upon. Ask him why he is here alone with your Sister Mabel."

"Yes, indeed—you Sir—what's your name? What do you mean by being alone with my Sister Mabel?"

Mabel went timidly across the room, and placed her hand on Mr. Tresillian's coat.

He turned angrily on Snow.

"Take that woman out of the room, Sir, and do not let her presence pollute your innocent sister."

"Oh bother! If you come to that," said Polly, "I don't see a pin to choose between the Quaker's daughter and me. I'll warrant Mr. Tresillian aint making sheep's eyes at her for nothing in the dead of night here."

Here Mr. Tresillian's patience was exhausted, and crossing the room, he seized Polly's arm, and taking the candle in the other hand, he led her out into the hall. He opened one of the doors, and found it led into the kitchen, in which there was still fire enough remaining to warm the shivering woman, and leaving the candle with her, he returned to the dining-room.

Mabel sat weeping at the table, and Luke, partly ashamed of his companion, partly defiant from finding out his sister's delinquencies, went on reiterating, "But what is that man doing here? What business has he to be with thee at this time of the night?"

"The right of being her future husband," said Mr. Tresillian, firmly, whose chivalrous feeling made what he felt to be a sacrifice of himself imperative for Mabel's reputation.

"*Thou* her husband! Thou art not a Friend?" said the youth.

Mr. Tresillian replied not, but placed Mabel's arm within his.

"I will start for London at once," he said, "and apply

for your parents' permission to marry you. Give me the address."

Mabel, sobbing, tore the cover from an old letter, and wrote it for him.

"Wine! you promised me wine," said Polly Best, putting her head in at the door.

"Give her the wine!" said Mr. Tresillian, angrily to Luke Snow, "and let her remain in the kitchen till the rain has ceased. For yourself, you had better retire to your room, and learn to treat your sister with more respect."

"Thou mayest be d—d," said Luke; "if Mabel is too fine for Polly, I'll sit in the kitchen with my girl. I think, however, fine Sir, thou countest thy chickens before they are hatched, when thou speakest of marrying Mabel Snow. Friends do not wear clothes like thine, and none but a Friend will be permitted to marry Walter and Rachel Snow's daughter."

Thus saying, he took the decanter of wine and retired to the kitchen.

Mr. Tresillian remained trying to comfort the unhappy Mabel, who, weeping yet from the agitation of the scene, was consoled by her reliance on her lover. All would go right in his hands, she was convinced. So she dried her tears, and Mr. Tresillian waited till Luke Snow had let out the woman, and they heard his heavy and uncertain steps on the stairs leading to his own room. Then Mr. Tresillian embraced Mabel tenderly, and bade her farewell, intending, if possible, to catch the night mail to London, if not, to post up, for the purpose of demanding Mabel in marriage of her parents.

When Luke Snow had dismissed Polly Best and finished the decanter of wine, of which I regret to say he drank the greatest share, he retired to his room and slept off the effect of his potations. He awoke next day with a cloudy sense of discomfort on his mind, on which the image became distinct by degrees, as the mists of sleep were dispelled, like as the figures on the glass of the magician gather themselves into form and consistency; but with this difference, that no enchanter's wand can, in real life, dissipate the disastrous combinations which swarm upon our awaking.

It was a proof of the intense selfishness of Luke Snow's character, that the only gleam of comfort afforded by his morning's retrospection of the transactions of the night arose from his conviction of his sister's transgression ; for in that transgression lay his safeguard from blame.

He set himself to address his father and mother as follows. It must be conceded that he was sincere in his statement ; that he knew nothing of Mr. Tresillian's acquaintance with his sister, for Mabel had not enlightened him on the subject, it being a fact of which she was chary of speaking, both on her own account, and because she did not wish to remind him of his degraded state, which had led to her meeting with Mr. Tresillian : —

" November 1, 18—.

"My Respected Parents,

"It is with deep sorrow I write that which will give pain to you both ; but without circumlocution I will inform you of what has come to my knowledge with regard to my dear but erring Sister Mabel.

"Last night, after I had been some time asleep—I retire to rest a few minutes before ten o'clock, not forgetting to meditate deeply before laying my head on my pillow, on all that I have accomplished or omitted in the day past, determined to act with increased diligence on that which is about to dawn—I heard amidst the beating of the rain against the window, a cry as if of a human being in pain or distress. My beloved parents have taught me to give to him that asketh not, and from him that is in want to turn not away ; so I dressed myself, and having obtained a light, I opened the back door, and found a poor wayfarer drenched by the rain and shivering in the bitter wind, and faint nigh unto death.

"So I said unto myself, 'When saw ye any a-hungred and athirst and gave not unto them, so much as ye did it not to them ye did it not to me.'

"I knew where Mabel had left the key of the sideboard, and I left the stranger at the door to get some wine to support her sinking frame ; but when I reached the dining-room what a scene met my aggrieved sight—Mabel sat there by the fire with a strange friend—if friend he may be called, who is a man of violence and wrong. First, Mabel strove to prevent my carrying the wine to the fainting 'stranger within the gate,' and then that man of Belial, when I persisted in my work of charity, smote me violently, sundry times, so that I was compelled to escape and place the poor wanderer for warmth before the kitchen fire, whence she departed shortly after nourished and comforted; for like the Good Samaritan I gave her sixpence from my pocket-money. With regard to my Sister Mabel, my dear parents, you will do that which seemeth good unto you; but I would prefer an humble petition that you would deal gently with this erring child. I do not know how she came to have knowledge of this violent man, but he professed a determination to marry her, which saying on his part appeared greatly to exalt her spirits. I believe he will shortly appear before you. He is a brother of that godless man Henry, commonly called the Lord Trelusa, whose days are passed in riot and drunkenness, in which particular doubtless his brother resembles him.

"The children are well. I grieve, dear parents, that this woeful intelligence should come to damp the joy which the preparations for my Sister Rhoda's prosperous marriage must naturally occasion you. Believe me that a strong sense of duty only both to you and to my sister could induce me to make this revelation; and in great sorrow,

"I remain your affectionate son,

"LUKE SNOW,"

The writing of this letter looked like copper-plate. Writing and accounts were Luke Snow's great points, and for his proficiency therein he had obtained the prize of a beautiful silver pen from the grammar school at which he had been educated.

Before Mabel had parted from her lover she had entreated him in his application to her parents to spare as much as possible all mention of her Brother Luke's irregularities. He promised that he would keep silence on the subject; or, if hard pressed, would refer her parents to herself for information.

CHAPTER XXVI.

" A slavery beyond enduring,
But that 'tis of our own procuring :
As spiders never seek the fly,
But leave him of himself t' apply,
So men are by themselves betrayed
To quit the freedom they enjoyed,
And run there necks into a noose
They'd break them after to bieak loose."

HUDIBRAS.

ALL the chivalry of Mr. Tresillian's nature had been called into play in the scene in the Quaker's dining-room, and though he had no intention of shrinking from his avowed determination to demand Mabel in marriage, because as a gentleman he felt he could not do otherwise under the circumstances, yet it must be confessed that the necessity filled him with depression. Beautiful and innocent as was Mabel Snow, she was not the creature whom his imagination had painted as the companion of his future life. No ! his wife ought to be highly descended, perfectly accomplished, and exceedingly clever and *spirtuelle*. Mabel was very beautiful, but only respectable in her connections ; and with all the affectionate interest he felt towards her, he could not deny that her simplicity was carried to an excess, which was charming in the young Quakeress, but would be out of place in the future Mrs. Tresillian, and the possible Lady Trelusa.

" But 'tis useless to look back," he meditated. " Perhaps the old Quakers will refuse me. What a blessing ! Yet if they know the state of Harry's health, I fear there is no hope of that. Yet it would make that poor girl very miserable not to marry me; so I must resign myself to my fate: after all, it will not be a hard one."

So Mr. Tresillian lost the mail coach, and posted up to London, which was a tedious manner of getting over the journey; and Luke's letter reached the parents twenty-four hours sooner than the subject of it.

Great was the grief and distress at Mabel's backsliding. Rachel Snow's anger was the greatest; Walter Snow's regret.

"Alas! Elizabeth!" he said, addressing Friend Snow, "we have overweighted that delicate child with the responsibilities we laid on her."

"Thou speakest as one bereft of judgment, Walter Snow," said his wife, whose will it had been to leave her home in Mabel's charge, and attend the Friends' quarterly meeting in London. "That evil-minded daughter must suffer for her sin, and repent, or be cast out from amongst us."

"It is said of the man Tresillian, of whom our Luke writeth, that his wealth is abundant," said Walter Snow, regretfully.

"'How hardly shall a rich man enter into the kingdom of heaven,'" rejoined his wife.

"Thou wilt hear what he hath to say?" suggested the meek husband.

"Verily, I will, and give him an answer also," was the decision of the wife. And the matter rested till the following day, when the female servant announced that a man not in the garb of a Friend, desired to have a meeting with Friend Snow, to converse with him touching an affair of importance. Men servants were not employed by Friends at the period of my story, as savouring too much of the pomps and vanities of the world.

As the maid presented the card to Rachel Snow, Walter Snow read "Mr. Wilfred Tresillian, Albany."

"Tell Friend Wilfred that we will receive him and hear his discourse," said the father of Mabel.

In another instant Mr. Tresillian had entered the room, of which the walls were drab coloured, the curtains were drab merino, the chairs were oak covered with drab stuff, a table stood on four legs in the centre of the room, square in its shape—for round pillar-and-claw tables were considered as dangerous, because a fashionable innovation; no pictures or glass ornamented the walls. The Friends took literally

15

the commandment, "Thou shalt not make to thyself any graven image, nor the likeness of anything which is in heaven above or in the earth beneath, or in the waters under the earth;" thus any representation of animal or vegetable life was considered sinful. Nothing could be more dreary and repulsive than this sitting-room, where, in addition to the Quaker and his wife, sat a maiden sister of the latter, to whom the house belonged.

There was a physical difference in the appearance of the sisters, though their dress was identical. Each sister had some gray knitting before them, which, from its being armed by four small shining pins and by its nondescript form, might be intended for a future stocking. The male Friend had just been reading aloud some serious book, which he laid on the table, carefully placing a mark in it first.

Mrs. Snow was plump and well-favoured; her sister, Miss Den, was evil-looking and meagre—withered in form, and sour in expression—more sullen, though less passionate, than Mrs. Snow.

A contrast was formed by the appearance of the young man who now entered, and who, bringing his feet into the dancing master's fourth position, made a bow of his head only, keeping his back erect, which brought his rounded chin on the deep cambric double-frilled shirt which adorned his chest.

Having executed three of these movements addressed to each person in the company, he stood erect, a fine specimen of beautiful and well-developed manhood, with blooming health to tint his cheeks, and a profusion of light curls, worn in what was called a Brutus crop, waving over his white and well-formed forehead.

The female Friends sat still, with a slight movement to acknowledge the civility, but Friend Snow could not forget his former habits, and with the instincts of a gentleman, he placed a chair for the guest, saying, "I beg thee to be seated."

When Mr. Tresillian had rung at the bell, he had wished in his whole heart that he might be refused the petition he was about to make; but the sight of the antagonistic countenances of the two women made him resolve to carry his point, were it only to overcome their opposition.

There was a moment's pause after he was seated, which was broken by Friend Snow, who said, "May I ask thee, friend, wherefore thou art come?"

"I am come," said Mr. Tresillian, "to say that I have become warmly attached to your daughter Mabel, and would gladly have your permission and that of her mother to woo her consent to become my wife. My means are ample, and I am, and ever have been on principle, free from debt. You shall have no reason to complain of the settlement I am willing to execute on your daughter, and on my children by her. For information on these points I would refer you to my lawyers, Messrs. Holdfast and Clutch."

"I thank thee, Friend Tresillian," said Mr. Snow, and was again silent.

His benevolent but rather weak expression was troubled. He would have given Mabel to her suitor, gladly, had his means equalled his statements, and had Mrs. Snow been out of the way. He was attracted by the charm of Mr. Tresillian's manner and appearance, and thought, as did Mabel, that he differed much from Joseph Sturm.

The female Friends only crossed their arms over their laps and gave expression to a deep groan.

"May I inquire," said Friend Snow, with some natural curiosity, "how thou didst first obtain speech of my daughter Mabel, and how long thou hast known her?"

"On these points I must refer you to her," said Mr. Tresillian.

"I have heard that thou wert seen in my house in her company at an unseemly hour of the night." (Deeper groans from the female Friends). "Dost thou consider it a fit time to see a young maiden, when sleep had fallen, as far as thou didst know, on every other member of the family? Dost thou consider such conduct as likely to recommend thee to the parents of the young maiden?"

"That my intentions towards your daughter were honourable, I am here to vindicate. Anything eccentric in the hour of my visits, Miss Mabel Snow can explain clearly to you."

"I trust she may be able to do so," said the father.

But Mrs. Snow, seeing that her husband was, as she imagined, losing ground in the conference, broke in.

15—2

"Friend Tresillian, we know nothing of thee, excepting this—that thou desirest to marry our daughter, and that thou hast visited her probably sundry times and in divers places without our knowledge or permission. In this thou hast sinned, and hast caused thy weaker sister to sin. Thou comest now, saying, what shall I do that you may give me your daughter to wife? Friend, consider thy appearance! Think of thy outward adornment, and how fearful a sin it is to waste so much of thought and money on striving to make thyself as much of an ape as those of rank higher even than thine own. Look at that high rolling collar round the top of thy coat, thy waist buttoned in till thy figure resembles that of a wasp, thy metal buttons, two useless ones behind, thy so-called Hessian boots, with things called tassels dangling in front, thy hat without a brim sufficiently wide to shade thy face. Friend, cast away these follies—unite thyself with a meek and teachable spirit to the Society of Friends—give to it a sufficient portion of thy wealth, such as the Council of Friends shall decide, and when they have admitted thee into our community, we will decide whether thou art a helpmate fit for our daughter Mabel."

Mrs. Snow's voice, in ordinary conversation, was agreeable; but when preaching in a full assembly of Friends, or making a speech as on the present occasion, her voice ceased to be impressive, and went off into a whine.

At first Mr. Tresillian, who was a singularly good-tempered young man, felt amused by her tirade against his personal appearance; but by degrees he became impatient, though waiting with exemplary politeness till she had finished. Then he replied—

"I think, Madam, you would have reasonable grounds for contempt of my principles, could I throw away the habits and convictions of twenty-eight years to adopt those of a peculiar sect, on no more serious basis than a desire to wed your daughter. Deeply as I value her, I fear my suit must be considered as ended, if such obstacles are thrown in my way. This must ever be a subject of bitter regret to me, for I love Mabel Snow sincerely, and would willingly make any sacrifice to ensure her happiness."

He rose.

"Remember," said the mother, pointing her finger impressively at the lover, " I forbid thee to see or to write to her."

" In that matter I shall do that which I see fit, without reference either to your wishes or your commands," said Mr. Tresillian, flushing with indignation ; and with less of ceremony than he had shown on entering the room, he left it, with a stiff bow to the Quaker family, and opening the door himself, he jumped into his *dennet*, and returned to his rooms in the Albany.

Thus, a few hours after he wrote to Mabel, believing that she would receive the letter before her parents could interfere to prevent it :—

"ALBANY, NOVEMBER, 18—.

" MY BELOVED MABEL,

" I have entreated for permission to marry you, and I have been refused with unmerited insult.

" Under these circumstances, I feel it will be kinder for you, as well as for myself, that all intercourse should cease between us. I shall never cease to love you, and earnestly to desire your welfare. If you are willing to marry me contrary to the wishes of your parents, and because I am dearer to you than those who have claims of kindred, write to me at ——, Albany, and I will contrive to meet you and carry out your wishes ; but I will not urge on you a course that may make your future life full of bitterness and disappointment. I cannot become one of your sect, sweet Mabel can you live my life and be happy with me, cast off by your parents, and dismissed from your community? Choose, dear Mabel, after due deliberation, and let me know your determination after the lapse of a week.

" Your ever affectionate

" WILFRED."

Mr. Tresillian gave a sigh of relief when he finished this. " Poor girl ! There, I have done my duty. I hope she will not accept my offer. At any event, I'm clear for a week, and now I'll enjoy myself."

To Mabel, accustomed to the scrupulous veracity of the Friends, and to their unexaggerated style of conversation, the letter seemed perfect in the expressions of love it conveyed. It was her first love-letter. The postman had brought it to the back-door when she had gone to the kitchen to give her morning orders to the cook. She took it unperceived by anyone, and with self command which astonished herself, she concealed it with the snowy kerchief which covered her delicate bosom, and wandered away through the autumn-tinted shrubbery till she was secluded from observation, to peruse and reperuse the letter till she knew it by heart.

A violent struggle took place in the mind of the young Quakeress. She had fully believed that her Wilfred would give up his convictions and adopt those of her family, simply because she knew that they were in the right, and fancied that he only required to be directed in a straight path to follow it without effort or reluctance.

The thought of her Wilfred, cast into outer darkness, where there would be weeping and gnashing of teeth, drove her to despair; and with every desire to rescue him from such a fate, she had no intention of sharing it. It would be too dreadful.

"Yet," argued Mabel, "is not the unbelieving husband sanctified by the wife? For what knowest thou, oh wife, whether thou shalt save thy husband?"

He had given her a week for her decision, and this power of controlling her own destiny, drove her into the tortures of uncertainty for twenty-four hours—for that period she knew herself to be free to write to him without constraint—but of this independence she was to be deprived.

"Friend Mabel!" said the wife of a respectable tradesman of the Quaker persuasion, walking to meet her as she was trimming the withered roses from their stalks in the garden which had been the scene of so many meetings with Wilfred, "I have a letter from thy mother, who, knowing it to be about the time when the drapery business would call me to London for the choice of winter goods, has commissioned me to take thee up with me, doubtless that thou mayest be present at the union of thy sister with Friend Joseph Sturm. Doth not thy heart rejoice, and is not thy spirit glad at the prospect? Thou wilt see all the pomps of the world and the vanities thereof; but thou wilt turn away thine eyes lest thou behold vanity."

Mabel quivered with apprehension at the thought of meeting her parents; but there was consolation. London did not seem to her imagination less circumscribed than the small town of T——, and Wilfred was in London. She should see him pass the house. She should watch for him from the window. Her aunt's house did not stand in a garden like her own home, but in a street, and through this street of course Wilfred would . frequently ride or walk. What pleasure to catch even a glimpse of his figure, to hear the sound of his voice speaking to an indifferent person. She must not marry him ; but oh ! to see him once more—— to feel the touch of his hand !

" I go up this evening, Friend Mabel. Perhaps thou couldest come in thy father's conveyance, and bring thy box and take me up with mine, to deposit us at Prout's Hotel at seven o'clock this evening. I will take two places in the inside of the mail-coach, and I trust we may reach London in safety in three days' space."

" I will not fail to be with thee," rejoined Mabel ; " and now I beg thy excuse if I leave thee, for I have much to arrange for the children and servants before I leave home."

Mabel had never before been inside a mail-coach, and the confined space and small windows seemed to suffocate her ; but under the experienced guidance of her conductor she was deposited safely at the door of Miss Den's house, which was situated in one of the smallest and dreariest of the streets at the West-end of London. A gaunt female opened the door, and Mrs. Milford, satisfied with having done her duty, asked if Friend Snow or Friend Den were at home, and hearing that the latter was, she left a message that she had brought Mabel, and hurried away to her own connections.

Mabel was shown by the maid into her aunt's sitting-room, which was at the back of the house. The front sitting-room was the best seemingly, and always kept locked and darkened, unless on great occasions. Miss Den kept the key ; the front bed-room was occupied by that lady, and a small one at the back was appropriated to the use of Mabel. The back-room looked into a narrow slip of garden, in which the beds were covered with patches of black and green mould and moss. There were a few straggling shrubs, which seemed determined to straggle, as all healthy growth was denied them. Some dilapidated trellis work, which had once been green, stood at the end of the bit of garden, and had once supported a virginian creeper, which, like other dependants, had succeeded in overturning its stay, by superior weight and wilfulness. This slight fence had been meant to shut out from view a stable which belonged to the house ; but as Miss Den did not keep horses, it was let, and the door for ingress and egress was on the other side from the garden. A window which lighted the harness-room, looked into the garden ; but as neither Miss Den nor her maid was particularly attractive, they had never found themselves troubled by any prying eyes directed towards their movements by curious grooms.

This account of the locality is necessary for the clear understanding of the story which is to follow.

When Mabel looked at her aunt's grim countenance, her heart sank within her. She had never met Miss Den since she was a child, and had forgotten her visage and gait.

"Is my father here, or my mother?" said the poor girl, timidly.

"Thy parents have returned to the house thou didst prove thyself unfitted to hold. They have gone to perform the duties to their younger children, which thou didst neglect. Thou wilt not see them again till thou art brought to a better state of mind, and hast shown thyself penitent for thy sin."

"Rhoda," inquired Mabel. "May I not see her?"

"Rhoda was united yesterday morning to Joseph Sturm. She has departed to her husband's dwelling, and is happy."

"Alas! my sister! thou hast no thought then of the unhappy Mabel."

"Rhoda has chosen the good part that shall not be taken from her. The part of fulfilling the duties of her daily life. Trouble her not, then, with the knowledge of thy misconduct. We have concealed it from her hitherto."

Mabel said no more. She was thankful for this at least. The rest of the day passed in silence.

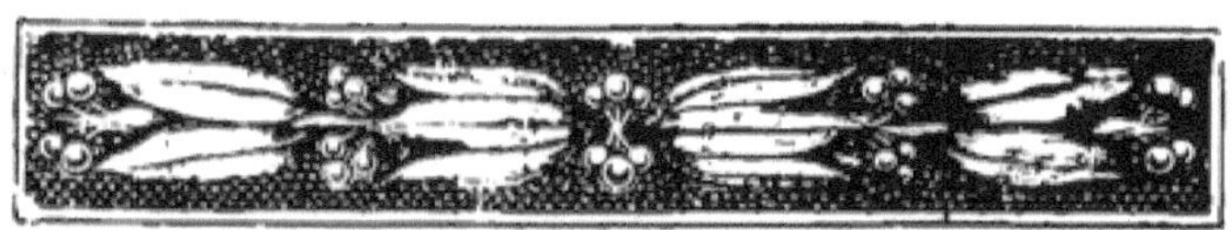

CHAPTER XXVII.

N the following morning, Miss Den brought into the sitting-room a large bundle of Irish, cut out into shirts, and gave Mabel a collar to stitch. Probably no lady of the present day is aware of the trial to the eyes resulting from stitching the collar of a shirt, when every separate stitch was severed and reunited by the industrious needlewoman. Mabel fancied, as these collars came up afresh, several in the course of each day, that the Friends to whom they appertained must have as many throats as the centipede had legs. Sometimes she rose and walked to the window, and looked into the little narrow garden bounded by its high walls. The stems of the virginian creeper delivered their fluttering leaves to the damp air and looked each day more naked and forlorn. Where were the populated streets on which she hoped to look down and find her lover? She was shut in a dungeon, as it were, a perfect prison-house, and her aunt and the gaunt maid were her jailors.

"I cannot bear it! I will seek him. I will marry him. I pine for a sight of him. Let me but see his face, but once, only once. Let me but feel his arms round me saying, 'Mabel, I love you.' Yet if I should entail on myself everlasting punishment for this love, if he is to drag me down to perdition, oh! let me be anywhere so it be with him!"

These were Mabel's thoughts, repeated to herself in every variety of language, but ever with the same meaning. The struggle between her love and what she conceived to be her duty, threatened to make her reason totter on its throne. The week had passed, and she had not succeeded in obtaining any news of her lover. She had decided to accept his offer to marry her. She wrote to him thus:

" —— Street, London, Nov.

"WILFRED,

"Like as the hart panteth for the water brooks, so longeth my soul after thee, my love.

"My soul is compelled to dwell with those who are enemies to its peace.

"Take me away, oh my beloved! Make me thy wife. I will be thine, and do thy bidding in all things.

"Thy wife that will be,

"MABEL SNOW."

Mabel watched the butcher's cart as it came for orders one morning. As the gaunt Jane left the door to ask her mistress's orders, Mabel stepped down, held out the letter to the boy who drove it, and, with an agitated voice, begged him to post it for her.

The boy did not understand what was said at first, but when he did, and held out his hand to receive the letter, a sudden and powerful grasp on Mabel's arm arrested it midway; and Jane, taking the letter from Mabel's trembling fingers, carried it off to Miss Den.

Deprived of this hope, and compelled to the incessant use of her eyes and fingers in her monotonous employment, Mabel's mind gave way.

One morning she tore her white dress in passing through a door, and proceeded to mend it with a darn of black sewing-silk. When her aunt looked at her in wonder, which upset her usual placid grimness, the unfortunate girl was momentarily conscious of her lapse from reason, and rushed to the upper window in her bed-room to throw herself out into the garden, hoping to end her misery in death. With wild eyes and frantic gestures she sprang on to the window seat, and placed her foot on the window-sill. The house-maid, who was busy in the room, threw her arms round her, and, at the risk of being precipitated down with her to certain death or mutilation, she held on, and dragged her back to the bed, fastening her hands behind her tightly with a handkerchief.

Left in silence and loneliness she slept, and awoke in wonder at the ligatures that bound her.

Miss Den came up, and seeing the softened expression in Mabel's eyes, she removed the handkerchief, and left her at liberty.

To the Society of Friends it was owing that those ameliorations in the treatment of lunatics were first instituted, which are now universally adopted. Miss Den saw in Mabel's symptoms excuses for much in her conduct that had been so faulty ; but with that conviction came also the determination to send her, with her parents' permission, to the asylum at York, where she might be restored to the perfect use of her mental powers.

Miss Den held frequent conversation with her maid. When there are three in a house, two will always band themselves against the third, even when there is not the excuse of a cause so valid as in the case of Mabel Snow. Terror quickened Mabel's perceptions. She was half conscious that she deserved coercion, but she believed that could she but attain to her lover she should be restored to mental health. She listened, and heard from Miss Den's communication to Jane, when they believed that she slept, that she was in a few days to be taken to the asylum at York, a week's journey from Wilfred. With dilated eyelids and hair falling over her naked shoulders, she had crept in her night clothes down the stairs and listened on tiptoe at the door of the sitting-room. They moved slightly, and Mabel regained her room, and when their steps were heard at her bed-room door she was in bed and breathing quietly in simulated sleep. But after that night she never rested for more than a few minutes at a time. Her aunt used to come and see her in bed and take away her candle. She contrived to secrete a piece, but she could not strike a light without making a noise which might alarm Miss Den. Sometimes she got up and dressed herself in the dark. Her bonnet had been taken from her, but she could put on the rest of her clothes, and she would sit up till the tardy autumn light warned her to undress and conceal her past watchfulness.

She was sitting up thus one night, about two o'clock in the morning, after her light had been removed for several hours, when she heard a carriage stop at the door—might it not be at the next house? No, it was for her—she was to be taken away quietly in the night—she knew it now, and could piece together the fragmentary speeches she had heard through the door.

Jane was going through the front hall to let them in—the cruel doctor and the attendants who were to convey her away. She stole softly down stairs. They were busy with lights in the front hall, and could not see her enveloped in her brown shawl. She opened the door going into the garden, and ran to the window of the stable. A groom, who had been bedding up his horses, saw the apparition of Mabel's white face at the window.

"Open, for the love of Heaven!" cried the girl, and the groom opened the window of the harness-room and drew Mabel inside.

"They are coming after me," she whispered, "do not say where I am. I want to go to a friend—wilt thou tell me how to go? Alas! I have only that to give thee," offering a five-shilling piece.

"Come this way, Miss," said the man, shutting down the window, "'spose them old Quakers are precious sharp on the young ones. I'll not peach; come here," and he took her arm and led her to a stand of hackney coaches and assisted Mabel into one.

"Now, Miss, where shall I say?"

Mabel replied by giving the number of Wilfred's address in the Albany, and the coach drove off.

CHAPTER XXVIII.

" Fill the bowl with rosy wine,
    Round our temples roses twine ;
    Let us cheerfully awhile
    Like the wine and roses smile.
    Crown'd with roses we condemn
    Gyges' wealthy diadem.

" To-day is ours !   What do we fear ?
    To-day is ours ! we have it here :
    Treat it kindly, that it may
    Wish at least with us to stay.
    Banish business, banish sorrow,
    To the gods belong to-morrow."

ROCHESTER.

THE HON. MR. TRESILLIAN was determined to enjoy himself, as we have before stated.   His spirits rose as he felt the week had elapsed, and Mabel had made no claim on him.   She was a sweet, innocent girl ; but he liked his freedom, and though he would not have acted in a cruel or ungentlemanlike manner towards one so timid and confiding, he was not sorry that she had not taken him at his word.

On that night he entertained a party of more than usual brilliancy.   His rooms at the Albany were furnished in the richest as well as the most gorgeous style of furniture.   Gilding on every article of furniture was the questionable taste introduced by the Regent.   Magnificent mirrors adorned the walls of his room, and reflected the cut-glass chandeliers quivering in their diamond drops, the elaborate beauty of which has never been exceeded by modern inventions. Heavy crimson velvet curtains with bullion fringe and tassels covered the windows, and the table was loaded with the choicest wines, the most luscious fruits, the most brilliant and fragrant of flowers. The party assembled was heterogeneous. On one side of the host sat a royal duke, on the opposite a beautiful singer, rather inclined to the autumn than the spring of life, with a magnificent bust and falling shoulders, so little concealed by drapery, that the spectator felt nervous as to the result of every movement. Luckily, she was tranquil and dignified, and unused to exertion, so she did not trespass on propriety to a greater degree than she had herself anticipated.

Next to the royal duke sat a lovely little actress, Mrs. M——, also dressed in the extreme of fashion, who had a few days before shocked the audience at Drury Lane by an accidental slip of her dress from her shoulder and breast. They had hissed her vehemently, and she had retired to the wing to re-adjust her clothes. Seemingly, she knew that such castigation would not exist at a private party, and she had acted on that conviction in the exhibition of her shoulders and bosom.

Next to her was seated one whom scandal had mixed up with her name, to the detriment of his domestic peace, one of the noblest of three heads, all noble, all intellectual, all of the highest character of beauty,—Goethe, Canova, and Byron. This last had not dined with the party, as he was adhering to his capricious regimen of biscuits and weak claret and water, but he had joined the company when the cloth had been removed, to enjoy what might be a feast of reason, but would certainly be a flow of soul. Mr. Tresillian was a Whig, and consequently in the Opposition, and he had some of the noted of that party amongst his guests.

Moore was there, with a bacchanalian twinkle in his blue eyes, and Sir F—— B——, in the glory of his recent martyrdom, having been committed to the Tower for his defence of the rights and liberties of the people.

He was singularly favoured by nature in a person on which gentleman seemed stamped from his birth, refined by education, and made irresistible to women by the charm of his manner, and the silvery tones of a finely modulated voice. These attractions he retained when youth had long been past.

Near him sat Bob ——, as he was familiarly called, a youth noted for fun and wildness, and for excess.

Near the bottom of the table sat a gentleman from the City, a man noted for shrewd business habits, which had made him useful in righting the labouring and nearly foundering vessels of his Royal Highness's domestic economy; and he was admitted to terms of intimacy, almost amounting to friendship, with more than one of the royal brothers. His indefatigable activity, decision, and humanity had lately rescued from death three unfortunate Irishmen, condemned, for coining, on the evidence of an informer, for the sake of the blood-money. This circumstance had extorted the admiration of those even who envied him, whilst the young applauded the undaunted courage with which, during one of the Burdett riots, he had plunged into the crowd, and seized a ringleader of the mob, narrowly escaping death from the loaded pistol which another pointed at his head, but which the staff of a constable jerked up into the air.

" The Syren," as the duke called Mrs. B——, sang at his request her celebrated bravura from the " Duenna," " Adieu, thou Dreary Pile," which was followed by his Royal Highness's voice in his favourite song of

> " The glasses sparkle on the board,
>   The wine is ruby bright;
> The reign of pleasure is restored,
>   Of mirth and gay delight.
> The night is ours ! then crown with flowers
>   The moments as they roll.
> If any pain or care remain,
>   We'll drown it in the bowl."

On the last line, repeated over and over again, he always pronounced drown as *drownd;* probably he would have spelt it thus had he ever had occasion to do so. But if he reasoned at all on the subject, he probably thought he might plead the privilege of near relationship to murder his papa's English.

When the applause, which had succeeded these jolly couplets, had died away into silence, the duke called on Mr. —— for a song, and the good-natured gentleman immediately complied, giving " The Wolf" with such magnificence of power, that Mrs. B—— applauded enthusiastically a voice which, always after dinner, created an Orphic dance amongst the wine-glasses and finger-glasses. Lord Byron now begged Tom Moore to give his favourite "When first I saw thee Warm and Young." He sang with but little voice, but with such exquisite taste and feeling, that tears started in the eyes of more than one auditor amongst the revellers. Several actresses had joined the party in the dresses in which they had appeared on the boards; but the most inveterate pleasure-seeker wearies sometimes, especially between two and three in the morning, and some were going to send for their carriages, when Tom Moore struck up "Fly not yet!" entreating the guests all to join in chorus, knowing that no music is so popular as that in which all can bear a part.

This was agreed, and the first verse went off well; but in the chorus Bob —— began a very drunken ditty of his own invention,—

> " Brandy I will not;
>   Royal gin for ever;
> Gin so gallows hot,
>   Gin has burnt my liver."

Mr. Tresillian rose from his seat, and taking the youth by the arm led him, too drunk to resist, into his bed-room, and flung him on the sofa.

The singing was waxing fast and furious,—

> " Thus should women's hearts and looks
>   At noon be cold as winter brooks,
>   Nor kindle till the night returning
>   Brings their genial hour for burning."

Lord Byron glanced at the beautiful actress, the royal duke at the Syren; wine and love, if such riot deserve the name, possessed the party, and propriety shrunk away aghast, when the door opened, and Mabel was ushered in by the valet. "A Bold Stroke for a Wife," had been represented at Covent Garden that night with a young _débutante_ in the character of Ann Lovely. Mr. Tresillian's valet, who was thoroughly acquainted with all the circumstances connected with both theatres, was aware of this fact, and when he saw Mabel Snow, and heard her inquiry for his master, he was by no means astonished or disturbed by the appearance of the fair Quakeress, but felt assured that the beautiful *débutante* had come to supper fresh from the theatre, and dressed in character.

Accordingly he ushered her into the supper room, at the door of which, as he closed it behind her, the unhappy Mabel stood, looking dazed and bewildered at the dazzling lights, the rich company, and the unwonted sounds of revelry.

" Oh stay ! Oh stay !"

shouted the guests in chorus,--and Mabel's entrance was for a moment unperceived, whilst she looked from one gentleman's face to another, in the hope of recognising Tresillian—in vain.

She began with hope,—she ended with perplexity. Her brain had recovered its natural state now that she felt that she had escaped from the terrors of her aunt. With her perfect sanity came the horror of what she considered sin as exhibited by this assemblage of men carousing, and women half-naked. Polly Best, with her soaked bonnet, muddy boots, and dripping shawl, was clothed to the chin. These women made her face crimson with shame for them who felt none for themselves. About Polly's profession she had had but a suspicion. Here was vice triumphant. Luckily, her Wilfred was not amongst them. She turned to leave the room, thinking the servant had mistaken what she said ; but her egress was prevented by a young nobleman in a state of semi-intoxication, who placed himself between her and the door, and who, staring impudently in her face, sang again the chorus, "Oh ! Stay ! Sweet Ann Lovely ! why turn from your devoted admirers ?"

With the gentlemanlike manners of the old school, Sir F B——t arose from his seat, and advancing towards her with a reverential bow, said, "Sweet Quakeress ! take a seat at this table, where are assembled so many of the most accomplished of your own profession. I feel convinced," said the kind gentleman, with a sweeping look at Mrs. B——, Mrs. M——, and the rest of the ladies, which implied his opinion of what they ought to feel, "that they will be delighted to admit you into their *coterie*, and make you feel at home." Mrs. B——n looked doubtfully at the new arrival.

" Does not sing, I suppose ?" was her thought.

" Pray, Madame B——," said the duke in his squeaking

voice, "say something to the poor girl. She looks quite dashed. I feel a filial tenderness for the Society of Friends. Dad was sweet on one in his youth."

Still the Syren was silent. She was as great a personage as queen of song, even though her supremacy was disputed by the Italian Catalani, as was the son of the King of Great Britain.

"Kind friend!" said poor Mabel, placing her small plump hand on the arm of Sir Francis B——t. "Thou seemest staid in age, and thy white hair deserves reverence; though I find thee amongst these sons and daughters of Belial, I will believe that thou hast no community with them in thy heart. I come to seek a friend, whom I see not amongst you. Canst thou aid me to find him?"

"That girl is modest," said Lord Byron, in a low voice. "No perfection of acting could simulate that beautiful simplicity."

Sir Francis B——t, however, being possessed by the notion that she was fresh from the impersonation of Ann Lovely, believed that the young lady only kept up the phraseology of the Society of Friends as a joke; and the noble poet himself was somewhat startled from his opinion of her innocence, when in answer to a question by Sir Francis —— as to the name of the friend she wished to meet, she answered, "Wilfred Tresillian."

"Lucky dog!" said one. "Sly fellow! Always first in the market when anything good is to be had! Where is he? Putting Bob —— to bed in the next room. Send her in, too; no, no, call him out. Let us see the meeting of the lovers." These were the speeches that rang round the room, whilst one of the company held a bumper of port wine to the lips of the Quakeress.

"'Drink, pretty creature, drink!'"

as Wordsworth says to the lambkin. Truly, friend, thou art a lamb thyself, it seemeth to me."

"Alas! amongst wolves," cried Mabel, with a quivering lip, putting aside the wine. "Be careful, friend; thou wilt spill it on my dress; and, wherefore, willest thou that I should be a sinner, even as thou art thyself in this matter? Knowest thou not that the wine-bibber is excluded from the kingdom of heaven with the rest of the ungodly?"

"Hark to the fair preacher!" cried one. "Doth the spirit move thee, friend?" said another.

"Put an *s* to it, and 'do' instead of doth," said Lord Byron, "and the motive power will be stated' of the whole assembly but myself, who only drink claret and water."

Mabel kept her hand on the arm of Sir Francis, as if for protection from the riotous assembly. He was embarrassed by this silent claim on his interest, and remained standing by her side, when the door leading to the bed-room opened, and Mr. Tresillian, with an amount of astonishment and dismay, which it required all the practised self-command of a man of the world to conceal, became aware of the presence of the girl who depended on him for love and duty, the first of which he no longer felt,—the second he was unwilling to fulfil.

He was shocked, too, to see Mabel, whose purity he reverenced, surrounded by such a set of men and women. Shocked that she should recognise these as his chosen associates—never, he thought, was such a *contretemp*. Where could he put her? Whither could she go? Why did she come? It was very provoking. This passed through his mind in an instant of time, as he walked towards her with every eye fixed on him in an amused expression of wonder.

Mabel, seeing him advance with a flushed face of grave displeasure, felt that she was unwelcome. Too timid to express the feelings with which her heart seemed bursting, before so large an assembly of mockers, she only put out her hand appealingly, and whispered, "Take me away."

"Will your Royal Highness do me the honour of taking the place I have unworthily filled as host to this festive meeting? I must restore this young lady to some friends of whom she is in search," said Mr. Tresillian, "and place her in safe keeping," not knowing exactly what he was saying, and abashed, notwithstanding his experience, by the roar of laughter which accompanied his departure, with Mabel's arm drawn through his.

"Devil damn him!" said his grace, "he does not seem too happy with his Quakeress."

"What a wonderful oath!" murmured Lord Byron.

"By no means," said the duke. "'Tis most according to our knowledge of the attributes of his Satanic majesty to suppose him to take that business on himself. The usual oath is blasphemy."

"But who is this girl? Miss Carew, the actress?"

"She acts well if it be," said his lordship.

"She's painted," said Mrs. M——d.

"And padded," cried Mrs. B——n, who was proud of her luxuriant bulk, which being more than half revealed to all spectators, vouched for its own truth.

"No chance of Tresillian's coming back to-night," said the duke. "Cigars and brandy!" and his Royal Highness prepared himself to spend the rest of the dark hours in such comfort, as his asthmatical complaint permitted, which made a recumbent posture disagreeable to him.

"A coach!" said Mr. Tresillian to his valet, as he drew Mabel outside the door, and wrapped her brown shawl over her. He placed her in it, after telling the man to drive about slowly till further orders, and jumped in after her. "Now, Mabel, what is it?" he said, with the smallest shade of impatience in his tone. It must be confessed that her advent had been very inauspicious.

Mabel felt it all, and wept silently.

"I came to thee because I loved thee, and I had thought thy love for me was abundant, in good repute and evil repute. My friends, those of my own household, have cast me off on account of thee. I have no one to go to, if thou dost not protect me."

"But why did you not claim my promise at the termination of the week?" inquired Mr. Tresillian, seeking some valid excuse for his irritation.

"Because the letter which I wrote to thee was stopped by my aunt's servant, and I had no means of communicating with thee."

Mabel, with the art so often found in those whose minds have lost their balance, said nothing of the intention held by her relatives to confine her in the York Asylum; and thus Mr. Tresillian was unable to account for her flight to him at such an hour of the night, but imagined that Mabel had chosen that time as being the period of the soundest sleep of her jailors.

"What was to be done with her?" he asked himself over and over. Her helplessness pleaded for her. A girl more self-reliant might have piqued him to overcoming her scruples to become his mistress.

"There is some pleasure in the pursuit of a deer or a fox," he thought, "but none in cutting the throat of a helpless sheep."

"Where wilt thou bestow me?" said the girl, in an agitated voice. "I fear they will pursue me, and take me from thee," and she placed both her arms round the arm which was nearest to her, and clung to it closely.

"They shall not take thee," said Mr. Tresillian, unconsciously adopting the language of the Friends. "When dost thou think thy aunt will find out thou hast left her house?"

"Directly," said Mabel, with a shudder. "I heard them coming after me."

"Mabel! you must be my wife directly; in no other way can I retain you."

"At thy pleasure, dear Wilfred!" sighed Mabel, gratefully; "but," with a little feminine perplexity, "I have no clothes."

"We must think of that afterwards," said Wilfred, who was also greatly perplexed.

Her having come unexpectedly, and shown herself to so many of his acquaintance, was most distracting. If she was to be his future wife, he must manage to set her right in their estimation. Yet he shrank from explaining the whole matter to his relations. Mabel Snow, though a sweet girl, was by no means one whom Lady Sarah would have selected for her daughter-in-law. Mr. Tresillian did not want a buttress to be built on the wrong side of the wall, by arguments against a marriage to which he was in his heart disinclined. No, they must reconcile themselves to it when it was done, and could not be undone. Mr. Tresillian knew a respectable woman who let lodgings. He drove to her house in Piccadilly, and ringing her up, he explained that he had carried off a young lady whom he wished to marry, and entreated Mrs. Smith to conceal Mabel, and to provide her with a sufficient wardrobe. He placed Mabel in her hands with strong injunctions to secrecy, and promised to return on the following morning. Mabel slept, worn out by all she had apprehended, all she had suffered, satisfied now that her lover was responsible for her safety.

CHAPTER XXIX.

N the following day Mr. Tresillian returned, and had a conversation with Mrs. Smith, whom by payment of a handsome sum, he prevailed on to accompany Mabel to Gretna Green. He did not choose to take a false oath, and in no other way, except by the publication of bans, could he marry a girl under age without the consent of her parents.

He knew that his chambers at the Albany would first be sought for news of her, and had taken care that safe answers should be returned to any questioners. He resolved that no reflection should ever be cast on his future wife which he could obviate by any carefulness in his own conduct, and starting at once on the long journey to Scotland, he never saw Mabel alone till he was united to her, and could honestly claim her as his wife.

When the ceremony was over they returned to town, Mr. Tresillian leaving his wife in the care of Mrs. Smith till he could obtain a suitable residence for her.

He advised her to address a letter begging forgiveness to her parents, and acquainting them with her marriage. This she did, appealing to her father, feeling him to be the tenderest parent of the two; but it was unanswered. The response which Walter Snow would gladly have made was negatived by his wife.

Mabel was not inconsolable. In the first deep happiness of her wifehood, she felt incapable of being stricken excepting through him. He was tender and fond of her — more tender, more considerate, than he had been to others more beloved; and in the first few weeks of matrimony Mabel, at least, was perfectly happy, and Wilfred was content. He had not yet avowed his marriage to his family. Mabel rather dreaded that any voice less beloved than Wilfred's should break on her enchanted dream, and did not express any anxiety on the subject. He took a small villa on the banks of the Thames, in which he enshrined his new saint, and in her small wifely care and new-born importance in having a home of her own, Mabel was perfectly happy.

But perfect happiness, or even that which is imperfect, was not to exist long for Mabel. The first interruption to it arose from Mr. Tresillian's suggestion that she should alter her costume and dress like other people. Whilst she lived in perfect seclusion he had not interfered; but what boy or man with a new toy is satisfied by its possession if it be not exhibited to extort the admiration and the envy of others?

Mabel had *un esprit borné.* She had been taught that her dress was part of her faith, and she could not bear to give it up.

"But why dost thou wish it, my Wilfred?"

"Because some men are coming to dine with me, and I do not like them to see you in a dress so peculiar."

"Men coming! Are they friends?"

"Yes," said Mr. Tresillian, "friends of mine."

"I cannot alter my dress, Wilfred," said Mabel, who had rejoiced her heart and soothed her conscience for the crime of choosing a husband for herself, by obtaining a fresh set of drab and French gray dresses. "If I appear to thy friends, they must take me as I am, in the garb of my sect."

Mr. Tresillian was provoked at her determination, and resolved to have his own way. He sent a dressmaker from the establishment of Messrs. Hogard and Amber to fit a dress on Mabel, which might be quietly yet fashionably made. The period was that when Lady Charlotte Campbell had contrived to undress all her countrywomen, and to make them *all* indecent, and three-fourths of them absurd, by a fashion intended to set off her own perfect figure, by an imitation of a Greek statue. Now, a Greek statue partly draped is very beautiful if its proportions are as correct; but put a Greek statue into a paper or a thick muslin bag, and it becomes ungraceful at once. To go about in fleshings, with soft muslin draperies, was even beyond Lady Charlotte Campbell, and the dress which was only tolerable on her became very revolting on such of the matrons of England whose forms were too ample in rotundity. Mabel, who had hitherto worn a full amount of flannel and calico in her petticoats, was told by the dressmaker that such were inadmissible, and must not be worn with the dinner-dress intended for her.

Mabel remonstrated once more with her husband; but he answered shortly that the first duty of a wife was obedience, and *that* he expected, if she took no pleasure in pleasing him.

He was evidently very angry, and Mabel was greatly distressed. Sometimes she was determined to do that which she considered a matter of vital importance — a point of morals — and appear in her usual costume; but she dreaded her husband's gloomy countenance, and remained in a pitiable state of indecision. The dinner-hour was at six, and Mr. Tresillian had taken care that it should be liberally provided and well appointed. At half-past four the dressmaker arrived with the dress, and, by an understanding with the master of the house, she remained, under pretence of trying it on to judge of the fit, to dress Mabel herself, as she had no reliance on the little Calvinist, whom Mabel, unable to obtain a Quaker servant, had selected as her attendant.

Mr. Tresillian had a good reason for his determination. He did not desire that Mabel should recall to his guests any report they might have heard of her coming to his chambers at the Albany in her Quaker costume. He meant to introduce her as Mrs. Tresillian—whether his lawful wife or not they would be too well-bred to inquire; and Lady Sarah or Lord Trelusa, if they heard of such a person, would feel no uneasiness at an occurrence so common with young men of that day. The circumstance of their not being called on to notice her would have satisfied them that the connexion was a temporary one. This would leave him free for the present to act as he liked.

Another effort, which resulted in constant discomfort on both sides, had been made by Mr. Tresillian to alter Mabel's use of the second personal pronoun — " Shall I give thee some cream ? "

" *You,*" interjected her husband.

" Is thy tea sufficiently strong ? "

" *Your* tea ! Yes, it is."

" Wilt thou walk with me after breakfast ? "

" Not unless you ask me properly. *Will you* walk with me ? "

Mabel coloured.

" On what day did you write to your father, Mabel ? "

" On fifth day, third week, tenth month," was the reply.

" Pshaw ! Could you not say Thursday ? "

" Why should I call a portion of time, which is God's, by the name given in honour of a heathen deity ? "

" Oh, Mabel, Mabel ! you drive me distracted," said Mr. Tresillian pettishly.

On the evening in question the little Calvinist servant announced to Mabel that a young man was coming up stairs to her bed-room, saying that a gentleman had sent him.

Whilst Mabel was lost in astonishment, and had a vague terror lest Luke, her brother, should have come to seek her, the young man entered with a bow and a smirk, and stated that he was come to dress her ladyship's hair. He was followed by the maid bearing a parcel from the jeweller's addressed to Mabel. She was seated when the hairdresser arrived, and a cloth was thrown over her shoulders before she was aware, and her beautiful hair, which had been smoothly banded over her brow and carried to the back of her head, was cut sufficiently to be curled by the iron into short circles. The braid was left in its undisturbed beauty at the back of her head.

" The very thing," exclaimed the hairdresser, as Mabel opened the jewel-case and showed a fine tiara of choice pearls. Mr. Tresillian had chosen them as being most likely to accord with the pure style of Mabel's charms.

Her hair was dressed before she saw herself reflected in the glass, with the coronet of pearls on her head. No movement of gratified vanity flushed her pale cheek. She thought herself like one of the idolatrous women denounced by the prophet as wearing " their hoods and their wimples and their round tires like the moon."

The hairdresser departed delighted with his work, and the

mantua-maker now began her task, and denuded Mabel of nearly all her clothes, and re-dressed her in the garments she had brought. Naked arms, uncovered throat and bosom, made Mabel think with disgust of the women she had seen at the rooms in the Albany. The clothes were so tightly-fitting that Mabel felt as if she should tear them if she moved. Whilst she looked at herself in the glass, her husband entered and almost started at the alteration in her appearance. Certainly, none of the company at the Albany could have recognised in this brilliant, elegant-looking lady, the timid and terrified Quaker girl. He came forward with a string of pearls to match the tiara, and fastened them round her fair round throat.

Mabel looked at him sadly.

"Canst thou really wish me to show myself to thy friends in this undress?"

"You are dressed like any lady of your own rank."

"I do implore thee not to put me to this shame."

"Nonsense, Mabel! I expect you to come down to receive my guests as you are dressed now, and remember— no *theeing* and *thouing*."

Mabel said no more; but she was strong in her sense of what was right. When the succession of knocking and ringing announced the arrival of the company, Mabel enveloped herself from her throat to her feet in her old brown shawl, which had covered her and been rain-drenched in so many assignations with her lover in the garden. "Surely, its remembrance will plead for me," she thought. "He cannot be angry when he sees it, and thinks of those evenings."

Women have much longer memories than men, who are never touched by sentiment when they consider that they have cause to be angry.

When Mabel walked into the room with an ill-assured step, and the shabby shawl pinned closely over her figure, her husband was exceedingly angry. It is true that her fair head, with its pearl coronet, shone out right royally from the dark-brown drapery. Her face, usually too pale in its excessive fairness, flushed on the delicately-rounded cheeks, and gave to her pure beauty the only quality it had lacked— that of colour.

Mr. Tresillian waited till they were all seated in the dining-room, and then said, pointedly, "Now, Mabel, you are safe from the draughts on the staircase, you can throw off your shawl."

The look which accompanied the observation admitted of no denial, and Mabel undid the pin, and shone resplendent in a satin dress, resembling that which Sir Thomas Lawrence has immortalised in a beautiful portrait of a lady leaning over a book with her hand shielding her eyes, fitting tightly over the bosom, of which the shape was made more evident from the sheen of the material.

Of Mabel's beauty there was but one opinion, nor of her want of conversational powers. She was depressed by the conviction that she was committing a sin in wearing such a dress,—by the knowledge that she dared not use the phraseology of her sect without offending her husband,—most of all by the dread that he, whom she doated on with a fondness amounting to idolatry, was drawing on himself Divine wrath by the life he was leading, and by his occasioning his weaker sister to err.

Mr. Tresillian, seeing her perplexity, exerted all his powers of conversation to amuse his guests. The give and take of playful wit,—

> "The lively pleasure to divine
> The thought implied, the hinted line,"

was as much lost on Mabel as if the conversation had been carried on in a language with which she had been unacquainted.

Allusions were made to celebrated authors of whose names she had never heard ; meanings were caught from sentences half expressed, and ready laughter was the tribute paid by the guests to sallies of wit, which they were pleased to applaud because the quick understanding of the jest proved their own talents in divining them.

The subjects on which Joseph Sturm and Friend Snow would have plodded over for hours, and scarcely have understood after much painful study, were tossed up and caught and discussed and thrown aside with the rapidity of lightning. As the dinner proceeded, the conversation became more rapid. Mabel sat sad and silent. When the dessert was placed on the table, Mr. Tresillian said kindly :

"Mabel, my love, you seem weary. You may leave us now, and we will come to you for some coffee presently."

Mabel obeyed; but kind as was the tone, she felt she was dismissed as a naughty child, who had misbehaved herself.

A few nights afterwards Mr. Tresillian insisted on taking Mabel to the opera, when was performed *Don Giovanni*. Seated quietly in the box, the young husband hoped to show off his beautiful wife without any distress to her, or exhibition of her *gaucherie*. But he had not calculated on the result. Sensuous in her nature, the music to which she was unaccustomed produced a vivid effect on her mind.

Her features became convulsed with horror when the corpse of the Commandant was revealed, with Donna Anna shrieking out her imprecations on the murderer. Her detestation of the hero was intense. In some unaccountable manner she connected the slaughtered man with her own father, and a gush of tenderness towards him and the home she had left filled her eyes with tears. She put aside impatiently the outstretched hand with which Mr. Tresillian sought to take and caress hers; and, irritated and offended, he got up and left her to speak to some friends in another part of the house. Mabel, for once, was indifferent to his departure. Her mind, highly strung, was entirely absorbed by the representation she was witnessing. When, at the conclusion, Don Juan received the visible punishment of his cruelty and lust, Mabel shuddered at the fate which she believed would also be that of her husband.

Mr. Tresillian took her home that evening convulsed by hysterical bursts of tears, of which she gave no explanation.

Her love for Wilfred now seemed changed to a vague terror; she believed him to be doomed, like the hero of the opera, to eternal reprobation, unless he gave up all his pursuits and companions, and joined the Society of Friends. Her maid was a Calvinist, and held the same gloomy views, and by her intercourse with her mistress deepened all her terrors.

"Oh! that I were as in time past, when God was with me!" moaned the unfortunate young Quakeress; and her thoughts wandered back to her home at Trevedra, her sinless hours, her dear innocent sisters, their constant occupations of working or gardening. Her name, doubtless, was never mentioned in that sweet domicile; she was as one dead— forgotten as though she had never been.

"My father! *he* thinks of me sometimes. 'I will arise and go to my father.'"

Thus she spent her weary hours in vain yearnings for home. She had loved her lover, and sacrificed her family for him; she had bitten the apples on the Dead Sea shore, and found the result but ashes and dust. She had not found the happiness she had anticipated, for Mr. Tresillian had not united himself to the Society of Friends. Had he ever loved her, she argued, he would have done so. Did not her father yield to the persuasions of her mother?

It was true that he might use the same argument. "Why did not she adopt his way of life?" To this she replied to her own thoughts, that hers was the right path, and his the wrong. His was the broad way leading to destruction, hers the narrow and thorny path leading to eternal life.

She wrote again to Walter Snow to beg for a few lines, granting her pardon, if not reconciliation; but no reply was granted. She spoke rarely to her husband, and seemed to be filled with a deep resentment at his efforts to unite her in his own pursuits and pleasures.

Tired with the dulness of his home, and at its perpetual gloom, uncheered even by the light of love—for Mabel, with the blind obstinacy of her character, believed that he would give to her displeasure what he had refused to her affection —Mr. Tresillian returned to all the wild company from which Mabel had for a while detached him, and plunged more madly into the vortex of dissipation from his previous abstinence.

Matters had been thus for some weeks, when electioneering duties took Mr. Tresillian to Cornwall. To Mabel the absence was scarcely a pain. She anticipated, so soon as he should have departed, that she might pursue her own course, attend the Friends' meeting on first day, and re-adopt the Quaker costume, which he had insisted on her laying aside in his presence. To her mind, warped and stiffened by religious prejudices, it seemed to her that her return to these duties was a return to the path of rectitude.

Mr. Tresillian, unruffled by any of the vagaries of a passion which he had never felt for her, was sweet-tempered and affectionate in his efforts to make her happy in his absence.

"You will write to me, Mabel?" he suggested tenderly.

"Truly, yes, if such be thy desire, Wilfred."

"If you should be ill, or require anything, you will let me know."

"I have all of the world's wealth that I can desire," said his wife, with a sigh.

And Mr. Tresillian kissed her, and departed with a sigh also,—but it was one of relief.

Whilst he was at Tregear he saw Sabina, and the circumstances occurred which we have related in the preceding chapters.

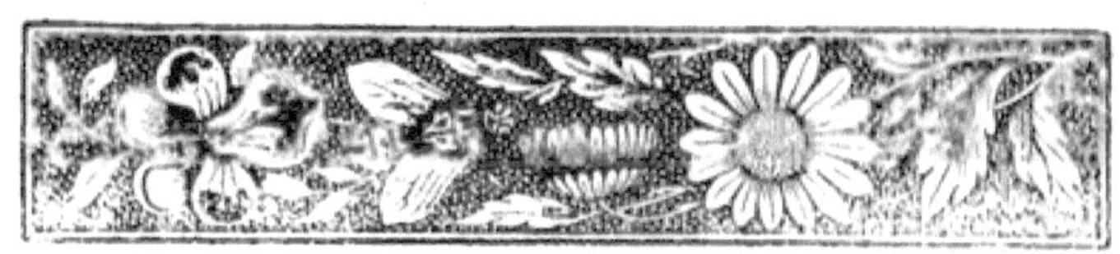

CHAPTER XXX.

"I CANNOT marry this one," said Mr. Tresillian, "because I have married the other. What a fool I was to be so honourable and chivalrous; it has not answered. I am like the French actress, who was induced by a friend to attend mass for the first time in her life, and found on her return she had been robbed of all her jewels and plate. She said it was the judgment of Heaven to punish her for having gone out of her ordinary course of life. I have not lost jewels, but I have gained a clog for life, all because for once I was high-minded and virtuous. If virtue is its own reward, I wonder at how long a date the payment is made. This is a sweet child! How sprightly, how intelligent! I might have made a fool of myself in marrying *her*, had I been free; but I am not. Heigho! what matters so long as I amuse my-self. She will not die of the disappointment, I dare say. Young as she is, she is quite sharp enough to take care of herself. Very unlike Mabel."

Perhaps it was lucky for Sabina, notwithstanding her instinct of self-preservation, that Mr. Tresillian found it necessary to return to London for a week or two; and as Lady Sarah said she could not support Tregear without her son's presence, she proposed to spend the period of his absence with some friends in Devonshire.

"You will promise to come and stay with me on my return, Sabina. And about the veil?"

"If your ladyship will permit, I will take it home with me, and I trust I may be able to finish it before your return."

"Good-bye, Mr. Tresillian," said the girl, holding out her hand frankly as she spoke, "I shall be off before you are awake to-morrow morning."

"Good-night," said the gentleman, pressing the small fingers placed within his.

He took care it should not be "good-bye," for he charged his groom not to bring round the dog-cart till an hour after the time at which Sabina required it.

This lively young girl was not easily put out of any intended plan by slight obstacles. After she had listened in vain for ten minutes in the hope of hearing the carriage-wheels, she went down into the drawing-room, and dropped from the window on the turf, and hastened away through the plantations past the Retreat, now silent and untenanted, opened the small oak gate, and hastening over the road, arrived at her uncle's dwelling in time to make his toast, and before Mr. Tresillian had bedewed himself with liquid odours at the completion of the toilette in which he meant to subdue all hitherto left unsubdued in the domain of Sabina's heart.

"Confound her! she's gone. I don't believe the little witch cares a straw for me!" was the result of his cogitation.

"I'm glad you're come back, Miss," said Susan. "Mr. Rock don't seem over well, and he's dull of the evening, Mr. Orellan being gone, you see."

"When did he go? I did not know it."

"No, master wouldn't have you told for fear you'd want to come home with him, and leave the great folks where you was so happy."

Sabina hastened to the sitting-room, and cheered the old man with her voice and smile, telling him all the little trifles of the life she had been spending, so amusing to her uncle as connected with herself.

She was to return to Tregear, it seemed, on the termination of Lady Sarah's visit to Devonshire, and this was a cause of joy to Mr. Rock, as it proved she was valued.

"Mr. Tresillian is very prompt in his kindness, Sabina," said the old man. "Mr. Orellan has got his appointment—

a friend at court, you see. I wonder how long merit would have pleaded in vain, unbacked by favour?"

"Very nice of him," said Sabina, cutting a slice of the semi-brown bread, which, without butter, served for her breakfast at home. How different from that at Tregear, which she left untasted from love of her uncle!

"Where is his command?" she continued.

"Near Saint Eve; and do you know, my dear, it is a long time since I smelt the sea, and I think a little change would set me up again for a bit. Suppose you and I were to get Orellan to take a lodging for us just for a week or so at Saint Eve. I should like to see how he gets on. He has only a small place—can't take us in."

"That is a blessing!" thought Sabina; but she only expressed the acquiescence which her uncle expected, to whom the certainty of the coming prize-money gave the wish of a sight of his beloved ocean again.

True, November was late in the season for pleasure-seekers, but neither the uncle nor the niece cared for appearance. "In darkness and in storms they took delight," and they were likely to have enough of both to content them; for the days of November are short and dreary, the nights long and tempestuous, and Saint Eve was beaten by the whole force of the angry ocean, broken by black rocks on the east, and sandbanks on the west, over which impediments the waves eddied and foamed.

Mr. Orellan speedily engaged them a lodging near the sea, and at the end of the following week the uncle and niece were settled in their temporary home.

On Saturday the small housekeeper got in her stores to provide for her uncle's comfort on Sunday, getting herself very wet in her shopping, for the weather had set in blowing and raining. On Sunday it held up for a little time, and they attended Divine service at the venerable old church. As they were returning home, Sabina stopped for an instant to listen to the singing of a dissenting congregation, of which the beauty struck her as they passed under the windows.

"There will be service there this evening, probably," said her uncle. "Those fellows know how to make religion attractive. We will go to-night, if you like."

"If you don't think you will catch cold, uncle." And thus it was agreed.

17

"The tide is out a long way, is it not?" said the girl.

Her uncle took out his pocket-book,—

"Yes, spring tide."

In the evening they proceeded to the chapel. The appearance of the venerable man and his beautiful companion attracted the attention of many, whose eyes gleamed round to catch a look at the new comers, though their heads were bent over their books.

The service began with a hymn, in which Sabina joined her rich and powerful voice, and many of the elders of the congregation hoped she might attend permanently.

After the singing came an extemporary prayer in which Sabina could not join, and doubted whether the congregation could, not knowing what was coming next, nor being able to guess the conclusion of the sentences, though their attention was awakened by a feeling of curiosity at the opening of them.

After the prayer the minister preached for three-quarters of an hour on "Justification by Faith." He was a sleek, dapper-looking little man, and delivered his doctrines respectably; but there were evident signs of weariness, and many noddings of heads that did not denote attention.

The concluding hymn was about to be given out, when a young man stepped forward towards the pulpit, and intimated a desire to address the meeting. He was tall, and rather bent in the shoulders, with wild blue eyes, and a magnificent outline of face. His likeness we once saw—an accidental one—in a print, once much a favourite with the religious public, named "The Resurrection of a Pious Family," where the youthful father's rapt face and extended hands are raised towards the heavenly habitation to which he is ascending.

His hair, flowing in dark curls, was dishevelled, and his dress, though clean, was wanting in the strict attention to order and neatness, which characterised the Methodists generally.

The congregation hastily and willingly reseated themselves, their eyes fixed on the young man, who seemed well known to them, and who immediately proceeded to address them thus :—

"'What meanest thou, oh sleeper? Arise and call upon thy God!' This was the address of the captain of the vessel to one who slumbered and slept, whilst the labouring bark threatened to founder in the deep waters. This indifference to the ruin which menaced him was a subject of wonder to his companions ; for each man is more occupied by the contemplation of his neighbours' sins, than conscious of his own. God was wroth with the sinner ; his terrible doom was imminent. You will say, ' What an insensate was this man !' The winds lifted up their voices ; the great deeps responded to their summons ; but he heard not the warring of the elements. He was sunk in brutish lethargy. Look at home. What is this that you do ? ' Arise ye sleepers ! arise and call upon your God !' Perhaps the slumberer was filled with the flesh of oxen, and drunk with the fruit of the vineyard. Perchance his sleeping thoughts yet lingered over the partaken feast. It might have been that his limbs were swathed in purple and fine linen, of which the gorgeous colour, and the delicate texture, had pleased his eyes, and rejoiced his sense of touch, and inflated his self-importance as he sank to rest. Look to yourself ! You come to the tabernacle of God heavy with food. You have sat down to eat and to drink, and you arise and come here to sleep; and this you call doing God good service. You come self-satisfied with your stainless linen, your superfine cloth, your irreproachable neatness of attire, and you think that you will be saved for your well doing. Might not half your feast, rich in its superfluity, have been given to the poor? Your outward appearance is fair, are your hearts as pure? You believe that you do not slumber in the face of a great danger. Task your memory to go over the past week. What thousands of small sins, evil thoughts, malicious words, petty oaths, commodious lies, little deceptions, you have committed ! They are forgotten whilst you sleep. The guilt of small reiterated sins is as great or greater than the committal of a great one. A man may strike his enemy in his anger, and take away his life ; but to hate your neighbour in your heart without cause, to take every opportunity of whispering scandal against his character, or of defeating his designs for his own aggrandisement, makes you as guilty in the Divine sight as if you had imbrued your hand in his blood. The frequency of these sins makes the guilt great : the danger extreme. The constant operation of evil deeds impairs the strength of the soul, and shakes the foundations on which virtue rests—wave succeeding wave undermines the whole fabric of virtue, and makes the building of God to fall."

Whilst the preacher had proceeded, the storm had increased with fearful violence, and the waves seemed by their sound almost to wash the walls of the building.

" Hark ! to the winds," he cried, " careering round the skies !   Listen to the angry waters that are rushing up the sands to wash away, if *He* might permit, the work of men's hands—the habitation they have made for his worship. Think what it would be for any of you to be quivering with terror, clinging to one single plank—perchance in yonder gloomy and terrible ocean—far from light, or help, or hope. Yet, were the poor castaway to sink in the sullen waters, the agony, though terrible, might be transitory ; but 'tis a fearful thing to fall into the hands of an angry God, who may make your punishment not momentary but eternal."

He paused to let the thunder of the checkless winds pass by in their course, and then, with a rapt exaltation in his eyes, he repeated the verses,—

" 'The mountains saw thee and trembled. The over flowing of the waters passed by. The deep uttered his voice, and lifted up his hands on high.' 'The sun and the moon stood still in their habitation. At the light of thine arrows they went, and at the shining of thy glittering spear.' 'Thou hast cast me into the deep, in the midst of the seas ; the floods compass me about ; all thy billows and thy waves pass over me.' 'When my soul fainted within me, I remembered the Lord ; and my prayer came in unto thee : even unto thy holy temple.' "

He concluded with giving out the words of the following hymn, which rose on the air more impressively from the silence within the chapel, and the turmoil of the elements without.

> " God ! our help in time of need,
>   Terrible in majesty,
>   Whilst with earnest prayers we plead,
>   Hear our supplicating cry.
>
> ' Christ ! who stilled the angry wave,
>   Bade its turbulence be still,
>   Stretch Thy hand the lost to save,
>   Let the tempest own Thy will.

> " Holy Spirit ! teach the heart
> To submit in life or death ;
> So, whene'er from life we part,
> Calm may be our latest breath."

The preacher then concluded with a short prayer for any who might be exposed to the fury of the ocean on this awful night, and dismissed the congregation.

They hastened to the doors of the tabernacle, but were at first driven back by the fury of the wind and rain, which were so violent, that not anticipating the force with which they were met, they staggered and clung to each other, and to the doorposts. Some were provided with lanterns 'and umbrellas ; but the last were useless, excepting as walking-sticks—the wind shattered the few put up to ribbons.

Whilst they had been engaged inside the chapel, others had been more actively occupied outside. Boys and women rushed about with frantic cries, and the cliff was covered by eager men, whose faces were lighted by the torches they carried in their hands outstretched over the giddy height at arms' length. A vessel had struck on a rock, which was visible only from the white circle of foam that eddied around it ; and when the moon shone out between the dark masses of clouds, it had been seen that many of the crew were clinging to the wreck, from which, in a short time, they must be washed away if help came not.

Mr. Rock and Sabina had allowed the congregation to pass out before them, wishing to avoid the rush of the crowd ; and thus it was that the preacher who had last addressed the congregation, came up to them as they were about to leave the chapel.

" A naughty night to swim in," said the old man, who had expended his pocket money as a youth, to purchase a small copy of Shakspeare. " What is it all about ? " he continued.

" Ah ! a ship ashore ! Where ? " he said to a man who was rushing past.

" On the Chough's Head, master."

" Where is that ? "

" To the east of the bay. You'll see it belike if the moon comes out again. I'll show your honour to a recess in the cliff where you can see, and not be blown off by the wind."

Before, however, the group had proceeded many steps, the moonlight illuminated the scene of the disaster. There was the dark displaced hull of the vessel, with the white waves dashing and sparkling over her. There was the broken mast, and several human beings clinging to it.

"Not above half there was when we saw it last," said the man.

"Hark! uncle!" said Sabina, as the wind swept by. "Do you not hear the cries of the poor creatures? Oh! uncle! can nothing be done?"

"Can nothing be done?" said the old man, repeating her words.

"A life-boat might save them! but even a life-boat would scarcely go out on such a night."

"Man! Man!" said the preacher, Mr. Ferrers. "Is there no way?"

"There's my boat," said the man. "There's no life-boat now: there was one, but 'tis broken up. I should not like to venture my boat, to say nothing of my life; and if I did, who would go with me? You see there's pebbles and sand, and the pebbles is large some on 'em; and the waves fall with such violence, and curl round a boat with the back wash, so that nothing has a chance agin 'em; and let one get away from the breakers near shore, there's the chance of dashing agin the rock where the vessel struck."

"I would pay you for your boat—you know me, I am Mr. Ferrers—but I cannot pay you for your life; that could not be more nobly bestowed than in trying to save your brethren exposed to such fearful peril. Where should I find two more if I were to go?"

"Have you a wife, friend? or any dependent on you?" said Mr. Rock, gravely.

"No: I am a single man."

"I can take an oar," said Mr. Ferrers.

"And I can steer," said the old lieutenant.

"Oh, uncle, uncle! do not go; why, 'twill kill you. Ah! Sir," she cried, seizing the arm of the preacher, "he is old and feeble; do not let him."

"If he be old he will have less of life to sacrifice. If he be feeble, God," said the enthusiast, "will put strength in his arms and warmth in his heart to fulfil this work of mercy. If he were on that mast, young woman, what would you think of her who interfered with an effort made to save him? Come James Brooks, show us your boat."

Sabina rushed to her uncle and flung her arms round his neck. She tore off her shawl and tied it round his throat. "I can get shelter, uncle, and you cannot. Oh, my uncle, forgive me for all my naughtiness, and bless me before you go."

"Fie, child; don't make me an old fool. There is no danger—nothing to speak of. Pshaw! you're not fit for a sailor's niece. Go back to the house, child, and go to sleep. I shall bring strangers back, perhaps, for food and clothing in the morning. Get plenty of hot water and roaring fires. Let me see you go before I go down the steps to the water's edge."

"Young woman," said Mr. Ferrers, impressively, "neglect not thy prayers for those who need them, and are in great extremity; pray for those at sea."

"Go back, Sabina," were the last words she heard her uncle utter. She seemed to obey him, but she only withdrew out of sight. She could not consent to be sheltered whilst they were exposed to the blast.

"Poor girl!" said Mr. Rock, with relenting tenderness, which made what he considered to be his duty very painful, —"she has not a protector in the world—not a relative, not a friend, on whom she can rely if I am taken from her."

His extremity made him confide this feeling to his companion as they descended the steps under the immediate shelter of the pier.

"I declare to you, old man," said Mr. Ferrers, seizing his arm, "if you should be taken and I should be left, the care and aid which a tender brother should expend on a dear sister shall be hers, if you die in thus doing God's bidding."

"Thank you," said, Mr. Rock, gruffly. "I believe you mean well."

"Great God! to whom darkness is as noonday," cried the young man, "we commit ourselves to Thy keeping, and appeal to Thy aid to lead our enterprise to a good result."

"The gentleman speaks very fine words about the Lord, said the tar; "'tis best to keep them in one's head such a night as this. No one can say I vallid my own life when there was danger afloat. Steady, gentlemen, steady," he cried, as Mr. Ferrers leapt too recklessly into the boat and nearly overset it in the tumbling waters. Mr. Rock stepped in with more judgment. It was not difficult to row the boat whilst under the shelter of the pier; but each of the men knew what perils would await them when they got into the line of angry breakers.

Sabina crouched down shivering, and clung to the railing on one side of the pier. Her uncle had desired her to return home. She would by-and-by, when she could no longer hear the splash of the oar coming occasionally on the rushing wind, nor hope to distinguish the boat should the moon give her light once more. She was alone, for the crowd, not anticipating that any boat would go out on such a hopeless errand, had congregated on the top of the cliff with lights, as if to give some assurance of neighbourhood and sympathy to the poor wretches who seemed beyond the reach of effectual aid. She sat leaning her head against the boarding of the pier, and watching involuntarily the line of white foam which followed the thunder of the advancing water as it struck the shingles, and curling them up in its remorseless play, carried them back into their ocean-bed. She had heard that the ninth billow was the greatest, and she mechanically counted from the last largest she saw. The shore was shelving, and the body of water thrown up by each advancing wave was magnificent; but to Sabina they seemed only like ministers of death to her uncle.

She found the sense of loneliness intolerable. She would try to get up to the cliff, to hear what the sailors and townsmen said of the chance of the safety of the boat and its small crew. It was difficult to face the wind.

Luckily, it blew in-shore, and Sabina was not carried over the verge of the headland. She crawled on her hands and knees, drenched with wet and shivering with cold; but at length she reached the group on the summit, and watched their eager faces illuminated by the torches they carried in their hands, the flames of which were blown towards them. There were no women, for the vessel was a strange one, and no familiar eyes were watching the return of the homeward-bound.

"Do you think they will ever come back?" said the girl with chattering teeth, touching the arm of one of the sailors.

"Who?—the poor souls on the mast? No, Miss; they'll never find any home now but the bottom of the sea."

"Oh ! I mean, will the boat live ? "

"What boat ? There is no boat could live in that sea."

"Don't speak like that ! " said Sabina, with a little cry. "They must, they will come back."

"Does the young lady say a boat has gone out ? "

"Yes," said Sabina, weeping.

"Whose boat ?—but there is but one—James Brooks's.' "

At that moment the sombre masses of vapour parted from before the face of the moon, and just where her divine radiance illuminated the dark waves a little spot of life was seen tossed up and down on the seething waters. The sudden light made visible the bald head of Mr. Rock steering the little boat—the rapt, enthusiastic air of the preacher, whose face was turned to heaven—and the stern, determined action of the noble sailor as he bent to his oar, in accordance with the eager but less skilful movements of Mr. Ferrers. A loud cheer burst from the lips of the spectators simultaneously, repeated again and again, till the echoes gave it back even on that wild night, and the sea-birds screamed with dissonant terror.

Sabina burst into tears of triumphant emotion : " If they die, they die in a glorious cause ; but oh, my uncle ! " and the feeling of triumph died away into sadness.

"Who, them with James Brooks ? " said one.

"That's the chap that preaches sometimes in our chapel."

"And the old gentleman ? "

"I don't know he, but he knows what he's about, he does ; he's used to a rough sea, I'd warrant. See how he gives the boat's head to the wave ; she'd have been swamped long ago if the wave had given her a broadside."

They were pulling painfully, but making but little way in that line of tremulous light. The wind was dead against them, and the clouds gathered over the face of the moon once more, and left the spectator in ignorance whether the frail vessel still lived on the troubled waters, or whether they had overswept the three men, who with different characters, different education, different views, yet were united in the common fellowship of unselfish devotion to their duty, even unto death, in the effort to save the lives of strangers in extremity.

"You think they'll come back?—you do think so ?—say

so. *Do* say something," said Sabina, clinging to the arm of an old sailor.

"Can't say, Miss. You see, suppose they ever reach the ship, which aint likely in such a sea, there's the chance that if they go the other side of the rock the waves will drive them against it and stave in the boat; if they go between the wreck and the shore the wind won't let them get close enough to get the men away."

"Could they not drop from the mast and be picked up?"

"They might if 'twas light, and they were not sucked under the hull of the vessel."

Sabina could get no comfort, and now the group of men, who had been at first so eager with their torches, began to drop off one by one.

"'Tis no use to stay," they said, in answer to a remonstrance from Sabina. "We're working men, Miss, and want our night's rest. If we could do any good we would stay, and gladly."

"Surely," said Sabina, "these lights would be useful in guiding the boat back if she were obliged to return. If you will not stay, at least make a bonfire which may keep in till daylight. Look, I will give you some money—a guinea between you three men—if you will get fuel enough to make a fire. Make haste; get it at once. Surely any of the people will give you wood and furze for such a purpose. Pray, pray, good people, do not go yet. Keep the torches burning till the bonfire is lighted. Do not let the poor men believe that they are quite deserted in their misery."

The promise of the reward stimulated the men to exertion, and she engaged one of them who went to the village for fuel to call at the lodging, and beg the mistress of it to keep up fires and hot water for the return of her uncle.

A peat fire was soon kindled and added to by old tar-barrels, furze, pieces of wreck, and faggots. The men regained some spirit and interest in their occupation, and when it was finished and blazed up boldly against the black sky, they gave a cheer of triumph that sounded to Sabina like the voice of hope.

They had fulfilled their agreement, however, and now prepared to depart, having taken their payment. No more was seen of the boat and its determined crew, and Sabina sat alone by the side of the beacon-fire, cowering over it, and glad of the fitful warmth it imparted to her drenched and shivering frame.

"Some of us will be out at daybreak to drag in the bodies and pick up the bits of wreck," said one of the men as he left Sabina—an ominous speech, which sank like lead on her heart.

One youth returned with a bundle in his arms: "Mother heard say you was here, Miss, and she have sent you her Sunday cloak, seeing as how you guv your shawl to the old gentleman."

It was the old scarlet cloak of the cottager of sixty years since, which is now gone out of fashion, for that fickle deity bears sway in the cottage as well as the palace. Very comfortable in its texture, and very picturesque in its colour, and unequalled in either by modern inventions.

Sabina felt inclined to weep with gratitude towards the unknown woman who had done her this kindness, and she wrapped herself up in it, and sent her thanks back by the youth who had brought the cloak.

Soon after the moon appeared again ; but the streaming line of light only made the shadows over the water look more ominously deadly in their intensity. The black hull of the vessel was no longer visible ; it might have sunk ; it might still be there, but buried in the darkness of the night, Sabina's thoughts pursued that small boat freighted with her only protector—the one person to whom all her duty was due, all her love was given. She was proud of him—proud that age had not lessened the beauty of his grand self-sacrificing character,—prouder of him tossing about in this night of storms in his threadbare, constantly brushed coat, than she would have been had he possessed land and wealth, and lived at his ease in his possessions, and been dressed in superfine cloth, and fared sumptuously every day.

Sabina had had no innate disposition to self-sacrifice; but as it is impossible to touch pitch without being defiled, so it is unusual, when two persons are brought into contact for years, for the weaker not to acquire some of the qualities of the stronger. Besides, she was a Rock, and the Rocks had ever proved themselves a sturdy race.

"He was a fine creature who had accompanied her uncle," Sabina thought. In the chapel his deep impassioned voice rang in her ears ; though she had felt a disposition to hate him when he took her uncle away, yet he was right to go. Her uncle was right also. "He who would save his life shall lose it, and whosoever would lose his life for *His* sake shall save it." Ah! that does not mean this living, breathing, warm sentient life; it means existence in some future state. Some future state! How vague that sounds! This life is like the bit of gold with which one crosses the gipsy's hand, and receives in return the promise of unknown good things. Ah! but one should have faith—in the gipsy, too, I suppose—yet, anyway, the determination to sacrifice one's life for another is half-divine. To do it deliberately, too—not with a sudden impulse, such as has led men to snatch the fuze from the fallen shell ere it burst, and save themselves and their comrades from the explosion. The effort here is continuous; they might return and rest their weary arms and warm their frozen limbs by the fires of their homes; but living creatures are clinging to the broken mast, and they go defying danger and fatigue to try to save them.

Sabina repiled her fire, and stirred it with a stick. "Could her uncle see it?" she wondered. He would never know that the bonfire was her institution—that she was sitting, exposed to the strife of the elements, in the loneliness of that cliff-top, to keep it alight. Her uncle was a strict disciplinarian, and no doubt he expected—if, alas! that dear old head had still any power of cogitating—that she had obeyed his orders, and had returned home to bed.

All kinds of old memories returned on her; amongst the rest, two lines in the favourite book of her childhood haunted her like an evil omen,—

> " Piled on the cliff the blazing faggots burn,
> To hail the bark which never shall return."

Then at that thought she covered her face with her hands, and rocked herself backwards and forwards in her agony. Strange to say, the loss of *her uncle* was the single misfortune she dreaded. The loss of the old man whom she loved so tenderly—the utter destitution in which that loss would plunge her—never occurred to her mind. Had it done so, it would have been thrust aside as trivial, for Sabina was unselfish in her way too. What was she, she argued, but a leaf quivering on the grand old trunk, which the bitter winds were upheaving to hurl it to destruction. How dark and dreary it was on the height! The wind had sunk and the rain had ceased for some time. It was impossible to perceive where the sea-line joined the sky—all was black alike. On the side of the village there had been a few twinkling lights in the windows after Sabina had been left in solitude, but those had died out, and with them her feeling of human companionship.

" Alone in this dark solitude! It is frightful," thought the girl. "Shall I say a prayer? Will God hear me?"

Sabina had always revolted from religious service because her uncle had enforced it so strictly. She set herself in silent opposition to all the doctrines he had inculcated.

" How often," she used to think, "should I have shared the fate of old Longlegs, and been flung down stairs, had all my rebellion been guessed at." Now she felt the want of a greater protection than man could give her; she was deserted by human aid. She turned her fine flashing face, illuminated by the peat fire, to the dark sky.

" God! if Thou art powerful! if Thou art merciful! hear my prayer. Save him! save my dear uncle!"—and her voice went off into a wailing sob—"Save the brave men in fearful peril this night! Give them success in their efforts! Restore them safely to their homes! And oh, Great God! —Great Spirit that movest on the face of the deep!—give me, if Thou carest for so small a creature—give me a sign that I am not forgotten in this vast solitude of storms and darkness! If Thou lovest Thy creatures, let the knowledge of it come on my mind!"

She prayed aloud on the bleak hill-top, and then she bowed her head on her knees and wept silently. When she raised her face from her covering hands, a long line of light, very slightly defined, was visible on the distant horizon. Day was breaking, but it seemed to Sabina that the Almighty had vouchsafed a sign by which she might recognise His protection. Her bosom began to palpitate with exultation. Surely the dawn would show her the boat returning to the shore. She watched the rim of light, which broadened into deeper colour, but it was as yet too feeble to illuminate distant objects. She buried her head again in her cloak. All was still now, excepting that the sea-birds, one or two, began their circling flight with harsh cries, to hail the rising sun. No one was moving in the village, and Sabina alone was watching to decide the question, " Is it life or is it death ? "

It was a gray expanse of water and sky, only broken by the saffron line of light. Now dimly discernible was the line of dark cliffs, and something blacker still, wedged upon one of the sunken rocks at their base. " That is the hull of the vessel," said Sabina, " but where are they ? " A fog hung like a filmy veil, over the proximity of the land, as yet not penetrated by the new-born sun. " They may be there, though I cannot see them," said the poor girl, clinging to hope.

The sun arose higher and higher. It pierced the fog, and with eyes almost blinded by her falling tears she ran over every nook, every shadow in which the boat might be concealed. It was nowhere to be seen, and Sabina twisted her hands in her dark hair, and looked upbraidingly to heaven in her despair.

She dropped her head again on her breast. What does she see? A speck on the heaving water, coming from the vicinity of the hull of the wreck. Now it is lost in the trough of the still perturbed billows. She stares breathlessly. 'Tis the boat ! It must be ! How slowly they approach ! Ah ! it is heavy—heavy with the rescued crew !"

" Oh God ! I thank thee !"

And on her knees, before her now useless beacon fire, Sabina extended her arms and turned her glowing face towards the heaven from whence the help had come.

CHAPTER XXXI.

WITH the first feeling of relief from the extreme tension of Sabina's mind came personal considerations of a perplexing nature. Her bonnet—her best bonnet—was spoilt. Her dress would wash,—everything, in fact, but her bonnet and her boots,—"and those," she said sadly, "have been washed enough already." She must go home and prepare for her dear old uncle. What a joyful thought ! He must know nothing of her night's exposure. She would go and trim the fires, and prepare the breakfast for him, and perhaps for the others, and come back in neat dry clothes to meet him at the pier, from whence she had seen him depart with so much anxiety and anguish.

"Bless me, Miss Rock, out all night ! A fine death of cold you must have caught, poor dear ! Drenched ! Law ! Miss, your nice bonnet is quite squashed with the rain ; that comes of going to them meetings," added the lodging-house keeper, in a low voice, for she was a High Church woman. "Mr. Rock coming back, you say, Miss ? Breakfast directly ? Certainly. No rolls till eight o'clock ; make some dry toast for the gentlemen. Eggs ? Yes."

Sabina was twisting her boots about in the effort to free her feet from their flabby folds, whilst the maid brought her the footbath. She was soon washed and dressed, and felt

the inestimable comfort of the warmth, which enabled her to
hurry to meet her uncle, and bring him to partake of it. She
ran out swiftly, knocking at the doors of the fishermen,
whose dwellings skirted the coast, to summon them to the
beach. They stretched their giant limbs and obeyed the
order, though not with Sabina's vivacity; but there were
nice pickings to be had on the days that succeeded a wreck,
and " early birds get the first worms," they agreed, as they
turned out.

When Sabina arrived at the pier, the beladen boat was
nearing it. It was fortunate—it was, as Mr. Ferrers said,
providential—that the wind had sunk before they attempted
to return with the load of helpless creatures, or the spent and
weary rowers must have failed to reach the land before the
waves had swamped the boat.

As it was, Mr. Rock had had to take the oar first of one,
and then of the other of his companions.

He was rowing, that gallant veteran, as they came near
the steps on which Sabina was standing, too much moved for
speech. He gave her one look of love, and then busied
himself with the boat and its helpless load. There were
many willing hands now to help to convey the half-insensible
crew of the wrecked vessel to the nearest public house; and
free from all present duties, excepting those of self-care, Mr.
Rock and his companions stood on the stout bulwark of
stone.

" Call on me to-morrow, James Brook," said Mr. Ferrers;
and the seaman knew that the order implied a coming gift.

" Oh, my uncle ! come home," said the girl, clasping both
hands round his arm; " you are so wet, so cold, and breakfast is ready."

" Will you take some breakfast with us ? " said Mr. Rock,
addressing Mr. Ferrers.

" I think I should prefer returning home first," said that
gentleman. " If you will permit me, I will visit you in the
course of the day. I am very wet, as well as yourself. Your
uncle has been mercifully preserved to you, young lady;
give God the thanks :—

> ' The storm was hushed, the winds retired,
>   Obedient to His will ;
>   The sea that rose at His command,
>   At His command was still.'

I was right in accepting the service which he offered ; but had it ended in the loss of his mortal life, my grief for your sake would have been heavy."

He shook hands heartily with Mr. Rock, and with a slight bow to his niece, he was gone.

Sabina had lit a fire in Mr. Rock's small bed-room, which was nearly filled by the four-post bed, with dimity curtains, and had placed him before the fire in his dressing-gown, with his feet in hot water. A glass of hot brandy-and-water was on the chair by his side, and Sabina chafed his numbed hands with her soft, warm fingers, and sometimes kissed the dear, bald head she had never expected to caress again, and sometimes prattled of the events of the night past.

"So, tell me, uncle, all about it. Did you hear the cheer the men on the cliff gave when they saw you ?"

"Yes, we heard it, and would have waved a handkerchief, only we were too anxious. It was ticklish work, you see, to avoid being swamped."

"And how did you manage to get the men into the boat ?"

"We waited in the lee of the shore till we could see to pick them up, and then we cruised about round the wreck, and called on them to drop. Some of them were more than half dead from cold, and nearly upset the boat as they were dragged in. That is a brave young man, that preaching fellow ; so is the owner of the boat. I can't make out the preacher. But, Sabina, my child, I think I will go to bed."

Sabina was out of the room in an instant, and returned with a pan of live coals to warm the bed. After she had done so, she took it down, and brought her uncle's breakfast to his bedside. He had drank the brandy-and-water, and refused to eat.

"I want sleep, my child ; I am exhausted. Seventy is rather late in life to play such pranks. I wonder what Orellan and Susan will say ?"

And he dropped off to sleep, whilst Sabina did justice to the neglected breakfast, and lying down by the side of her uncle, from whom she feared to part, lest he should awake and want any aid, she slept also the sleep of happiness ; her outstretched hand on the top of the shoulder which was turned from her.

Mr. Ferrers was the grandson of a man of large estates

and a fine fortune. The grandfather had an only son, who
was the rightful heir to the whole of it ; but Squire Ferrers
spent the fortune first in riot and contested elections, helped
on by a passion for hunting, to indulge which he kept a pack
of hounds, and a large stud of horses. Hunting employed
the mornings, hard drinking the nights. His son was a youth
of refined tastes, loving music, poetry, and painting. His
father called him a milksop, and essayed " to make a man
of him," by making him drunk every evening.

The boy resented the experiment, and ran away to sea.
There were no competitive examinations in those days ; men
and officers being required in the navy, were thankfully accepted, and no questions asked. The captain of the ship
soon found out that he had a gentleman's son on board, and
the Admiralty made him a midshipman ; in due time he
passed a brilliant examination as a lieutenant. During this
time he had received but a small sum yearly from his father ;
but providence is not a virtue that takes root on board of a
man-of-war. During a fortnight's stay on shore, whilst his
ship was refitting, he fell in love with the penniless daughter
of a general officer. The father refused his consent, so the
young couple took their own way, and married without it.
They were very happy so long as they lived ; but a malignant
fever closed their lives within a few days of each other,
leaving but one child, the Mr. Ferrers of whom we spoke in
the preceding chapter. Mr. Ferrers imagined that he should
inherit a large property at his grandsire's death ; but he found
himself possessed only of a ruinous farm which had been
built amongst the crumbling and ivy-covered walls of an old
abbey. The bulk of the property, though entailed, had been
sold illegally. This was not detected till after the death of
the grandfather, who had sacrificed the greater part of the
paternal property to the hounds, having, as his friends observed, literally "gone to the dogs." When Edward
Ferrers came of age, he was informed by his lawyer that he
might reclaim the property by a proceeding at law, in which
the success would be certain, the transaction having taken
place when his father, from his prolonged stay in the East
Indies with his vessel, was incapable of signing any permission, or of invalidating his own claim to the succession.
The young man answered that he would think about it ; and
he used his great share of intelligence in trying to discover

the nature of the transaction. He found that the lawyers on both sides had been rogues ; but that the client who purchased, having been an honest, simple-minded man, knew not that he was party to a fraud, and had at his death divided the property amongst his children, who then possessed it. The loss, of course, with all the back rents, would have been ruinous to them.

Edward Ferrers pondered deeply. He had but little money, and knew its value, but he decided on not claiming for himself that which would bring suffering on the innocent. At college he had always been of a grave and thoughtful character. Several young men of similar tendencies banded themselves together to make a stand against the intemperance and dissipation of their companions. They met at each other's rooms to discuss religious subjects, and aided each other "to live soberly, righteously, and godly in this present world."

Highly strung and enthusiastic, the services of the Church seemed, to young Ferrers, too cold and inanimate to express the wants and necessities of his ardent soul. He separated himself from her, and joined the Methodists, to the appointed preacher of whose chapel he was so liberal a yearly donor, that they made no objection to his sometimes usurping the pulpit to deliver discourses, which with their wild eloquence, put to shame the jog-trot effusions of their appointed pastor. How could that man-fearing man have ventured on such an attack on sleepers, who provided him with the means of living, and gave him the good dinner, the partaking of which had produced frequently such somniferous effects on the donors ?

Mr. Ferrers seemed, either by conviction or inclination, to spend nearly all his substance on others. He had yet an income of about fifteen hundred a year, of which he spent about a hundred only on himself. The tailor at Fowey made his clothes ; one female servant did the work of his house, and waited on him. As he knew nothing of farming, his land was let, and, fortunately for him, to an honest tenant, who felt a pity for the young man, of whom, when speaking to others, he always sighed and tapped his brow with a significant nod, which indicated "all is not right there." He had given a life-boat to Fowey, but it had been borrowed by Mevagissey, and had broken down from its car on the road home. The crew had been sent with it, or his services, and those of Mr. Rock, would not have been required to rescue the drowning seamen.

He had instituted a school for boys, in which orphans were clothed and educated gratis; but those parents who could pay a small sum were required to do so, as experience had taught him that benefits, to obtain which no sacrifice is made, are little valued. Those persons who were simply unfortunate, were sure to find advice and pecuniary aid at the Abbey Farm; but those whose conduct could not bear investigation, shrank from the questions of an inquisitor so shrewd and unsparing as Mr. Ferrers.

This was the gentleman who, in the course of the morning, came to visit Mr. Rock. Sabina had arisen and dressed herself afresh, and had come down stairs, a little uneasy that her uncle had not moved even in his sleep.

"How is the gentleman, Mr. —— ?"

"Rock is my uncle's name. He is a half-pay lieutenant in the navy."

"Ah! I guessed his profession from the nautical skill he displayed in steering the boat last night. Where is he?"

"My uncle is asleep still," said Sabina, with a look so anxious that Mr. Ferrers answered it.

"Shall I go up and see him? Will it disturb him?"

"I wish you would. I have no one to consult," said Sabina with a quivering lip, "and I am so anxious about him."

"Show me the way," replied the guest, and he followed the girl on tiptoe.

He looked steadily at the movement of the bed-clothes for a few minutes, and then came out as softly as he had entered.

"Your uncle is doing very well; he is only exhausted by fatigue." Then with a kindling eye, he exclaimed, "What a magnificent old man he is! How few at his age would have braved death so gallantly!"

The praise of her uncle made Sabina's cheeks glow, and Mr. Ferrers seeing it, thought for the first time that she was beautiful.

"Were you very anxious last night, or could you manage to get any hours of sleep?"

"No; I did not sleep."

" No, indeed, poor young lady !" said the loquacious landlady from the adjoining room, through the open door of which she had listened to the conversation, in which she now joined without scruple. "How could she sleep, I should like to know, when she was out on the top of the cliff all night, keeping up the bonfire, when all the rest of the folks was in bed? Drenched with rain and quite blue with the cold she was when she came back. And you gave your uncle your shawl ?"

" Ah ! some kind woman sent me her cloak. I don't know her name, but her son brought it to me. I was not very cold, really; you see I had the fire; only it was lonely."

Mr. Ferrers looked at her with admiration. "You knew you were not wholly alone ? You knew that you were watched by an eye that never sleeps ?"

Sabina was silent. She could not discuss such subjects with a stranger. He looked at her inquiringly as if expecting an answer.

" I cannot talk on subjects so—awful," said Sabina, trying to find a word, "with a perfect stranger."

" Pardon me," he replied, with much sweetness, " circumstances gave me such interest in you, that I have been impertinent. Where I found so much, I could not endure to think that anything should be lacking."

To this Sabina made no reply but walked to the window, and looked out on the bit of garden bordered by sea-pinks, the bunches of withered carnations, and the purple berries of the laurel, now gleaming in the midday sun, the more vividly from the rain that had fallen on the previous night. The sun being nearly vertical threw out slight shadows, and beyond the small enclosure the waves glittered and danced, as if they had never felt storms, or occasioned death.

" How beautiful is the sunshine !" exclaimed Sabina. " How it pervades everything with happiness and glory. How different from the turmoil and gloom of last night !"

She was silent, and he did not immediately answer; she looked towards him to see if he were attending. He answered to the look.

" As the world is wrapped in darkness and gloom, so is the unregenerate soul; but when God has shed the beams of his grace on the heart, it is flooded by sunshine, which no clouds can obscure, no night withdraw."

The sentiment was so raised by the enthusiasm of the speaker above the ordinary level of conversation, that Sabina was silent. Her companion had seemingly ceased to think of her, and was gazing out on the horizon with far away thoughts. So she stole out of the room, and went to her uncle's bed-side, and had the comfort of seeing him open his eyes.

She prevailed on him to remain in bed whilst she prepared his breakfast, and Mr. Ferrers, catching sight of her as she was going up with the tray in her hands, thought how beautiful she was, and how useful to her uncle, and dim half-thoughts arose in his mind, which had never before obtained admission therein, as to whether he should be happier with a wife. Sabina saw the look he cast on her, and only thought, "Mr. Tresillian would have offered to carry the tray for me himself."

When she returned to the sitting-room, Mr. Ferrers had his hat in his hand. "I wish you good-morning, young lady. I am going round to collect subscriptions for the families of those left orphaned by the storm. I shall call again in the course of the day, when I hope Mr. Rock will be awake, and when he will doubtless be glad to add his contribution to that of the others."

"Pray, do no such thing," said Sabina. "My uncle cannot afford to given even a sixpence; he is a very poor man."

"Everyone can sacrifice something out of the smallest income for those who want it more, having nothing," replied the gentleman, gravely.

"Yes, he risked his life, and has probably shortened it by what he did last night; that was all he could give. Do you think there is no self-sacrifice except in giving money you do not want? Is not the daily effort to keep within a pinching income, the painful struggle 'to do justice,' as much as 'loving mercy' in the manner you propose? My poor uncle," continued the girl, the glow with which she had spoken fading from her face, "goes without nourishing food, lest he should go in debt even a half-penny. I will not have him asked for money; he cannot give without starving himself."

Mr. Ferrers was silent in admiration of the old man whose character was thus described, and of the girl who so boldly and indignantly had warded off an attack on her uncle's purse.

Silent, too, from many perplexing considerations; he wished to ask Mr. Rock to dine with him, but he knew nothing of housekeeping, and depended for his food on a wilful old servant.

Had he been unshackled by that domestic thraldom, he would have ordered a leg of mutton and baked potatoes, which was the only dish that ever suggested itself to his memory. Once cooked, the leg appeared and disappeared daily till it was finished, and Mr. Ferrers never thought any variety necessary. He could not remember when the leg had last been cooked, and on this point he was resolved to call Alice, the maid of all work, into consultation on his return home, to draw up the statement as to the wreck.

So he left Sabina in silence, and she felt a little ashamed of the warmth with which she had spoken, and feared she had offended her new acquaintance. But she knew that, though the manner of her speech might have been faulty, the substance of it was right, so she took Lady Sarah's veil, and went on with her mending till her uncle joined her in the sitting-room, a little pale and tired, yet with such a look of satisfaction in his face, that Sabina told him that a night's exposure on his favourite element had made him ten years younger.

Soon after, Mr. Orellan arrived, very fussy and important, and rather vexed that his absence, occasioned by the necessity of looking after some smugglers, had prevented his being present the night before.

He was eager to show Mr. Rock his small house, and the two old sailors walked out together, talking over past and present times, and feeling as if the separation of a few days had been lengthened out into years.

Mr. Rock was grateful to Mr. Tresillian, and Mr. Orellan was grateful to Mr. Rock, though with a vague thought that his great services had no doubt clinched the success of the application, so soon as his antecedents had been inquired into, and that his merits had been at length appreciated by the ungrateful Lords of the Admiralty. From his friend Orellan, Mr. Rock heard full particulars of his eccentric companion in the past danger. His peculiar character found little favour with either of the old sailors, who were staunch Church-and-King's men. To leave the Church and its long services, and pray after his own fashion, they both agreed, must be little less than profane. " A conceited fellow !" Mr. Orellan declared he must be, to think that he knew better than the fathers of the Church, all those great and pious men, who had given their sanction to the form of words called " Morning and Evening Prayer." He wondered, for his part, why the Almighty did not express his anger by a thunderbolt falling on that schism-shop, and confounding all the seceders from Mother Church.

" He is very brave," said Mr. Rock. " And you say he gives most of his substance to the poor."

" That's no reason why he should set himself up as knowing better than the fathers of the Church," interposed Mr. Orellan.

" That is true," said Mr. Rock, meekly ; and as he did not like the small slandering which few think wrong in conversation, he turned Mr. Orellan's attention to nautical subjects.

" Bring that flimsy fabric with you, Miss Rock," said Mr. Ferrers, " for I cannot promise you any amusement at the Abbey Farm excepting what you may provide for yourself." This was uttered as Sabina and her uncle were preparing to accompany him to dine at the Gothic hour of three o'clock at his home, the difficulty about the leg of mutton not having been found insuperable.

Just as they were sitting down to dinner Mr. Ferrers remembered that there was no wine on the table, and dashed off to the cellar, from which he returned with some cobweb-covered bottles of port and sherry, the relics of his grandfather's stock. Mr. Rock stopped him as he was about to draw the corks. " My niece and I are water drinkers. Pray, do not decant the wine on our account, for I hear that you avoid all fermented liquors."

" It is true," said Mr. Ferrers. " I keep the wine for the old and infirm. Yet, I think you need support——"

" I never take such, thank you."

The conversation turned on the wrecked vessel, and the number of men lost. Warned by his previous conversation with Sabina, Mr. Ferrers said nothing about the subscription, but conversed very agreeably on politics in general, and on the local interest of the place. Each thought the other a mistaken man, for Mr. Rock was a Tory, and Mr. Ferrers, whose quick sympathies were given to the lower classes, was a Radical, which in Tory interpretation meant a revolutionist. But, as each was a gentleman, they kept to themselves their respective opinions, which were that Mr. Rock was the servant of a' corrupt government, and that Mr. Ferrers would go to a hot place in the next world for wishing to subvert it.

After dinner Sabina wandered into the inner-room, which might be called the withdrawing-room in its original sense, for no little feminine niceties marked the room in its modern acceptation of the word. It had been the chapel of the abbey, and having suffered less from decay than the rest of the building, had been allowed to retain its old proportions. Sabina thought it charming. The windows were lanceolated, and the mullions of old gray stone were partly covered with ivy and virginia creeper. The upper parts of the windows were rich in the glorious dyes of old stained glass, and between them there were shelves of books, some speaking of college studies, and others the remains of his grandfather's and father's library.

New books were like new companions for Sabina. The lace veil was folded up and put safely away, whilst she enjoyed the delight of taking down one volume after another, which, though old, had to her the charm of novelty. She sprung down from the chair on which she had mounted, feeling a little ashamed, when the gentlemen entered, and looking carefully lest she should have scratched the old oak chair with her boots.

" I defy you to hurt anything here, Miss Rock. If these books amuse you, you are welcome to take any of them to your lodgings, or to come here and read them if you prefer it. No one will disturb you, for I do not occupy this room; and as it was a chapel and the dignitaries of the abbey were buried here, old Alice thinks the room is haunted, and does not enter it oftener than she is compelled."

Before they separated in the evening, Mr. Ferrers proposed prayers. Mr. Rock agreed, on condition they were selected from the Prayer Book. To this Mr. Ferrers assented, though he would have preferred trusting to his own inspiration. He walked home with them to their lodgings; on the way thither they were joined by Mr. Orellan, who walked on with Mr. Rock in front, whilst Sabina and the other gentleman followed.

The girl dropped out of earshot of their elders, and said,—

"Is it usual to pray together at the end of a social evening?"

"I do not know that it is usual. In the world certainly not; but I trust we are not of the world. Do you not like the custom?"

"I do not think I do," said Sabina. "I had rather pray when I am alone. Somehow I feel ashamed in company, unless it be at church, whither we go for the purpose of prayer——"

"'Those who are ashamed of Him in this world, of them also will He be ashamed in the world to come.'"

"It was all very well," said Sabina, "when public acts of devotion to Christ subjected the devout to imprisonment and death, then there must have been something sublime in praying even in the corner of the streets or on the house-tops. But in the present day, when the religion proclaimed by Him is that sanctioned by government, I think the least said about it the better, except amongst bosom-friends, or at seasons appointed by the Church itself. Otherwise one feels inclined to think of Little Jack Horner, who said, 'What a good boy am I!'"

Mr. Ferrers felt affronted, but did not know what to answer at the moment. At length he spoke in a tone of pique,—

"Pardon me if I have transgressed the usual rules of society. I felt towards the gentleman, for the time at least, with whom I had been placed in such imminent peril, as one might feel towards a bosom friend, and with such even you admit such a custom is allowable. I will not forget for the future to observe towards you and Mr. Rock the distance which you seem to desire."

"I am very sorry if I have offended you," said Sabina, humbly.

She remembered how much pleasure she had anticipated in reading his books, and she held his hand an in-

stant, in the hope that he would forgive her and shake
hers cordially. But he did not, and thus they separated.
And he returned to the Abbey Farm to think of Sabina half
the night, and to dream of her the rest of its hours ; and
she, after a moment's vexation, gave her uncle his insipid
gruel, and then slept quietly without dreaming of anything
in particular.

CHAPTER XXXII.

"Thou robb'st my days of business and delights,
  Of sleep thou robb'st my nights;
  Ah! lovely thief, what wilt thou do?
  What—rob me of heaven, too?
  Thou e'en my prayers dost from me steal,
  And I, with wild idolatry,
  Begin with God, and end them all in thee."

IS residence at Saint Eve improved Mr. Rock's health, and gave him almost a rejuvenescence. They remained there a second and then a third week. The two old lieutenants were inseparable, for each was interested in the interests of Mr. Orellan. Happiness, too, is a great lightener of the heart and sweetener of the temper, and the poor lieutenant, relieved from the cares of house-rent and with increased pay, felt disposed to make his old companion partake of the comfort he had been the means of procuring. The bedridden wife had obtained increased strength from change and improved food,—and all this good had resulted from Mr. Tresillian's interest at the Admiralty.

But of that gentleman we must now speak. He had returned to Tregear, and, at Lady Sarah's suggestion, he rode over the following day to look for Sabina, and to hasten her return to Tregear.

"I hope she may have finished the veil by this time," said the lady, thoughtfully. "Whether she have or not, she had better come back; for her voice is beautiful, and the house is dull without her."

So Mr. Tresillian called at Mr. Rock's house, and made acquaintance with Susan. He wanted to hear all about

Sabina, and leaving his horses at the hotel, he walked to the house with this determination. He asked leave to come in and drink a glass of water, when he had heard of the absence of Mr. Rock and Sabina, which fact he had learnt from the groom at the hotel. Susan was much flattered, and opened the shutters of the sitting-room in a hurry, and dusted a chair with her apron; after which she departed to pump the water afresh, and left Mr. Tresillian alone. He looked round. "What a very poorly furnished room it was, now that the light and beauty of Sabina's childish grace was no longer there!" There was her shabby little work-box on the sideboard. Mr. Tresillian opened it, and took out a small bow of blue ribbon, which Sabina had worn on her white muslin dress on the night when he had last seen her, and crushed it into his waistcoat pocket.

"Here's the water, Sir; beautiful spakling clear water as ever you drank. The lieutenant is very particular what water he drinks, and 'tis excusable, as 'tis all that he cares for except coffee and tea. Have I heard from them, do you say, Sir? Oh, yes! no, not exactly from them, but I have a nevey, a sister's son, living at Fowey, and he comed over to see me last Sunday, and he said,—would you believe, would you believe it, Sir,—that master went out all in that storm that day sen'night, to a wreck to save lives, and that Miss Sabina was at the top of the cliff for hours to keep up the watch-fire that they might see the way back. And they do say," said Susan, with a knowing look at Mr. Tresillian, "that a gentleman, that went out after the poor drowning folks along with my master, is very sweet upon my young missus, and well he may be, for there is not a girl so good nor so pretty behaved if you was to hunt Cornwall over, or Devonshire either, for that matter."

"Indeed! I'm very glad to hear it!" exclaimed Mr. Tresillian, with a little forced laugh. "And who may this fine gentleman be? What is his name?"

"Oh, Sir! perhaps I shouldn't have mentioned, for 'tis only town talk, you see; and I don't suppose anything is settled yet. The gentleman's name, Sir, is Ferrers, Sir; a gentleman what does a deal of good in Saint Eve and the neighbourhood."

"Ah! I think I've seen him. Stout fellow,—stout,— squints!"

"Dear me, Sir! why, my nevey says he's a tall well-favoured gentleman as ever you'll wish to see!"

"Damn him!" said Mr. Tresillian, *sotto voce.* "You don't know when Mr. Rock is likely to return, then?"

"No, Sir; they only went for a week, and they have stayed three. And I reckon, if there is anything in what my nevey says——"

"Good-morning! you will say I called. I have no card," said Mr. Tresillian, breaking off the conversation abruptly. "A little ungrateful,"—he began, and then he paused. What right had he to complain? Was he not married,—married to that lump of insipidity? What an accursed fool he had been to marry her! He had never loved her,—he had never really loved till he had known this child. Yet, his love would be destruction to her,—he could not marry her. She did not know that,—she might love him, believing him to be free, if he kept his own counsel,—and then? Well, then she must be his mistress, and he would marry her if ever he were free. He did not say when Mabel died, but he meant it, for he saw no other chance of freedom.

The next day Mr. Tresillian drove his dennet down to Saint Eve. He did not arrive there till the evening, and after putting up his horse at the hotel, he walked hastily to Mr. Rock's lodgings.

"Mr. Rock was gone out with Mr. Orellan, the gentleman belonging to the coast-guard," the woman said. "Miss Rock was on the beach somewhere with a book; she often sat there for hours."

He asked in what direction she had gone, and hastened to find her. The beach in the direction she had gone was deserted, for the townsfolk of Saint Eve, when they had time for walking, preferred the pier, where most was to be seen.

Thus he walked on uninterruptedly over the soft, yellow sand, and round the dark headlands, till he saw in the distance a small figure seated, which might have been taken for a sea-bird.

He wished he were one for the time, to skim over that broad tract of sand, and reach her side, whom his thoughts sped onward to meet so eagerly.

He began to walk so fast, that he was out of breath. He could distinguish her clearly now in her light gingham dress, dark hair, and hat thrown back. She was seated on the sands, her hands clasped over her knees, looking at the waters, as the waters danced nearly to her feet and then swept back again. If she had had a book, she had laid it aside. What would not Mr. Tresillian have given to have found, on creeping softly behind her, that, like Astarte, she had traced the name of her absent lover on the sands,— and that name his own. She does not look around, and she does not hear anything but the washing of the eternal seas.

He will soon reach her now. She moves, but her head is turned to the opposite side of the beach from the one by which he approaches her. She stands up, and her head is thrown back with eager, seemingly with painful attention.

At what is she looking? A darker figure is descending the face of the cliff, over a path seldom used, from its danger.

"That must be he—Mr. Ferrers—confound him! I wish he would break his neck!"

But Mr. Tresillian's wicked wishes were vain. A tall figure stood by Sabina's side, and clasped her hand.

"Will he never drop it?" was Mr. Tresillian's angry query. "How I should enjoy knocking him down."

He had given her something—some wild flower from the face of the cliff, which she had been unable to reach. Oh! they were walking slowly this way. Mr. Tresillian recognised him now. He had been at Cambridge with Mr. Ferrers, a third-year man, when he, Wilfred, had been a freshman. People had spoken of his great talents, and that he was over-reading himself, which seemed proved when, though a high wrangler, he had missed being senior. Mr. Tresillian had thought of reading for honours, but it had ended in thought. He thought he would enjoy the first year, and make up for lost time in the second. He was full as clever as Ferrers, with whom he had been at Harrow. The masters had said he, Tresillian, might do anything, and attain any honours, and he received the dictum with satisfaction, and rested on it.

In the meantime Edward Ferrers had worked steadily from the time of his leaving Harrow till he went into the Senate House. He had trusted to being senior wrangler, but before the end of the second day's examination he had been carried to his chambers in an attack of inflammation of the brain. What he had done, however, had entitled him to a high position, and he received the illness as a punishment from the Almighty for caring too much for the praise of men.

Mr. Tresillian felt that he should do great things; but the second year passed, and nothing had been attempted, and then he thought it was too late to try. He took a respectable place amongst those who did not try for honours, and had passed the three years in great dissipation and great enjoyment; but he had neither injured his health nor involved his fortune, and considered himself a lucky fellow.

Now looking at Ferrers as he walked by the side of Sabina, stooping his great height to bend over her, he envied him his college honours for the first time.

"He's handsome, too—confound him! But such a maypole! She cannot like him," he exclaimed, as he felt a strong suspicion, from her upturned face, as she replied to his words, that she did so. "I wonder when they will find me out; they are too much occupied to see a man walking straight towards them."

They did see him at length, and Sabina gave a little rejoicing cry, and ran towards him with a cordiality for which both gentlemen could have shaken her, each interpreting her innocent greeting to his own displeasure.

"She loves him too tenderly to conceal her delight at seeing him again," thought the enthusiast.

"She does not care a straw for me, or she would not express her pleasure at meeting so warmly and openly," thought Mr. Tresillian.

After Sabina had precipitated question after question on the new comer about Lady Sarah and Tregear, and a thousand trifles connected with her stay there, she saw that there was silence and gloom between the two gentlemen, and attributed it to her ill manners in not having introduced them to each other.

"I beg your pardon; Mr. Tresillian, permit me to introduce my friend Mr. Ferrers; Mr. Ferrers, Mr. Tresillian;" and the gentlemen bowed stiffly to each other, and looked like embodied thunder storms.

"I have had the honour frequently of meeting Mr. Ferrers when we were at college, but I dare say he does not re-

member one who was but a freshman when he was at the
conclusion of his career."

Mr. Ferrers bowed, and said nothing. He had been
struck with Mr. Tresillian's beauty of person, charm of
manner, and reputed talent ; but their ways had been different, and he had heard of him too frequently as leading
every mad prank amongst the wildest of the Trinity men.
So he was grieved that Sabina should be on terms of cordiality with a man of evil reputation, or what was considered
to be more than folly by the grave set of young men who
judged him.

Sabina found it impossible to make any general conversation between two persons so discordant. She stooped
and picked up a cowrie shell, and Mr. Ferrers was reminded
of the myriads of small shells that covered the field of
Marathon, strings of which are sold for a trifle to the travellers by the women and children who collect them. He
had some he would show Sabina. Mr. Tresillian picked up
some broken bits of slate, and began to play ducks and
drakes in the water, and Mr. Ferrers was provoked to see
that Sabina watched how many times each stone skimmed
the surface of the water, and showed interest in an amusement so trivial. At length he looked at a part of the cliff
which he considered accessible, and taking off his hat stiffly,
he bowed to both his companions, and took his leave. He
might have been consoled had he seen Sabina's white face
and parted lips as he achieved his perilous enterprise ; but
he was compelled to keep his face to the cliff in ascending,
and was too proud to turn when he had reached the summit, to see whether Sabina had cared to ascertain his safety.

Mr. Tresillian finding himself master of the field, or rather
of the beach, began, like other triumphant animals, to make
himself disagreeable, and thus to indemnify himself for the
vexations he had previously suffered.

" A very pleasant acquaintance you seem to have picked
up, Miss Rock," he said, with a perceptible sneer in his
voice.

" I do not know what you mean by 'picking up.' If you
think Mr. Ferrers' acquaintance may be 'picked up' by any
chance passenger, I should think you must have observed in
the last few minutes enough to negative the idea. I do not
either assent to the fitness of the epithet by which you de-

signate him.   Pleasant applies to something soft and agreeable. A pleasant evening is made up of sunshine and gentle
airs ; a pleasant man is benignant, generally plump and
smooth-faced.   Certainly, I never should call Mr. Ferrers
'pleasant.'"

"What then ?"

"Sublime !"

"Sublime ! ha, ha, ha !" with a sarcastic laugh.   "Good
Heavens !   I wonder where he got that coat—a coat made
by Noah's tailor in the ark, I should think."

Sabina smiled and looked at the fashionable dress of her
companion—a high rolling velvet collar to his coat, stiff
neckcloth, and high shirt collar ; a padded chest and pinched
waist.   She thought how careless and unstiffened was the
dress of Mr. Ferrers ; how low his collars, how uncompressed
his waist ; his linen was white and spotless, but his dress
was threadbare and poverty-stricken.   Mr. Tresillian did
not understand the smile, and after a pause he said,
"Well ?"

"I was thinking," replied the girl, "that neither dress
was picturesque—not half so much so as that of a common
sailor ; but of two ugly dresses, I rather prefer his as having
least pretension."

"Indeed !   I congratulate you on your taste."

"I was also wondering," continued Sabina, rather nettled,
"what the men thought of his dress when he saved their
lives at the risk of his own ; what the poor think of the cut
of his coat when he feeds the hungry and clothes the
naked."

"Enough !" said Mr. Tresillian, in a fury, for, as Horace
has observed, nothing provokes a lover so much as the laud-
ation of qualities in his rival which he does not possess.   "I
suppose you love this man, Miss Rock !"

"I really am at a loss to know on what grounds you interrogate me !" replied Sabina, now thoroughly angry—
"there is but one person in the world who has a right to do
so.   When he considers it his duty and undertakes it, I
shall know what to answer."

Mr. Tresillian was silent.   How could he speak of the
love which was trembling on his lip and boiling over in his
heart when he had a wife, and could not woo the girl,
whom he felt that he adored, honourably?   He was con-

vinced that hers was an intellect which could not be baffled by any excuses or hoodwinked by any subterfuges, and that if he told her what was the truth—that he doated on her— she would refer him to Mr. Rock, if indeed she did not refuse him at once, from her preference of another. So he kicked the pebbles before him like an irritated schoolboy, till Sabina suggested quietly that he would cut the tips of his delicate boots, and then he left off with a muttered oath, not intended for Sabina's ear, but which she heard nevertheless.

The sight of Mr. Rock and Mr. Orellan walking in the distance softened Sabina's heart towards her companion, and smoothed her temper.

She addressed some observation to him about a horse which had been lame, and aided him to recover from the perplexity in which the difficulties of his situation had thrown him, so that when the old lieutenants came up he greeted them so politely, and threw such cordiality into his address to Mr. Rock, that Sabina forgave him his exhibition of ill-temper, and repaid him for his kindness by such sweetness of look and manner, as completely turned his head.

Before he left Saint Eve he obtained Mr. Rock's permission that Miss Rock should visit Lady Sarah as soon as she returned to Deepindale. He tried to hasten Sabina's return to the following day; but Mr. Rock had taken his lodgings to next Saturday, and not before that day would he consent to move. Sunday they would attend divine service at Deepindale, but on Monday Sabina should be ready whenever Lady Sarah would kindly send the carriage. Mr. Tresillian gnashed his teeth at the thought of the opportunities Mr. Ferrers would have before Saturday of pressing his suit; but he had no excuse for staying at Saint Eve except as the acknowledged suitor of Sabina, and that, alas! as the husband of another, he could not be.

Yes—the husband of another, and the future father of an infant to be born of his Quakeress, whose situation of coming maternity struck him on his return home. At the time when Sabina went to Saint Eve, Mabel had made no communication to him on the subject. It was the source of grief and anxiety to her whether the future infant might be trained to heaven, or discarded to perdition. She was too moody to show much pleasure in Wilfred's return; but she was bent on carrying her point that the future infant should be brought up according to the doctrines of the Society of Friends.

It was not in Mr. Tresillian's nature to be otherwise than tender in his treatment of his wife under such circumstances. He deserved more credit for his forbearance, as he knew nothing of the infirmity of intellect which she had evinced before her marriage. He set down her ill-health to the caprice often shown by women under the like circumstances. Whilst, in Mabel's belief, the salvation of himself, herself, and their coming infant, depended on the adoption of the carriage and habits of the Society of Friends, her husband treated her somewhat after the manner in which a kindly parent treats a fractious child. Mabel felt it, and was more irritated by the careless tenderness of Mr. Tresillian than she would have been had he gravely entered into the question and argued it with her.

The point on which she insisted after a conversation which, in her earnestness, she forced on his unwilling ears, was that her infant, of whichever sex, should be educated as one of the Friends, commonly called Quakers.

Mr. Tresillian hated the controversy; if he could not give his poor Mabel love, he could give that which was more constant and continuous, the spurious tenderness which is afforded when there is the consciousness that the root of love from which its real blossom should spring, is not in the heart. He never could be jealous—never could be miserable lest her love for him should suffer diminution. He could even be polite and sweet-tempered, and if she did not oppose him openly in his presence by wearing the Quaker garb, he cared not to inquire what happened in his absence. The thought of a baby heir to his future title, gave him additional tenderness towards her who should bear him this gift, but the idea of the future Lord Trelusa (for his brother was rapidly sinking into the grave), abjuring the title and going about in a straight-cut coat and broad-brimmed hat, was too much for his gravity, and he exploded in a fit of laughter, the impropriety of which he felt himself, whilst the levity which gave rise to it deeply shocked his simple-minded wife.

"No, my child," said he, kissing Mabel's hand. "I will make this concession: if the infant be a girl, she shall be educated in your faith; if a boy, in mine. Now be reasonable, little woman, and keep your mind easy, and let me have a cheerful home when I return to you."

Mabel could only wish—prayers being contrary to her creed, which considers importunity for that which might be wrong as sinful—that the infant might prove a girl.

The clothing of the future infant occupied her neat fingers now incessantly ; she liked to see Wilfred, but did not grieve much during his absence. The regulation of her quiet household had attractions for her, and she felt, though she could not have expressed it, rather *génée* by the presence of one whom she feared to offend, and knew not how to amuse. He salved his conscience for leaving her by the present of a magnificent set of baby clothes, forgetting that every adjunct of work or lace would be an offence to his plain-dressing wife ; but Mabel was probably more amused by getting rid of the obnoxious ornaments than she would have been had the clothes been originally made for one of the Society of Friends.

CHAPTER XXXIII.

" There is a monarch stern and cold,
   Whose empire with this earth shall last ;
His subjects are the brave and bold,
   The famous men in ages past ;
Nor less in present hours—the best
   Seek in his realm their final rest.

" And Duty is this sovereign's name,
   And, though severe his frozen rule,
Purest their lives, most free from blame,
   The noble students in his school ;
And as he swayed with precept true,
   And as they bent to Duty's sway,
Love with increased obedience grew,
   And easy seemed his rugged way."

R. FERRERS, when he left Sabina and Mr. Tresillian, did so with a tempest in his bosom, to which that of the elements which he had braved on that night of storms was a calm. He was a man of great depth of feeling, and of stern determination.

When he was thrown into the society of Sabina, he loved for the first time, and fancied he had found a pearl of great price, who would enter into all his views, and aid him in carrying out all his projects. It is strange that even the most virtuous and modest of men never doubt their power of winning a girl if she be poor.

Sabina had stated her uncle's poverty openly, and Mr. Rock had said that she depended wholly on him for support—*ergo* she was destitute, and would accept him, he being comparatively rich, were he to ask her to be his wife.

He had to consider the subject gravely. He did not spend

more than one of his fifteen hundreds a-year on himself, and by the expenses of marrying Sabina another hundred at least must be deducted from his works of charity—would this be right? Whilst he hesitated, Mr. Tresillian came, and he saw and imagined enough to disturb all his calculations. He left them in a transport of jealousy, which made his bosom seem a hell; it was no longer whether he chose to marry Sabina; she seemed already engaged to a man superior to himself in rank, and wealth, and beauty. He would not contend. He would never see her again. He would leave Saint Eve till Mr. Rock had taken his niece away. He knew that Saturday was the limit of their stay. He would keep out of the way till then.

They were to leave on Saturday morning, and on Friday Mr. Rock spent some hours as usual with Mr. Orellan. Sabina took her lace veil and sat in the abbey drawing-room, looking out sometimes on the fitful gleams of sunshine which illuminated the dark ivy, and threw chequered lights of orange, blue, crimson, and purple through the stained-glass on the wall of the quaint old room, sometimes reading Franklin's translation of the Greek tragic theatre, which seemed to take her into a new and wonderful life, and sometimes thinking with awe and admiration of the austere master of the house. Old Alice had told her that her master was not expected home till Monday, so there was no chance of seeing him again, and the girl felt a gentle sorrow that this should be the case.

The windows looked out into a little garden, where the last of the autumnal flowers still lingered. Sabina went out and picked some buds of the china roses, some lavender, and southern-wood, and put them into a glass of water; nothing could be more sad than the little attempt at a nosegay, but it would remind Mr. Ferrers that she was grateful for his kindness. She placed them on the table, and then wrote a note of farewell :—

" DEAR MR. FERRERS,

" I am sorry not to see you again to thank you for all your kindness to my uncle and myself. I have so much enjoyed your room and your books, and I should have enjoyed your conversation also, but that I felt it above me. ' Such knowledge is too excellent for me; I cannot attain

unto it.'　I fear you have often found me trivial and imper-
tinent, for which pray pardon me, and believe me to be,
　　　　　　　" Yours sincerely and gratefully,
　　　　　　　　　　　" SABINA ROCK."

" My uncle would unite with me in every good wish and
expression of thanks, but that he is unconscious of my
writing this note."

She sealed and left it by the flowers on the table, and
making a little present to Alice, she bade farewell to the
Abbey Farm.

CHAPTER XXXIV.

MR ROCK and Sabina returned on the following day to Deepindale. On Sunday they attended divine service, and their return gave rise to various observations amongst the congregation. The doctor thought Mr. Rock looked ten years younger. "These old fellows who have been accustomed to salt water so long that it has become a second nature, always ought to live where they can breathe the air impregnated by saline particles," said he with an air of profound wisdom. Mrs. Cressy thought that "Miss Rock was burnt as black as a coal, and was not a bit pretty now," and she looked with satisfaction at, 'Melia's skin of cream and roses. The men, however, thought Sabina beautiful, though her cheek had a tinge of ruddy bronze, which gave a rich glow to her loveliness.

On Monday the carriage arrived from Tregear to take Miss Rock back, and Mrs. Cressy hearing the sound of its wheels, prophesied that no good could come of such high visiting, and that Sabina would find herself "in the wrong box."

She, all unconscious of evil prognostication, felt her spirits rise at the prospect of seeing Tregear and its inhabitants again. The days were short, and the weather frequently inclement now, and her uncle, when she kissed him, insisted on her not returning daily to make his breakfast.

"You see it vexes Susan, my dear, that you think she cannot make my toast, and it is not fair on the people at

Tregear to make them send you over daily. I shall be very busy, and shall not feel the want of you so much till Monday next, when you will come to remain, will you not, Sabina?"

"I will, my uncle," said Sabina, unconscious of the future.

She was shown up into Lady Sarah's room on her arrival, and found that placid lady surrounded by dresses of the past, and dresses for the present. Sabina's taste was appealed to, as to whether the sea-green assorted well with pale pink, and whether a trimming of brown velvet tulle looked well on a clinging white crape.

The lace veil was inquired after, and found to have been repaired to perfection. The lady was really grateful. "Hogard and Amber," said she, "would have charged me a hundred guineas for it. I never saw anything so wonderful. I cannot detect the joins."

They dined alone, for Mr. Tresillian did not return till the evening; when, with instrumental music and singing, the hours sped swiftly away; but by a thousand acts and looks, unnoticed by Lady Sarah, he contrived to evince towards Sabina such reverential love, such timid devotion, that the girl, who had always felt previously that he had treated her as a child, was at first gratified, and then was conscious that she loved her dangerous companion in return. Not that she saw the danger. How could she? He had plenty of money: he was independent. Lady Sarah seemed to like her. She could not mistake the preference she showed Sabina. She was the daughter and niece of a gentleman, and though she was poor, yet that could not matter to those who knew no privation, and to whom the word poverty presented no definite idea.

Each day Mr. Tresillian loved the girl more passionately. Had he been free he would have gone to Mr. Rock and demanded the hand of his niece; but he was no longer free to do a chivalrous act, and never having been accustomed to refuse himself any gratification, he was determined that Sabina, as she could not be his wife, should consent to be his mistress. If she loves me, and I swear she does, he said, in his thoughts, she will be happier with me, unmarried, than married to anyone she does not love, like that fellow Ferrers; but even he did not dare to start such a proposition to a girl so high-minded and spirited as Sabina. She would reconcile herself to living with me afterwards when she found there was no remedy, he thought. She must be deceived, or coerced in the first instance. "And that old man?" asked conscience. "Confound him! I wish he were out of the world," said Wilfred Tresillian, leaving the question unanswered.

With all the homage of eye and hand paid by Mr. Tresillian to Sabina, she could not help wondering why he did not speak of marriage. It was not till the Sunday previous to the day on which she was to return to Deepindale, that he spoke to her of his perplexities on this subject. It was delicate ground to go over, and he did it artfully. He dared not suggest any likely opposition on the part of Lady Sarah, the placidity of whose temper, and whose evident liking for Sabina, would have contradicted such an assumption. Nor did he venture to say that his family would consider such an alliance beneath him. At such an idea Sabina would have rebelled, and separated herself from him at once; so he spoke of his brother, ill, wilful, yet devotedly attached to him, and bent on marrying him to a younger sister of his deceased wife. The opposition to his wishes might shorten his life, and condemn that of Wilfred to eternal gloom from having been the cause of such a misfortune. If Sabina would consent to a private marriage, he would avow it so soon as he could reconcile his brother to the idea, or as soon as his death took from him all reason for secrecy."

Sabina listened, and believed; but she suggested that she should consult her uncle first on the subject: there could be no harm in telling *him* the truth.

"Ah! my darling! you know your uncle better than I do; but, judging from his general character, I do not believe he would consent to my marrying you in any way except with the honours of war—of matrimony I mean, full consent of parties, white favours, wedding cake, gloves, and cards."

"I should like the wedding cake myself," said Sabina, thoughtfully. "I don't care much for ribbons and gloves."

"You greedy little thing," said her lover, laughing; "you shall have a great cake and eat it all yourself, if you like. Now, listen. I will tell you my idea, which is this :—Instead of going home on Monday, I will take you to Bodmin, where I will marry you by special license, and you shall return home on Tuesday for a day or two, and then you shall come back here."

"But I promised my uncle to be home with him on Monday, and I would not vex him for the world ; besides, I do not fancy such an out-of-the-way kind of marriage. I had rather never marry you at all," and she released herself from the effort he was making to seat her on his knee.

They were talking in the library in the dusk of the evening, Lady Sarah having retired to fit on a new dress from Hogard and Amber's.

"I do not think you love me at all," said Mr. Tresillian. "If you did so, you would not object to what would make me so happy."

"I should not love thee, dear, so much, loved I not honour more," the girl replied softly.

"I do not see how honour could be outraged by your marrying me."

"No, of course not," said Sabina, simply. "The honour to which I referred, was that of keeping my word to my uncle."

"Then you will do what I wish, Sabina ? "

"No, I think not. I must deliberate," and Mr. Tresillian was satisfied with the promise to reliberate, relying on the proverb.

About fifteen miles from Tregead there was a house near the sea, which had been fitted up as a summer residence by a friend of Mr. Tresillian's. Now at the beginning of December, it was untenanted, excepting by an old woman put in to keep it aired. The owner was wealthy, and it contained all that the most luxurious could require for comfort. Mr. Tresillian borrowed the house from his friend for a short time, and directed the woman to light fires, and procure food and forage for horses. It was to this lonely dwelling he intended to convey Sabina, either by her own consent, or against it, and delude her by a mock marriage, trusting to time to reconcile her to the truth when she should discover it. He would have much preferred that she should accompany him with her free consent ; but anyway, he was determined she should make the journey.

Sabina fulfilled her promise of thinking the matter over, and determined *not* to marry her lover at the risk of grieving her uncle. What would he say if a niece of his should marry in such a hole-and-corner fashion. She could fancy his mortification. "No, no ; all fair and above board," he would exclaim. "No relation of mine shall marry a duke, if she has to ring the back-door bell to do it." She had heard him express such like sentiments, and in her heart she agreed with him. True, she loved Wilfred Tresillian—she loved to believe in his devotion to her—she played a thousand graceful kitten-like pranks around him when they were alone, which made him half distracted; but she saw no reason why, if he loved her as he said he did, he should not either brave his brother's displeasure, or wait till it was obviated.

Poor Sabina believed what she was told, and could not know that Lord Trelusa, seldom sober, neither knew nor cared whether his Brother Wilfred were alive or dead.

The Monday on which Sabina intended to return home was a day of pouring rain and beating wind. The water was driven in liquid sheets against the panes of glass, and the sky was overcharged with heavy vapours. Sabina was sad and tender in her feelings towards all she was about to leave, and made herself particularly agreeable to Lady Sarah, that she might be missed, and asked to repeat her visit. She did not, however, wish to prolong it now. Her heart was with the old man at home, from whom she had been for seven days separated, and of whom she had heard nothing in the interim. Lady Sarah proposed that she should remain till after dinner, and suggested dining half an hour earlier,—an immense concession from her ladyship.

"You will not mind, my dear, going home in a post-chaise. Wilfred says one of the carriage horses has a cold, so he has ordered a hack chaise from Deepindale. You will not mind, will you?"

"Oh, no; certainly not. I'm very grateful to your lady-ship for sending me at all," said Sabina, who began to fear that difficulties might be thrown in the way of her getting home at all on such a stormy night.

When they were at dinner Lady Sarah said—

"You don't mind storms, my dear, I suppose, nor your uncle either?"

"Oh, I suppose my uncle prefers sunshine, as I do always; but my uncle never minds being exposed to in-clement weather if any good can be done by it. I never knew till several days after the wreck, that he persisted in remaining long after the boat was well-laden by the drown-ing crew, because he believed there was a cabin-boy some-

where clinging, or fastened to the wreck. He induced the
sailor who went out with them to climb up the mast in the
dim morning light, and cut the ropes which kept the lad up,
for he was insensible from cold, and he was brought safely
to the boat; and my uncle," added Sabina in a choked
voice, "took off his coat and wrapped him in it, that any
lingering warmth might be preserved."

A clatter of glasses was heard behind Sabina, and Mr.
Tresillian looked up and rebuked his servant by a glance
for his awkwardness.

"Fetch that box of French sweetmeats," said he to the
valet, when the dessert was placed on the table; and they
were brought and placed before Sabina.

"Oh, what beauties!" said the girl, opening the box, and
taking out imitations of luscious fruits, in the form and
colour of the originals, and filled with a delicious syrup
when opened. Sabina pushed the box towards Lady Sarah,
who declined to take any, as her son had mentally pre-
dicted. He knew how carefully any compounds of sugar
were avoided by her ladyship, who guarded her remaining
teeth with maternal tenderness, which became the greater as
the number which claimed her care diminished.

"The box is your own, Miss Rock. Keep the contents
for your own eating. You are the only person who ap-
preciates them here.. I, like my mother, have no taste for
innocent pleasures."

Sabina took the box to herself, thinking how pleased old
Susan would be to see them, and that perhaps her uncle
would like one. And the box! "What a beautiful box to
keep Susan's ribbons," thought the girl.

"Your servant, Wilfred, looks very surly, does he not?"
said her ladyship, timidly; for Mr. Tresillian did not admit
of interference, in a general way, with his part of the
establishment.

"Yes, he is surly. If he does not mend his manners, I
shall dismiss him; but he is useful in his way, and one cannot command willing service always. If one has a good-
natured fellow he is a fool, and lets one be cheated; if a
clever one, he is ill-tempered, and cheats you himself. Of
the two evils, choose the least; *i.e.*, the clever one."

They adjourned to the drawing-room, and Sabina sang
"Angels ever bright and fair" so thrillingly, that tears came

into Lady Sarah's bright eyes. Then she sang, with exquisite tenderness, the plaintive air with which Mrs. Jordan beguiled the ears of our great-grandfathers, from the *Spoiled Child* :—

> " Where'er I go, whate'er my lowly state,
>   Still grateful memory long shall linger here."

Then they sang together some trios, which had delighted Lady Sarah's youth ; and at length Sabina, with her brown eyes filled with tears, returned to the drawing-room cloaked and muffled up in a hood, which made her look exceedingly pretty, and timidly offered Lady Sarah a kiss, which was cordially returned.

"You must come again soon," said her ladyship, kindly ; and Sabina accepted the invitation thankfully.

" I have some accounts to go through to-night, and shall not see you again, my mother, till to-morrow, so I will wish you good-night now ;" and he kissed her white soft hand gallantly and gaily.

" What a dreary night !" exclaimed the young man, as a burst of rain and wind opposed their passage from the hall-door. " I cannot let you go home alone ;" and handing in the girl, he leapt in after her, and desiring his valet to get upon the box (which he did not do till he was thoroughly defended by a many-caped great coat from the pouring rain), they started.

" Poor men !" said Sabina, " I hope they will not be very wet. Luckily, it is not far to Deepindale."

CHAPTER XXXV

MR. ROCK had enough to do in turning himself about in his own domain on his return home. On the Wednesday after his arrival, he set to work to replace all the articles that had travelled with him, in the exact angle which they generally occupied, and to look out the clothes that wanted Susan's neat fingers to repair. Besides, he had to listen to her vituperation of the Saint Eve's washerwomen, who had sewn up the holes of his socks without drawing them together, as Susan declared a Christian washerwoman should ; while she asserted that the clothes generally looked as if they had been dipped in peasoup, and should go into the wash-tub before either her master or young missus touched one of them. Then came the *Times* paper, and then Mr. Rock went out to have the ends cut from his gray hair, which had run riot in his three weeks' absence. On Thursday the great object of his thoughts arrived from London—the upright grand piano by which he was to surprise and delight his darling, ordered without reference to price. Why should he not, at the close of his long, self-denying life, have the gigantic pleasure of giving Sabina this treat ? It had been purchased by the risk of life and limb. The harmony of peace had been obtained by the discord of war. He thought of the past hours when the prize-money so long delayed had been won. He remembered the lugger privateer which he and his brave companions saw to the north-west, eight or nine leagues from Heligoland. He felt in idea once more the parching thirst which had dried his mouth, and the weary labour of the rowers in overpassing this extreme distance, before the side of the lugger could be reached, bristling with weapons and armed by determined men. He recalled the struggle up the side of the vessel, the hoarse cries, the howl of agony as some man fell forward, wounded, on the assailants who swarmed up the defended ship. He thought how, as he hung by his left arm on the edge of the deck, he saw the Frenchman's face close to his, cool and determined, with fierce glittering eyes, and his sabre raised to decapitate him, and how he drew his pistol from his belt, and put its muzzle to that livid countenance and blew it to atoms, whilst he mounted safely, and dragging down the enemy's colours, shouted "Victory !"

That was years ago, and now he had the payment so long delayed, and his darling should play on the piano so purchased, the loved songs of his nautical manhood. She sang them well, and loved to hear the old man tell of past times, whenever he could be induced to do so.

Here it was, safe at last within that small room. How beautiful it looked, so new and bright; and then the old man unlocked it, and touched one key after another, and grieved a little that he could not strike a chord to be able to judge of the tone. He had told Mr. Broadwood's people that he was no judge, but the piano was for a lady that was, and he trusted they would not take advantage of his ignorance, but send him a fine-toned instrument, as he trusted himself in their hands; a trust ever well-placed in that firm, for Mr. Rock received as fine a piano as ever had left their establishment.

Now the old one was to be disposed of. He offered to restore it to Mrs. Cleverly; but she found its absence so much more agreeable than its presence, that Mr. Rock ended by placing it in Sabina's bed-room as a convenient sideboard for flowers, work-basket, or small volumes. So he arranged his sitting-room and his niece's bed-room, and this took him on to the end of Thursday. On Friday he had to preach patience to himself. The day dragged wearily.

Susan doubted whether her master had really done himself any good at Saint Eve ; he seemed so moped now he had come back, and yet he had that beautiful music-box to look at. She said to herself, "Well, he'll be all right when Miss Sabina comes back."

"On Monday she will come back," he said to himself as he awoke, "and this is Saturday; she will come in the morning." But Monday morning passed without Sabina's arrival to gladden her uncle's heart. "What a stormy day it is ; the glass down to 'much rain.' She will be here by luncheon-time ;" but, as we know, Sabina was about to dine at Tregear.

"Poor girl ! She cannot come till they let her have the carriage," he said, apologetically, to himself.

The evening closed in. "Surely she will come soon," said he, as he sat in the thickly-gathering gloom of the winter's twilight. Economy would have prevented his ordering his candle had she been at home, and he had an additional reason now. He could not bear to shut out the remaining light, because it would make it seem so very late.

"Will you have tea, master ?—'tis five o'clock," said Susan, after an hour had been spent by Mr. Rock in listening for the sound of a distant carriage that came not. He could only hear and be irritated by the click of the pattens on the pavement, as the saturated umbrellas passed the window, concealing the women who carried them.

"It can't be five o'clock yet," he said, hastily, and took out his chronometer. "Yes it is, Susan," he added, meekly ; "but we'll wait a little longer, perhaps she may be here by six o'clock ;" but at six o'clock he drank his cheerless cup of tea alone. From that hour till eleven he sat before the fire, his dim eyes refusing the effort to read that which could not then have chained his attention, and straining his imperfect hearing to receive the most distant sounds. Once a carriage was heard approaching, and he started up, and Susan, who was listening in the kitchen, ran to the front door ; but it bore some one to happier expectants, and the old man swallowed down his disappointment as he best could. At eleven he gave up the hope of seeing her that night.

"Poor darling! I dare say they did not like to send her out in such a rain. I am sure she would have come if she could;" but the poor old lieutenant's heart was heavy as he went slowly up to bed, and prayed fervently for his dear child, and then laid his head on a sleepless pillow. It was well for him that he knew not the fate of Sabina.

What helpless rage—what uncontrollable agony—would have been his!

CHAPTER XXXVI.

"He hath profaned the sacred name of friend,
   And worn it into vileness ;
   With how secure a brow and specious form
   He gilds the secret villain !   Sure that face
   Was meant for honesty ! but Heaven mismatched it,
   And furnished treason out with nature's pomp,
   To make its work more easy.
   See, how he sets his countenance for deceit,
   And promises a lie before he speaks."

A FEW days before the fact I have here narrated Mr. Tresillian had intrusted his valet to perform some unusual duties, and the latter, after promising to fulfil them, reminded his master of his promise at some future time to procure him the situation of coal meter, with a hundred a-year in cash and allowances of coal and candles, besides the greater attraction of receiving a bribe from the master of every vessel which came into port, for the payment of the owners depended on the number of chaldrons measured by the coal meter, and a prompt and liberal present to the man in authority greatly diminished the numbers accounted for to government.

Mr. Tresillian did not deny the promise, but said, carelessly, that he had given the metership at Fowey, which his valet wanted, to a voter, and he must wait.

The man had before found waiting an unprofitable occupation, and had become morose and discontented in consequence.

" I could not let you go home alone, you know, Sabina," said the lover gaily.   Indeed, there was such a sparkle in his eyes, and such a flush in his handsome face, that Sabina looked at him with wonder mingled with admiration. " What is this in your lap?" he said, for the lamps were blown out before they had proceeded many steps.

"The box of sweetmeats."

"You are eating them now, you greedy little thing! How many have you taken—four? Pray don't eat any more ; you will be quite ill. Let me have the box," and he let down the window and was about to empty the contents of it into the road, but Sabina prevented him.

"Oh, don't! My pretty box," exclaimed the girl. "Oh dear, I'm so giddy," and she laid her head against the side of the carriage. "I'm so stupid and sleepy," she scarcely articulated.

Mr. Tresillian put his arm round her and laid her head on his breast. How he loved the beautiful helpless creature who reposed there. She was his now; she *would* be his. The sweetmeats were drugged to make her sleep, lest she should find out that she was not returning to Deepindale ; but the taste had tempted her to eat more than her lover had anticipated, and he was somewhat alarmed at the heaviness of her insensibility. He kissed the half-open mouth, so unresisting and unconscious. "Gracious powers ! if I have killed her," was the horrid thought that flashed through his brain.

He let down the glass and turned her face toward the current of air that blew into the carriage, and felt a slight shiver thrill through her frame. He covered her bosom with her shawl, and pressed her towards him—his own now and for ever ; she could not escape him. How beautiful and spirited she was. How she would rave at first ! but she loved him—she owned to that. A woman forgives everything to a man whom she loves. He was not quite easy in his mind. It was cowardly to kiss this unresisting semi-insensible little creature. He should be glad when he reached Carlew and carried her into a lighted room, and dashed water in her face, and restored her to consciousness. The way led across a lonely heath. Had Sabina recovered she would have been helpless, for she would have seen no one to whom she could have appealed for assistance. He had directed his valet to provide a special license, and a man to simulate a clergyman, should Sabina refuse to be his on other terms ; but he was really unwilling to have recourse to this last deception, lest it should be brought

ıp against him unpleasantly in the future. At length the
carriage drove to the house ; the bell was rung, and the
servant appeared at the door.

"The lady is ill," said Mr. Tresillian to the woman.
'Show the light into the sitting-room," and he lifted Sabina
n his arms out of the carriage and carried her to a sofa.
Her head hung on one side, and her eyes were half open.
He laid her down and called for cold water, and dashed it
on her face, and looked with terror at the still unquiver-
ng lids. He groaned aloud and knelt by the side of the
sofa. What would he not have given could he have
recalled the last three hours, and have restored her safely
o the house of her uncle.

Medical assistance? Ah! there was none nearer than
wenty miles. With the helpless female servant at his side
ıe wrung his hands in his terror, and in the despair of his
nability to remedy the mischief he had perpetrated. But
Sabina's fine constitution was doing for her more than all
he doctors of London or Paris combined could have accomplished. Her brain began to rally from the stupefying
effects of the drugs she had taken, now that the motion of
he carriage no longer aided its effects. She sat upon the
sofa shivering, and wrung the dripping curls from her
ace.

"Where am I? Uncle!" she cried, in a timid, terrified
voice ; then louder, "Uncle! Susan! who are you?" to the
strange woman.

Mr. Tresillian kept behind her lest she should be alarmed
at his appearance, so guilty was his conscience. She started
ıp and saw him, and looked puzzled,—

"*You* here! Where are we? Where is Lady Sarah?
This is not Tregear! Take me home, Mr. Tresillian." The
woman left the room. "Why have you brought me here?"
—for her brain, recovering from its stupor, became excited
oy terror—"Tell me, man! why am I here? Uncle!
ıncle!" she cried aloud, and then feeling Mr. Tresillian's
arms thrown round her, she struck at him madly with all her
small strength.

"Listen, Sabina!—look!—I leave you free. You promised to marry me ; you will, you must do so. To-morrow
promise I will take you back to Deepindale if you wish it ;
out this night you must be my wife," and again advanc-

ing, he flung his arms round her and covered her face and her bosom with kisses.

She disengaged herself, and turned on him with fury—

"Do you think I love you now? Why! I *hate* you. You have made me deceive my uncle,—you try to make me marry you stealthily. I doubt your intended marriage. I hate you more than I fear you! Let me go?"

"You cannot escape from me, Sabina. All the people here are at my orders; they know that the clergyman waits to make you my wife." He rang, and in answer to the female servant said—"Tell Mr. Norris that we are ready for the ceremony."

"This is a dreadful jest," said Sabina, struggling to steady her reeling brain; "but I can come to no harm if I am true to myself." She ran to the window, and let down the bar of the shutters, and strove to lift the sash. Mr. Tresillian's arms were round her in an instant to drag her back. Irritated and terrified, she screamed aloud, uttering repeated and prolonged cries for help. Though her lover had no fear that any assistance would reach her, he could not bear those agonised shrieks for aid, and strove to stifle them with his hand. "Hush! hush! nothing shall harm you,—you need not fear me. Surely, you love me, Sabina, and will be my wife."

But Sabina continued to cry out for "Help! help!" the sound becoming more agonised, as her terrors increased from the uselessness of her appeals for aid, when the door of the inner-room opened, and a soft voice said—

"I will give thee help, poor, deceived maiden! come to me!" And Mabel drew Sabina towards her gently, whilst Mr. Tresillian sank down, and covered his face with his hands.

"Who are you?" said Sabina.

"Thou dost not recognise me, friend! Indeed, I am not sure I should have known thee, had not my informant given thy name and that of thy uncle. And now, what course wilt thou adopt? I heard enough to know that thou desirest not any portion with this sinful and godless outcast from grace. The horses, which brought me hither, have rested, and, albeit the night is dark and stormy, they can convey thee to thy home, and I will send with thee this Godfearing woman, who is my attendant, that no further evil may befal thee."

"But you? I don't know you?"

"In the time when God regarded me, my name was Mabel Snow. Now, by the wrath of Heaven, I write it Mabel Tresillian."

"You are his wife?"

"His legally wedded wife!"

Sabina stepped quickly up to the sofa on which Mr. Tresillian sat, with his head buried in his hands, and touched his arm—

"Listen to me! tell me if what this lady says is true, or is it a slander? Are you married to Mabel Snow?"

"I am!" groaned her lover.

"Oh, Wilfred! And I have loved you so!"

This was Sabina's only reproach. She told Mabel that she should like to go as soon as possible, and would prefer being alone. She was shivering painfully from the immersion she had suffered in Mr. Tresillian's efforts to recover her, and her clothes were wet about the neck and shoulders. Mabel made her cloak warm, and wrapped her carefully in it; and herself placed her in the carriage which was to convey her to Deepindale.

CHAPTER XXXVII.

> "Oh, sacred rest!
> Sweet pleasing sleep, of all the powers the best.
> Oh peace of mind, repairer of decay,
> Whose balms renew the limbs to labours of the day,
> Care shuns thy soft approach, and sullen flies away."
>
> DRYDEN.

T was nearly four o'clock in the morning when the old man, awaking from a painful doze, heard a carriage stop at the door of his house. He started up, and put on some of his clothes, with anticipation of some great misfortune. How his withered hands shook in trying to produce sparks from the flint and steel! The dampness of the weather had affected the tinder, and each was extinguished as it fell.

"Susan! Susan!" he exclaimed in a quavering voice, feeling his way to the door of her bed-room.

Susan awoke, and struck a light at once; for that wise virgin always kept her tinder-box during the night by the side of the kitchen fire.

"Susan! give me a light! there is some one at the door! Make haste!" And Mr. Rock descended, an old yellow pair of Maltese slippers flapping at his heels, and threatening to throw him down, and unbarred the front door, and received Sabina, who had, in her eagerness, descended from the postchaise, and stood within the shelter of the porch in his arms.

"Oh, uncle! dearest uncle!" she cried, in an agitated voice, "I'm so glad to get back!"

The opening of the door had, by admitting the blast of wind, luckily extinguished the candle, so the joy of getting his darling home was not damped by the expression of her wild and worn countenance.

"My dear, what made you so late?"

"Oh, uncle, it was so dark; and they did not like to send out the carriage horses. So they ordered a postchaise, and the lamp blew out, and the man lost his way. But 'tis all over now, and I hope you have not been uneasy, my uncle?"

"All right, my dear child. Susan, bring another light! mine is gone out. Don't go in there," as Sabina was going towards the sitting-room. "Not there to-night, my dear. To-morrow morning we will go in together," with a tone of joyful importance, which the unhappy Sabina did not understand, and was too miserable to care about.

"I am cold, uncle. I should like to go to bed at once." She did not ask for a hot bottle to place at her stone-cold feet, because she knew the fire must have been extinguished for hours, and she would not give Susan the trouble of re-kindling it. She kissed her uncle and embraced him, as if she feared to be torn from his arms; and then took a lighted candle, and locked herself into her solitary room, whilst he, happy man, retired to bed, and slept in comfort for the first time on that night. Sabina felt her head aching fear-fully, and her thoughts wandering. Sometimes she started up after a short slumber, aroused by the sound of her own voice, talking loudly and eagerly. She was going to be ill, she knew, for her strong health had mentally and bodily suffered severely from the events of the past night. She got out of bed, and unlocked her door. If she should be unable to get up she must provide against contingencies. She loved Mr. Tresillian, but was filled with horror at the deception he had attempted to practise upon her, and was distracted by the dire necessity of loving without limit one whom her judgment pronounced to be unworthy of love.

"Married! married secretly! married to the Quakeress Mabel Snow!" how utterly incredible it seemed! Her head whirled round. What if she had been ill from the time she had entered the postchaise, when so deadly a sleep had fallen upon her, and all that had passed subsequently had been delirium. In that case she must be very ill in-deed—better thus. She tried to argue with her aching head. "Better that I should be mad than that he should be so wicked. And that was Mabel Snow, was it ?" she went on wandering. "Mabel S—now!" and she drowsed off into temporary slumber, only to start up, screaming for her uncle and Susan—"Help! help!" They did not hear her at first, for they slept the heavy sleep which follows release from anxiety. "The dark hours would never go," Sabina thought; and yet there were but four to pass before the dim twilight of a wintry day might dawn. Susan found Sabina, when she came down stairs at half-past seven to light the kitchen fire, standing in the scullery trying to pump some water to drink, that in her room not being fresh or cold enough to tempt her to slake her burning thirst with it.

Susan led her back to bed, and in doing so touched her feverish hand, and heard her unnatural tone in speaking; and, when she had covered her up, she went to her master's room, and told him that Miss Sabina seemed very ill indeed, and should she go to fetch Mr. Dent?

Mr. Rock's heart sank within him. He had slept so happily in the conviction that his child was safe under his roof, and the Almighty had rebuked his confidence by sending this visitation on him.

He hurried on his clothes, and went softly to Sabina's bedside. Her face was crimson, and her arms tossing about wildly. She did not seem to see him, but looked beyond him, as if to see if anyone were following him into the room. He spoke, but she only muttered unintelligibly in reply, and with a swelling heart the old man hurried to the house of Mr. Dent, and entreated him to come at once to see Miss Rock.

As the clothes she had taken off were reported by Susan to be drenched with rain (as she supposed), Mr. Rock imagined that she had exposed herself to it, when she got out of the postchaise before the door was opened on the previous night.

"A violent cold and feverish attack," Mr. Dent sagely determined the illness to be, on these data, and sent in his draught to be taken every four hours, &c., &c., which did only the good of amusing poor Mr. Rock, who seemed to believe that Sabina's life depended on her swallowing diluted spirits of camphor and water at the exact moment prescribed by the apothecary.

In the course of the day Sabina's luggage arrived from

Tregear, with a note from Lady Sarah to Sabina, saying that Mr. Tresillian had told her that the servants had forgotten to put it into the carriage. She wished to know how Sabina had reached home on so inclement a night.

The old lieutenant answered it, with too much grief in his heart to care for the manner of his communication. Had he, in fair weather, been required to write to an earl's daughter, how he would have hunted for a sheet of the finest cream-laid paper, and tried to mend a pen to his liking, and have begun with a flourish at the top, and a broad space left on the margin, as if he were going to address the Board of Admiralty.

Now his anxiety made him careless even of a round blot, that fell on the paper from the pen quivering between his shaky fingers. He said simply, with many thanks to her ladyship, that his niece was very ill, out of her senses in fact, from cold and fever. If she ever recovered (for the old man was inclined to despair, and wanted Lady Sarah to suffer a little also), she should have Lady Sarah's note delivered to her.

Lady Sarah was as sorry as a lady of very placid temperament could be, and sent daily to enquire after her ; and every day the answer was, "much the same," or "no better, many thanks to her ladyship."

When Sabina's carriage-wheels were heard driving off, Mr. Tresillian felt his misery was unsurpassable. His shame, his humiliation in the presence of a wife whom, unjustly enough, he despised, was nothing compared to the loss of the girl on whom he doated. She was gone—gone from him in anger. He longed to throw himself at her feet, and beg pardon for the outrage he had been foiled in—to cry aloud for her pity and forgiveness. He hated his wife, whom he knew to be standing there looking at him with the magisterial face, given by the sense of being in the right in the opinion of everyone.

Mabel might have been contented with a quiet triumph, but she was not. The injudicious young wife wished to improve the occasion, and after a short pause thus addressed him—

"Dost thou not think thou makest a contemptible figure, even in thine own eyes, Wilfred Tresillian? Thou hast been detected in perpetrating a cruel fraud, by which thou intendedst to commit a wicked act of adultery. I might have known, unhappy man! what to expect when thou refusedst to dress thyself as a Friend, and walk in the quiet paths of the children of peace. Now I will leave thee to work out thy iniquities with greediness, and separate myself from thee for ever in this world. Perhaps some light may be vouchsafed to thee which may guide thee to eternal happiness in the next. In this my soul disdains to consort with thine, and in future we must be separated in body, as alas, I have felt we have been in mind for many months past."

"Just as you please, Mabel," said her husband, starting up; "I shall not trouble you with my company in future. I never loved you. I married you only from a feeling of weak pity, because I knew that you were compromised in the sight of the world by your own imprudence and the advantage I had taken of it. I have been sufficiently punished by finding a girl, for whose sake I would peril body and soul, and think them well lost if she were won."

"Thou meanest that poor child, Sabina Rock, who was received by my family in charity," said Mabel, who was irritated by the influence she heard attributed to one whom she had thought below her.

"Yes; I love Sabina Rock as I never loved before, and shall never love again," said Wilfred, who felt pleasure in trying to inflict misery on another when he himself felt so much. Seemingly he had succeeded, for Mabel's self-command gave way, and she said, softly—

"If it might please God, I should like to die." She turned away and retired to her bed-room, and Mr. Tresillian sat by the fire in the sitting-room with a thousand wild images chasing each other through his brain. Sabina returned home alone in the carriage, with wet clothes, and scarcely recovered from the injury to her brain from those cruel sweetmeats; angry with him, struggling, striking him with all the power of her weak hands, and injuring him about as much as an infant hurts his nurse; Sabina saying only, when convinced of his perfidy—"Oh, Wilfred, and I have loved you so!"

All these succeeded each other in his troubled memory, but there was inexpressible sweetness in the last. She had loved him; she must love him still. The thought of her leaning on his breast, though she was unconscious, gave him uncontrollable pleasure.

His wife—he almost hated her for being a barrier between him and his wishes. He would send her back to the villa on the Thames, and, returning to Tregear, would try to obtain Sabina's forgiveness of the past, and get matters back to their old standing. He felt assured she would not complain to her uncle; she loved him—she loved her uncle. She must know that such an attempt, if known, must lead to a duel with an old man of Mr. Rock's nice sense of honour. She was a sensible girl, and would be sure not to mention it. He must wait there till morning, he supposed; so he arranged the sofa before the fire, which he made up, and stretched out in its warmth; he sometimes listened to the wind, which roared round the desolate house, or the sheets of water that were dashed against the windows.

He had just fallen into a sound sleep, in which he dreamed that he saw Sabina leaning her head on the breast of Mr. Ferrers, as she had in reality rested on his, when a slight noise awakened him, and he saw his wife's maid standing by the sofa. The lady was taken in the pangs of premature labour, and medical aid must be procured. Mr. Tresillian started up, and, glad to do some kindness to her whom he could not love, he had one of the carriage-horses saddled, and rode to the next town for assistance. He returned to Carlew with the doctor, and after some hours of anxiety, Mabel presented her husband with a son and heir.

"Not a boy?—not a boy?" said the poor mother, eagerly.

"Yes, Ma'am, a fine boy;" and Mabel hid her face on the pillow and wept.

When Mr. Tresillian refused the metership to his valet he disappointed two persons—his own servant and his wife's maid, whom his valet was engaged to marry. The man was entirely in his confidence, and had by his master's desire arranged everything for the reception of Sabina at Carlew, and provided a man in the dress of an ecclesiastic to perform the marriage, should Miss Rock insist on that ceremony; but his attachment to Mabel's maid had made the occupation repugnant to him. He declared 'twas a sin and a shame to take in the poor young lady in such a manner, and any lingering of fidelity towards his master would have melted before a reason less cogent than that which we are about to relate. When he had been a very young man he made himself a father without the tie of matrimony. The mother had died in child-birth without avowing the name of her companion in guilt, and the infant had been brought up by the parish. When the boy had been old enough to be removed from the burthen on the ratepayers, he had been sent to sea. The valet had never lost sight of the child, and without embarrassing himself about his support, he sent him occasional presents of clothes and money, and loved him the more for every added benefit he bestowed, as is the nature of human creatures. It was this boy who had been rescued with others of the crew from the wreck by the instrumentality of Mr. Rock and his companions, and every latent instinct of good revolted from his permitting the old man's child to be sacrificed, when he had hazarded his life to save that of his own son. The circumstance of Mr. Rock's taking off his own coat to protect the boy from the cold became known to him only by Sabina's narrative as he waited at table at Tregear, and occasioned his clatter with the wine-glasses, which awakened the wrath of his master. It could not alter anything then, for his arrangements had been made by agreement with Mabel's maid, and Mabel's journey to Carlew had been decided on between the valet and the attendants. The mistress was plastic in the hands of the stronger-minded woman, and acted by her suggestion and advice.

Mabel had been urged herself to appear on the scene, in order to deter Sabina from a mock marriage by proving her own prior right, and to strive, as she imagined, to lead her husband in the right path, by pointing out to him the enormity of his conduct. She had expected to find him overwhelmed by contrition, and ready to fall at her feet and implore for pardon—a pardon, which she would after a while grant, when, as a mark of a changed heart, he should abandon all his old associates and his fashionable attire, and join the society, and wear the garb of those Friends called by the world Quakers. When she proposed to separate from him, she did it in the hope of being contradicted; but she had failed in every effort to awaken his conscience, and had forced from his irritated mind only the outpourings of his love for another woman. Her wish to reclaim her husband was not a single desire; by it hung another even more intense—the salvation of her infant, should it prove a boy. The number of strict Friends has greatly diminished within the last sixty years, and those who now hold the tenets of that sect have greatly modified the extreme views held by the founders of the society, and by their early and more enthusiastic followers. Now, salvation would probably be considered, by the Society of Friends, attainable by a man in a fashionably-cut coat; but to Mabel's bounded intellect, it seemed that there could be no inward purity without such outward and visible signs as could be found in drab cloth and a broad-brimmed hat.

Her experience of fashionable life had not been a happy one. The half-dressed women and intoxicated men who were, as she afterwards found, friends of her husband, revolted her taste and terrified her mind, alienating her from Wilfred, who could associate with persons she considered so licentious.

She had made a mistake in her marriage. She had committed a sin in uniting herself to Wilfred Tresillian without the consent of her parents; but of what a gigantic crime should she not be guilty if she permitted her offspring to be reared in such iniquity. Had it been a girl, the child might not have perished utterly; but it was a boy, and the mother's anguish was intense.

Her love for her husband faded from her heart, in the deeper feeling which pervaded it for the infant. He was there lying on her arm, his small lips sucking nourishment from her bosom. How tenderly she smoothed that silky hair which only covered the back of the round head, with its glossy brown, cobweb texture. The small finger clasped her own, so that the mother's gentle hand could not remove it till the infant's relaxed in sleep; but was this goodly creature she had brought into the world to be an outcast from the face of the Almighty—to be plunged into everlasting perdition if he grew up and followed the footsteps of his father? "Ah! better he should die! better a thousand times he should die in his infancy!" and at the thought the mother covered his infant head with tears.

This contest between the natural instinct of maternal tenderness, and the convictions of a morbid and distempered mind, was too much for the feeble intellect of Mabel to sustain. The idea that she ought to sacrifice her child's life to secure his immortal happiness pursued her unceasingly. An internal injunction seemed to command the destruction of the infant. She wrestled against the thought; it pursued her night and day. She wished for the boy's death without the agency of her own cruel fingers. If she slept, she hoped when she awoke to find him cold and breathless. At other times she almost crushed him to her bosom, with eyes brimming over with tender tears; her very love was an instrument to urge her to his destruction.

Mr. Tresillian was proud of the infant, as young fathers, unworried by money cares, often are proud.

He saw in the small features and rounded limbs a future likeness to himself. The boy would be Lord Trelusa. His brother could not live many weeks. He did not care whether Mabel lived or died, and he dared not ask himself whether he wished her out of the way of his forming a dearer tie; but the boy he felt disposed to love. He rode over daily to see his little son, and to observe how well he throve in that bleak, deserted house. He must acknowledge his marriage now; he must think about breaking it to his mother. Lady Sarah would have been more resigned had it been Sabina, he thought, and he grieved to remember that there would be no mutual liking between the mother-in-law and daughter.

Mabel seldom noticed her husband, excepting by a look of dislike, when he entered her room. He did so, because the infant was always there; and as his visit was to his little son, he would not leave the house till it was accomplished.

One day both mother and child were asleep on his arrival, and he stole in softly and sat down, concealed by the curtain of the bed, till they should awake. Opposite to the foot of the bed was the toilette table, and as the curtains were put back, the father could see what passed within their folds. He had taken a paper in his hand, and had begun to read, when he looked up, hearing a slight movement. Mabel was leaning over the boy on her left arm; the fingers of the right hand were grasping the infant's slender throat, and the noise heard by the miserable father was the choking gurgle made by the gasping victim. In an instant he was kneeling on the bed, and had unclasped the cruel hand;

but the boy was black, and gave tokens of life only in convulsive struggles. Mr. Tresillian ran down with him in his arms to the kitchen, calling for hot water.

"A fit—a convulsive fit! Haste, haste! he may yet be saved!" And at length Wilfred was relieved by seeing the respiration return to the heaving breast, and a more natural colour to the livid face.

Yes, it was, he said, a fit; but he was determined that the child should not be exposed to a recurrence of such a seizure, and he took the infant himself away in his carriage, and deposited him in the care of a cottager who had a young infant of her own, and on whose nutriment for the babe he could confide. Not till the child was in safety did he think of the mother. She was mad, evidently, and the hands that had been raised to murder her infant, might destroy her own life. He returned, and desired her maid to obtain additional nurses, that her mistress might never be left; saying that suckling her child had weakened her so much as to endanger her health, consequently he had removed it. He said nothing of the true cause of the act, and the maid thought he was a brute, as he ever had been to her mistress, to take the infant from her. The loss, though inevitable under the circumstances, was disastrous in its effect on Mabel's senses. She became ungovernable in her actions, and requiring restraint; the medical attendant believed her to be suffering from a delirium which would pass away when a few days had elasped, and deprecated the absence of the infant, to whose sudden separation from the bosom of the mother he attributed the violence of the symptoms. Mr. Tresillian bore the reproach, and said nothing. His mind was racked by ceaseless anxiety about Sabina, of whose health he heard daily, and never any improved account. He had sent her a beautiful bouquet of flowers, and old Susan, thinking to please her poor young mistress, had placed them in her room in a large blue jug, on Mrs. Cleverly's piano. Sabina saw them when she first awoke from her sleep, and her intellects were clear. She saw the flowers she most preferred clustered together by some skilful hand.

"The gentleman from Tregear brought those, Miss," said Susan. "Aint they beauties?"

"Take them away, Susan; they make my head ache, the

perfume is so overpowering, and the colours are too bright for my eyes. Take them away at once."

And Susan pitied her young mistress for being so fanciful, and carried away the disgraced flowers to Mr. Rock's sitting-room, where Mr. Tresillian saw them next day when he called with a self-invented message from his mother ; and hearing Mr. Rock's statement that his niece had said the perfume was too overpowering, he understood that his gift was rejected by Sabina.

The poor girl was haunted by the dread that her uncle should find out the fact of Mr. Tresillian's outrage, and should demand satisfaction in the way then common for less injuries than those Sabina had sustained. It seemed un-likely that such a fact could be concealed, and whenever Mr. Rock was out of her sight or her hearing, she grew nervous and partly delirious. So the old man, with tears of tenderness in his eyes, gave himself up to sit idly by her bed, whilst she slept with her hand clasping his—a sleep so light and unrefreshing that she started up when he made the slightest effort to release it.

The townspeople hearing from Mr. Dent that Sabina was likely to die, forgot their jealousy of a person no longer likely to excite any, and felt concern and pity for one passing away so young. So the butcher sent her a present of a nice fresh sweetbread, because he thought "the poor young thing might fancy a bit, if it was well cooked ; not that he supposed that old woman they called Susan could do much. Why, they didn't buy a joint more than once a fortnight ! So she could have no practice. His missus should have dressed it with pleasure, only he was afraid of offending the old gentleman."

The lawyer, Mr. Grinde, who was a sportsman, sent a couple of wild ducks to Miss Sabina, and Mrs. Cressy a basket of beautiful apples, just such as the young lady liked, she knew ; and, as it was near Christmas now, " apples were apples," a speech which Sabina had often heard without understanding, as she knew not how they could very well be anything else at any period of the year after the blossoms had fallen from the young stems.

One day, sad at heart and weary, Sabina lay still and contemplated Mrs. Cleverly's piano against the wall at the foot of her bed.

"Why did you bring the piano up here, uncle?" she said. "Were you tired of it?"

Mr. Rock cleared his throat.

"Ahem, my dear, yes. I thought it would be a little treat, you know, to you to have it in your own room."

"Very kind of you, uncle," Sabina replied, languidly, and closed her eyes again; but she was a shade better, her uncle thought, or she would not have observed it, and the old lieutenant was comforted.

CHAPTER XXXVIII.

"But now the fulness of its failure makes
  My spirit fearless; and despair grows bold,
  My brow beneath its sad self-sorrow aches."

OWEN MEREDITH.

HEN the fever incidental to Mabel's state had subsided, the violence of her mania abated; but the prevailing idea still existed in her mind—a love of her infant, and a determination to show that love, by destroying his life before sin could deform the blossom which she hoped would in its innocence bloom eternally in heaven. If he lived, she saw in him a reduplication of his father,—careless, unscrupulous, and sinful. The last act of Wilfred's life, with which she had become cognizant, had filled her with the greatest horror of his conduct, and terror lest his disposition should live again in her child.

Her attendants were kind and attentive, and Mabel knew that if she were to escape, it must be by the simulation of the greatest composure. With the wonderful sagacity exhibited by the insane, she became outwardly placid in her manner, and grew quietly cheerful. She was no longer disturbed by visits from her husband, who was not attracted to the house now that his infant was no longer there, and who was satisfied by hearing from time to time that Mrs. Tresillian was progressing favourably, without a personal interview. Indeed, as the father became more and more wrapped up in his infant, his feelings towards Mabel became intensified from indifference to hatred. He knew this to be unjust, but memory ever presented to him her face, usually so statuesque and placid, with a look of stern determination, which seemed foreign to her character, bending over the infant with a cruel glitter in her blue eyes, and her white, soft hand grasping the little helpless throat. He rode daily to the cottage of the woman in whose care he had placed the child, and dismounted to impress a kiss on the little unconscious brow. His mother's hatred had endeared that helpless morsel to the father, whose fortunate interference had saved his life, and who had thereby obtained additional claims on his love.

Mabel was resolved to escape—to escape and find her infant, and finish the work she had begun. When she had arrived at Carlew she had money, and this she now remembered. Mr. Tresillian, on suspicion of his valet's treachery, had dismissed him, and he had married Mabel's maid, who had consequently left her mistress ; but Mabel seemed to have transferred her preference to one of the nurses hired to attend her, and nothing was thought of the departure of her favourite servant.

The nurse slept in the room next to Mabel's and usually retired to rest at ten o'clock.

The weather was inclement, and the snow on the ground. One morning Mabel saw a boy occupied in sweeping a path from the entrance to the garden gate. She wrote a note, ordering from the next town a postchaise, to be in the stable-yard at eleven o'clock the following night, and gave the boy a shilling to post it.

The nurse liked bottled ale much, but hot brandy-and-water more. Mabel had often vexed her by her refusal to accept the tempting stimulant, the partaking of which would have given an excuse for the nurse's indulgence in the same beverage.

After supper was concluded on the following night, and a tumbler and a half of strong ale had been imbibed, Mabel expressed a desire to taste brandy-and-water hot with sugar, which the nurse had often assured her would " get up her strength nice."

" Make it strong, nurse, or I shall not fancy it," she said.

And the nurse made it according to her own notions of strength, which were liberal.

" Ah ! what nasty stuff ! It takes away my breath !" said the young Quaker lady. " 'Tis a pity to waste it. You had better drink it yourself, nurse." The nurse drank it, and was glad when her mistress had hurried to bed, and she had liberty to follow her example.

Mabel waited till she heard a prolonged succession of snores in the ante-room, and then she listened till she became aware, from distant sounds, that the postchaise she had ordered was approaching the stable-yard. With trembling hands she opened the wardrobe which contained her bonnet and shawl, and with some of her money carefully hidden in her bosom, and the rest more accessibly placed in her pocket, she undid one of the drawing-room windows, and stepping out on the lawn she went to meet the carriage, and had entered it, with a bundle of linen she had collected for her flight, before she remembered that she knew not where the infant she sought had been deposited.

She had, however, no power of seeking him whilst she remained at Carlew watched by her attendants. She determined, therefore, to drive to a little village called Calcuik, about a mile and a half from the town of Trevedra, where she might remain quietly, and consider what course to adopt in the future. She felt convinced that the nurse would not discover her absence for twelve hours, and that, when discovered, she would do nothing without consulting Mr. Tresillian, which could not take place till he called at Carlew, as he had left no address for letters to be sent after him.

Thus Mabel counted on some considerable time for the carrying out her plans, and was not mistaken. She arrived at the small public-house, which was the only home she could claim for the present, and dismissed the chaise. It was lonely enough, but she begged to remain in the bed-room, because there was only one public room for all the guests, those being the miners and labourers of the neighbourhood. She had often looked idly on this small dwelling as the waggon had passed it, whilst conveying her family and herself to the Friends' meeting on first day. She remembered them all—her rosy sisters, her grave mother, her sweet-tempered, placid father. She longed to see them once again. There was no truth, no godliness out of the pale of the Society of Friends. Their tranquillity, their sobriety, their truthfulness in word and deed, all impressed her memory, and melted her heart towards her own family. It was very sad to be within a mile and a half, and not to be with them. She was very dull in that hot, close, small-windowed room, and Mabel, whose ideas of cleanliness were, like those of all Friends, exceedingly nice, was shocked by the sight and the odour of all the house. In going to Mr. Tresillian she had exchanged from comfort to luxury—now, she felt as if she had sunk into squalid poverty. In her variable mind the thought of her husband, and the idea of violence to her infant faded away, and an unspeakable longing to see her family took possession of her.

She would wait till evening—evening came now at four o'clock, when daylight faded from the gray snow-containing clouds; snow was on the ground, too, and there would be few travellers abroad. She went out at that hour, and walked to the town of Trevedra. How familiar all the houses looked, and the names over the shop-doors. Those queer Cornish names, in comparison to which those of other counties seem common and vulgar. Few folks were moving about on that dreary winter's afternoon. She walked down Crypt Street, and looked at the market garden, over which, when a child, she used to spell the announcement that *Lucerne* was for sale there, and remembered her un-satisfied wonder that Mr. Polperrok, the market gardener, should be empowered to sell a Swiss canton, of the existence of which she had just learnt in the Abbé Gautier's geography. Like many children, Mabel remained ignorant from being too timid to ask for information. She crosses the bridge and sees old Betty, the waterwoman—waterman she might almost have been called in her masculine hat, light nankeen jacket and petticoat, and hoarse voice. Her face is wrinkled, like one of the old women painted by Myeris, and looking at Mabel she recognised her, and her wicked old blue eyes twinkled; for she laughed internally to think how often she had rowed Luke Snow and ladies of loose life and conversa-tion, down to the woods of Polperro to spend summer-days. The weather was against such freaks now, but a debauch at a small public-house down the river was less known and less talked about than it would have been in the town itself.

Merry parties went out on that tidal river, and the old woods re-echoed with the glee—

> "A boat, a boat unto the ferry,
> And we'll go over and be merry,
> To laugh and quaff and drink old sherry."

Old Betty knew the air quite well, and often rose from her bed and pushed off her boat, on hearing the summons to convey the revellers to and from the romantic shore.

Mabel hastened on, passed the beautiful church by the old Church Lane, through another street, passed some poor habitations, till she got to the leat. She crossed the bridge, slippery and unsafe from frost and snow, and saw the mill-wheel, a beautiful incrustation of icicles. She was intensely cold—every sight was cold. She was near her father's garden now—she wondered if the garden-gate was locked. She stood behind a buttress of the wall where she had concealed herself on the night when she first saw Tresillian. Presently she heard a wheel scraping over the hard gravel, the door opened, and the gardener wheeled out a barrowful of stones and rubbish, to deposit it on the opposite side of the road. Whilst he was intent on tilting it, Mabel entered the door, and concealed herself under the snowladen evergreens, whilst the man unsuspiciously passed her, and re-locked the gate.

The Snow family had not been prosperous in Mabel's absence. It was true that their wealth was increasing rather than diminished, but they had been "tried," Mrs. Snow said. Every small ruffle on the surface of her life was a "trial," sent with the purpose of adding to the lustre of her virtue.

Mabel's conduct was a bitter grief both to her maternal love and her feelings, as regarded her position amongst Friends. She had taken a high hand in all their meetings, had promulgated severe codes of discipline, and was supposed to have brought up a model family on model principles.

About Mabel's defection as little was said by them as possible. It was a tender subject, and avoided at all the meetings, monthly and quarterly. Mrs. Snow felt the silence like a dead weight on her heart.

Before their return home, and after Mabel had left them, their house had been broken into, and much that was valuable in linen and plate had been abstracted. It was against the principles of the Friends to prosecute, and the loss was submitted to. But other burglaries were committed where the sufferers were not so quiescent, and the thieves were put into prison. Before their trial Polly Best, in order to screen one for whom she had a peculiar regard, declared who were the persons whom she had, by her information, enabled to enter Mr. Snow's house ; and, utterly careless of Luke Snow's feelings, told how frequently she had been admitted by night into that hitherto stainless household, and in what manner she had managed to undo the fastenings when her entertainer was sleeping off his debauchery.

Mr. and Mrs. Snow heard, and were crushed by the double disgrace. Luke was sent to a friend's house in a distant county to board, which it was imagined would cut off his connection from the dissolute men and women who had led him away. Having been sensual and selfish in one locality, they hoped he would be pure and well-conducted in another. A pitiable delusion ! neither men nor women, young or old, are "led away except by the disposition to sin in their own natures." Those naturally wicked may speed the downward tendency by associating with the depraved, but no good man, woman, youth, or maiden was ever "led away" into sin. There must be the fuel before the fire can be lighted, and evil sparks expire on snow.

However depressed were the father and mother, they allowed but little to be seen in their outward appearance.

The dinner had been removed, and the couple sat by the fire in the winter twilight ; the simple dessert of apples and nuts in their china dishes were reflected in the highly polished mahogany dining-table. It was too dark for work, too light for candles ; so they sat and gazed into the fire, in which the newly introduced cannel coal made a sudden and fitful blaze, whilst the little Quaker girls were trimly peeling the single apple allotted to each, with a silver pocket knife, with which every child was provided, lest damage should accrue to small fingers by the use of steel ones.

To the outside of the window of this room Mabel crept, and, placing her face against the glass, she shivered and looked in. The home she had left had an air of comfort and tranquillity, which she had never valued so much before. We all have felt a sensation, almost of envy, in passing the warmly curtained and brilliantly lighted home of a stranger, when hurrying sad and weary to our own, which we feel will be dull, dark, and cheerless, and probably without the adjuncts of wealth, and the attendance of servants, to render it alluring on our return.

How much more attractive was this tranquil dwelling to

poor Mabel, who had been so tempest-tossed and shipwrecked since she had quitted its sterling shelter. She leaned her head against the pane of glass and wept. The flame of the cannel coal leaped up, her face, white and sad, and the tears that covered her cheeks, were illuminated by the flash, and the youngest girl who saw it all, sitting opposite the window, cried, with a voice which seemed to the parents, always believing in divine inspiration, to be supernatural—

" Sister Mabel is crying ! "

Mabel had caught the expression of intelligence in the face of her little sister, and had removed herself into the shadow before the awe, which had fallen both on the father and mother, had subsided, and they had turned to inquire what was meant.

" There ! but there ! " said the child ; and Mr. Snow left the room, and went tremblingly along the passage, and opened the door into the garden.

He saw nothing, and called, " Mabel ! " in a voice almost inaudible from agitation. There was no response, and the cry was repeated with an expression of mingled anguish and hope still more intense. Then a rustle in the bushes, and Mabel threw herself into her father's arms, weeping herself, and bathed by his tears also.

" My daughter ! my Mabel ! she was dead and is alive again ! she was lost and is found ! "

They brought her to the fire, and chafed her numbed fingers, and warmed her frozen feet. All anger had left their hearts when they had heard from Miss Den of the wandering of her intellect, which accounted for so much in her conduct otherwise incomprehensible. They were above measure touched by seeing that she still retained the garb of her sect, though the materials were new and of richer texture than she had worn when she left home' proving that they had been thus fashioned to please her, and not worn because she had none other wherewith to dress herself.

They were weary of questioning her, fearing to overset the tottering brain by exciting painful emotions

" Doth thy husband know that thou hast returned to the house of thy father ? " her mother asked.

" No-o," was the reply, given with a startled look around her, indicative of terror.

" Dost thou fear him, poor child ? " asked Mrs. Snow.

"Father! let me stay with thee," was the reply.

When he was alone with his wife, he suggested that it would be better to tell Wilfred Tresillian that Mabel was with her relatives, both to reassure him as to her safety, and in order that he might deal gently with her, instead of ordering her to return to him. They recognised his right to do so as her husband. They dared not ask as to the circumstances of her journey; it might have been taken with his consent; it might have been a flight from his persecution. So Mr. Snow wrote thus :—

"Wilfred Tresillian,

"Thy wife Mabel has returned to our home; if it seem good to thee we wish thou wouldest permit her to remain with us, for she seems to require ministration with a gentle hand to soothe her wandering mind. I write lest thou shouldest be uneasy on finding she has left thee.

"I am, thy correspondent,

"Walter Snow."

To this Mr. Tresillian answered :—

"Dear Sir,

"I am glad to hear of Mrs. Tresillian's safety, and that she is in the care of those whom she has herself chosen to minister to her comfort, and I beg that no expense may be spared to procure her the best medical attendance which her state may require, for which you may hold me responsible.

"I remain, your obedient servant,

"Wilfred Tresillian."

CHAPTER XXXIX.

" Thou hast deceived an honest heart, whose strong
  And trusting faith reluctantly is broken;
Yet lingers love, although respect be gone,
  Cherished like memory of some kind word spoken,
By hearts now coldly tutored to forget,
  Or as the skies retain their glowing light,
  The sun's reflection when his orb is set."

WE leave Mabel in such tranquillity as her sad circumstances permit, and return to the sick bed of Sabina.

Like the Queen of Carthage, like all unhappy creatures who are disappointed in love, she loathed the light of day. It was irksome to her to watch the line of sunshine as it passed over the opposite wall. " Her days were days of vanity," *i.e.*, of false images—things unreal—and wearisome nights were appointed unto her. She could not rest without stealing out, as if impelled by some spell to see once or twice during the night that her uncle was safe in his bed. She thought he would have found out the truth about Mr. Tresillian, would steal away and fight a duel, and be wounded or killed for her sake, or wound or kill her lover. She could not conceal from herself that she loved Mr. Tresillian with all the passion and tenderness of which her nature was capable ; yet she recoiled from the treachery with which he had treated her, and shrank from the contemplation of such baseness.

" How could she hate the crime, yet keep the sense ?
How loathe the offender, yet detest the offence ? "

She wished she could forget him, and tried to turn her thoughts to other subjects. The wreck, the Abbey Farm, the coast at Saint Eve ; but over-riding them all was the image of Mabel Snow—Mabel Tresillian, the lawful wife of the man she felt she had been loving since her childhood, without being conscious how deeply her affections had taken root. Mabel Snow it was who occupied consciously the place she longed to fill—Mabel Snow, the playmate of her childish hours, when she had stayed at Trevedra with the family who had pitied her destitute condition, and been kind to her. Why should she not have loved him ? How could she help loving him ? How cruel it was to play with her attachment as he had done ! How kind Lady Sarah had always been to her ! In what a fool's paradise she had lived at Tregear. He could not have loved her ? Love does not seek the disgrace, the destruction of its object. She would forget him ;—and overcome by bodily weakness she turned away and wept.

"Would the days never pass ?" Here was Susan with a tray. "What ! only one o'clock ? Pheasant ?"

"Yes, Miss ; a beautiful brace, sent yesterday from Lady Saran with her compliments."

"Oh, Susan ; I can't eat it. Take it to my uncle. I wish some one would tell them not to send the nasty things. I hate flowers and grapes, and game, and everything."

Sabina felt like a disappointed legatee, to whom the heir sends a present of a hundred pounds to console him for the loss of a hundred thousand.

She had no wish to get up ; no spirit to employ herself. Mr. Dent told her she must make an effort, she would be better for getting up. He brought a song for her to try for him. "She must be partly dressed, and there was the piano quite handy. He should look in in the evening. Miss 'Melia Cressy sang it beautifully." Sabina smiled faintly. She did not care who sang and who did not ; but she let Susan draw on her stockings, having nearly toppled over once in the effort to do so herself, and was partly dressed and wrapped in her dressing gown, and seated at the old piano. Her fingers were very faint and feeble over the keys, and they hit random notes at first, but at length they recovered some of their cunning, and her feeble voice murmured rather than sang the air, whilst her fingers fell on the chords of the accompaniment. Mr. Rock came and listened silently, and thanked Heaven for his child's amendment, looking forward to the day when he should have the triumph of leading her into the sitting room, and showing her the new grand piano.

Mr. Dent prided himself on his craft. The next day a difficult piece of instrumental music was brought, of which he professed himself utterly unable to understand the flute accompaniment if Miss Rock was not kind enough to play the concerto.

"Ah ! what a pity this piano cannot do justice to it. It wants the additional keys."

Mr. Rock looked on with an air of satisfaction. The unseen, unheard blessing down stairs, had every added improvement of which pianos were then considered capable. Sabina promised to study the concerto. She had, poor girl, the feeling always found to be illusory, that the doctor would charge less in his great bill at the end of the illness, if the patient was gentle and obliging, and not given to worry him by irritating claims on his time and attention, or complaints of the nastiness of his drugs.

My own impression is, that they always charge more, from the idea that if patients are meek they are helpless, and may be easily trampled on. The gouty gentleman who flings his crutch at the head of his doctor, or the peevish old woman, who has him waked from his first sleep, to declare she is attacked by cholera, when she had dined on gooseberry tart—these are the folks who obtain most attention at the smallest rate of charge.

However, Sabina's experience was small, and her dread of the bill great, for her uncle's sake ; so she worked away at the difficult crashing concerto of Griffin in three sharps, till she came to the pathetic air, so wonderfully arranged that beauty is added where it seemed impossible to beautify the original, and on to the brilliant rondo at the end. It was strange how she recovered her strength in this occupation. She would get well quicker yet if she could be tempted into the air, Mr. Dent said, but Sabina fought against going down stairs. She knew there was a chance of Mr. Tresillian's calling, and as her uncle would as soon have signed his name to a deliberate falsehood, as have ordered Susan to say, "Not at home," she knew there was no escape for her if he did call. Had she tried to get up stairs, she would have met him in the passage. Mr. Tresillian, however, felt that there was now no excuse, as Sabina was getting well, for his calling daily, so he contrived to find out what progress she was making towards perfect health, by sending for Mr. Dent to attend a groom boy, whom his horse had kicked in the leg. The bruise was nothing. The parents were not disturbed by it ; but the tender-hearted master was determined to have the best advice, and sent for Mr. Dent from Deepindale accordingly. He was in the seventh heaven of rapture. His talents were at length appreciated. He knew he had done well in calling attention to himself at that celebrated concert. His fortune was made.

Sabina, finding that Mr. Tresillian ceased to call, was glad to escape from the confinement of her room ; and one morning before one o'clock, she dressed herself, and asked for her uncle's arm to walk down stairs. "Wait a minute ! wait a minute, my dear, till I have been down and seen the doors are all shut," said the artful veteran, who in reality was fumbling to find the key, which had sunk into the recesses of his capacious pocket. There it was at last, and with shaking hands he unlocked it, and erected the music-stand, and placed the music-stool, and then, standing back, he shaded his eyes from the sunshine to see the effect.

"Yes, nothing could be better," he thought, and he went up, with a glow on his old weather-beaten face, to bring his child to see the much-prized purchase.

Sabina came down very slowly, for she felt giddy from the unusual exertion, and her knees bent under her. Her uncle placed his arm round her waist, and led her into the room, making a full stop before the grand piano.

Sabina gave a little cry, and then burst into tears. She understood all the love, all the sacrifice involved in such a gift, and I doubt whether its magnitude did not produce more pain than pleasure in her mind. The old lieutenant at first was shocked by those tears, but attributed them to bodily weakness, which made them indications of pleasure, which otherwise would have been shown in smiles—for smiles indeed succeeded them—and expressions of pleasure and gratitude were precipitated one over another, till the old man's heart was full, and he almost wept too.

"What an old fool I am, child ! As Shakspeare makes a young girl say somewhere, ' I am a fool to weep at what I'm glad of.' You will get well now, quite, my darling, and sing to me, the 'Heaving of the Lead,' and 'The Lizard Lights,' and 'Sweet Poll of Plymouth.' We shall be so happy, my dear!"

> " A pair of friends, though she was young,
>   And he was seventy-two."

Some days after, when Sabina considered herself quite strong again, a note was brought to her from the great house, with a tremendously black border. Sabina recognised Lady Sarah's hand in the superscription ; but some terror, lest anything should have happened to Mr. Tresillian, made her tremble in tearing the paper round the seal—a large seal with a widow's lozenge, as was the fashion in those bygone days.

The letter was as follows :—

" MY DEAR SABINA,

     " I am sure you will sympathise with me in the *great* loss I have sustained by the death of my *dearest* Robert, of which a courier has *just* apprised me. Wilfred started *immediately* to the seat of his late brother, as of course much *painful* business must devolve on him with regard to the funeral. I can scarcely see what I write, my eyes are so *swollen* with weeping. I have a great deal to think about, my dear, and really if your uncle could spare you to come over, I should like you to be here to support my spirits, at the trying moment when the people come from town to bring my mourning, when the benefit of your taste in the selection I must make will be the greatest assistance to me.

" I hope your uncle does not attribute your *serious* illness to any want of care on my part during your last visit. You shall not travel except in *my own* carriage this time, for I dare say that nasty postchaise was *damp* and *mouldy*, or let in the water, which accounts for it all. So pray induce Mr. Rock to *spare* you, if you can come without *much* inconvenience to him or *risk* to your own *health*.

        " Yours sincerely,
            " SARAH TRELUSA."

Sabina gave the note to her uncle. He was pleased at the consideration expressed on his account, and flattered that Sabina had been thought of by her ladyship in all her

22

troubles. Probably, the kind-hearted veteran gave her credit for more feeling than she really possessed, and thought the difficulty in the choice of mourning arose chiefly from her anxiety how to show her respect in choosing the deepest.

"You must go, Sabina, it seems to me," he said, meditatively.

"Oh! uncle, do you think so? I had so much rather not. You see, I cannot get away when I like, being dependent on Lady Sarah for her carriage."

"That is true, my dear; but she may be a good friend to you in future, when, when "—but the unselfish old man did not like to pain his niece by suggesting when she would be so useful.

"I will go, uncle, if you think I must; but I am not so well able to walk as I was, and the weather is so very cold and dreary."

"No! you must not return every day to see me. You can go for a week, and then come back for good. Let Lady Sarah understand that before you go."

"Yes; and, as her ladyship only wants me in Mr. Tresillian's absence, I can return sooner if he returns before the expiration of the week."

"True, my dear. Remember, you must not call him Mr. Tresillian any more; he is Lord Trelusa now."

"Yes; I had forgotten that he succeeds to the title," observed Sabina.

When Sabina, on the following day, reached Tregear, she was ushered up to the lady's dressing-room, in which the shutters were half-closed. Lady Sarah greeted her in a plaintive voice, and passed her delicate handkerchief over her beautiful eyes, and then kissed Sabina kindly and set to work on the business in hand, having summoned a young woman arrived from town and her own woman to assist at the deliberation.

Her ladyship had more opinion of Sabina's judgment than of her own, or that of the milliner or her own maid. Wilfred had said "that girl's taste is perfect," and Wilfred must know. Sabina was glad to be of service, and admiring the still beautiful daughter of the Earl of Canonbury sincerely, she took pleasure in seeing the dazzling fairness of her shoulders and full bust set off by the deepness of the non-reflecting black texture of her dresses.

When all the orders were given, and the patterns tried on and retried, and decided on, Lady Sarah dismissed everyone but Sabina, and taking her softly to a drawer in a wardrobe, she said, wiping her eyes—

"My dear, mournings are so dreadfully long—twelve months for a son! However, no one shall ever say I did not do my duty to the poor boy, and I must say black is becoming to a fair skin; but, as I was going to observe my dear, here are two lovely silks—a blue and a pink. I was just going to have them made up for dinner dresses, and there is a brown gros de Naples for a morning dress. All these will be quite out of fashion before twelve months are over, and so I will give them to you if you will accept them. I should like to see you in them, my dear, since I canno' wear them myself."

Sabina suggested that her ladyship might keep them, as there was nothing about the patterns of the silks likely to bear date; but her patroness assured her that she should loathe the sight of them if she kept them by her, and Sabina could not do better than to take them in the same spirit as they were offered.

The girl did not object to the present. She had been assured by Lady Sarah that the work she had accomplished on the veil was worth a hundred pounds, by doing which she had saved her friend that sum, so she did not care to refuse what the lady meant as a kindness. She did not care much for the costly silks, and meditated whether she could dispose of them in some way to pay Mr. Dent's bill for attendance during her illness.

Sabina, though treated with the greatest kindness by her hostess, pined for her home. She felt she had lost ground in the command of her mind since her return to Tregear. The discussion of chromatic scales, and occasional and unexpected discords revolving into concords, with Mr. Dent, had driven out in some degree the thought of her unprincipled lover; but at Tregear she saw his daily letter to his mother every morning on the breakfast table. Every book, every flower, every garden path, reminded her of him—of some circumstance which was linked with his remembrance. In the library, he had taken down and left on the table the then newly-published volume of "Rokeby," to show her the outlaw's song, and to inquire jestingly whether she

22—2

would follow the example of "The Lady on the Turret High." This led them to Prior's version of "The Nut-brown Maid," and Lord Trelusa had repeated those charming lines, containing the question of Henry, with a tone of tenderness which increased the exquisite melody of the poet—

> "Didst thou but purpose to embark with me
> On the smooth surface of the summer sea,
> And to forsake the bark and seek the shore
> When the wind rises and the billows roar?"

She remembered the love and the inquiry blended in his eyes, which she then could not understand. Now, the meaning supplied by subsequent facts was a painful one; it was a tentative question, for the purpose of seeing how she would take the situation for which he intended her—that of his mistress.

It was so hard to hate him when she loved him so dearly; yet she loathed his treachery with all the revulsion of an honest heart. The weather was bitter outside the house, but in the hot-houses summer still bloomed. They had stood there under the tangles of the passion flower, and he had playfully twisted one of the long branches, laden with its yellow pods and starry blossoms, round her head as a wreath, without detaching it from its stem, and said she was imprisoned by passion, and could not be released. She had undone the garland carefully, but could not replace the long, twisted creeper, from which the small tendrils had been separated. The flower, removed from its support, hung sadly, with retroverted leaves, looking pale and dishevelled. Here it was as they had left it that morning when they had been so happy.

"I knew not I was walking on a volcano," said the girl, to herself.

He had climbed upon one of the stages of the hot-house to take down the pitcher plant, a specimen of which Sabina had never before seen. He had dipped his fingers in the fluid in its cup, on her saying that it might serve as a font to the fairies, and flung some of the drops over her brow, saying that he baptised her afresh by the name of Sabina Tresillian.

She had been unwise, she felt, to dare all these memories by her visit to Tregear, though she did not exactly see how she could have avoided coming. He could not return before the funeral of the late lord, and consequently she should have at least a week or ten days clear. At the expiration of the week Lady Sarah entreated her to stay till after the funeral, driving into Deepindale herself to prefer her request to Mr. Rock. The old man was overwhelmed with confusion at such an honour, and consented before he knew what he said. He did not, however, wish to recall it. It pleased his old Tory notions that his niece should live in society so refined, and so far above any he could procure for her in Deepindale.

"The child was getting quite womanly," he thought "folks will be falling in love with her soon—not yet though' (with a saving thought of comfort)—"she is so *very* young and Lord Trelusa knows she is quite a child."

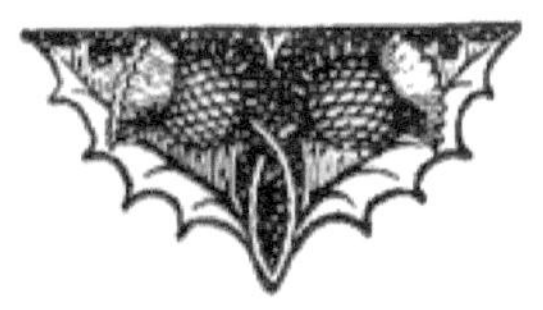

CHAPTER XL.

"To subdue th' unconquerable mind,
    To make one reason have the same effect
    Upon all apprehensions : to force this
    Or this man, just to think as thou and I do ?
    Impossible ! unless the souls which differ
    Like human faces were alike in all."
                                    DRYDEN.

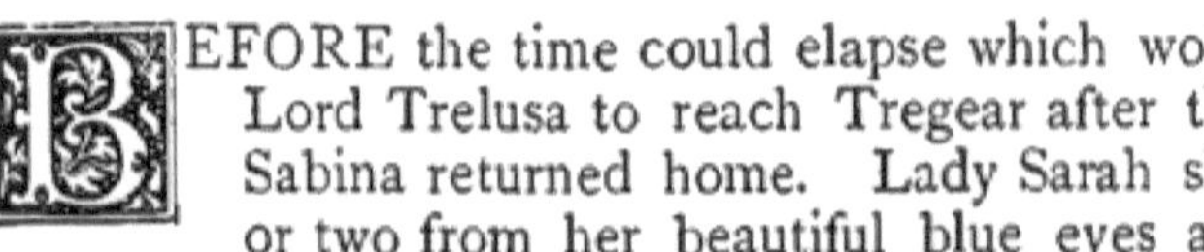

EFORE the time could elapse which would enable Lord Trelusa to reach Tregear after the funeral, Sabina returned home. Lady Sarah shed a tear or two from her beautiful blue eyes as she said good-bye, declared she had been of the greatest comfort to her in her affliction, and placed a fifty-pound note in her hand. She had not meant to get rid of her obligation to Sabina by the gift of the silk dresses only.

"Don't scruple to have it, my dear. Buy something for that dear old man at home ; say that I gave it to him, but *you* know what would please him best. I have plenty of money always. I do not want it. Trelusa will be wonderfully rich now."

And a quiet look of satisfaction settled on her face ; for her eldest son had been plain in his person, coarse in his manners, and degraded in his habits, besides being undutiful to herself. No wonder that she thought her youngest the perfection of a gentleman, and the very best son who had ever lived.

Soon after his brother's funeral, Lord Trelusa received the following letter, addressed to " Wilfred Tresillian, commonly called Lord Trelusa : "—

"WILFRED TRESILLIAN,

"It seemeth good to me, and also to my wife Rachel, to have some communing with thee on a subject which must be as important to thee as to us; and if it seemeth fit to thee, be pleased to call at the house of my sister-in-law in —— Street, by name Jane Den, when, if thou art there at one of the clock, we shall be ready to receive thee.

"I am, thy correspondent,

"WALTER SNOW."

The object of seeing him in London rather than in Cornwall was to avoid any collision between Mabel and her husband, as he surmised, which might have disturbed her mind.

When he reached the house, nothing seemed changed, either outside or inside. The same gaunt maid ushered him up stairs, and in the same room in the same places sat Walter and Rachel Snow, and Jane Den. Fifteen months had passed since he had gone thither to demand the hand of Mabel in marriage, and how much of disturbance to him and distress to others had arisen since!

He sat down, the servant having placed a chair before she left the room; and he waited for his father or mother-in-law to begin the conference; but heavy sighs, first from one Friend, and then from another, were all he could hear for the first few minutes.

"'Tis lucky I'm not in a hurry, or these folks would drive me distracted," said the young lord mentally.

Rachel Snow first began to speak.

"Thou art here, Wilfred Tresillian, in the same room and with the same persons thou didst meet fifteen months and twelve days ago. Thou has controverted our wishes, and taken from us our daughter since that day; and has thy heart been lighter, and thy spirit more glad, because thou didst take thy own pleasure, and lured a simple girl into thy snare? I believe if thou wert to tell the truth, thou wouldest say that thy heart is heavy with the weight of a great care."

"Are you aware, Madam," said Wilfred, " of the circumstances which led to my meeting your daughter? It was to shield her brother that she wished all the past to be concealed; but as without any act of mine you are, as I am

informed, aware of all your son's conduct, you can receive
no greater pain than he has already inflicted. I saw your
daughter first outside the gate of your garden, striving to
induce your son, who had a prostitute on his arm, and was
exceedingly drunk, to return to the house. She was insulted
—your pure-minded, delicate daughter—by his inebriated
companions, and in defending her I was struck and wounded
in the face. At her request I followed the misguided young
man, and some hours later two of my servants picked him
up insensible in the road, and carried him to his bed at your
house. His state of insensibility gave me serious apprehensions as to his life. I remained with him all night, nursing
him with care which he did not deserve, and your daughter
was grateful. We loved—she, probably, for the first time—
and her love, I need hardly say, was truer and purer than
my own; yet I meant well by her, and on your son bringing
that woman at night into your house, I avowed my intention of making Mabel my wife, and as her future husband
insisted that no insult should be offered to her. I demanded
her hand of you in marriage, as an honourable man should.
You received my proposition with scoffing and expressions
little short of insult. I gave way to your wishes, and saw
nothing and heard nothing of Mabel, after I had told her
that for a week I should consider myself bound to act by
any suggestion of hers, till at the expiration of some considerable time she came to me in the middle of the night,
agitated and distressed, and threw herself on my protection.
I did that which I felt was due to her purity—that which
few young men, whose lives have not been conducted on
the strictest principles of morality, would have done—I
married her. I gave her a commodious house and a command of money ample for every want or wish. I should
have been an attached husband, as I ever was a tender one,
but she repulsed every attention, because she could not
prevail on me to adopt the tenets of the sect in which she
was educated. The prospect of her bearing me a child was
an additional source of disquiet and grief to her. She
wished, whatever might be its sex, that it should be educated
as one of the Society of Friends. The child was born, and
a few days subsequently" (and here the father became pale
and spoke low) "she grasped the little helpless infant by
the throat, and but for my stronger hand, which unclasped

those murderous fingers, she would have strangled my son.
I took the child and placed it in safe keeping. She will
never see him again."

A groan burst from the breast of each parent of Mabel
when they heard for the first time the terrible proof of her
insanity, of which they had known the existence for sixteen
months, but had not suspected that it had evinced itself in
a manner so frightful. They sat some time in silence, not
doubting the truth of the account given them by Lord
Trelusa, but overwhelmed by grief and concern at the facts
stated.

At length Mr. Snow spoke.

"I have no doubt, Friend Wilfred, that the poor girl's
brain had been disturbed by the too great responsibility with
which we invested her, in leaving the cares of a family on
one so young; but our eyes were holden, that we should
not see the misconduct of that unhappy youth.

"Our object in meeting thee to-day was to suggest to
thee that as Mabel showed symptoms of mental alienation
before thy marriage with her, it would be in our power to
dissolve such marriage in a court of law, and this would
prevent that which has been hanging over us for some time,
the disgrace of her being excluded from the Society of
Friends, in consequence of her marriage with one not of
that sect. Of course it would simplify matters very much
if thou didst not raise any legal objections to such a
course."

He was silent and looked at Lord Trelusa, whom astonishment rendered speechless.

"Good Heavens! Mr. Snow. What grounds have you
to go on? How can you prove my wife to have been
insane, when the first symptoms came on after her confinement?"

"Not the *first* symptoms, friend. If thou wilt interrogate
Jane Den, her aunt, thou wilt find I have not advanced anything which cannot be proved by her evidence, and that of
her servant."

Miss Den, with many sighs, told of the eccentricity of
Mabel's conduct, and of the effort she had made to accomplish her self-destruction.

"Why was I not warned of this?' was the natural
question asked by Lord Trelusa.

" We thought," said Mabel's mother, " that her marriage with one whom she greatly loved, would probably lead to happy results as regarded her sanity, and that if we interfered to take her from thee it might precipitate the evil we feared would fall on her.   It is only now that she comes to us broken in spirit, and heavy in heart, that we feel we would do much to restore her to the fold whence she so unhappily strayed, poor wounded lamb ! "

" But do you not see," said Lord Trelusa, "that should your efforts bring forth fruit you bastardise my child ?—the child whose prospects are so fair—who is now the next heir to a peerage ? "

" It is on that very ground we wish it," said the couple in one breath.   " Excuse me, Walter Snow," said the more eloquent female Friend, as her husband was about to speak. "We feel with our dear Mabel on this point, and though it was an act of madness to attempt the poor infant's life, we think his chance of ultimate happiness would be greater, brought up in the Society of Friends, as the natural child of Mabel Snow, considering the circumstances of her marriage, than if he were the person called by men Lord Trelusa, educated in the pomps and vanities of the world, and habituated to all the sinful lusts of the flesh.   If everything that a man hath will he give for his life, as the Scripture says, how much more for life eternal.   'What will a man profit, if he gain the whole world, and lose his own soul ?' "

Lord Trelusa felt his brain reel with the momentousness of the proposition as stated by his father and mother-in-law. His feelings were mingled, for he loved his little son, and could not but feel a pang at the idea of the injury he should inflict on him by his assent to the wishes of Mabel's parents.

So differently did the two parties judge.   Lord Trelusa believed that a mortal injury would accrue to his boy should he be deprived of his peerage.   The Snows were convinced that he would be lost immortally should he be brought up to hold that worldly honour.

Lord Trelusa begged to take time to consider the point. This was accorded, but Mrs. Snow reminded him that though he might delay and embarrass their proceedings, he could not prevent their arriving at the conclusion desired by

Mabel's family. They should attain their end, even should he oppose them, though at greater loss both of time and money

To be free, to be able to inthral himself again—this time under happier auspices—this thought made his eyes flash, and his footstep light, as he left Miss Den's house. He heard from her servant before he left, of the effort made by the unhappy Mabel to destroy herself, and shuddered when he saw the window, from the ledge of which the maid had saved her from precipitating herself. Poor Mabel! his conscience was clear on that score. He had behaved exceedingly well to her. Not one man in a hundred would have thus acted under similar circumstances. But Sabina! ah! there he flinched, and recoiled from the investigation urged by conscience. His mad passion would have made him a scoundrel to that darling child. But she would forgive him, would marry him, if he could make up his mind to do this injustice to his boy. Why should he not? It would be done, without him probably. How fond his mother seemed of Sabina. The daily letters were full of her. "Sabina had written her orders for her to her tradesmen. Sabina had selected her mourning. Sabina had sang to her all the evening like an angel. She did not know what she would do when Sabina returned to her uncle." He would hasten home. He could go now the funeral was over. He would go down unexpectedly and find her with his mother, and tell her all the truth about Mabel; and she would make excuses for him even more than he should make for himself—"she loved him so." She had owned that, even when most angry, justly angry with him for the deceit he had practised upon her. Yet the thought of his boy haunted him. Poor little infant! He loved him the more that he had saved his life. He thought of feeling proud of him when he grew up; of the personal resemblance to himself, which was strong even in those infantine features; he thought what his son's career in Parliament should be. He would be a cleverer, or in any event, a more industrious man than himself. He had a boy, an heir, which his deceased brother had ever longed for in vain, being blessed only by a female progeny. He might have a score of useless girls like his brother, and never again a beautiful male infant like his own. Before he sought Sabina, he would see the child again. Well! but would not the boy be happy enough as a broad brim? No; he could not reconcile himself to this idea. The boy could only be happy and prosperous in the way he thought more fortunate. They might take the child from him—what then?

He knew not how to decide, "and found no end in wandering mazes lost;" but he came down to Cornwall with the knowledge that he would have to return to London immediately. That did not matter. He must see the little Wilfred and Sabina. His heart bounded at her name, like that of a happy bridegroom, expecting a fond welcome from the chosen of his heart. It was his habit to visit his boy unexpectedly, that he might be satisfied as to what treatment he received from the nurse, and judge whether the scrupulous cleanliness he enforced was attended to.

He found no reason to complain. The infant was dressed, to the pride and delight of his foster-mother, in the most stainless of robes, and the richest of lace caps. A clean white bib was under its chin, and a piece of pink flannel covered it with its outward folds.

"Is the baby well, nurse?" said the father, looking contentedly at its round arms and dimpled fingers.

"Ye-es, Sir, that is, my lord?"

"What do you mean by *ye-es?*" said Wilfred, impatiently.

"I can't rightly say," said the woman, looking puzzled. "The babe sucks well, but he never takes no notice, and his mouth hangs open, and his head goes a' one side, and he can't hold nothing in his hand! I ne'er seed but one so before, and that was a natural——"

The father turned pale.

"Take good care of him," he said, placing an additional fee in the nurse's hand.

"Gracious Heaven! that grasp on his throat made him an idiot! Everything has united to punish me for having acted honourably towards that accursed woman!" But he repented the adjective as soon as it was uttered. "Poor Mabel! Well! 'tis really a warning to me never to try for being a good man, a character which brings penances so peculiarly crushing. I might save myself the trouble of thinking about my boy as the future Lord

Trelusa. Quaker or not he will never be capable of holding the title."

There was comfort, however, in the thought of his freedom. He would communicate at once with the Snows, and say that he would not oppose their wishes. Mabel did not care for him—rather feared and avoided him. She would be happier with her own family.

CHAPTER XLI.

"Early, bright, transient, pure as morning dew,
She sparkled, was exhaled, and went to heaven."

YOUNG.

BUT a mightier power than that of human law was at work to free Mabel from all earthly ills.

She seemed on her return home to fall somewhat into her usual habits and occupations, but with an indisposition to speak or move, even greater than had been the case when, in her happiest days, she had ever been more tranquil than cheerful. She dropped asleep over her book, or needlework, and awoke with a start, with a flushed face and dilated pupils. One morning they found her unwilling or unable to rise. Her eyes wandered unconsciously and without speculation from one object to another. She uttered the name of her married sister, and then of her father. Her father came to her bedside, and wept over her; but she was unconscious of pain or sorrow. In a few hours effusion on the brain supervened, and Lord Trelusa was a widower.

It was a consolation to Mrs. Snow that Mabel, whose supposed defection from the doctrine taught by the Friends had never been made public at the quarterly or yearly meeting, was buried in the graveyard belonging to the Quakers' meeting.

Lord Trelusa's mourning for his brother made an alteration of dress unnecessary, and made unnecessary also, as he remembered with comfort, any communication of the very unpleasant story to his mother.

No delay now! He would seek his darling, and plead

his cause successfully. He gave a half laugh at the notion that it " could be anything but successful," standing before the large glass in the solitary London drawing-room, which reflected the very handsome person of a young man of thirty years, fair-haired and fresh-looking, a peer of the realm, with wealth which seemed fabulous. But he did Sabina the justice to think that he owed more to her love than to any personal or adventitious advantages.

He was disappointed on arriving at Tregear to find Lady Sarah alone.

" Miss Rock has returned home, I suppose ? "

" Yes," said the lady, with a gentle sigh. " She is so fond of that old man ; I believe she hates to be away from him."

Lord Trelusa thought of the loneliness of the veteran lieutenant when his niece should be Lady Trelusa, and sat musing a few minutes as to whether there could not be a suite of rooms fitted up for the old man both at Tregear and in the London house.

" The old lieutenant is quite a gentleman of the old school in manners," she went on to say. " It is rather agree-able to meet such an one after the carelessness towards ladies, and the absence of reverence in manner, which are creeping into the society of young men in the present day."

Her ladyship had been flattered by the extreme devotion shown by the old sailor (always susceptible to female charms) to her beauty rather than her rank.

" Yes, he is a gentleman every inch of him," responded her son. He would be his father-in-law very soon, and he must exalt him to make him worthy that position.

It was at night that this conversation took place.

" I shall ride over to Deepindale before your eyes are open to-morrow, my lady. Can I do anything for you ? "

" No, my son ; unless you ask at the coach-office if my parcel has come from Hogard and Amber."

Lord Trelusa promised to remember but forgot, in the vivid interests which occupied him.

When he reached Mr. Rock's house, Susan met him with a smile and a courtesy. " He was such a pleasant gentle-man," she thought, "and sent so many nice things from Tregear, though to be sure, she should have been thankful if he had kept the game to himself. No one could tell how hard those birds were to pluck, nor the time it took to do them well! Then, to be sure, master, poor, dear gentleman, seemed to enjoy them, though *she* could never touch a bit, after drawing, and trussing, and roasting them herself. There was the bread-sauce, too! such a quantity of crust it left! If it wasn't that Miss Sabina's teeth were beautiful, they never could have got through them crusts."

All these thoughts ran through Susan's head as she smiled and courtesied to the young lord.

"Will you like to walk in, Sir? We've got a new piano, —such a beauty! Master got it for Miss, but she being so ill, poor dear, hasn't played much on it as yet."

"But where is Miss—Mr. Rock?"

"Lor, Sir! don't you know?" For, with the usual circumscribed notions of ignorant folks, she believed the affairs of the family in which she lived to be sufficiently important to be known to the whole world. "Master was so grieved when he saw how bad Miss looked when she came home from Tregear, that he took her away next day to Saint Eve. She will catch her death of cold, says I,—but he didn't take heed of me, and so they went."

"And how did Miss Rock seem to be?" said Lord Trelusa.

"She seemed wonderful down-hearted, if I may say so, Sir—that is, my lord. My young missus hasn't been the same since her illness. Mr. Dent—that's the doctor—says he don't like the looks of her."

"But why Saint Eve—that bleak place? Ah! I see— Mr. Orellan. My piece of virtue has stood in my way there again. Why did I get that place in the coastguard for that old fellow, just to tempt the other old man to go after him, and take his niece away from me?" thought the young man to himself. "Good-bye, Susan," he said, cheerfully, giving her half-a-crown. "Do you think they will soon come home?"

"Can't say, Sir—hope they will—for now I've done cleaning the house up, 'tis wonderful dull without them."

It was too late to go to Saint Eve that day, so Lord Trelusa returned to Tregear, and had to confess his forgetfulness of Lady Sarah's commission.

It was true that Mr. Rock was shocked by the alteration for the worse in Sabina's appearance; but that was not the only reason for their sudden removal to Saint Eve.

" Dear Rock," Mr. Orellan wrote, " I think I never have wanted your valuable counsel so frequently as I have done lately. In these confounded long dark nights the smugglers reap their harvest as completely as the labourer does in long bright summer days. I am so driven about from one point to another, that I'm like a boy playing ' What's my name?' I'm pulled behind; turn to catch my adversary, and get another poke from another direction. In the meantime the revenue is defrauded, and my chief will soon begin to think me a lubberly landsman instead of a sharp officer. The chief reason of my failure is want of hands. I have not men enough allowed me to guard the different points where tubs are landed. I was speaking to Ferrers—that preaching fellow is not so bad when you come to know him—and he said, ' Why don't you ask your friend to come and stay a few weeks here ? The air was very beneficial the last time, and I dare say he would be glad to be of use to an old friend. I am going to see some friends in Yorkshire for a couple of months, and the Abbey Farm is quite at his service and that of his niece. Alice will be glad of companions in these dreary winter evenings.'

" I believe the invitation was heartily given, and I need not say how pleased I shall be if you can find it convenient to accept it.

" With my compliments to Miss Rock, I am, your obedient servant and faithful friend,

"STEPHEN ORELLAN."

Mr. Rock read part of this letter to Sabina, passing over the part about the smugglers, lest she should be alarmed. He wished to go to Saint Eve, but doubted whether Sabina would like to leave the neighbourhood of her new piano so soon. He knew not that the poor girl carried in her bosom a hidden wound which provoked as much restlessness in her movements as the same cause produced in those of the Tyrian queen. She was glad to get away from the neighbourhood of Tregear—glad to leave the home where her illness had been so wearying—glad to have the thought of the fresh salt breezes playing on her feverish brow. She seemed to feel, poor girl, that she might care less for her lover in a fresh place. Mr. Rock had had a new assortment of linen since the payment of his prize-money, and she had not the compelled attention to mending his socks and putting buttons on his shirts every Saturday when they came from the wash. The socks used to spread themselves over the following week in former days, and Sabina half regretted they did not do so now, so she took to working over the toes and heels, as she had been taught to do in Mrs. Snow's family.

It would be a comfort, she thought, if the poodle would tear some more lace, for her to mend for Lady Sarah. She had the great pleasure of paying Mr. Dent's bill before they left Deepindale, which she only got by sitting down in the surgery and saying she would wait there till it was made out. A distant time is so agreeable to the creditor when some of the items may be considered doubtful. To do justice to Mr. Dent's penetration, he knew both uncle and niece too well to think of *lumping* the charges, so pleasing a plan to a medical practitioner, who says when he has made up the account to four pounds seven shillings and sixpence, "May as well call it five pounds; they won't feel the loss of the shillings as much as I shall the benefit of them!" So his account was not unreasonable, and Sabina having paid it, began to think whether she ought to buy her uncle anything with Lady Sarah's money. She would have desired nothing better than to expend it all on her uncle ; but he was so touchy on money obligations, that she dared not confess to having received that fifty pounds.

Lady Sarah's little speech, she knew, had only been made by way of inducing her to receive the gift, and on consideration she determined to provide small comforts for Mr. Rock without his being cognizant that they did not come out of the weekly expenses, rather than that he should feel overwhelmed by an obligation which he could not repay.

CHAPTER XLII.

" How many hearts have here grown cold,
    That sleep these mouldering stones among ;
How many beads have here been told ;
    How many matins here been sung !

" At this gray cross by time long broke,
    Methinks I see some pilgrim kneel ;
I see the curling incense smoke ;
    I hear the organ's solemn peal.

" But here no more soft music floats,
    Or solemn anthem 's chanted now ;
All hushed except the ring-dove's notes,
    Soft murmuring from the beechen bough."

THEY arrived at Saint Eve one wintry afternoon, and were welcomed by Alice.

"Master only went away yesterday, Sir, and said that you were to have everything as comfortable as I could make it for you and the young lady. The beds are well aired, and dinner will be ready at five o'clock."

Mr. Rock wanted to go and see Mr. Orellan at once, but the walk was a long one, and led over the cliff, and, to please Sabina, they dined together and played chess in the evening.

"You play as well as Orellan now," her uncle said, one day, rather sadly. "Those young brains always beat the old ones, if they have the same amount of strength to start with."

It may be so ; but in this case Sabina's head had been better supplied by nature in quickness, than that of either of the veteran lieutenants; and this more than balanced the skill earned by experience.

On the following morning they breakfasted early, that Mr. Rock might have a long day with his old friend.

The Abbey Farm had been built on the extreme point of land at the north of Saint Eve, and consequently commanded an extended view of the British Channel. The town stood away at the back of the abbey, and there was something grand and commanding in the isolation of the old building, which had been erected in former years, that the sound of its bells and the glimmer of its lights might warn vessels from the treacherous sandbanks, over which the sea broke, at the base of the cliff on which it stood.

It was a bright, clear day, and Sabina looked sadly over the wide extent of waters, which, like futurity, offered no defined objects of thought. She sat within the recess of the old arched window, and remembered how many hearts had offered their griefs at the throne whence alone can be obtained pity and consolation. In that chapel how many lives had sunk into vacuity in the daily successions of conventual duties? Were they happy? she wondered.

> " Where moving shadows mock the part of men."

She wished she were a Catholic, and could bury her sorrow in the cloister.

Ah! that dear old man! She could never leave him whilst he lived; but what was to be her fate at his death? She could not care; she would go out to service somewhere. She felt in such a disposition of mind, that any bodily discomfort would lose its power to wound her.

How black those rocks were—variegated with veins of crimson and green, brightening in colour as the white waves broke over them, and fell in a cascade on the other side. She looked at them till she grew giddy. Then she strove to find occupation in the room. She opened a book, of which the leaves parted too easily to do so without cause, and found within them the dead flowers she had placed in the glass on the morning she had left the abbey. There they were, with a faint dead smell about them. She might not have recognised them to be the same, but that she had tied them together with some netting silk, of which

she knew the texture, though the colour, like that of
the flowers, had faded. So he loved her — this grand-
looking, high-souled enthusiast. She supposed so, or he
would not have treasured her flowers. She was slightly
sorry for it; but forgot it again directly. Lord Trelusa
alone occupied her thoughts. She did not care whether Mr.
Ferrers loved her or not. How beautiful and sleek and
guileful her lover was! like a wild animal—a panther—or
like a serpent crawling stealthily towards its object, and
then finishing with a deadly spring.

"Oh! 'tis useless! 'tis useless!" she cried, walking
swiftly up and down the room. "I love him in spite
of his wickedness. I loved him when I hung round
his neck, when I was a little child. I loved him then,
when I entreated him to let me live with him always. I
would give the world to fling myself into his arms now,
and tell him how dear he is to me. How beautiful he
is! How kind—except in that weakness!" Then she
tried to excuse him to herself, but could not. It was
not an act of momentary forgetfulness of right conduct, but a
determined course of seduction. "There was no truth in
him." He had loved Mabel Snow, or he would not have
married her. He fancied that he loved Sabina Rock now,
but in a few months she would have been thrown aside for
some other newer beauty. Sabina meditated on this, and
hardened her heart against her lover.

She thought Mr. Rock would never come back, and went
out to look for him. Mr. Orellan lived on the western side of
the town, over the cliff, and Sabina was seized by a sudden
terror lest her uncle should fall over it. Her mind was
relieved by seeing two figures, standing out against the gray
sky, coming towards the Abbey Farm, still at some considerable distance. Sometimes they stopped, and talked
earnestly. Then out came their spyglasses, and they peered
over the edge of the cliff into the distant horizon. Then
they disappeared altogether over the cliff, and Sabina gave
a cry of terror, which Alice heard, and, smiling, assured her
that there were steps cut here and there in the rock, and no
doubt Captain Orellan (for he had that title there by courtesy), had gone down to look into the caverns, and see what
he could find.

"What could he find—seaweed or shells?" said Sabina.

"Kegs of liquor, Miss. You know the captain is put here to prevent their being landed, or to seize the cargo if it is landed. Now, the gentleman that was here before used to whistle and look another way when a boat pulled in ; and, bless you ! the folks at Saint Eve got their brandy from Holland, and their whisky from Ireland, wonderfully cheap ; and they made no complaints. Many's the twenty pound Captain Cole put into his pocket, and all was kept quiet. But this Captain Orellan—I don't say nothing against him, Miss, as he's a friend of your uncle's—*he's* for doing his duty, as he calls it, and the consequence is, that there's nothing but watching and waiting, and spying and informing, and quarrelling and shooting, from sundown to sunrise, amongst the Preventive Service men and the sailors that come in the smuggling boats. I think we were happier when Captain Cole was here ; we were certainly quieter ; but I suppose it is a fine thing to do one's duty, even when 'tis in killing or sending to prison poor fellows, who only want to help a poor soul to a drop of comfort on a winter night."

Sabina smiled, and thought she should soon be demoralised if she listened to Alice. Indeed, she thought her morals must be in a shaking condition, considering the efforts made to undermine them on all sides.

"Mr. Orellan is a fine old fellow, though I never liked him," she thought. "How very convenient a few of those hush-money twenty pounds would be to him and to Mrs. Orellan."

Here, however, she was mistaken. When the old men had reappeared on the summit of the cliff, and had advanced slowly towards the house, Sabina saw that his old uniform navy blue coat had a piece of faded black crape pinned round the arm, and on Mr. Rock coming in, he told Sabina that poor Orellan had lost his wife.

"Afflicted, but relieved, probably," said Sabina.

"I don't know, my dear ! He is afflicted. I don't know if there is any relief in the feeling. Folks like what they protect and make comfortable ; and if he has lost a care, he has lost someone who always looked for his coming back. I don't think Orellan has even a dog now—he had one once, but the dog put his paws up, and dirtied his trowsers. You see sailors grow particular about neatness and cleanliness ;

it is one of the chief duties on board ship, and comes next to godliness. I think he might have a dog, though, now. It is such a comfort to have something to love one, my child !" And Sabina, whose feelings were easily aroused at that juncture, put her arms round her uncle's neck, and sobbed aloud. The thought of Lord Trelusa was in her mind, as " something to love one."

On the following days she went out and made her abode in the clefts of the rocks. She was not compelled to employ herself, and she preferred being idle ; a sign of the sickness of her mind, for her natural disposition was excessive activity.

It was not cold when she got into some sheltered nook, where she would sit listlessly for hours. She tried to take interest in the smuggling question that occupied the old sailor friends ; but her sick heart refused to care for any subject but one—Lord Trelusa was all in all to her.

Her mind was engrossed by this all-prevailing topic one day as she sat in the seat she usually chose, from its being retired and sheltered. To attain unto it, she had to pass round a point of rock, where the footpath retreated inward, and the part to which her hands clung overhung the sea, beating a hundred feet below. She liked the danger of the access, and felt convinced she should have her retreat uninvaded.

There was ample space to stand or sit when this small cavern in the bay was reached; and there she spent her hours of wasted time.

One day she heard some fragments of rock falling with a splash into the ocean below—that space of deep water so deeply green. To her dismay, she saw Lord Trelusa clinging to the points of rocks round which she managed to pass harmlessly, but which his added size and weight made a process of great danger.

She was silent, knowing that a cry or exclamation might precipitate his fate, and watched him breathlessly till he achieved his difficult undertaking, when, with an impulse that seemed irresistible, she seized his arm and drew him as far as possible from the edge of the cliff, with a fervent " Thank God."

His face was pale, for he had seen his peril in the rottenness of the stones to which he clung, when it was too late to retreat, and in his heart he echoed the expression of thankfulness. He was very grave, too; for he knew not how Sabina would receive him, and if he had to speak of love, he had also to tell of death—of the death of her who had interfered by her gentle majesty of virtue to rescue Sabina from his stratagems and violence.

"You are glad I am safe?" he said timidly, sitting down by her side. His lips were trembling with agitation, and Sabina could not refuse him a seat by her side which his nervousness seemed to render necessary to his safety.

"Why are you come here?" she said, not replying to his question. "It is very wrong in you to come—insulting to me—false to your wife."

He told her all—how he had been led into a marriage with Mabel Snow, whom he had pitied, but never loved —how he had never felt for any woman the passionate love which filled his heart for Sabina. He spoke of his release from thraldom by poor Mabel's death, concealing, from pity to the deceased, her attempt on the life of his child. He spoke of her tenderly, and Sabina wept over the fate of her early friend. Then, his arm stealing round the girl's slender waist, he entreated her to be his—to give him an answer at once. He implored her not to keep him in suspense.

Sabina was troubled in mind, from a simple circumstance which made every word he spoke seem as if coming in a dream.

She was miserable lest he should not round the point of rock safely in returning, yet did not like to express that degree of interest in his safety that would account for her nervousness.

She put away the encircling arm gently, and said, "I cannot talk to you here. We will return to the Abbey Farm, if you please—at any event, not here."

"She fears me," he thought, with a feeling of mortification. "She cannot forget that she had cause to do so."

He withdrew his arm, and suggested to Sabina to precede him round the point of rock.

"I have already displaced some of the stones and loosened some others, and if more fall from my weight, the return will be more dangerous for you."

He looked up at the cliff, to see if there were any means of ascending it, but it was hopeless.

"I think I would rather you went first; so little supports me, and I am so used to it."

He obeyed her, and arrived safely on the other side of the point, and then Sabina followed with a lighter spirit. They descended to the beach, and walked over the quiet yellow sands, unmarked by any footsteps save their own. Now, that he had hope of winning Sabina for his wife, she was as safe from importunity in his company as if her uncle were by her side.

"Sabina, will you marry me?"

"No," she replied gravely and promptly.

"*Not?*" he exclaimed, with a cry of astonishment and terror. "Not marry me? Why, you *love* me, Sabina—I *know* that you love me," and as he gave that assurance to himself he felt more satisfied. "I saw how pale you were when I rounded the point of the cliff. It is nonsense to refuse me—quite foolish to say so," and he was growing rather angry at the recollection of that prompt "No."

"I do not deny that I love you, Lord Trelusa, but I do not love you well enough to marry you and spend with you the rest of my life. I could not trust—pardon me, I do not want to go into particulars; be satisfied with the simple denial, and do not let us discuss the question."

"You are very hard, Sabina. I am not a bad fellow, take me altogether. Hang it! no one is perfect. There are many in this world with fewer temptations, who are much worse than I am."

"I don't know with what manner of men you must associate, Lord Trelusa," said Sabina, with her eyes flashing fire, "but when I think of the events of the last six weeks, and particularly of those on one night, when I left the shelter and protection of your mother's society to return, as I thought, to my own home—when I remember the extraordinary heaviness and stupor with which I was overwhelmed, after those French sweetmeats, of which no one partook but myself—when I recall my struggles, my cries for help, and your efforts to render them unavailing, I cannot but feel insulted by your having inflicted your company on me on this occasion. Heaven has, ere this, I trust, repaid to that pure-minded woman who saved me from your violence, a hundredfold for her kindness to me. No irritation against one, whom she knew to be her rival, had any effect in diminishing her benevolence. She wrapped her own cloak over my dripping and shivering frame, and treated one, who had diverted from her her husband's fickle fancy—('tis profanation to call such a feeling love)—not as an enemy, but as a sister. I tell you truly, I do not love you sufficiently well to forgive the insults you have offered to a defenceless girl."

Lord Trelusa was silent. He was angry and mortified. He had not thought she would have suspected the sweetmeats to have been drugged; nor would she have done so, had she not overheard, before she quite recovered, some words exchanged between Lord Trelusa and his valet, the treachery of whom his lordship had not then discovered. Lord Trelusa had desired him to see if any had been left in the postchaise, and desired that they might be destroyed, lest anyone else should partake of them.

He loved Sabina, and was resolved she should marry him; but he was sagacious enough to see that the moment, when she had increased her anger by the enumeration of her wrongs, was not that in which he could successfully plead for her forgiveness. So they walked along in silence towards the house, when Sabina ventured an inquiry after the health of Lady Sarah, which he answered curtly, and relapsed into silence.

Sabina left him when, as they drew near the Abbey Farm, they overtook Mr. Rock, who had not been aware of his lordship's arrival, and received him with a degree of cordial wonder.

"Anything stirring in the political world, my lord? I suppose we must not ask who is to occupy the seat left vacant by your removal to the Upper House?"

Lord Trelusa gave him sundry bits of information, which gave the lieutenant a feeling of importance as he thought of communicating them to Orellan.

Wilfred then went on to say, that his thoughts were not at present occupied by the duties of his new position—the truth was, that his hopes of happiness were centred in the desire he felt to obtain the favour of Miss Rock, and the possession of her hand in marriage. Might he ask Mr. Rock for his consent to win his niece?

The old man was completely taken aback.

"Eh! What! my lord! Surely I do not understand. My

niece! a mere child! Your lordship *must* remember 'tis only a month or two ago when you kindly sent her home, silly child—well, it might be a year—two years. But, dear me, she's too young—I assure you, she is much too young for anyone to think of marrying her for the next five years."

If anyone had proposed to Mr. Rock to take from him his ninety pounds a-year, and leave him destitute in the world, he could not have been more concerned than he was by Lord Trelusa's proposition to make his niece a peeress.

His own darling! What right had anyone to take her away from him? She loved him better than any lord in the land, he knew, and she was to him as dear as daylight to his eyes.

But his second thoughts were less selfish. First, Lord Trelusa assured him that more than five years had elapsed between his visits to Deepindale; and that Miss Rock, being turned of sixteen, might be called seventeen. This Mr. Rock objected to as a subterfuge. However, it did not matter, as the question was only discussed between the two gentlemen. Then Mr. Rock remembered that he was in his seventy-second year, and that he had no fortune—no provision, in fact, beyond the few hundreds left of his prize-money for her support. These considerations made him very thoughtful and sad.

"She is my pet lamb," he said; "she is the only bit of pleasure I have in the world. 'Tis hard to give her up to this handsome young man, who is titled and wealthy. Why should he have everything, and I nothing?"

But he said if his niece consented, he should be happy to confirm it by his own.

"I assure you, Sir," said the artful peer, "though Miss Rock is, in my lover-like eyes, perfect in all her own exceeding grace and virtue, a great inducement to make her my wife is afforded by the connection it will give me with one so distinguished for his valour and high character, as a gentleman and man of honour, as Mr. Rock."

The old lieutenant coloured and bowed low at the flattering speech. He did not believe it; but it proved that the young lord loved Sabina so well as to wish to propitiate her old uncle, he thought.

When Lord Trelusa left Saint Eve, he shook hands cordially with Mr. Rock, and held his hand timidly towards

Sabina to receive hers. She could not refuse it without attracting unpleasant observation from her uncle; but she yielded it so coldly that the young lover knew that no forgiveness was implied by that act of courtesy.

It was a strange phase of human feeling, but not at all unnatural, that Sabina, whose tender relentings towards the man who had intended her such deadly injury were ungovernable, when she thought him utterly placed beyond her reach by the circumstance of his marriage with Mabel Snow, should, when she saw him at her feet, recoil from him whom she loved, but for whose character she had a contempt.

When they had finished their tea that evening, and Sabina had set out the chessmen, Mr. Rock, instead of taking the two pawns within his ample hands, to give Sabina the choice which was to determine the move, pushed back his chair from the table, and looked at his niece sadly.

"She really does look older than I thought," he said to himself, after some considerable time spent in meditation.

He was swelling with his feeling of importance. He did not know that Trelusa had been pleading his own cause; besides he had become aware of various little bits of intelligence on political matters, confided to him by the young lord, with which he meant to overwhelm his friend Orellan next day.

Altogether, he was not unhappy, but very busy in his mind.

"My dear!" and he cleared his throat. "Sabina?"

The girl, who had no idea that Lord Trelusa had ventured to speak to her uncle after her decided refusal, thought, "What has the old darling got into his head now? There can't be two grand pianos."

"Sabina, Lord Trelusa came here to-day to speak to me on a point—a very important point as regards his happiness, he says—in fact, my dear, he wants you to be Lady Trelusa."

"Indeed!" replied Sabina. "I am exceedingly obliged for his politeness, and I prefer to be Sabina Rock."

Her voice had a scoffing tone in it, which filled her uncle with amazement.

Sabina was indignant with Lord Trelusa for his applying to her uncle in spite of her refusal, and thereby running the risk of embroiling her with her only relative, who might naturally resent her refusing an offer, of which the advantages were so patent, and the evils so unseen.

"My dear!" said he, at length, "you know when a man asks a girl to marry him he does her great honour, pays her a great compliment. I'm sure I don't want to lose you, Sabina"—and his voice became unsteady—"but I can't live much longer, my dear, and I am very poor, too poor to leave you anything sufficient for your own support when I am gone."

"Never mind that, uncle."

There was a silence. At length he continued, "Do you dislike him? He is very handsome."

"Very," she agreed.

"Very good-natured and courteous in his manner?"

"Very."

"He must love you, you little witch, for it will be a match which the world will consider below him, though the Rocks are of a good family and pure descent."

"*Would* it, uncle? But the world will never have the opportunity of criticising his choice in my case, as I shall not marry him."

"Sabina!" in a penetrating tone; "there must be some reason for your refusal."

A long silence. The girl was worried, and irritated at having her feelings thus tested.

"I am sure you seem to me too young; but I don't understand the ways of women, I suspect. Oh, Sabina! tell me the truth!"

Sabina was in agony lest he should probe too near the truth.

"Well?" she said, in desperation.

"I suspect that you must love that long-legged high-shouldered fellow who preaches in the conventicle?"

Sabina laughed a laugh of relief, but she was but feminine after all, and the laugh became ungovernable, and ended in tears and sobs, and then bitter laughter again.

She was a sensible girl, however, and she retired to her room and dipped her head into cold water two or three times, and returned shaking the moisture from her dark curls, "like dew drops from the lion's mane." She thought it was better to relieve her uncle's mind, and settle the matter at once and for ever.

He was still sitting with a puzzled look of distress on his
face. He knew nothing of women but what he remembered
of his dear strong-minded mother, who kept her tears for
her own chamber, and had never more than a wan smile on
her face after the death of her husband, and was not likely,
therefore, to go off in an hysterical fit of laughing and crying.
She was too old for that when he knew her ; and Valerie ?
Alas ! his imagination only had been able to supply what
her conduct had been in distress and disappointment. Thus
he was puzzled, and feared to speak lest he should do more
harm than good.

" Dearest uncle," said the girl, coming in with a watery
smile, and very red eyes, " I think you might speak more
respectfully of our host." Here a little laugh made her stop
and swallow down a disposition to cry. " I confess to his
having long legs and high shoulders, but he is very handsome and very good. I do not love him, however, and I·
could not marry him. Set your mind at rest on that point ;
besides, he has not asked me to marry him ; and it is a little
premature to declare I will not do so."

Sabina was stringing words together to gain time.

" Will you tell me your objection to Lord Trelusa ? " said
her uncle. " Pray, my dear, confide in me ; you cannot
have a tenderer friend."

How much she loved him ! Yet she never could have
told him what was in her mind, even had she not feared, as
in this instance, he would act with hostility towards her
lover, did he know the extent of the intended wrong.

" Uncle," said she, at length, " when you live as a guest
with people who are kind to you, do you not think it is
treacherous to reveal the opinions you form of their conduct,
which is commented on by the guest who sees the people in
all the undress of their domestic life, when they are not
made up for company."

Mr. Rock was in the clouds. He had never been made
up for company in his life, otherwise than in putting on his
best uniform coat when he went on board the Admiral's
ship. That honest old man had never had anything to conceal from friend or foe. Sabina ¡saw she must illustrate
her meaning by an instance.

" Uncle, could you ever love a woman who told you a
falsehood ? "

This was *mal apropos.* It sent the old man's memory wandering tenderly to Valerie. Supposing Valerie had made a little slip in her truthfulness, had told her mother that she was going out to buy a yard of ribbon, when it was really to see the boat come off from the ship—the boat which she trusted might contain *him?* So he answered doubtfully, "My dear, I might overlook one sin against truth, but not a habit of lying."

"Oh, uncle! suppose when you were commanding a ship of your own——"

"I never did command a ship of my own, my dear; only when the 'Star' was refitting at Plymouth, and the commander was away on leave, and I had the duty as first-lieutenant."

"Well, suppose under those circumstances the second-lieutenant told you an untruth?"

"An untruth!" said the old man in a voice of thunder.

"Yes, uncle, a lie."

"Why I should say he was a dirty dog and no sailor," said the old man, flushing at the possibility.

"I do not wish to marry Lord Trelusa," said Sabina again, quietly, and her uncle gave a long whistle, which had no particular tune in it at the beginning, but went off into "All ye jolly sailors bold, whose hearts are set in honour's mould."

"I wish I could get a sailor for her," he thought. "She is worthy to be the wife of one." He imagined that she had detected Lord Trelusa in untruths. "Maybe that he would lie through a nine-inch plank," thought he. "She is right to refuse him; a liar is as bad as the dry rot in a ship—can't tell where 'tis sound and where unsound. All fair outside, all crumbling within."

"Uncle," said Sabina timidly, "perhaps you would not mind writing to Lord Trelusa to tell him I cannot marry him. Perhaps he may come again for a verbal answer, and that would be painful, or at any event unpleasant to him and to me."

"Certainly, if you wish it," said her uncle, "but it would come with more decision from yourself. Suppose you write, and I will enclose it with a few lines. You see he has been very civil to me, poor fellow!"

Mr. Rock did not like the occupation. When he had

seen a man flogged on board ship he flinched from every cut of the cat, as if it had been his own back which was lacerated, and when the executioner swung himself round to give more impetus to the lash, the sensitive lieutenant quivered over all his frame, and turned sick and faint, a feeling which was shared by many an iron-limbed sailor besides.

But Sabina could be obstinate sometimes ; the old leaven had not died out entirely. She could not write herself, she felt, without showing some relenting of tenderness.

Mr. Rock had to give way ; and, after spoiling so many sheets as to make him hope that Sabina would never entail on him again a similar expense from a similar cause, he wrote as follows :—

"MY LORD,

"My niece and I are very sensible of the honour you propose to confer on us by making her your wife. I regret to say that for some unexplained cause she is unwilling to alter her present condition, of life, and begs me to say that, with your many advantages, you have the power of choosing one who is your equal in rank and more fitted for the sphere in which you will move. She expresses the most fervent wishes for your future happiness, and says she must be ever grateful for the kindness with which she has been treated by Lady Sarah Trelusa. I have the honour to be

"Your lordship's most obedient
"Humble servant,
"MICHAEL ROCK."

He did not show the letter to Sabina. He felt rather afraid of the criticism of this child. "If she don't like it," he thought, "I shall have to write it over again, and this would be the fifth sheet of letter-paper I have spoilt— eighteen-pence a quire, and very coarse too for the money."

Neither did he show the answer. Where was the use of worrying her with it. The old man had calculated when it would come, and called at the post himself. This love affair was tending to demoralise Mr. Rock. Not that he had made up his mind not to show it. The truth was, that he had gone over the words of his composition so frequently, that they failed to convey much meaning to his mind, and was doubtful what conclusion Lord Trelusa would come to on reading it. If he were a very determined lover he might not take such a "no" for an answer, and Mr. Rock felt that his niece meant no, and would be vexed with him for not having conveyed it explicitly.

Sabina was satisfied when she had explained herself and put the matter into her uncle's hands.

Lord Trelusa was more in love than ever, and less likely to give up his determination to marry Sabina. Had she accepted him, even after a show of hesitation, he might, after his first burst of joy, have seen reason to doubt the wisdom of his choice, but her spirited refusal to become his wife had enhanced her value in his eyes, and made him more than ever determined to overcome her reluctance.

He wrote courteously to the old lieutenant, telling him that deeply as he regretted the temporary delay to his happiness conveyed in his letter, he should never, whilst the affections of Miss Rock remained otherwise unengaged, consent to forego the hope of calling himself his son-in-law. To Sabina he poured out all his passionate entreaties that she would forgive him, and consent to be his.

" To Sabina.

"An unspeakable depression seized me when I received your uncle's letter. I am not usually the prey to presentiments, but I felt on this occasion that some misfortune was looming in the distance. Had I not felt how great would have been the insult, I should have liked to send it back, and say,—' Do not let me have an answer yet. Think well before you decide. You have written too speedily for my happiness.' But I have read the repetition of the refusal you compelled him to write. I know the kind-hearted old man hated the occupation of depriving me of all hope.

"Have you no pity, Sabina? I think your unawakened heart has no perception of the agony you inflict. I might as well discourse to a native of Iceland of the horrors of the arid sands and the vertical sun in the torrid zone.

"I have loved you, too, so long and so tenderly. When you clung round my neck as a little child—when kneeling at my feet you entreated me innocently to take you home to live with me. When you grew up, your beauty, your wonderful musical talents, enchained me,—all the nameless perfections which I see not in any other woman, though I have had the *élite* of London society to choose from for years past.

"I was at a party some time since. A grand ball, in a brilliantly-lighted saloon; a corridor, with marble pillars, led to it; and each column was hung with encircling wreaths of beautiful flowers. I fancied myself like one of those pillars, so cold and unmoved and insensible to the loveliness of the fragrant creatures who surrounded me. I only observed them to compare them with the half-child, half-woman, I had left at Deepindale, and to pronounce them to be immeasurably your inferiors.

"But you can never have responded to the passionate love I bear you. Did you do so you would have pardoned me the fault which arose from that passion's intensity. You weary of my professions. I can see you in imagination skimming over these words, not reading them, not understanding half the meaning they would convey. You read them, I know, as you would a language of which you understand a few words only, and do not think it worth while to take the trouble to find out the whole signification. I do not ask you to see me again as yet. I do not ask for an answer. I will not read the answer if you send it. I will merit your love, and when weeks have passed over, and your just indignation is mollified, I will ask again for your pardon—for your hand.

"Trelusa."

Mr. Rock said nothing of his letter, and Sabina placed hers in her desk at the close of the day. When she received it in the morning she laid it in her bosom, whilst she made the breakfast for her uncle; boiled the egg to an instant, and toasted his bread as no one but herself could. Then when her uncle went out to go his rounds with Mr. Orellan, she took her usual station in the recess of the cliff and read and re-read her lover's letter.

She loved him, and she kissed the characters his hand had traced and the paper on which it had rested, but she did not repent of her determination. She was too subtle not to see how selfish was the passion which had actuated him. If, she thought, a man were to take the woman he professes to love and fasten her up in the crowded streets in some ridiculous dress or position, making her, without any fault of her own, a mark for the finger of scorn to point at, a subject of scoffing and derision, I wonder whether she would accept, as an excuse, that he did it out of the intensity of his love for her. Here is a man who would have placed me in a far worse state, who would, by force, have compelled me to forego the society of the pure of my own sex ; and more than that, would have broken my uncle's heart in this world by the disgrace he had brought on me, and endangered my eternal happiness in the next, because he believed that he loved a girl with a smooth skin and brown eyes, and could not forego the gratification of his desire.

The result of this deliberation on Lord Trelusa's conduct was, that Sabina took the letter from her breast, and quietly and softly tore it to pieces bit by bit, and watched it fly away over the cliff ; some fragments loitering a few minutes entangled in the sponge-like blossoms of the sea pink ; some nestling in the recess of the cave, beaten against the surface of the cliff, too high for Sabina's reach, where, for days after, they disturbed her by their presence, which kept alive, too vividly for her comfort, the remembrance of the writer.

CHAPTER XLIII.

"See nations slowly great, and meanly just,
To buried merit raise the tardy bust."
JOHNSON.

LORD TRELUSA had hit on an idea that he considered particularly lucid. In conversation with Sabina at Tregear, he had frequently led her to speak of her uncle's services in action, because he enjoyed to watch her kindling eyes, as she narrated some act of heroism by which Mr. Rock had distinguished himself. Most of these anecdotes she had heard from Mr. Orellan, for her uncle seemed to consider it disgraceful to speak of anything which might be considered to infer self-commendation. Mr. Orellan had told her how, in a fearful storm in the Bay of Biscay, a vessel was seen labouring in the gale, and firing repeated signals of distress : how the captain looked in silence on the ruthless waves, and thought no boat could live in such a sea : how Lieutenant Rock entreated permission to try to save the crew, and the captain said he would order no one to go ; they might volunteer who liked to risk their lives. Then Lieutenant Rock appealed to the men, and they were silent. He called aloud, ' My lads, will you see those brave fellows go down, and make no effort to save them ? " And then how *two* men only out of the crew answered from the mast-head, and the boat was safely lowered, and the seamen held their breath as it dipped in the trough of the sea, or quivered on the crest of the billows. Three times did that gallant little crew commanded by Lieutenant Rock return to the sinking ship, and bear away her almost despairing crew, till,

in the last venture, the boat was nearly engulphed in
the swell of the devoted vessel as, like an animal
wounded in the brain, it rushed madly round and
round, ere it sank for ever. What cheers rang through the
vessel when the last cargo were brought up the ship's side !
what eager hands enclasped those of the lieutenant and seamen who had so nobly devoted themselves !

"Your promotion is safe, Rock," said the captain. "Your
fortune is made !"

Alas ! the recommendation was passed unnoticed by the
Admiralty.

On another occasion, Mr. Rock had been sent home in
command of a prize, and being attacked by the enemy with
a superior number of guns, and finding his sailing powers
inferior to those of the Frenchman, Mr. Rock ran his vessel
up, and crossed his adversary's bow, so that the vessels
came on board each other nearly midships. Then Rock
secured the enemy by a hawser, with which he lashed her
bowsprit to his own capstan, and the fight raged fiercely all
through the hours of night, till the morning's dawn lighted
the victory of the Englishmen, who carried two prizes into
port instead of one.

When Lord Trelusa arrived in town, he went to the Admiralty, and inquired if anyone knew anything of the services of an old officer, Rock by name. His lordship purposely addressed his inquiry to a veteran clerk, *au fait* for
years at the routine of the business, for he knew that to
younger servants of that useless body, the name was too
bygone to awaken any remembrance.

"Rock? let me see. Rock? Ah! yes; I remember;
has not been afloat these ten or twelve years. Gallant old
man ! Here is the memorial of his services, modestly put,
when he humbly petitioned to be employed again."

Lord Trelusa ran his eye over the memorial. "Good
Heavens ! Sir ! are men like these set aside and neglected
in the navy?"

"Dozens of them, my lord. They are fine fellows ; but
what can we do with them all? Borough interest carries all
promotion."

"Oblige me with a copy of this memorial."

And the obliging clerk supplied it to the young lord.

Armed with this, he went to the First Lord of the Ad-

iralty, and put forth Mr. Rock's claims for the honour of
night Commander of the Bath.   He urged it as a per-
onal favour to himself, saying that he hoped in a few weeks
—so soon, indeed, as *etiquette* for the mourning of his brother
dmitted—to ally himself to a near relative of the old lieu-
nant.

The request was attended to without any difficulty ; for
hat could be denied to landed and funded property, rank,
nd interest?   Lieutenant Rock's virtues and valour might
ave gone unrewarded to the grave, along with Orellan's
rvices, but for the discriminating penetration of the young
an who had fallen in love with Mr. Rock's niece.

There were some usual forms to be gone through, but the
elay would not extend, he was told, beyond a week or ten
ays, and Lord Trelusa enjoyed in anticipation the pleasure
abina would feel in learning the honours of her uncle.

CHAPTER XLIV.

"Fresh and strong the breeze is blowing,
    As yon ship at anchor rides;
Sullen waves, incessant flowing,
    Thund'ring dash against its sides.

"So my heart, its course impeded,
    Beats in my perturbed breast;
Doubts, like waves by waves succeeded,
    Rise, and still deny it rest."

SABINA spent all the hours of daylight not required by her duties towards her uncle, out of doors on the beach, or wandering about the cliffs; she went alone for miles along that desolate coast, and knew every cavern and recess within the bay of Saint Eve, and round each of the promontories that bound its extremities. She saw much without observing, for her eyes were with her memory, far away at Tregear, singing with Lady Sarah and her lover, or listening to conversation which ever trembled on the verge of confessed passion on his part. The smuggling vessels, who held out to sea during the daylight, used with their glasses to detect the white figure of Sabina—for the light gingham dresses showed white at a distance: she was always there; always alone; and they believed her, not unreasonably, to be a spy in the interest of the preventive officer, Captain Orellan. Inquiry confirmed the suspicion—inquiry amongst those who favoured the contrabandists, conveyed to them the fact, that Miss Rock's uncle and Captain Orellan were staunch friends, and always laying their heads together to prevent the landing of the tubs of liquor, or to seize them when landed. However,

eir names were legion, and Captain Orellan had but twelve
en at his command, and he was not well assured that there
ere not traitors in that little company, small as it was.
ike an unhappy general of modern days, he had to fortify
o large a tract of country with his small force. He could
ivide them in fours, and keep with him the least loyal, to
verawe them by his presence; but, whilst he was in one
art of the bay, the daring free-traders ran their little boats
pon another part of the beach, and at a preconcerted and
reviously-delivered signal from the vessel, the country
eople came down in companies, with horses, mules, and
onkeys, and loaded them with the kegs, or, if such means
f transport were not at hand, with long tough poles they
ung the kegs or tubs between them on their shoulders,
nd carried them in triumph inland. The darker the night,
ie greater the traffic in the forbidden fluid, for, by the cover
f the obscurity, the smugglers could manage to land their
argo where their brethren on shore could find it; they both
aving the advantage of a perfect knowledge of the locality,
hilst, to prevent his men from being tampered with by
ocial influences, Captain Orellan was compelled to obtain
iem from a distant part of the county.

The captain was unpopular. The service in which he
as engaged made him so, and neither his manners nor his
emper were likely to make friends amongst those who knew
ot his real worth. The good sense of the country, more-
ver, had declared itself in favour of free-trade, by the want
f sympathy it showed toward those who obstructed the
fforts made to oppose the tax imposed by government.
he people liked spirits at a cheap rate, and woe to him
ho attempted to prevent them from obtaining their ac-
ustomed supplies.

There was, moreover, a charm in the wild life of the
muggler which captivated the young and brave by whom
ieir vessels and boats were manned; and even by the ma-
istrates who committed them to trial, and by the judges
ho condemned them to death, these wild sons of the sea
ere regarded with pity, and never considered in the light of
iieves.

One evening, when the wintry sun was sinking into the
cean in a circle of fire, and a soft gray mist hung over the
ind and sea, Sabina was warned by the evening light that

she ought to be at home to welcome her uncle on his return to the Abbey Farm. She was on the sands, and hastened along by the side of the cliff, as the tide had risen since she came out, when she heard the sound of a rough song come on the quiet air, joined to the splash of the oars, and saw a boat come round the horn of the bay, beyond which the lugger lay, from which the crew were bringing part of her cargo. They came up near where Sabina was standing ; but occupied by their song and their boat, they noticed her not. She was wise enough to remain motionless ; any flutter of her petticoat or shawl would have betrayed her ; and as they were between her and her home, she was obliged to wait till they had achieved their undertaking and pulled off again.

Sabina saw their faces distinctly, and observed, with a shudder, that one who seemed to command the boat was the former gamekeeper at Tregear, who had excited Mr. Tresillian's wrath by addressing her on her return home the day when she had been in the plantations at Tregear. He had been dismissed from his situation in consequence of the supposed insult offered to Sabina, and being without a re-commendation to another service, he had joined a smuggling vessel, and had been sent in command of the boat.

The song they sang was spirited, and the words were distinctly audible to the girl, who trembled as she listened, lest she should be discovered by those lawless men.

SMUGGLERS' SONG.

1st Verse.

" A blustering night and a rolling sea,
　When the moon goes down and the craft rides free ;
　Then we pitch the kegs till the boat is full,
　And, ' Hist ! away ! with a pull ! boys, pull ! '

Chorus.

" Pull, boys, pull ! no cause for fear,
　The country is quiet, no land sharks near."

2nd Verse.

" The old wife sits in the chimney nook,
　Nursing on knee the Holy Book ;
　One eye she turns to the skies without,
　For the night is dark—strange steps about ;
　A tap at the door—there are spirits near ;
　But they are not the spirits old women fear.
　On her nose comes the dawn of a kindly glow,
　As she sips the drops from the kegs that flow.

" Then pull, boys, pull ! " &c.

3RD VERSE.

" The squire he sits in his lofty hall,
He hears the whistle, he knows the call ;
The guineas we find in a hollow tree,
And the kegs are rolled in stealthily.
Then back we go to our mates afloat,
With weary arms to fill the boat ;
And then we pull, when the boat is full,
For fortune is kind and bountiful.

" Then we pull," &c.

4TH VERSE.

" There's a wedding goes on at the ancient grange,
But the bride is coy, and the guests are strange ;
The parson looks round with a sadden'd gaze—
No spirits he sees his spirit to raise.
Hark ! there's a tap ! and a merry brown face
Cries out ' Amen ! ' to the minister's grace.
The keg he presents to the friends who preside,
And the payment he takes is a kiss of the bride.
Then back we go with an empty boat ;
The cargo's discharged, and we go afloat.
Joy to the sailor with pockets full,
Who skims o'er the sea with a ' Pull, boys, pull ! '

" Pull, boys, pull ! " &c.

It was getting dark ; but Sabina dared not pass the cave, because the sailors were constantly coming back from it to the boat, in which one man remained. At length the crew were all safely embarked, and then the girl, too soon for prudence, shot past the aperture, and fled away over the beach skirting the cliff.

" There goes that d——d spy," cried one. " She'll tell the news to all Saint Eve before an hour is over, and we shall have the sharks down on us."

" Send a bullet after her ! " said another ; and, suiting the action to the word, one of them fired, and the shot just grazed her elbow, and then rebounded harmlessly from the cliff. She was sufficiently alarmed before ; but her footsteps were now winged by fresh terror. She tried to increase her speed, but her steps were now over the dry sand, above high-water mark, for the sea had diminished her choice of paths. She sank up to her ankles, and could not, without an effort, withdraw her labouring feet. At one instant, she fancied the boat was returning, and that the men would seize and murder her ; but they were only keeping under the lee

of the shore. The lights were twinkling in the windows of
the Abbey Farm as a turn of the cliff brought it within her
scope of vision. There were safety, and love, and home,
and she struggled onwards to reach it.

Long before she had ascended the cliff, she met her uncle,
hurried and anxious. " Why, Sabina ! child ! Where have
you been ? What has kept you ? Do you know how late it is? "

Sabina excused herself, somewhat out of breath, as they
walked towards the house, telling her uncle what had occurred.

He said nothing; but walked quicker. "Sabina," he
said, " you must go to the inn—the 'Ferrers Arms;' see
the landlord yourself, and tell him to send a man and horse
off directly with a note which I will write to Captain Orellan."
He wrote hurriedly, and gave her the note. " Now, run ; I
would send Alice, but you will go quicker. I must go and
see if the farm servants have all left, as I fear they may have
done ; if not, I must send to the Quicksand Point, for the
rest of Orellan's men. He will want them all."

" Uncle ! uncle !" said Sabina, with a terrible apprehension which she would not put into words. " I shall find you
here on my return? "

" That depends on how long your errand may take," said
her uncle, with a forced smile ;—" but go, my dear ; obedience is a woman's first duty ; we'll talk afterwards."

She kissed him, and went. She knew how important he
considered her going, by his sending her, when he was so
chary of her communication with persons of rank inferior to
her own. When she reached the small inn, which called
itself an hotel, and inquired for the landlord, she was shown
into a room where he sat smoking and drinking with some
guests who had treated him to some of his own liquor, which,
to tell truth, had never paid duty to government. Sabina
waited till he had puffed a high volume of smoke from his
mouth, and tried to read the address of the letter, but gave
it up at length, having mislaid his spectacles. Irritated by
the delay, she read it aloud, and heard many a significant
" A-hem !" from the circle of carousers, who surmised the
order it contained.

" All right, Miss," with a wink at a man behind Sabina
" I'll send directly." But he made no sign of rising.

" Are you not going to send at once ? If you are busy,
I'll go to the stable, and tell one of the men to go."

" 'Scuse me, Miss, no one gives orders in my house, or my stable, but myself."

" Then pray go—for the love of Heaven, go. There may be mischief if you don't."

" Lor' bless your pretty face, there'll be a sight more mischief if I do. But give me a kiss," for he was getting very drunk ; " 'tis but a forfeit for coming amongst gents that are taking their pleasure."

Sabina twisted herself from his grasp, and fled, hearing a roar of laughter from his companions at his disappointment.

" Oh, my uncle !" she said, as she ran back to the Abbey Farm. She scarcely knew what forms her fears were shaping. She ran up the steps. " Alice ! Alice !" but she saw no one. Alice had, perhaps, been sent to summon some of the farm-servants from their cottages. She ran up into her uncle's bed-room, after lighting a candle, and saw an empty space over the chimneypiece, and in the corner of the room. The pistols and broadsword were gone, which her uncle had one day brought from Captain Orellan's dwelling.

" He is gone ! gone !" she cried. " Oh, uncle ! how could you cheat me so ? How dark it is all along the cliff and the beach !"

She was thinking of pursuing her uncle, but felt afraid. Then the idea of his danger drove her terrors for herself out of her thoughts. " I must go and see what has become of him. Alice ! Alice !" She had a wild notion of asking old Alice to accompany her, but Alice was nowhere to be seen ; so, after a moment's hesitation, she wrapped a black shawl round her, remembering that her light dress had made her a clear mark for the pistol of the smuggler, and went out into the darkness—away down along the beach—away from all the cheering little lights which sparkled in houses in the town, and its cottage outskirts,—away from all hope of aid from the dwellers therein.

" Where he is, I must be ! dear old man ! He has no business to mix himself up in such scenes ; " and thus stumbling over fragments of rocks, splashing into the edges of the billows as they washed up to her feet, shivering with the cold of a January night, but still more with the apprehension that weighed on her heart, Sabina returned towards the mouth of the cavern.

CHAPTER XLV

DRYDEN.

WHEN Mr. Rock had dismissed Sabina on her fruit-less errand, he armed himself, intending to join Orellan, so soon as he could satisfy himself where he could find him. He knew the cavern to which Sabina had referred in her report of the smugglers, and knew also that it had an outlet running up the interior of the cliff, in the direction of the Abbey Farm, of which the aperture was kept carefully closed, by faggots of furze and dead branches, to conceal it from those not in the secret of the contrabandists. He walked along the top of the cliff, that small obstacles might not interfere, as they would have done had he been on the beach, with his view of the sea. It was covered with the soft mist, still retaining a gleam of the set sun, and was quickly sinking into a unity of gray colour that defied inspection. A few stars began to glimmer in the quiet sky, and the sounds from the distant village died away in the louder roar of the billows as they advanced towards it. He got to the side of the cliff, and peered over it, so that in his anxiety he had almost toppled over that treacherous crumbling edge of the rock.

There was a flash ! Yes ; that was the single pistol shot that called on the men to surrender ; then the report ! Now the flashes and reports follow in quick succession. The rocks take up the reverberation, and multiply the sharp sounds, a million times repeating them. The old man shouted, with the enthusiasm of his youth.

"Courage, my lad! Fight on, and shoot down the scoundrels! Fight for King George, and your Captain Orellan!"

Cries and exclamations arose from the water, blended with the roar of the sea and the report of the fire-arms.

"I must join him. He must be in the thick of it. He will want a true man to back him. This struggle would make an old man young."

He thought of the covered entrance. They were fighting at the mouth of the cavern. Probably Captain Orellan had come down to make a seizure of the kegs, and the boat's crew returning, a skirmish had ensued. He could get to the cave much faster by removing the obstruction artificially placed there, and running down the declivity, than in descending in the dark over the face of the cliff, or returning to the gently inclined path from the farm.

When he reached the opening, generally so carefully concealed, the furze faggots and poles had been removed. He stayed not to wonder why this should be, but rushed on as fast as the darkness would permit, till he saw a glimmer of light at the end of the covered way. He ran towards it. There was a crowd of men and boys, and some unsexed women, peering forward with white faces into the cavern, in which a couple of torches, their ends pushed into fissures in the rock, shed a fitful light. There were oaths and cries, and shouts for help. Amongst the voices, Mr. Rock heard that of Orellan, in rage and despair, as it seemed to him. He tried to push through the crowd which stood between him and the affray. A woman caught his arm, and held him back, with a whisper,—

"Let them alone. Let them alone. *They're doing for him!*"

"Scoundrels!" cried the old man, swinging his arms round him and forcing a passage through the crowd. "Cowards! do you stand here, and see a brave man murdered?"

"We don't meddle nor make; 'tis no job of ours," they cried.

But Mr. Rock had thrown himself against every impediment, and reached his friend, who stood with his back to the cavern, with a face pale but unflinching, defending himself with his cutlass against two assailants. Two lay dead, or mortally wounded, at his feet. He looked up, with a half-smile of welcome, at the familiar "What cheer!" of his friend, who brought down one of the smugglers with his pistol; but the flickering light, playing on Orellan's face, showed a frightful contraction of pain that passed over it. He staggered forward, and his old messmate caught him as he was falling. For an instant the weight made him unable to defend himself, and the smuggler, snatching Mr. Rock's other pistol from his belt, placed it at his breast and fired. The old man fell, mortally wounded, by the side of his old companion. The fight was over, and the smugglers had won.

The kegs, already deposited at the head of the cavern, were carried off by the crowd without, who being liable to imprisonment and transportation, or if, as in this case, blood was shed, to the punishment of death—hurried off, leaving the wounded men without aid, and at the mercy of the tide, should it rise so high as to lift their helpless bodies and carry them seaward.

The smugglers made off to their ship. There would be a "hue and cry" soon. They took up their wounded and dead men lest any traces about them should lead to the prosecution of their own families, and the discovery of more of their gang.

The tarred rope torches flared their red light above the heads of the two old friends, now left in the solitude of that cave of death. Mr. Rock, though gasping for breath, addressed a few words to Orellan, who had dragged himself up to the side of the cavern, against which he supported his head.

"We are near port now, old messmate. 'Twill soon be over with us both. You have sacrificed yourself for me. Rock. Well! I would have done as much."

"I know it."

And the dying men sought out each other's hand, and grasped it with all the force possessed by their languid frames.

There was a pause, for Mr. Rock was thinking of Sabina. His companion spoke:

"I'm glad Betsy's gone," he said, at length.

Mr. Rock saw his countenance altering.

"Orellan, can you say a prayer?" he said.

"Our Father!" gasped the sailor, looking up. The eyes retained their upward look, but they were fixed. Orellan had preceded his friend to the ocean of Eternity.

Mr. Rock stretched out his hand, and gently closed the sightless eyes. "Farewell, old trusty friend!" he said. "We shall not be long apart."

Then he tried to move into an easier position, for the pain and suffocation prevented his turning his thoughts heavenward. There was no sound now except the roar of the sea, and the hissing noise made by the waves as they ran up over the sands. He supposed it was about seven o'clock—it must have been dark about three hours. He wondered whether Sabina had missed him, and if she would send any people to look for him and for Orellan. Then his thoughts wandered to Deepindale, and he thought he was playing chess with his old messmate, but both the black and white men were turned red, and the squares on the board were red also, so that they knew not where to place the men—then he fancied he heard Sabina singing—

> "'Tis night, and the mid-watch is come,
>   And chilly mists hang o'er the darkened main,"

and he shivered. Then he dozed for a little, and woke with a start of wonder, not remembering where he was — awoke and saw Orellan's dead face by his side.

"Ah, yes, he knew all about it now. Poor fellow," he said, looking lovingly at the body. "Oh, if I could kiss that dear child once more!"

The wish was gratified. Sabina entered the cave by the side opening to the sea. She was drenched by the waves that rushed up to the sides of the cavern, but her anxiety made her insensible to the risk of being washed away by their violence. She was dazzled at first by the glare of the torches, coming from the intense darkness outside. She advanced bewildered, not knowing what to expect, but gathering a vague hope from the light and the silence.

"Sabina," cried her uncle in a choking voice, and she rushed forward and flung herself by his side on the sand.

"Oh, uncle! uncle!" she cried, "where are you hurt?

Why do you lie here? and, oh, God! what is *that?*" pointing with a look of horror at the corpse. "Is *that* Captain Orellan?"

"It was—my child," gasped Mr. Rock, "but he is gone —gone to heaven, I trust—before me."

"Oh, uncle! you must not—shall not die! What *can* I do? What can I do?" she cried, wringing her hands. " Shall I go and get help? I will run for a surgeon."

She sprang up, but her uncle held her softly by the arm, and at that moment his gentlest touch had the force of a giant for her.

"'Tis useless, my child! I should only lose the comfort of having you with me for the last half-hour of my life. Sit by my side, Sabina, and lift my head upon your knee, so that I may breathe better. I've made a will—twenty pounds to poor Susan—the rest, only a few hundreds—prize-money —and £90 to bury me; perhaps it would defray the expenses of Orellan's funeral too. If we could be buried together, my dear—'tis foolish—but 'twould seem like company—and in the churchyard of Saint Eve, we might be near the roaring of the sea—that's nonsense, as we could not hear it; but I should like it, and so I'm sure would he. There, that's more comfortable," he said, as Sabina tenderly placed his head against her breast.

These were the last words dictated by consciousness. He seemed to slumber, but at length he cried out in a loud voice, which caught the echoes of the cavern—

"Orellan, I am coming!"

Sabina listened awe-stricken, but there were no other sounds, and the head sunk heavily on her breast.

She was there with her two dead companions. Was it strange that the young girl's brain rocked and reeled with its unnatural tension? The waves were running up the interior of the cavern—they might come and wash away the bodies. They should not, if she could withhold the corpse of that dear old man. She would cling to him—if the waters took him, she would die also. Why should she live? Those torches were going out—one was already extinguished. She should soon be left in darkness, with the sound only of the advancing waves, and the company of the dead, yet she had no terror of her uncle's corpse, though she shuddered at the recollection of Captain Orellan's face as she had last seen it. The light flared up suddenly and was extinguished and she was left in gloom. She felt for her uncle's heart, but it had ceased to beat—there was still warmth about it, but the hand she had touched was growing very cold. How many hours would there be till daylight? She knew not— she was beginning not to care, and was becoming only sensible of exceeding cold and numbness.

CHAPTER XLVI.

"I fruitless mourn to him who cannot hear,
    And weep the more, because I weep in vain."

GRAY.

WHEN Sabina recovered consciousness, she was being conveyed on a shutter towards the Abbey Farm. The unusual movement made her feel giddy, as did the swinging of the lanthorns carried by the people who walked by her side. They carried her into the kitchen, and she staggered up and said, "Where is uncle?" forgetting for a brief moment her irreparable loss.

Alice was wiping her eyes with the corner of her apron. She said nothing, but Sabina staggered to the door, crying out, "I must go and find him," and met the men bringing in his corpse. Then she was satisfied, and allowed Alice to put her into her bed, and chafe her numbed feet and hands, and she was conscious of a feeling of bodily comfort, and then she wept bitterly to know that her uncle could never again enjoy any earthly pleasure, or any alleviation of bodily or mental pain; but she felt too feeble and exhausted to suffer much.

A few days after, when the old farm servant had nursed her back to some of her lost strength, grief began its usual power of tormenting. She remembered a thousand things which she might have said or done which would have made him happier; for even in the extremity of her self-torture she could not recollect of late years any intentional unkindness of act or word. It is this which makes the sting of death to the survivors.

There was much to be done, and she felt very helpless—undertakers to be employed—a lawyer, she supposed ; she knew nothing of what ought to be done ; but before she was compelled to act, Mr. Ferrers, informed by Alice of the death of Mr. Rock, came back to the neighbourhood of his own house, though he respected Sabina's destitution of friends and wealth too much to reside under his own roof, whilst she remained there. He did more—he went to Deepindale and prevailed on the weeping Susan to give up the care of the house to a trustworthy woman, and brought her to his home, that she might impart to, and receive comfort from the destitute girl.

I do not know that the arrangement produced any amicable feeling between the two old servants—Alice giving herself airs of consequence from having done everything for the dear gentleman in the last days of his life, which made Susan, who had spent nearly the whole of hers in his service and that of his mother, frantically jealous. Alice was a younget woman, and gave Susan to understand that Miss Rock was very particular, and could not eat her toast if she saw a bir of black fluttering on it, to which Susan retorted, that she had made toast before Miss Rock was born, and there was no occasion to teach her how to prepare Miss Rock's breakfast.

Sabina strove to soothe down the perturbed spirits of the belligerents, by promising them both mourning for her uncle, and sending them into the town to procure it for themselves. Over the various articles for choice they became friendly again, and left Sabina at peace.

Mr. Ferrers saved her all trouble—all anxiety about the arrangement for the funeral, and when Lord Trelusa, who was in town, came down immediately on receiving the intelligence, to see of what use he could be to Sabina, there was no more to be done.

On the day of Mr. Rock's death, the Gazette came out, announcing to the world that the King had been pleased to confer the honour of Knight Commander of the Bath on Lieutenant Rock, lieutenant on half-pay in his Majesty's service. The old man did not live to hear of the tardy recompense of his many services. Lord Trelusa had intended to give himself the reward of telling Sabina this piece of intelligence, to see her face brighten as she heard it.

" She shall read it to her uncle out of the paper herself,"
he said, with a not ungenerous impulse. He was becoming
less selfish from attrition with those to whom that failing was
unknown. " Then perhaps Sabina will not think so badly
of me," he continued, but he said it doubtfully to himself;
for he knew she judged him with more justice than mercy.

Both gentlemen sent their names up to Miss Rock,
asking if she had any commands for them. She declined
with grateful acknowledgments, and excused herself from
seeing either. She meant, after the funeral, to return to
Deepindale, and release Mr. Ferrers from her occupation of
his house; but before the two-high-minded sailors were laid
side by side in the churchyard at Saint Eve, Sabina was insensible from an attack of fever, brought on by exposure to
the weather, and by the trying scenes through which she had
passed.

She was for weeks unconscious of the changes from the
rush candle at night to the dulled light through the closed
shutters by day. Time went on, but she took no note of it.
The two women, frightened out of the indulgence of their
little asperities, felt they had enough to do in trying to save
the flickering spark of light which trembled on the lips of
their patient.

Lord Trelusa and Mr. Ferrers grew almost cordial in their
mutual fears lest death should rob them of the prize so
coveted by each.

His lordship had an object which he pursued with stern
determination. This was the arrest of the ringleaders of
the smugglers, especially of the *ci-devant* gamekeeper who
fired the shot which resulted in Mr. Rock's death. They
were caught, and three of the principals were tried and condemned to death for the murder of Captain Orellan and of
Lieutenant Rock.

Mr. Ferrers could not endure, with his notions, then so
peculiar, now so universal, that the sentence of the punishment of death should be carried out on these men. Justice,
stern and unpitying, however, was to claim her victims,
unless some great effort were made to arrest its course.
Lord Trelusa had sufficient influence to divert the punishment from death to transportation ; but when Mr. Ferrers
applied to him on this subject, he utterly declined to interfere. The men deserved their fates for a brutal murder ; if

they were not hanged, every man who suffered on the gallows was unjustly executed.

It was a grief and mortification to Mr. Ferrers to do anything which might bring Sabina into correspondence with Lord Trelusa, far more that she should ask a favour of him; yet he never flinched from what was right according to his idea of duty, and he asked for an interview with Sabina, whilst she was yet feeble and exhausted, but sensible. She was partly dressed, and laid on the sofa to receive him, and awaited his approach with some degree of nervous agitation.

He was shocked to see what an alteration sickness had made in her person, but her eyes flashed out with even more than their usual brilliancy and size, from contrast with her attenuated face. She began to talk hurriedly to her companion, with excuses for her long intrusion on his property, and expressions of hope that she would soon be enabled to return home. But at that word, and the thought of the desolate house, where her uncle would never more meet her on the threshold, she buried her face in her pillow, and wept aloud.

Mr. Ferrers was inexpressibly affected. He longed to take her hand, and say "All that I have is yours, do with me and it as you will," but he felt it would be ungenerous in her present unprotected state, and when, with all her proud spirit, she felt herself humbled and at a disadvantage.

She knew nothing of the prosecution of the smugglers, nothing of the circumstances of the murder which had been obtained from one of the men who had turned king's evidence. He told it all, and Sabina sat up on her sofa with a flush on her face and a look of impotent rage flashing from her eyes, which made her look like a beautiful fury. She said nothing, and waited till she heard of the trial and condemnation to death of three of the ringleaders. Then he told her of the funeral of the two old officers. How the flags on the ships in the bay hung half-mast high—how Lord Trelusa attended, and the mayor and corporation, in their robes, and how many tears flowed from the eyes of men and women when the earth rattled on their coffins, and "Dust to dust" was pronounced.

She spoke at length, her words coming from compressed lips—

" They wept for them, whose lives they would not stir a step to save."

Mr. Ferrers now took from his waistcoat-pocket some trifles which he had taken from that of her uncle after his death. Sabina knew them well. She had seen them during the occasional illnesses of her uncle placed carefully at n exact angle on his dressing-table—a pen-knife, a little end of black lead pencil (he had never been able to afford a silver one), a well-worn wedding-ring which he had taken from the attenuated finger of his dead mother, and a small rough cornelian, connected with some tender memory of his youth—what none knew. Perhaps he had picked it up when walking up from the boat with Valerie one day, and it had been hallowed since by her remembrance. Sabina seized these treasures. She felt jealous that Mr. Ferrers should have touched them. She placed them in the palm of her hand and laid her wet cheek on them. Now that her heart was softened he thought he would plead for the condemned men.

He spoke of their hot, ill-trained manhood, and the general feeling in favour of their contraband occupation which seemed to, though it did not in reality, excuse them. He spoke of their confinement in the condemned cell—those men, so accustomed to light and sunshine and out-door occupation ; and he told Sabina that by her influence with Lord Trelusa she might succeed in arresting the course of justice, and exchanging the punishment of death to that of transportation for life.

"*Never !*" cried Sabina. " Those two gentlemen were foully murdered by your own account. My uncle was shot by his own pistol when he was trying to support his dying friend. Hang the ringleaders !" she exclaimed, with a passionate cry. " Why, I would gladly hang every man and woman also, who looked on at that frightful butchery and never stirred to save my poor uncle and his friend. I will utter no jargon, Mr. Ferrers, about the benefit to be derived to society by the infliction of the punishment of death in deterring others from crime. Were I in a desert island, where none could be benefited by example or injured by future outrage, I should, if I could, destroy those men from a feeling of vindictive justice. Do not ask me to forgive. I *cannot.*"

" ' Vengeance is mine, saith the Lord, I will repay it,' "
replied Mr. Ferrers in a low voice.

" If we are to wait for a special interposition from Providence," said Sabina, " for the punishment of every offence against life or property, what is the use of law? "

" In this case," suggested the minister, " law would take care that punishment is inflicted; but that it shall be of a nature to enable the sinner to repent and turn away from his wickedness."

" They gave my uncle no time for thought—no time for repentance. Let them die."

Mr. Ferrers was shocked at the determination of the young girl, and desisted.

She then asked eagerly for an account of what money remained belonging to her as legatee to her uncle, and for the bills of the funeral of both Mr. Rock and Captain Orellan; also for the memoranda of every expense incurred by her during her illness, and for any sums of money spent for her by Susan or Alice.

Mr. Ferrers promised to supply her with particulars, and took his leave.

She wrung his hand, and wept bitterly at parting, and thanked him for his *disinterested* kindness. She suspected how little the epithet was deserved, but she was not bound to seem to understand what he had never expressed in words.

For kindness she was grateful, but not for the love. However much we may persuade ourselves that we are, we are never really grateful for anything we do not desire to have.

When all her debts were paid, she found that not much more than five hundred pounds remained for her subsistence. It seemed imperative on her to give up the house at Deepindale and sell the furniture. What then would become of Susan and herself? She thought long and anxiously. Five hundred pounds in the funds in those days meant twenty-five pounds a-year. She thought whether she could exist in a cottage at Saint Eve, for which she might pay three pounds a-year rent, and feed and clothe herself with the remainder. Susan would be valuable anywhere as a servant to a single gentleman or lady.

She could not bear the idea of her uncle's poor furniture

being put up to auction, nor the thought of all the observations and sorry jests to be passed on its worn appearance ;
and she intended to procure a broker who might consent to
give her a certain sum for it as it stood. In the meantime
Lord Trelusa had not forgotten Sabina.

At his suggestion Lady Sarah wrote a cordial invitation to
her to come and take up her residence with her ladyship,
which, Lady Sarah said, would be conferring a favour on
her, as her dear Wilfred thought of going abroad for some
months and she should be very lonely without a companion.
" Of course I might have either of my grand-children, my
dear child," she wrote, " but Edith's voice is scrannel, and
Adela squints. I must confess that I like to have all I can
of beauty and talent near me. Do come. You know how
happily we get on together."

Lord Trelusa wrote : " If you refuse me the forgiveness
which I crave, do not let my sin against you make my mother
a sufferer. You know how much she prefers your society.
Do not refuse her this pleasure. I will not come to her
residence, wherever she may choose to make it, without your
permission."

Sabina answered Lady Sarah, with due expressions of
gratitude for her kindness, but declined at present to avail
herself of her ladyship's invitation. Some intuitive perception of Lady Sarah's character showed the girl that she
would have no more clear idea of her feelings on the subject
than would one blind from the birth of the different grada-
tions of colour.

Lady Sarah, whose lot had been to tread only on the velvet
path of fortune, and had never had to want for home or
money or friends, could not enter into Sabina's distresses.

It was a different thing, that young lady knew, to visit at
Tregear when she had her uncle's home to return to, and to
live for ever as a dependant on Lady Sarah's bounty ; besides
the unpleasant feeling of keeping Lord Trelusa from his own
seat or placing herself in his way to solicit, as it were, a re-
newal of his offers of marriage.

CHAPTER XLVII.

THOMPSON.

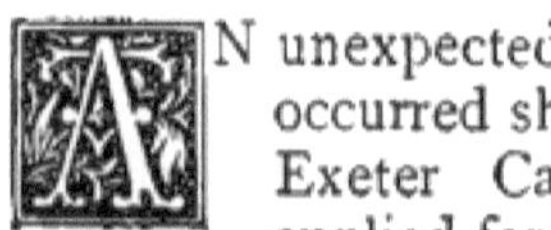

AN unexpected solution of some of Sabina's difficulties occurred shortly after. The place of organist at Exeter Cathedral became vacant, and Sabina applied for the situation. A trial of the various candidates was determined on, and Sabina, unattended by any friend, went to that fine old city and performed before the churchwardens and such of the magnates amongst the dignitaries of the Church, as interested themselves in the cathedral musical service.

Sabina's sad story had predisposed the judges in her favour before she appeared, and her beauty, modesty, and the deep but quiet and inexpressive mourning in which she was attired, increased their admiration. She played well, and they were satisfied; but when her magnificent voice pealed through the groined arches and distant aisles of the venerable building, they became enthusiastic in her praise, and elected her organist at the usual salary of seventy pounds a-year.

"Now I can keep Susan," she said to herself, as with a light step she descended the flight of steps leading from the church. Before her return to Haven House, she looked at and engaged a small cottage on the outskirts of the city, to which she had removed such of her uncle's furniture as she required, and, happier than she had been since her uncle's death, she prepared for her new life.

She did not answer Lord Trelusa's letter. She feared her

own want of resolution to continue to say no to a lover so determined and strenuous. She turned her attention to the improvement of her musical powers, feeling that in instrumental music she had much to learn, though the early foundation laid by Mr. Temple had fitted her for the performance of cathedral service far better than any common teaching could have done. He had taught her what he most preferred, and as that style had suited the magnificent volume of her voice, and its power of long sustentation of the notes, she had always practised from choice that style which she was now to perform from necessity.

Her uncle's grand piano was the great comfort of her life, and blending its fine tones in skilful combinations, Sabina passed many of the hours of summer and winter nights. She was companionless, excepting Susan, for her cold, self-sustained manner kept at a distance all those who would have intruded on her privacy, or sought to draw Sabina within their domestic circles.

Thus two years passed, and Sabina was nearly nineteen, but in character and feeling more like twenty-eight. All she had enjoyed, all she had suffered in life, was wrapt in silence beneath the mask of her beautiful but impenetrable countenance. Her ambition was to make her choir the most perfect of any cathedral town in England, and she succeeded. The Bishop and Dean and Chapter complimented themselves on their penetration in having elected so talented an organist, and considered the execution of every perfectly performed anthem as a credit reflected on themselves.

Her recreation was to wander alone in the sunsets round the most beautiful environs of that city, so rich in undulating ground, stately parks, and picturesque views. Then from amongst the luxuriant pastures, by the side of the Exe, she would look back on the old cathedral, veiled partially in a mist of soft purple, and rising majestically from the crowd of inferior buildings which surrounded it, till the waning light reminded her that old Susan would be uneasy at her long delay.

She was very tranquil in her life ; and if the thought of her lost lover rose sometimes before her too vividiy for her peace she sat down to a difficult composition in music, and turned her restive memories into hard facts.

But "her lone and loveless life" was not to continue thus for ever.

There was evening service at the cathedral, and the anthem
to be performed was that beautiful one of Kent's, in which
the words and the music speak equally the necessities of
human weakness appealing to superhuman strength : and the
terrors of coming death calling for aid on the Fountain of all
light and life.　Sabina's voice in the first treble pealed out
through the dim aisles its rich tones of supplication,

"Hear my prayer.　Hide not thyself from my petition ; "

whilst the congregation listened breathlessly and wept, at the
voice which seemed to interpret their wants and wishes at
the throne of grace,

" My heart is disquieted within me, and the fear of death is fallen upon me."

In the last movement, which seems triumphant in its conviction of futurity—of a place of rest from trouble, a refuge
from earthly grief and sorrow—Sabina seemed inspired in
the earnestness she threw into the wish—

" Oh that I had wings like a dove ! then would I flee away and be at rest."

The second treble took it up, and it ended with a perfectly
executed chorus of voices, at the termination of which even
the most insensible of the congregation heaved a sigh of
relief, from their tension of admiration.

Sabina played out the people to Handel's fine movement
"The dead shall live ; " and as the congregation was a
numerous one, they were some time in departing, and leaving
the cathedral clear.　Then she wrapt her cloak about her,
and prepared for her long walk in the direction of the village
of Ede, near which her cottage stood.　She had just descended the last step of the cathedral, when she saw by the
lamplight a servant, in the Trelusa livery, mounted on a
horse covered with foam.　He touched his hat to Sabina,
and said,—

" If you please, Miss, my lady is very ill, and as her ladyship is always asking for you, the doctor said you had better
be sent for."

Sabina, whose feelings had been in consonance with the
words she had poured forth, felt the summons to be like the
announcement of doom.

"' My heart is disquieted within me,'" she said, "'and the fear of death is fallen upon me.'"

She asked a few questions as to how long Lady Sarah had been ill, but the man knew only that the doctor had been attending her at Tregear, to which place she had recently returned from London for two days only. Lord Trelusa had been travelling abroad for some months, he said, and it was uncertain when any intelligence of his mistress's illness would reach his lordship.

Sabina felt that she could not hesitate; and, dismissing the servant, with orders for fresh horses at every successive post-house, she walked to the residence of one of the churchwardens, and, telling him the circumstances, asked permission to fill her place at the organ by one of the pupils, of whom she had many.

The churchwarden, much impressed by the title of Miss Rock's friend, promised that there should be no fault found, should the substitution be disliked; and then Sabina, relieved from this anxiety, ordered a postchaise to follow her to her home, that she might pack her small wardrobe, and inform Susan of her intended absence.

She did not reach Tregear till the gray light of a summer's dawn. The clouds, dappled with pink, were rolling away from the yet unrisen sun, and the old building, backed by the full-leaved trees, looked sad and ominous to Sabina's apprehension, who could feel no pleasure in the influences of morning, when she knew not what those venerable walls might conceal. It was a relief to be admitted, and to ascend the old oak stairs, and enter on tiptoe her ladyship's room, where she slept the troubled sleep of fever.

Sabina left the room again, drawing Mrs. Stephens, the maid, away with her, to try to obtain from her some account of her ladyship's seizure; but the maid could only say that Lady Sarah had left town, because, from the death of her aunt, Lady Penruddock, she could not, according to etiquette, join in any of the gaieties of the season. Mrs. Stephens's own idea was, also, that the death of Lady Penruddock, who was about her ladyship's own age, had made her nervous about herself. Whether or no that was the case, Lady Sarah had complained of headache and general indisposition on the journey, and Doctor L—— being sent for from Exeter had pronounced her to be dangerously ill.

It was then that her ladyship had called repeatedly for Miss Rock; and the doctor inquired if that were any relation to the young lady organist, and finding it was the same, he had advised her being sent for immediately.

When Lady Sarah opened her eyes she saw Sabina, who had put on a most cheerful expression of face, lest her friend should think that the girl considered her to be looking very ill.

Before she had been many hours by her bedside, she felt convinced that the complaint was in a great degree nervous, and would give way to cheerful society and fresh objects of interest.

Lady Sarah's face had expressed a great amount of placid pleasure at seeing her young favourite again ; and when Doctor L—— spoke of her wonderful talents for music, and magnificent voice for singing, her ladyship said that she had found out her extraordinary proficiency more than three years ago, when she had sung with remarkable power and skill at a concert at Deepindale.

Doctor L—— returned to Exeter more than ever impressed by Sabina's merits, as they had been recognised by so fine a judge as Lady Sarah Trelusa ; for even the strong-minded hesitate sometimes to pronounce an opinion, when they feel they will have no seconders to their resolution, and give their vote most boldly when they vote with a majority.

Lady Sarah began to sit up, and then Sabina's taste was constantly in requisition on the subject of caps and morning wrappers. She began to hint that she must return to her duties, but her ladyship became so much more indisposed in consequence, that Doctor L—— persuaded her to remain a little longer.

After about a week, Lady Penruddock's jewelry arrived, and a large quantity of fine old lace. The jewels were a great comfort to the lady, and consequently to Sabina, as the way in which they were to be reset afforded many days of amusement.

Nothing had been said by his mother about Lord Trelusa. She seemed entirely occupied by her indisposition, and by Lady Penruddock's death and legacy.

After a fortnight had elapsed a change to sea air was recommended ; and, after a feeble attempt to retire from her post of nurse and companion, Sabina consented to accompany her ladyship to St. Eve, where a commodious house was engaged for herself and her servants, some of whom preceded her thither, that the dwelling might bear an appearance of comfort, more like that of her son's residence.

Many recollections crowded on the mind of Sabina when they drove into St. Eve. Those that were sad preponderated. She had spent many happy hours at the Abbey Farm, but also many of unspeakable agony. Lady Sarah was pleased by the change, and liked to watch the vessels as they passed in and out of the bay, and observe the small sailing-boats, looking like illuminated spots on the water, as the sun struck their white sails. Part of the day Lady Sarah spent in sleep; and then Sabina hastened out, to have the luxury of thinking unrestrainedly. She had been trying to save money out of her small income, and for that reason had taken pupils. It was slow work that of accumulation, however; and the sum she wanted was, for her efforts to obtain, an enormous one.

She strolled towards the church, in the churchyard of which Lieutenant Rock slept quietly, after his life of storms, by the side of his friend. She wished to look round the church and see if there were space for the monument to her uncle, to obtain which she was up early, and so late took rest, and ate the bread of carefulness. A woman was washing the pavement of the side aisle, and moved her pail of water and broom for Sabina to pass.

"Up this way, if you please, Miss," she said; and the girl with a languid wonder why she should be required to go one way rather than another, passed on.

The reason soon became obvious, for a beautiful monument of white marble, with a suitable inscription, told the spectator that near that spot were buried the mortal remains of Michael Rock and Stephen Orellan, with a modest summary of the acts of gallantry which had marked the career of each, and the friendship which had existed between them in life, and which had united them in death.

Sabina leaned her head unseen against the pillar of the church, and wept tears, not altogether bitter, at the tribute to her uncle's memory.

She needed no prompting to reveal the author of this act. Mr. Ferrers would not have considered such a sacrifice to the dead admissible, when so many living creatures lacked food and clothing. It must have been the work of Lord Trelusa ; and had he pleaded for pardon with the tongue of men and angels, the eloquence, though divine, could not have been so effectual as the silent prayer of the insensible marble, erected to the honour of her deceased uncle, and of the friend he had most loved in his life-time, and whose honour he would have preferred to his own.

Sabina returned very softly to Lady Sarah, and was particularly patient and gentle to her for the rest of the day—indeed, she was ever sweet and considerate to her ladyship ; but on this day she felt that she was indebted to Lord Trelusa for the greatest pleasure of which, since the death of her uncle, she had been susceptible, and she longed to repay it to his mother.

Her thoughts, however, dwelt on the monument, and on him whom it was intended to commemorate ; and Lady Sarah, in the course of the evening, observed her preoccupation and inquired its cause.

"I have been in the church, and seen the monument to Captain Orellan and my uncle," said the girl.

"Ah ! my dear ! Do you like it? Poor Trelusa drew the design himself before he went abroad. He was so anxious that it should be done well. Does the inscription satisfy you ? "

Sabina expressed admiration and gratitude, as well as her choking voice would permit.

" Poor Trelusa ! " continued her ladyship. " He was so very much upset at the intelligence of your uncle's death— so much disappointed."

Sabina did not understand the disappointment, and looked up through her tears inquiringly.

"Why you see, my dear, he had been working so hard to get the K.C.B. for your uncle, and he had counted on his having that little pleasure, and the 'Gazette' came out that very day ! "

"I thought," said Sabina, with a little natural mortification, "that it had been given to my uncle for his services."

"And so it was, my dear. Trelusa could not have obtained it, with all his borough interest, had there not been good grounds for its being conferred ; but the good grounds would have told for nothing without interest, or it would have been given before, and your uncle would have died an admiral instead of a lieutenant."

Sabina tried to say how much she was obliged, but broke down utterly.

Lady Sarah looked at her kindly, but suggested that she herself was in weak health, and required cheerful conversation.

In this she was not altogether selfish, for she saw that, in the effort to amuse her, Sabina would be most likely to forget her own sorrows.

So the girl fetched the box of lace, and arranged part of it for the trimming of a rich dress of gray satin, to be worn as half-mourning, when that period should arrive.

"Ah! Sabina!" said her ladyship plaintively. "The Countess of S—— gives such concerts! She has a niece who is musical, and sings with all the hired Italians. She is no more to be compared to you——"

And Lady Sarah's thoughts went off to future concerts, at which Sabina should appear, and display the critical acumen of her taste in having brought to light so bright a gem from the depths of Cornwall.

In the meantime Sabina wandered about St. Eve with a heavy heart. She avoided the side of the beach, which was so fraught with terrible memories; but she climbed to the cleft in the rock where Trelusa had broken in upon her solitude. Probably he had forgotten her since then. It would be quite as well that he should have done so, for Sabina's heart melted with tenderness towards him, when she thought of his efforts to please her uncle, and the monument which commemorated that uncle's virtues, his gallantry, and his fate. She did not think of his intended crime so much as of the loving eyes that had looked so mournfully at her when they had last parted, conveying a look of tender reproach for her implacability.

As she sat and looked out on the turbulent waves rolling up and retreating, she saw that their action had undermined the granite cliff, and she felt that the continuance of Lord Trelusa's passionate efforts to win her love would undermine her resolution, if continued sufficiently long.

A distant shout of juvenile voices came from inland, and Sabina, in returning, saw a troop of boys bounding in their delight at freedom from the restraint of school hours. They

26

were the scholars clothed and educated out of Mr. Ferrer's income of £1,500 a-year.

Sabina recognised the grandeur of the self-sacrifice, but she could not love the man ; her heart yearned for the softer features of Trelusa's character. Mr. Ferrers would never have conceived the idea of the crime which Lord Trelusa had nearly perpetrated ; but Mr. Ferrers would have thought the effort to obtain the small honour for her uncle (small, as compared to his deserts), as "foolishness," and the erection of the monument to his memory as sinful waste.

I am sorry for my heroine. She loved the wrong man ; and was more attracted by Lord Trelusa's character of mingled good and evil, than by that of Mr. Ferrers, which stood out on the horizon a perfect monolith, without crack or flaw.

Surely, thought Sabina, the vessel sailing prosperously without a fault to be found in her shape, rigging, or management, is an object of less interest than that of the one which

> " Howling winds drive, devious, tempest tost,
> Sails rent, seams opening wide, and compass lost."

And if such a one be saved, what a subject of rejoicing to those who have hazarded something for the rescue !

" But probably he has forgotten me," she said ; but she hoped he had not.

She visited Alice at the Abbey Farm, who entreated her to come and stay a little while there, that she might wait upon her, and have some company. Her master was always doing some good deed in different places, and was seldom at home. She was afraid he would go after the savages in the hot countries some day ; and Alice was sure there were savages enough at home.

This was getting near a subject too painful for discussion ; so Sabina made her a small present, which so wrought on her mind, that she sent her respects to Mrs. Susan Sorrel— a great concession, of which Sabina made the most in repeating it.

It was time now to return to Tregear, for Lady Sarah had grown weary of the sea.

Sabina, who feared Lord Trelusa might return, and find her with his mother, made a desperate effort to return to Exeter, instead of accompanying her friend.

"If he finds me here, he will think I am awaiting his arrival, to put myself in his way," she argued to herself.

Lady Sarah only begged she would wait till she had a companion.

"If Trelusa were here I should not be so lonely," she said.

One day her ladyship received a letter, announcing his arrival in London.

"I wonder why he has not come down at once?" she said, meditatively.

Sabina said nothing, for a thick letter, on foreign paper, was on the table by the side of her plate, but she did not like to open it then.

After breakfast she wandered out under the trees, now full-leaved, in the luxuriance of their midsummer glory, and opened her letter. It ran thus:—

"It depends on you, Sabina, whether I return to Tregear, or continue a wanderer for a few years longer. I owe you gratitude, for having taken the place that I ought to have occupied by the side of my mother. Yet, but for you, I should not have left England; and you only fulfilled the duty your unkindness had caused me to neglect. Do not, I implore you, refuse your pardon for a fault so deeply deplored, and so greatly punished, as mine has been.

"Oh! I do so long to see you again, my child! Sometimes I feel so sick at heart—so utterly depressed at our separation—that life is distasteful to me. Then I remember that you may yet be won—that you cannot be altogether and for ever implacable. When will this separation end?

"Two years have already passed since I saw you; saw your face flushed with anger—your lips compressed with resolution—resolution adverse to my hopes. Will you never soften with womanly tenderness?

"I have mixed with society, both foreign and English, since we met. I have tried to interest myself in other people and other circumstances; but one thought, one desire, pervades my whole existence. I knew not till now, tha I had such capabilities of constant devotion to one person. You cannot tell with how incessant a yearning I pine to be with you once again. May I come? Perhaps if I saw you again, and again you repulsed me, the charm might be broken, and I should love you less. I will not force myself on your society without your permission. I will, if you decline seeing me, ask Lady Sarah to join me in town.

"If you have no sympathy with what I suffer, you must forgive the expression of it. I have given no sign now for many months. Vesuvius is not always in a state of eruption, though the elements are ever burning in its depths.

"TRELUSA."

This letter had been delayed, and Sabina felt grieved that he must have expected to find an answer of some kind in town, and have been disappointed.

Lady Sarah wrote :—

"MY DEAR WILFRED,

"You must really come down as soon as you can. It is far too hot to be in town now, especially as I am in mourning for your great aunt, and therefore I cannot go out just yet. Sabina has been so good as to nurse me back to health, but she seems very impatient to return to her home.

"Have you brought me that Genoa velvet I mentioned to you? It will be useful next winter; and, as Sabina says truly, there is nothing which makes the skin so dazzlingly fair, where the complexion is like mine. She is really an excellent girl, and a first-rate musician, and suits me exactly. If, my dear son, you could get over her want of rank, and your dislike to a dark beauty—a taste in which I entirely concur—you might find her rather agreeable than not, as a wife.

"I shall expect you as soon as you can make it convenient to come."

Lady Sarah closed her letter, and sealed it.

"Put it into the bag in the hall for me, my dear," she said, addressing Sabina.

She obeyed; but first wrote four letters over the seal— "Come."

Sabina settled on Susan the interest of her five hundred pounds, and proposed that she should continue to live with her. She found, however, that Susan preferred a cottage of her own in Deepindale, in the occupation of which she could amuse herself by exasperating Mrs. Cressy and the inhabitants generally, by the account of the wealth, magnificence, and happiness of her dear young lady.

Sabina furnished Susan's house with those articles which had done duty so long in Haven House, and which it had been her happiness for so many years of her life to clean, and polish, and mend.

*　　*　　*　　*　　*　　*

Our heroine married her lover, and had no reason to repent her choice. He had sinned from the wilfulness of a nature which from long indulgence could brook no control. She led him to choose the right path in his future life, and infused into his children much of her own strength of character. The infant child of the unhappy Mabel had died during Lord Trelusa's travels on the continent, and he was thus released from a painful portion of the past. His eldest son by Sabina was named Michael, after the old man whose memory he respected and Sabina loved. With her boys clustering round her knees, the young mother would relate the daring and unselfish actions performed by their great uncle, and rejoice in the eager looks of interest, and the glistening eyes which expressed their yearning sympathy with all that was great and good.

THE END.

W. H. SMITH AND SON, PRINTERS, 186, STRAND, W.C.